BLACK
December

BLACK DECEMBER is beautifully intertwined with a wonderful novel by J.P. Malan titled COLD CASH and acts as its sequel. The story will continue in a third in the sequence coming out soon titled DAWN OF THE FIFTH WORLD co-authored by C.H. Williams and J.P. Malan.

BLACK
December

by
C.H. Williams

First Printing November 2011
Copyright All rights reserved

C.H. Williams (Camille Osterhout)
Black December Fiction ISBN
9781466486652.
Set in Garamond

Cover Design by Alisha Treasure

Printed in the United States of America

This book is dedicated to my family.
To my mother, my inspiration and best friend, my dad
and my brothers who are truly my champions, my
daughters who are my everything and to my husband,
the love of my life.

Chapter 1
Early Spring 2012

Rebel burst through the door onto the front porch of her mother's ranch house startling her brothers and uncle who were sitting around sipping coffee and enjoying the crisp early spring morning.

"It's happening! It's starting!" she exclaimed trying to breath through the panic threatening to consume her.

Her brothers stood up, their faces drawn with concern and her mother, Kira, rushed up the stairs nervously, knowing that something was seriously wrong. Rebel wasn't easily agitated and rarely got this upset.

Darien, her oldest brother stepped toward her. "What is it Rebel? What happened?"

"That massive filament that we've been watching on the sun's surface just erupted and ejected a monstrous coronal mass ejection straight at us! It's the big one Darien. Jade isn't answering her phone. I'm going to get her!"

Rebel moved toward the door determined to somehow get to her daughter who was all the way across the country in Washington D.C.

"Rebel," Kira said soothingly, "just calm down a second. Why do you think this coronal mass ejection is the big one?"

Rebel turned back to her mother, alarm screaming through her and trying to explode into full-blown panic. "Mom, it was huge! Nothing like the others. The shockwave from this eruption is traveling toward us at the speed of light and will be here in minutes. It will bend back the magnetosphere, opening us up to the radiation that will follow and take out the satellites. After that, the magnetically charged plasma cloud will slam into the earth and take out the entire power grid."

"In a matter of minutes our cell phones won't work and I won't be able to contact Jade," she added as she dialed her daughter again then shook her head in frustration when it went straight to voicemail. She stared at the phone helplessly trying to keep her tears in check as she slumped into a chair.

Dylan, the middle of her five younger brothers, stepped in front of her and asked, "Are you talking take out the cars big?"

Rebel looked up at him and nodded sadly. "It would be a catastrophic Y class flare if they had such a thing. I'm talking global electromagnetic pulse big. Take out cars, the power grid and every piece of electronics big. This thing is a monster and the plasma cloud will be here in eighteen to thirty six hours. Then it's lights out."

She stood up and started pacing again. "The sun's magnetic field is in the same alignment as the earth's which makes it all worse. There is an unusually high number of sunspots on the sun right now too. That's why we've had so many earthquakes this last week. Have you been watching them?" she asked anxiously.

All of her brothers nodded.

"The magnetosphere is at its weakest point ever in recorded history and it has endured constant bombardment from the many CME's that have impacted earth in the last few weeks. We are in for a major hit."

"What about Cayden and Shane?" Kira asked thinking about her youngest sons who were hanging iron on a construction site in Nebraska. "They aren't due to come home till next week."

Dylan walked to the edge of the porch and stood next to his uncle. He trusted his sister's instincts, knowing that she had put hours of research into the heated 2012 theory and had come to the conclusion that something was going to happen. He turned to his older brother and said, "Warrick, call the boys, tell 'em to pack it up and get home."

Warrick looked at his brother for a second then strode toward the door. He paused and said, "I'm with Rebel. We should go get Jade." Then he entered the house.

"I'll go with you to D.C., Rebel," Dylan said. "Darien and Warrick can help mom, Evie, and Uncle Neil get moved up to the cabin."

"No, Dylan. Mom needs all of you here. Stay and

get everyone settled in at the camp and make sure the boys get home safe. I will fly to Washington, pick her up and be back home before the sun rises in the morning." Rebel unlocked her phone again and started pacing as she tried to call Jade.

"Rebel!" Warrick bellowed from the living room. "Get in here!"

Kira and Rebel raced into the house expectantly then turned to the T.V. in horror as the news announced that a magnitude seven earthquake had just leveled Washington D.C.

Rebel's face paled and her hands started shaking as she listened to Jade's voicemail take the call. "Jade, call me as soon as you get this," she said desperately then looked at her mother. "She still isn't answering."

She slid down onto the couch and fell victim to the tears that finally overcame her. "That will have taken out the landlines. If her cell is dead, I won't be able to call her at all. I need to go get her. What if she is hurt?"

"I'll book you a flight," Dylan said picking up the house phone. "Just pray they still have planes that can fly without satellite navigation."

Darien turned to Kira, "Mom, let's get your stuff together and get you ready to leave. We need to get you moved up to the property right now. If Rebel is right, this solar storm will take out all of the rigs."

"Ya, and it's a three hour ride to the cabin, so we only have time for a couple trips," Warrick added.

Dylan looked at Rebel worriedly as he finalized the plane reservations. "Rebel, go get your bag. There are very few planes still scheduled to fly out today and yours leaves in three hours. That's barely enough time to get you to the airport."

Rebel took the stairs three at a time as she hurried to her room. She grabbed a bag and stuffed in a change of clothes. She threw in her emergency cash and credit card. "I wish I could take my handgun," she mumbled as she gathered some toiletries.

"Let's go!" Dylan yelled urgently from the bottom

of the stairs.

Uncle Neil walked up and handed her a radio. He smiled and said, "Take this just in case and I'll leave my HAM radio on. Be careful." Her uncle was a retired Army radio specialist and always kept in touch with the family and his friends on his radio.

Rebel hugged him and then her mother. "I love you guys," she said then turned to Warrick and Darien. "I'll be home soon."

Dylan was silent as they drove to the airport in Salt Lake City. Both of them knew the severity of the situation that they would be facing over the next few years if the CME took out the electronics system and satellites. He tried to calm the growing alarm that seeped through him.

"Rebel," he finally said as they pulled into the airport parking lot, "keep the time in mind. You don't want to be stuck in the air when this thing hits. Even if you can find a plane that will fly manually, it won't stay in the air after an impact from this kind of geomagnetic storm. The electronics will fail."

Rebel hugged her brother and said, "I will. Keep in touch."

Jade was shocked out of a deep sleep when her bed came alive, bucking like a bull trying to throw her out. Her alarm clock fell off the table and her little nick knacks tumbled off their shelves. She bolted to her feet and instinctively ran for the door. The quake was so bad that she could barely stay upright. The floor seemed to rise up underneath her in a wave like motion finally toppling her over. The lamp shattered to the floor and the bookshelf crashed over beside her. She climbed up and grabbed the bag that hung next to the door and ran outside onto the lawn trying to catch her breath.

She turned around and froze in dismay as a loud groan and popping sound escaped from the building. It moaned and creaked like ice on a pond bearing too much weight. Then the building started to come down. Bricks crumbled to the ground and windows cracked and shattered.

Jade stumbled back in horror as she watched the structure collapse. Dust surged into the air from the ground beneath it as it settled into a pile of debris. "Oh no!" she breathed thinking of the little lady that lived next to her. She ran toward the crumbling pile of steel and concrete that had been her home a moment ago. "Mrs. Manning!" she screamed, frantically digging through the rubble looking for her neighbors and trying to suck at least some oxygen from the dust billowing around her.

She didn't hear the fire trucks pull up as she searched the debris and was surprised when she looked up and noticed the flashing lights and firemen that surrounded her. Tears flowed freely down her cheeks as she moved bricks and lumber knowing that no one would have survived this tragedy.

Hours later Jade wiped the dirt and sweat off of her face and tried to smile at the very large fireman that handed her a towel. She had worked side by side with them all morning finding only bodies.

Fresh tears stung her eyes as she thought about her mom. Rebel had been fanatical about being prepared for disasters, and earthquakes were on top of her list. She had insisted that her apartment be on the ground floor and her emergency bag be by the door. She had made exit plans and evacuation strategies and gone over them with the family so that they would be prepared for anything. Jade had made fun of her because D.C. rarely experienced earthquakes.

Funny thing was though, it had happened. Jade had felt the ground start to shake and without thinking, had run for the door instead of crawling under the table, barely making it out before the building started creaking under its own weight.

The fireman beside her handed her a bottle of water and said, "You should get some rest."

Jade tried to smile again but failed miserably. "Thanks, but I'm fine." She had no intention of leaving until everyone was accounted for, just in case. Besides, she had nowhere to go. She hadn't taken the time to make many friends since she had arrived here almost a year ago. Suddenly she realized that she was stranded here with nothing but the emergency bag that she happened to grab on the way out the door. She shook her head when the thought crossed her mind that her mom may have been right all along about this 2012 thing.

"What's your name?" the fireman asked.

"I'm Jada," she said quietly, "but my friends call me Jade."

A huge explosion up the street brought their focus back to the disaster in front of them. The fireman took off on foot toward the new flames and several others jumped into the fire truck behind her.

She stood there alone in the street watching the chaos that surrounded her. The sound of people crying and men hollering into the rubble, of sirens blaring and lights flashing engulfed her. It all seemed to flicker and grow dim as if she were dreaming. Then it hit her. This was no random earthquake. This was the beginning of devastating disaster to come.

Jade thought about Rebel and knew that her mom would read this quake like a book and be worried sick. She needed to let her know she was ok.

"Shit! I don't have my phone!" she moaned as a feeling of hopelessness enveloped her. She was alone and very far away from her family and the worst was still to come. She remembered the strain on her mother's face the day she left for D.C. and though her mother would have never held her back from the fantastic opportunity of moving here to work as an intern, she had been worried. Worried about this very thing.

Rebel felt her tension build as the plane launched into the air. Her head was pounding and her stomach wasn't handling the stress well. To top off the bad luck from the day, Salt Lake City was being pummeled by a wicked spring storm that would ultimately dump inches of snow. She eased back in her seat trying not to think about the events that she believed were in their near future.

The 2012 end of the world theory was full of hype and myth but she had thoroughly researched it and was able to sort the crap from some of the theories that she believed were plausible if not inevitable. She had dug up facts and read every point of view she could find written by credible sources. There are many very educated, well-informed people out there that believed the earth was in real danger in the coming year.

Suddenly, the plane jolted and lost altitude and airspeed.

"Microburst," Rebel said out loud. "God, I hate to fly."

The weather had been unpredictable lately and there had been a huge increase in large earthquakes, tornadoes and category five hurricanes in the past several years, a fact that had fed the 2012 frenzy on the Internet like fuel to a fire.

The plane recovered and she let loose her grip on the armrest.

"As if I'm not already lit up enough," she mumbled to herself then waved to the stewardess and asked for a drink.

The woman returned with a smile. Rebel quickly downed the liquid trying to keep the inbound solar storm out of her head. The flare had erupted with a coronal mass ejection, exploding a large cloud of electrified particles off the surface of the sun and shot it on a path straight toward earth. The billion-ton plasma cloud was traveling millions of miles per hour and would be here in a matter of hours. Normally a CME wouldn't do much damage because the earth's magnetosphere protected it. A large one could destroy satellites and possibly bump the power out in some locations. But this one was different.

The sun was entering the peak of its solar maximum and had been extremely active lately. Many people on the Internet believed that it was being perturbed by several outside sources. The theory was that the entire solar system was passing through the galactic equator and the theoretical Planet X had entered the solar system. If you added it all up, it equaled the worst solar activity in human history.

On top of everything else that was happening, Planet X would have displaced many comets and asteroids on its path toward earth and sent them flying toward the inner solar system. Without power, no one would be able to track them.

Rebel looked around the aircraft and realized that none of these people knew that in a matter of hours, they would be without power and most likely without any kind of electronics at all. Most people didn't believe that a CME would destroy the sensitive electronics that were a part of everything in a modern society but she believed that this one would.

The aircraft started its decent and Rebel drew in a shaky breath as she felt the reduction in speed. She only had a few hours to find Jade and get home or they would be stuck out here. Her apprehension resurfaced and she had to close her eyes tightly to get the images of her daughter alone and hurt somewhere, out of her head.

Jade was a smart logical young woman and Rebel clung to the fact that they had gone over the emergency plans many times and she would know what to do if a disaster occurred.

Rebel had pre-rented a truck to be waiting for her and had ordered a supply of food and water to be ready for her to pick up. She hadn't been surprised when the car rental clerk had laughed at her for wanting a four wheel drive pickup.

"We aren't in Idaho anymore, Toto," she said out loud as she exited the plane. The man walking next to her glanced over at her curiously.

She looked back at him and couldn't help feeling out of place. All of this fast paced electric car crap. God, she hoped that she didn't have to deal with anyone from the so called political class. They were all a bunch of idiots, always trying to grow the government and make people completely dependent.

She had been raised in the country where for the

most part, people took care of themselves and theirs. They worked for their money and didn't expect more than their fair share. To her, everyone was equal. Having money didn't make one better than anyone else. Some of the best people she knew didn't have anything but a good heart. Her attitude about the elite had gotten her into trouble before because she really had a hard time keeping her mouth shut and her opinions to herself.

An event of this magnitude would definitely level the playing field though. Money wouldn't save anyone from the devastation that would ultimately cripple their technological world and send the entire civilization back into the 1800's.

As she walked through the massive, crowded airport she couldn't help thinking about what would happen to all of these people if their food and water supply were cut off. How would they survive with their money all tied up in investments and banks. Without power they wouldn't have access to anything. No ATM's, no credit cards. And even worse, the electronics in the cars would be fried so soon there will be no transportation.

Someone online had claimed that if the worst of this really happened, ninety percent of the population could parish. She watched the people ignorantly hustle past her and was crushed by the math. Nine in ten of these people could die! Nausea over took her and she ran to the bathroom.

Jade was grateful for the blanket and food that the fireman had given her. He had insisted that she come back to the station with them when they returned to fill the trucks. He gave her a sandwich then raced out to another call.

She was alone again and exhausted from searching the rubble all morning. She leaned her head against the wall and pulled the blanket up around her neck feeling very anxious. The power was out and the phones weren't working so she had no way of calling home. Her mother had told her that if anything ever happened, she was to stay put and wait for her. The plan was to be in a police or fire station close by. She snuggled deeper in the blanket somewhat comforted by the thought that her mother would find her and finally gave in to the exhaustion, falling sound asleep.

Complete devastation marked the path from the airport to Jade's apartment building. Fires burned from broken gas lines and way too many buildings had fallen to the earthquake. Many of the roads were impassable and power lines were down all over.

Panic ripped at Rebel's throat as she pulled the big 4x4 around the corner and took in the ruins that were once the beautiful building that her daughter had lived in. She gripped the wheel tightly and tried to steady herself. 'Jade is fine,' she told herself over and over as she turned the truck around.

She drove feverishly to the closest fire station and prayed that Jade had followed the plan and had gone to one of the places that they'd talked about. She could hardly breathe as she walked into the empty room where the trucks were usually parked. Jade had to be here.

Anxiously, she scanned the room until she saw her daughter curled up in the corner sleeping. She rushed to her side, trembling with relief.

Jade was dirty and looked completely disheveled and exhausted as she slept so peacefully. 'Thank god, you followed the plan,' Rebel thought, grateful that it had worked.

The giant doors suddenly opened behind her and two huge trucks rolled into the building. Before the first truck rolled to a stop, a very large fireman jumped off and headed toward them. Rebel was struck by the concern on his face as he quietly approached them.

"I'm Stewart," he said softly to Rebel reaching out his hand.

Rebel shook his hand. "You brought her here?"

He turned back to Jade and replied thoughtfully, "Yes, she was so determined to find everyone in her building after it collapsed and wouldn't quit until everyone was accounted for. I'm sorry to say that no one else made it out alive." He glanced back at Rebel. "I don't see selflessness like that every day."

The bells in the firehouse went off, the loud ringing jolting both of them. Stewart cursed under his breath and turned to go.

Rebel reached for his arm and said, "You seem pretty selfless yourself. Thank you for helping her."

He looked into her eyes and said, "Thanks and your welcome. We don't hear it very often either. I assume you are her mother. She told me you would be coming. Take good care of her."

Rebel smiled, taking comfort in the fact that Jade had known she would come for her. She looked at the fireman and said in a solemn voice, "You need to leave the city. If you have family, get them and get out. I know it is hard to hear, but you won't be able to save everyone. This isn't over yet."

Stewart looked at her with a strange expression on his face, but didn't respond. He just nodded his head to her, picked up his hat and started for the truck that was already pulling out of the garage.

With a heavy heart, Rebel watched them pull away then shook Jade awake.

"Mom, I knew you would come for me," Jade said jumping up to hug her. "I shouldn't have come here. You were right all along. I have put you in danger, I'm so sorry!"

"Don't you dare say that Jade!" Rebel said firmly hugging her again. "This is not your fault. We will be just fine. Come on. Let's get you out of the city before we get hit with another aftershock. It's a long drive back to the airport. Some of the roads are completely closed from debris and others just aren't there anymore. I have food in the truck though, and you can sleep a little longer."

"The truck?" Jade repeated as they walked outside then laughed out loud when she saw the big four wheel drive pickup. "God mom, you are such a redneck."

They giggled at each other, both of them feeling a sense of relief as they climbed into the pickup.

Rebel pulled the truck onto the road and headed toward the freeway.

Jade turned to Rebel and said, "So really mom, how bad is it going to get? All this stuff you talk about, is it all really going to happen?"

"Well," Rebel sighed then replied, "It's bad. We are about to be impacted by a major solar storm. The magnetic waves that it generates will induce currents that will rip through the power grid and take out the entire system. It will cause a global blackout. We will also see more earthquakes because there are so many sunspots facing the earth right now."

"Sunspots? How do they cause earthquakes?"

"They are like massive magnets and have significant affects on earth. It is also possible that a coronal mass ejection could cause ground based magnetically induced volcanic eruptions. It could even set off all of the slip faults and subduction zones as the current flows through the crust of the earth."

"Are we close to any of the subduction zones?"

"Yes, many of them. The closest one to Idaho is the Cascadia Subduction Zone on the pacific coast, and the San Andreas Fault that runs along the coast of California but from here, the New Madrid in the Midwest is the most dangerous. If all of them go at the same time, the wave energy could cause volcanoes to erupt all over including Yellowstone which, as you know, has been in the red zone for years."

Jade paled and said, "Mom you said we wouldn't survive if Yellowstone went off."

"True," Rebel said trying not to visibly show her anxiety. "We will deal with that when it happens. The most pressing issue today is that when this electrified plasma cloud hits, it will leave us with no power." She paused not wanting to alarm Jade. "It will probably take out the cars."

"We won't have any cars?" Jade breathed nervously. "I never really believed you mom. You know, about all of this 2012 stuff. I still don't understand it all."

"Don't worry, there aren't many people who do," Rebel said. "But I believe we will survive. Life will just be a little harder now."

"Didn't this happen before? Some big solar flare that wiped out communication?" Jade asked. "I remember you saying something about it."

Rebel nodded. "You are talking about the Carrington event back in 1859. It wiped out the telegraph system and actually burned some of the operators. The big difference is that now, we have satellites and cell phones and airplanes and computers and credit cards and a one hundred year old electric grid. And this CME is way bigger than that one was."

"What are we going to do? What is the plan?" Jade asked trying to remain calm.

"We are going to fly home and hunker down. Our property is fully stocked with supplies. Hopefully, we can find another plane that can fly old school because we have already lost our satellites and navigation. We need to hurry though, because once the solar storm hits we won't be able to fly at all. If it comes in like I think it will, it will fry the electronic systems and the planes will literally fall from the sky." Rebel smiled encouragingly at Jade. "We just need to make it home before it all comes down. Don't worry, it will work out."

Jade nodded solemnly and looked out the window. "Look at the devastation out there. People aren't used to earthquakes here." She watched as they drove by crumpled buildings and downed power lines throwing sparks onto the road. People were walking around scared and confused, displaced from their homes and without power. "How much time do we have?"

Just as the words came out, the ground shook again turning her words into a scream. Rebel quickly pulled the truck to a stop at the side of the road. The pavement in front of them rippled and buckled, crumbling into pieces. A car that was driving behind them flew by like nothing had happened. Rebel watched as the little tires hit the loose material on the broken road and flip the small vehicle upside down.

"Jesus!" Rebel said as the car skidded into the median on its top. "Why don't people think when shit like this happens? I swear to God, their brains just shut off." She turned to Jade and said, "Stay here and keep your seatbelt on cause someone could hit the truck from behind."

Rebel got out of the truck just as another car slammed on its brakes and was rear ended by yet another. The driver of the first car climbed out rubbing his head and staggered toward her. She put a clamp on her tongue so that she wouldn't call him the idiot he was and simply asked, "Are you ok?"

"I think so," the man replied then turned toward the other wrecked cars. She left the man to check on the others relieved to hear the sirens coming toward them.

She waited until the police got there then got back in the truck. "We have to hurry. We don't have time for this shit." The truck took the rough terrain with ease and Rebel couldn't help but ask Jade, "What do you think of my big ass 4x4 now?"

Jade laughed and couldn't help feeling respect for her mother who had obviously thought things through as usual. "Right on, mom," she said as they turned onto a freeway entrance.

When they finally reached the airport, Rebel couldn't believe the madness. The airport had more people in it now than when she had landed. Everyone wanted out of the city. Flights were delayed or cancelled because most of the runways were broken up from the earthquake and many of the planes had been damaged. At least the power was on out here.

Rebel looked at her ticket then at the display board. "Our flight has been cancelled! God damn it! We will be lucky to get out of here now!" She fought to control the nausea and panic that pounded through her as she walked up to the ticket line. "My flight's been canceled and I need to get to Boise or Salt Lake City," she said with dread.

"I'm sorry," the woman at the ticket booth said after

a moment of searching. "I can reschedule your flight but it won't leave until morning. That is the only thing I have going to Idaho or Utah."

"Fuck!" Rebel swore not caring who heard her. "That's not good enough. We need to leave today!"

The woman arrogantly looked down her nose at Rebel and said, "Look around, what do you expect?"

Rebel grabbed a hold of her tongue and tried to breathe through her anger. She tried to be civilized when she asked, "Anything to Colorado?"

"Not today," the woman said with attitude.

Rebel wanted to reach across the desk and throttle her but Jade put her hand on her arm and said, "Mom, it's not her fault."

She fought to control herself and turned away from the woman. "Let me think here for a second," she said pacing back forth in front of the booth then exclaimed, "How about Nebraska?"

The woman raised her eyebrow at her but looked into the computer screen. "I have one seat leaving in an hour to Omaha. It was a cancellation."

"I'll take it!" Rebel said somewhat relieved. At least Jade would be halfway home.

Jade grabbed her arm and cried, "Mom! No! What are you doing? You're not staying here, I won't leave you."

Rebel grabbed the ticket out of the woman's hand and led Jade out of line and toward the gate. "Look, Jade, I can drive toward Nebraska or try to get a flight somewhere on the way. Your uncles have been working on the Air Force base in Omaha and haven't left for Idaho yet. They can pick you up at the airport and take you with them and I will be right behind you."

Jade stomped her foot and started crying. "Mom, now I'm afraid. You came here to get me and now you are stuck here. You said the CME would be here soon. What if you can't get out?"

"I will be fine. You know that," Rebel said firmly as she hugged her tight. "I need you safe, Jade. I will be there as soon as I can. I love you. This will work out, just stick to the plan."

Her heart almost stopped beating as she watched her daughter walk up the loading ramp alone and afraid.

Conner unloaded his firearm, put it in its storage case and packed it in the trunk with his bags. His job was dangerous and he always traveled with his weapon. That's why he traveled by car instead of flying. He worked as a mercenary for the government. His most recent assignment had been finding a group of rouge marines that had gone a-wall. They were well trained and highly skilled and had kept him on the move for the past two months.

He had finally cornered them and let the military take it from there. He wasn't paid to kill, just to subdue. His job was done here but he had one more stop before he could head back home. A little unfinished business.

He hated being in the cities. The noise and chaos drove him crazy and he couldn't wait to be on the road home. He settled behind the wheel and headed toward Charleston. It was a couple hundred mile drive from Cleveland but he planned on staying the night in Parkersburg. He pulled the car onto the freeway thinking about the vacation he planned on taking from work. The beautiful mountains of Montana were calling his name. He had been on the road for so long he couldn't remember what they looked like. He leaned back and started to really relax for the first time in months.

Rebel knew that Jade had not been happy about being stuffed on the plane, but there were no alternatives. She walked through the lobby toward the doors trying to add up the miles to the next airport. She knew in her heart that she wouldn't be able to fly out of there either. The runways wouldn't be much better and time was not on her side. Her only choice then would be to drive until the flare hit. She dug her phone out of her purse out of habit then threw it in the trash, sighing in disgust when it didn't have service. She walked over to a pay phone and dialed her youngest brother,

Cayden.

"Hey, it's Rebel," she said when he answered. "I just put Jade on a plane to Omaha. There was only one seat out of here so I am going to drive until I find a flight home. I told her not to leave the airport until you got there."

"I'll get her sis, don't worry," Cayden said convincingly. "But there is a problem. The plasma cloud is coming faster than they thought it would. We may only have another four hours and I'm having a problem booking a flight from here because the weather is so bad."

"Shit!" Rebel said worriedly.

"And sis, the ACE satellite read the polarity of the cloud and the magnetic field of the particles is in direct opposition to earths. It's going to slam us like a bolt of lightning. It's big Rebel, bigger than they have ever seen." Cayden said softly

The concern in her brothers' voice made Rebel homesick for him. He and Shane hadn't been home to visit for a while and she suddenly realized how much she missed them. Shane was a couple years older than Cayden, but the two were inseparable.

She struggled to remain calm and answered softly, "Ok. Call the brothers and let them know. Forget the plane because if its coming this fast, you don't want to risk being in the air. Drive as far out of the city as you can, you don't want to be stuck there. It will be dangerous. And Cayden, this CME will take out the cars so you will be on foot as soon as it hits."

"You just take care of yourself sis. Don't worry about Jade, we will guard her with our lives," Cayden said determinedly.

"I found the number to the pay phone at the airport in Omaha. Wait there until I call so I know you're safe. I love you, bye," she said fearfully, trepidation building up inside her again. She knew her youngest two brothers would take care of Jade. They had been raised with her almost as siblings because of their close age. Cayden had only been four years old when Jade was born.

Although they were mature young men, they were

still considered the babies of the family and were therefore fiercely protected by the older brothers.

Cayden hung up the phone and looked at his brother. He could tell that Shane was as concerned as he was. "Rebel may have been right about all of this 2012 shit. She is sending Jade to us on the only seat out of D.C. and she is going to get stuck on the East Coast!" He picked the phone back up and dialed his brothers in Idaho.

"We are almost out of here," he said when Dylan answered. "Rebel couldn't get a flight to Idaho or Utah but found one seat out of Washington to Omaha, so she sent Jade here. As soon as she lands, we are on our way. Rebel is going to drive out."

"God damn it! Rebel is so stubborn!" Dylan said shaking his head regretfully. "She wouldn't let any of us go with her."

"I know but she was worried that something would happen at home and you wouldn't be there for mom," Cayden defended her.

"Well, do what she said then. Get Jade and drive as far as you can. I will keep tabs on Rebel. Take care bro."

Dylan hung up the phone, thankful that he had left his landline on all these years even though he rarely used it. He got in the truck and headed for Kira's house where everyone would be gathering for coffee. He was extremely worried about Cayden and Shane and gripped his coffee cup tightly as his tension mounted.

Being stuck in Omaha was not good and they would have no way to communicate. He was worried that the younger boys didn't have enough experience to keep themselves safe and now they would have to protect Jade. They would probably end up without transportation very soon and the city would be dangerous.

His mother's house was bustling with activity as Uncle Neal and the brothers prepared to take Kira and her best friend Evie to the property. He looked at the big front porch where he'd spent hours with his family and felt a sense of nostalgia. He waved at Kira as he stepped out of the truck.

"Hey mom," he said giving her a hug. "I have an update on Rebel and Jade."

"Oh, good, I've been so worried. I'll grab you some coffee."

Darien stood as Dylan walked up the porch steps. "What's the word?" he asked, concern pulling his brow into a scowl.

Dylan glanced at Warrick then accepted the cup from Kira. After a pause and a sip of coffee, he looked back at Darien's impatient face and said, "There was an aftershock that took out most of the runways at the airport in D.C. Rebel got Jade out on a flight to Omaha, but she's going to have to drive out. She is going to try to get a flight somewhere on the way but most likely, she will end up on foot when the CME hits."

Kira sucked in her breath and cursed softly.

"Shane and Cayden will meet Jade as soon as she lands but we have another problem. The storm is coming faster than they had anticipated. They will only have four or five more hours in the car. It's not enough time to get home so they will be on foot as well," Dylan answered.

"Son of a bitch!" Warrick roared. "They won't make it on foot." He got up and jumped off the porch. "We will have to go get 'em! We will finish up the evac and get mom and Evie safe up to camp then we'll go get them. Come on Darien, let's load the horses and get them up to the property."

Darien looked at Kira's worried face then back to his brothers. "It's a three hour drive we will only have time for one trip before we lose the truck. We will have to leave for Nebraska from the cabin."

Kira was trembling so hard that she almost spilled her coffee. She knew that Rebel could take care of herself but she would be alone and in danger for weeks.

"Don't worry mom, Rebel has trained in the gym for years and can protect herself. You just finish getting ready and we will worry about getting everyone home," Dylan said encouragingly. "It will work out cause Rebel's been planning for this for years."

Everyone laughed as they remembered how tenacious Rebel had been about the preparations. They had all done their own research though and come up with the same conclusion and had jumped right in and helped her pull off what she called a 'just in case' plan. Now it looked like they would need it.

Rebel pulled out of the airport and knew she was in deep shit. The city would turn to hell any minute. The general public didn't react well to disasters like this. People were displaced from their homes and without supplies or money. More than likely, they would soon be looting and rioting. She had read a story once about the New York blackout in 1977. The power had only been out for one day and the city fell to an entire breakdown of social order. The police had been completely outmatched and lost control.

The police had their hands full here already and that meant that the streets would be deadly after the CME hit. Rebel knew that she needed some protection. She had spent years learning to box and studying mixed martial arts and was in extremely good shape for her age, but that kind of self-defense wouldn't count for much in this situation. She needed guns and ammo. She needed weapons.

She pointed the truck west and was just about to set the cruise when she spotted a pawnshop on the corner up ahead. She slammed on the brakes and pulled in. It was a dumpy little store but hopefully they would have what she needed.

The man behind the counter sneered at her as she walked into the dingy, dimly lit store and said, "I'm about to close, what do you want?"

Rebel tightly gripped her anger and calmly walked up to the man, stepping within inches of his chest. She was a little taller than he was so she looked down at him and said in an intimidating voice, "You wretched little man. Are you so miserable that you have to pass your nastiness on to others?"

The man was so stunned that he jumped back and growled, "I'm not miserable!"

He was so pathetic that Rebel laughed out loud. "Whatever! I need a weapon and ammunition." She looked him square in the eyes and added in a growl, "I can't wait three days."

It was his turn to laugh. "That's funny! There are laws you know."

"I know!" she shot back. "It's an emergency. I'm in danger and so are you." She pointed her finger at him to exaggerate her point then leaned closer and said, "I'll trade you this favor for a secret."

He stepped back again as he looked her up and down, staring at her for several seconds.

Rebel held his gaze looking right back at him with a scowl.

"Fine," he finally said, "but only a .22 caliber. I'm not losing my ass for nobody."

"Fine," she mimicked him trying to hide her disappointment. "Do you have a vest?"

He seemed to calm down a little and pointed to the back wall.

Rebel walked to the back and picked out a bulletproof vest that fit close enough. She grabbed a duffle bag and packed in several flashlights, lighters, a hunting knife and a denim coat to ward off the chilly early spring nights. She picked out an impressive Ruger .22 caliber semi automatic handgun and an extra clip with plenty of ammunition.

She waited for the man to swipe her credit card then said, "I need some tinfoil and a box. Do you have something in the back?"

The man shrugged and walked into the back room. He returned a moment later and handed the items to her.

She put the flashlights and batteries next to the 2-way radio that her uncle had given her into the box and wrapped it with plastic and then the foil.

"What are you doing?" the man asked curiously

watching the process.

"I am making a faraday cage," Rebel said without looking up. "It's used to keep the electromagnetic pulse of a nuclear bomb from destroying the circuitry inside the radio."

When she was satisfied with her box, she stuffed it in her bag and turned to the curious man and said, "The power is going off in a few hours and it's not coming back on. If you're smart, you will pick out a weapon for yourself and get out of the city." Then she strode away leaving him standing there wondering what the hell she was talking about.

She climbed into the truck and pulled back onto the highway reminding herself to stay clear of people from now on. She would have to avoid cities and populated areas for the rest of her journey. The only problem with that is that you run into the bad people who are avoiding the law for hostile reasons. She glanced at her newly acquired weapon and decided that she would have to find a real outdoors store soon to better arm herself. She looked at her watch and tried to figure out when Jade's plane would land in Omaha.

As she picked her way through the looters on the road who were now out in full force, she mentally prepared herself for the trip back home. She knew that a woman on her own was a target and she would be facing extreme dangers. The worst would be the gangs that would probably take over the major cities. The second would be the fact that men always turned on each other in times like these.

The police force would more than likely fall apart because the officers would be worried about their own families. Who could blame them? It would take the National Guard days to assemble and they wouldn't be able to cover every town. She had no doubt that the entire social structure would break down completely in the coming days.

She sighed in frustration and looked at her watch again. Jade should have landed by now. Hopefully, the storm that dropped five inches of snow and closed the freeways in Utah this morning wasn't causing trouble. It would be hitting Nebraska by now. She turned into a grocery store and walked to the pay phone. She dialed Cayden hoping that everything had gone smoothly.

"Hey sis," he answered instantly. "We've got her. Great timing, we just walked up to the phones."

Rebel nodded her relief, "Thank God, I was worried that the storm would cause problems."

"Well, it is creating tornado's," he yelled. "There is a tornado warning at the airport right now..."

Rebel gripped the phone tightly when it went dead.

"Cayden," Rebel yelled into the phone. "Cayden, can you hear me?"

No response.

She leaned back against the wall trying to regain her composure. "This is really too much," she said to herself. "First Jade is in an Earthquake, then she ends up in a tornado. What else? No, don't ask, cause it can and will get worse!" She hung up the phone and dug in her pocket for more change. She gathered herself up, clinging to the fact that Shane and Cayden would protect Jade with their lives then looked into the sky and thought about the last few hours. She had seen severe unpredictable weather in the past months, but everything happening now and all at once was pretty hard to swallow.

She picked the phone back up and dialed Dylan at her mother's house and gathered strength from his voice when he answered.

"How are you doing Rebel?" he asked.

"The boys and Jade were in the airport and I think they were hit by a tornado," she said almost losing control. "I was talking to Cayden and the phone just went dead."

"Calm down, sis," Dylan soothed. "The boys can handle themselves. They will call me as soon as they get to another phone."

"K," Rebel said taking a deep breath. "I've armed myself sort of. It's just a .22 but at least it's something. I got a vest too just in case."

"Good. Look Rebel, I will see to the kids, you just see to yourself. We have decided to head to Nebraska and get them. We need some time here to get mom and the family set up at camp then we will head out."

"Dylan, what about the nuclear plants there? Will they get them shut down in time?" Rebel asked very concerned.

"It takes several days to safely shut down a nuclear reactor and those two in Nebraska are both cooled by the Missouri River. But I'm sure they will have enough fuel for the generators to get them safely off line," he said. "But we do have over a hundred nuclear facilities in the United States. Hopefully, we won't have a major incident."

Rebel tried to think positive as she said, "We only have a couple more hours of communication so just know that if I'm not in Omaha when you get there, don't wait. Just get the kids home. You will get to Nebraska before I do."

"No deal. We will keep heading east after we pick them up and meet you. Here's the plan. Safeguard the radio and after the CME hits, put it on channel nine. Turn it on at sunset every night when you get close. Now, get out your map and let's find you a road home."

Dylan proceeded to mark out the roads for Rebel to follow so it would be easy to find each other. Then with a loving goodbye, hung up the phone.

Rebel felt the heavy weight of concern sitting on her as she once again headed west. It was going to be a long summer.

Cayden dropped the phone and grabbed Jade to the ground as the tornado crashed into the huge front windows in the lobby of the airport. Everyone around them shrieked in fear as glass shards flew past them.

"Fuck!" Jade yelled and ducked her head into the wind as it blew freely through the now open structure.

"Jade! I've never heard you swear like that," Shane reprimanded as he pulled her to her feet.

"Well, you try being in an earthquake in the morning and a tornado that night!" she spit out then stomped her foot trying to gather her hair out of her face.

"Thank god it just side swiped us. Oh no, look at

the parking lot, there is no way our car made it through that," Cayden said after the raging wind calmed.

Shane looked around at the hundreds of stunned, injured people. "We need to get out of here," he said. "Let's find the closest standing motel and hole up till we figure out what to do. We need to call the brothers."

"And Rebel too, the tornado hit and the phone went dead while I was talking to her so she is probably freaking out," Cayden added.

Jade rushed over to a bleeding woman and said, "These people need our help here. Cayden, move that luggage off of her leg."

"Jade, we need to move out," Shane said urgently.

"After we help them, Shane," Jade said smiling sweetly at her uncle.

He shook his head in frustration but knew better than to argue. He shrugged and moved to help an older gentleman up off the floor.

An hour later, Shane pushed debris out of the way ahead of them as they picked their way through the lobby and headed for the door. Outside, rain pounded down on them as they found the car upside down underneath a fallen light pole and covered in tree limbs. They dug their duffle bags out of the back seat and headed toward the street in hopes of finding an available taxi.

The closest standing motel was several miles away from the airport. They settled into their rooms relieved to be inside and away from the wind that continued to howl outside.

"There is a pay phone down the block. I'll go call the brothers," Cayden said.

"Brother, I'm glad to hear your voice," Dylan said when he answered the phone. "Are you guys ok?"

"Yes, we are, but the car is totaled. We are holed up at a motel," Cayden explained.

"I was afraid of that when Rebel told me it was a tornado that cut off your call. We have a new plan. We have decided to come get you because I don't want to lose track of you while you are on your way home. The phones won't work for much longer so you will be on your own. I want you to gather up some supplies and stay put. Pack your wakis in a faraday cage and don't pull them out until after the flare hits, then listen for us on channel nine. It will take us a few weeks to get there so find a spot you can make into a fort. That city is going to be dangerous and you will need to protect yourselves. No one knows what is coming so use the time to prepare and dig in," Dylan instructed.

"What about Rebel," Cayden asked, "and what about mom?"

"We will get mom all set up before we leave. Rebel is going to head toward you and if we get there before she does, we will continue east until we find her."

Cayden sucked in his breath nervously. "Ok bro, we will handle things here. You guys be careful and tell mom we love her." He hung up the phone unhappily and walked back to the room. He looked at Jade's expectant face and said, "They are coming for us."

Rebel looked up into the night sky and was taken back by the sight of the red, green and purple lights of the aurora that suddenly slithered across the sky. It was rarely seen where she lived in Idaho so the beauty of the event took her by surprise. She knew that the aurora was created when electrically charged particles interact with the earth's magnetic field and like many other beautiful things, preceded deadly danger.

It was so bright that it turned the night sky into day. An orange tint colored the clouds and she was reminded again of the 1859 Carrington solar storm. She had read online that the crew on the clipper ship, The Southern Cross, described the clouds as glowing red and the ocean looked to be bathed in blood. They said that the light pierced through the clouds and illuminated the lightning.

She pulled the truck off of the road and tried to mentally prepare for the invisible impact of the incoming plasma cloud. "Here it comes," she said out loud as she watched natures display of lights rise up again.

Sparks exploded out of the transformer on the power pole next to her from the aurora induced power surge. The street lamps turned off one by one as the power grid started to fail. Block by block the city lights went out until total darkness enveloped her. Then it happened. Her worst fear. The engine in the truck shut down meaning that this electromagnetic blast just took out all of the electronics on this side of the earth as if they were simultaneously hit by lightning.

"Fuck!" she breathed out loud as the aurora swelled again, glowing brightly, swirling above the darkened city as if laughing at the chaos it had caused.

Nasa had warned everyone to be prepared for a once in a lifetime solar event. They had also predicted the most intense solar maximum in fifty years and combined with the increased magnetic disturbances caused by the solar system crossing galactic plane, the sun had just created the largest geomagnetic storm ever seen in human history.

She got out of the truck and looked around. "Now the chaos begins," she said to herself and with a sigh of resignation pulled the handgun out of the bag, loaded it and stuffed it in her jeans. She stuck the knife into her boot and put on the vest and coat. Then she filled the bag with the remaining bottled water and food then took one more look back and walked into the beautifully colored night.

Conner had settled into his motel room in Parkersville and stood on the balcony looking over the city lights. He was still trying to metamorphosis from a brutal killer into a human being. It usually took some time and was somewhat difficult for him. He lit a cigarette and leaned on the railing, enjoying the calm night.

As he scanned the scenery in front of him he noticed a section of the city go dark. He stood up and watched in amazement as every sector darkened until finally the lights in his hotel went out. He looked down at the streets below him and listened as the city turned to chaos. Sirens simultaneously sounded across the blackened space as cars impacted each other from the lack of streetlights and fear took hold of the population.

He went back into the room wondering why the power had failed across the entire city. He picked up his cell phone. It wasn't working either. 'Weird,' he thought.

He paced the room for several hours then shrugged and undressed for bed, deciding to figure it out in the morning. He lay in bed unable to sleep listening to the mayhem in the city outside his window.

Chapter 2

The next morning back in Idaho, the brothers were preparing for their long trek across the country. Mom, Evie, Uncle Neil and a small group of close family and friends were all set up at camp, which was more like a ranch.

The family had spent several years preparing the property for this day. They had built a three-bedroom cabin next to the entrance of a massive cave that reached a hundred yards deep into the mountain as well as a six-bedroom bunkhouse. The cabin faced a large valley with a big rolling river flowing through the bottom of it.

The cabin was completely self-contained and supplies were stacked high along the cave walls. A massive covered barbeque pit stood waiting for steak and the garden was planted. There was a spring emptying into a small creek about thirty yards from the front door.

They had built a shelter for the horses that doubled for a hay shed and was enclosed by a log pole corral. Sixty head of cattle grazed in the large pasture that surrounded the entire mountainside. Kira's chickens roamed freely in front of the cabin and several goats scattered them from time to time.

"I have a surprise for you guys," Warrick said as he walked out the door and dropped his saddlebags on the porch."

"What is that?" Darien laughed as he pointed to the saddlebags. "I always knew you were born into the wrong century, but really, don't you have a duffle bag?"

"Do you want to see it or not?" Warrick said giving him a fake punch in the gut then headed for the hay barn.

Dylan looked up from his coffee curiously. Warrick wasn't quite the type for surprises so this had to be good. He stood up and followed them to the barn.

Both men shook their heads when Warrick opened the door to reveal a large black hummer.

"Come on man, really?" Darien laughed.

Warrick just smiled and got behind the wheel. He put the key in the ignition and started the engine, glancing at his brothers through the windshield. He laughed as they realized that the truck started and turned to him in surprise.

"How did you do that?" they asked in unison.

"I thought all electronics were fried as of last night," Darien said.

"Rebel found out how to do this online one day last year. She showed me the plans and asked if it were possible. I didn't say anything to you guys because I didn't know if it would really work until last night after the fucking thing actually hit," Warrick said proudly, grinning at his accomplishment.

"But how the hell did you do it?" Darien asked.

"I bought the hummer and modified the engine. Not many people realize that because it's basically a military type vehicle, it is easily protected from EMP's. I used a faraday cage to keep some of the parts safe and the rest was just putting it together."

"I never thought it would be you that saved the day, Billy the kid," Dylan teased.

Warrick glared at him then pointed into the truck. "Look, I made sure it had a hair spray and comb compartment just for you, Johnny Bravo."

Dylan glared back, "Funny, you fucker. You're just jealous because I'm what will make this truck look good."

Warrick laughed at his brother and said, "Whatever."

"Come on you two, let's get moving," Darien said shaking his head.

Warrick turned back to the rig and said, "I put a 55 gallon gas tank in the back so we will get as far as Cheyenne before we run out of fuel. But that saves us a couple weeks ride."

Darien and Dylan looked at each other for a second then started laughing.

"What the fuck is so funny?" Warrick pouted.

"We just didn't expect this from you," Dylan exclaimed.

"Fuck you both!" Warrick sulked.

"No, dude, this is really cool. Let's get the horses loaded," Dylan said excitedly.

It didn't take long and they were on their way. They waved good-bye to their mother and uncle as they pulled out of camp.

"Please keep them safe and bring them back home," Kira prayed out loud then turned her attention to the group of people she was responsible for here at home.

Rebel had been walking all night when the pre dawn silence was pierced by a blood-curdling scream. She quickly stepped behind a parked car and squatted down glancing around. The scream came from someone close by so she crept up to the alleyway and looked around the corner. There they were, three men holding a woman at knifepoint.

"Shit! So much for avoiding people," she said under her breath cursing the bad luck. It wasn't in her nature to turn away so she crept forward leaning against the wall of the building.

One of the men ripped the woman's shirt open and pushed the knife against her throat so hard that Rebel could see the blood from thirty yards away. She quietly pulled the handgun from her waistband and scowled at it annoyed. A .22 caliber pistol wasn't much as weapons go, and wouldn't mortally wound a man unless it was a close shot and damaged a vital organ. But a precise hit would definitely get someone's attention.

The woman screamed again urging Rebel into action. She pointed the gun at one of the men and fired, hitting him in the thigh. The shot rang out louder than she expected in the still morning but she quickly fired two more rounds. All three men howled in surprise and fell to the ground.

The woman took off running the second she was loose and didn't look back. Rebel ran the opposite direction, seeing no reason to wait around for the men to realize they weren't fatally injured.

She sprinted down the street for a couple blocks then ducked into a doorway. She peeked out to see if anyone was following her and found the street empty so she stepped out and started running.

Normally, she could run a mile in six minutes, but her bag was heavy and she had been walking all night. She slowed to a jog but kept going now thankful that she had spent so much time in the gym over the last few years.

The streets looked like a snap shot out of one of those zombie movies. Cars were just randomly left in the street. The windows in the buildings looked hauntingly empty. But it was the silence that freaked her out. It was as if the CME had wiped out all sound on earth. No cars running, no jackhammers, no sirens, no one talking. Just silence.

As she jogged deeper into the city pondering the distance she'd traveled so far, she suddenly became aware of yelling and gunfire ahead of her. She slowed to a walk, the yelling growing louder as she crept down the empty streets. She stepped into the doorway of a corner building and looked down the street, startled by the scene in front of her.

Two hundred people were engaged in a vicious bloody battle. They were shooting each other and slashing with knives and throwing firebombs. Buildings were on fire, filling the streets with smoke. People were breaking windows out of the storefronts and taking whatever they could carry. It was an out of control gang fight in the middle of a looting mob.

The fighting swarm started moving in her direction so she stepped back looking around for a place to hide but there was nothing. She slid into the door entrance of a large glass faced building hoping they would move the other direction. Suddenly the door opened behind her and she was yanked inside the building. She spun around and pulled out her pistol, pointing it at the man who had grabbed her.

"Quiet!" the man hissed unconcerned by the weapon, "or I'll put you back out there."

Rebel hesitated then lowered the gun. Obviously he was trying to help her.

He reached over to lock the door and looked out the window just as bullets riddled the side of the building.

They both dropped to the floor, glass raining down on top of them.

Rebel peeked out the window as the battle raged in front of her and once again reminded herself to stay out of the cities and away from people. She scanned the block and bit her lip as she watched a large group of men pull a woman out of one of the buildings.

"Help me!" the woman wailed hysterically.

Rebel glanced at the man beside her and said, "They'll kill her."

He shrugged, "Can't help her. They'll kill us."

"Maybe," she said walking to the door, "but I won't just stand by and watch."

He looked at her curiously. "Lady, why would you risk your life for her?"

"Why did you help me?" she asked, glaring back at him angrily.

"God damn it," he said picking up a shotgun leaning against the wall. "You are poorly armed and I have no range. We are walking to our own funeral."

Rebel looked back out the window wondering how the hell she was going to pull this off. She looked at the .22 again and scowled knowing that she would have to acquire one of their weapons. "I will take one of their guns, you just back me up. I'm Rebel, what's your name?"

"I'm Dave, "he sighed as he followed her out the back door and around the corner of the building.

The main fight had moved down the block and the group of men that had taken the woman had hidden themselves in an alley across the street. Rebel crept to the building beside the alley and heard the excruciating terror of the woman struggling against the sexual assault.

Rebel picked up a piece of chain laying at the edge of the alley and wrapped it around her knuckles. She snuck up behind a very preoccupied man on the outer edge of the group and tapped him on the shoulder. As he turned to her, she swung her fist hitting him square in the chin. His eyes rolled back in his head and he slowly tilted backward, toppling over unconscious. She snatched his weapon and immediately opened fire on the group of men with the fully automatic rifle, aiming low so that she didn't slaughter them, although she wanted to.

Ten men dropped instantly and several more grabbed wounds and ducked out of the way. She advanced into the group and grabbed the woman to her feet, keeping the weapon leveled on the surprised men, then backed out of the alley slowly with the woman behind her. She eyed the group, watching for anyone to move.

One of the men caught her attention as he stepped from the shadows toward her but a shotgun blast suddenly echoed through the narrow space between the buildings and the man dropped, his weapon rolling out of his grasp.

Rebel turned to Dave in surprise, silently thanking him with a nod then grabbed the woman's arm and raced across the street and out of sight.

"This way!" Dave yelled leading them toward the back of his store. He led them to a stairway that went up to what she guessed were apartments on the top floor.

"Come in," he instructed pointing to one of the doors.

Inside, Rebel was surprised to find about fifteen terrified people huddled together. A small boy scooted closer to his mother and hid his head in her arm as Rebel walked in.

She helped the woman to the couch then looked at Dave. "Do all of you live up here?"

"Yes," he replied and shrugged, "and damn sick of it. I've replaced those windows twice this year. Different day, different altercation."

"So this happens a lot around here?"

Dave sighed dejectedly, "Every damn day, but it's always worse when the power goes out."

Rebel walked over to the window and peeked down to the street at the violence that was disappearing around the next block. She looked around the room at the frightened people and felt sorry for them. Normally, she didn't talk to anyone about the 2012 stuff because so few people could grasp it. But now that it was happening it was time to start warning them.

"Can I talk to you in the other room?" she asked leading Dave to what must have been the kitchen.

"Who the hell are you?" he asked before Rebel could say anything.

"My name is Rebel. I was just passing through when I heard the ruckus. Thank you for helping me," she said. "Look, even though I'm not from here, I can imagine what you go through and I know that it's going to get worse out there. This is not just a power outage. We were hit by a severe geomagnetic solar storm that took out the entire power grid. We aren't going to get power back for years."

The familiar look of disbelief was plain on his face, but Rebel continued. "That isn't the only thing. The blast was so bad that it fried every piece of electronic equipment in its path." She paused wishing she wasn't the devil's postman. "We are going to face more earthquakes and tornadoes and maybe a pole shift before this is done," she explained regretfully.

"I've heard something about this, the world is going to end in 2012 right?" he said and started pacing the floor. "I thought it was all a bunch of bullshit."

"I'm not suggesting that the world will end, but it will change drastically. You are all in danger here and need to get out of the city. We have only been without power for a few hours and look outside. What do you think will happen after a few weeks?" Rebel paused to let it sink in. "I don't know where to tell you to go, but the city is dangerous. If you have friends or family in a rural area, you should try to get there."

"You're serious!" he said shaking his head.

"Yes, I'm serious. I'm only telling you because you helped me and I want to return the favor," Rebel said then sat down in a chair.

Dave looked at her in disbelief for a moment then shrugged, "You look tired, you might as well crash with the rest of us for awhile."

"Thank you," she replied realizing that she hadn't

slept for two days. She stood up to find a couch to sleep on. He would either believe her or not. It was out of her hands now.

A few hours later, sunlight pierced through the window waking Rebel from a restless sleep. She felt better though, even if it was just couple hours rest. Silently she crept down the stairs and out the door. She was careful to lock it behind her even though all of the windows were broken out.

The police were out in full force and from the looks of the blood on the street, had picked up many dead and wounded people. The buildings stood tall above her looking hauntingly empty and the fires continued to burn spilling ash like snow on the sidewalk.

An officer walked up to her and said, "This isn't over, we are just following behind them picking up the pieces. We can't stop the riots so stay off the streets. The National Guard has been notified but until they get here, there's nothing we can do. They were headed south last I seen."

"Thank you," Rebel said. "I'm heading west." And with that she headed up the road.

Conner opened his eyes just as the sun peeked over the mountain. He had barely slept, anticipating that something else might happen. He dressed and walked down to the lobby to see if they had heard anything there.

"What's the word? Why is the power out?" he asked the clerk.

The man shrugged and said, "No one will tell us anything. All I know is that now nothing works, including the cars. There isn't a car on the road this morning."

Conner stepped back in confusion, "The cars aren't working either?"

The clerk shook his head, "No one knows why."

"What the fuck is going on?" Conner mumbled then walked back to his room to get his keys. He tromped down to the car and tried the ignition. Nothing.

"This is the weirdest thing I've ever dealt with," he said out loud as he gathered all of his belongings out of the car. He went back up to his room, unsure of what his next move should be. No power, no phones, no cars. Something was definitely wrong here.

He stepped out onto the balcony and watched the chaos below him, pondering his new situation.

Shane and Cayden had decided to stay at the motel. It had a perfect little apartment tucked in the back. The windows already had bars on them and the patio had a built in barbeque. The manager hadn't opened the motel this morning because there was no power and everything was eerily quiet.

Cayden looked out the window and said, "I can't believe that no one is out moving around. I hope it stays that way."

"One could only hope," Shane snorted then turned serious and said. "I don't think we have enough food and water."

"What you got in mind? We gonna rob the Wal-Mart?" Cayden jested.

"Yes, we are," Shane answered seriously, "and we need to do it before people realize what is going on. The longer they are without power, the more looting will take place. We are just going to be first in line."

Cayden looked at Shane in amazement. "Not good bro. I don't like it."

"Dude, if the power was on, we would go shopping and pay for the shit, but without power, they won't even open the doors."

The logic made sense but Cayden was still uncomfortable with the deal.

"We have to make sure Jade has food and water for at least a month, maybe a little more," Shane reasoned. "A man can only walk thirty miles a day and it is eight hundred and fifty miles from Idaho to here."

Cayden did the math in his head and realized that his brother was right. "Shit. Ok then, let's do it."

They sat down to make a plan. If they were caught and jailed for looting, the brothers would surely pull off a jailbreak, but they would never hear the end of it.

Suddenly Jade walked into the room and they both jumped like small children in the cookie jar.

Jade laughed and asked, "What the hell? What are you two up to now?"

Shane looked at Cayden who ducked his head. "Well, we are…, we are planning our supply list for the next month."

Jade sauntered over to take a look at the list. "So where are we getting this stuff?"

"Jade, we are gonna rob the Wal-Mart and you aren't going," Cayden said anticipating her argument and standing up to emphasize the statement.

"I am to going with you!" Jade said standing as tall as she could to counter him.

"Shane, she can't go," Cayden said looking at his brother for back up. Even though he was pushing a foot taller than her, she seemed to be over powering him.

"Cayden, you won't win this fight. You know how she is. When she makes up her mind, its final," Shane said with a sigh.

Jade smiled at Cayden as he collapsed back into his chair. "You might need me Cayden, don't get mad." Then she pouted her lips and said in a soft voice, "I want to help. I'm tired of having to be saved."

That was it. Cayden caved. All of his reserve was gone. That's how it always was with Jade. She could take your heart out of your chest and work it over a little, then hand it back to you with a smile. Thank God she was so sweet because if she were wicked, no man on earth could be saved.

"Fine, but you don't leave my side!" Cayden said fiercely.

"All right, jeeze, you don't have to be grumpy. What's the plan?" Jade asked excitedly.

After an hour of deliberating, they were no closer to

a plan. Finally Jade asked, "So why Wal-Mart? Why don't we find a little store and just buy the stuff?"

Shane and Cayden looked at each other then they both looked at Jade. "We need a month's worth of supplies and we didn't get a chance to cash our checks so we don't have much cash. Besides, I doubt if anything would be open," Shane said.

"Oh, I'm sure someone will sell us supplies," Jade said. "And I have money." She giggled at the look on the boys' faces. "Mom made me pack an emergency bag and I grabbed it on the way out of my apartment." She paused and turned serious. "Now that I think about it, I didn't even consciously think about getting it, I just grabbed it on the way out the door. It was just hanging there like she told me and....," she trailed off sadly.

Cayden stood and hugged her. "Don't worry Jade, your mom will get here." He looked at Shane over her head with sadness in his eyes.

Shane stood up and said, "Ok, Jade, we will do it your way. How much money do you have?"

Jade let go of Cayden and pounced on her bag. She dug around for a moment and pulled out a wallet with a thousand dollars in it. She looked up at the boys and said, "This should get us whatever we need. Let's go shopping."

Both boys laughed and they headed for the door.

Rebel sighed with relief as she reached the edge of the city. Now that she was in a rural area, she may be able to find a horse. She walked well into the afternoon before she finally did. A little house sitting back off the main road with a pasture sporting two head of horses stood out ahead of her. She walked up to the door and knocked, unsurprised when the door opened and she found herself staring at the business end of a rifle. The older man holding the weapon peered at her suspiciously.

"Sir, I'm friendly. I've come to ask if you will sell one of your horses," Rebel said calmly.

"Not interested," the man responded. "I might need them. Never know what's going to happen now."

"I understand your concern," Rebel soothed. "I may be able to help you understand what is going to happen. I assure you, I mean no harm."

The man slowly lowered the rifle looking cautiously around her to see if she was alone.

"Why are you here alone, and on foot?" he asked.

"I was stuck in Virginia when the power went out. I'm on my way back to Idaho," Rebel replied. "It's a long way. That's why I'm asking about the horse."

He looked at her somewhat surprised, but his expression softened as he said, "I don't use those damn horses anymore. They just sit out there and eat. You can have 'em both if you need 'em."

"Thank you," Rebel said relieved. "I'd be glad to pay you. Do you also have tack that I could purchase?"

The man set the rifle down and led her to the barn. "You said you know what the hell is going on?" he asked waving his hand toward the sky. "This ain't just a power outage is it? Somethin's happenin ain't it?" He looked past Rebel and whistled out into the pasture.

As the horses came thundering into the corral, Rebel said, "Yes, we have experienced an impact from a very large coronal mass ejection. It has wiped out the entire power grid and all of the satellites." Rebel paused not knowing how much to say or how to say it.

The man bridled a big muscular buckskin gelding and led him to the tack shed then glanced over at her and began saddling the animal.

"We won't have power back for a very long time. Do you have a food storage?" she asked. "We will more than likely experience more severe weather, earthquakes and possibly large volcanic eruptions. I believe it is possible that we could see a geomagnetic pole shift in the months ahead."

Rebel held her breath expecting him to laugh or argue or something. But he just kept to his task so she went on feeling like a broken record, "I also believe that something is perturbing the path of the orbiting asteroids and comets possibly sending them toward us."

The man looked at her for a second then walked into the tack shed and returned with saddlebags and a rifle scabbard. When the horse was fitted he handed her the reins and said, "That is quite a tale. The worst part about it is that I have no doubt you could be right. Isn't that a god damned shame." He shook his head dejectedly then said, "Wait here a minute." He walked back to the house and returned a moment later with a 243-pump action rifle.

She couldn't believe his kindness. "Thank you so much," she said completely surprised. "But it's going to be dangerous living for awhile, maybe you should keep it for your own protection."

"I have a backup little lady. You take it and keep yourself safe," he said haltering a stout little mare. He handed her the lead rope and said, "This is Punkin and this is Jake. Jake is a little older but he is a good boy, loyal and strong. Take good care of him, he was my wife's horse before she died."

Rebel dug into her pocket for money but he waved his hand again.

"I don't need your money. I don't need much of anything anymore." He looked up into the sky sadly then turned and walked toward the house.

She paused for a moment sensing his anxiety then swung onto the animal's back. She glanced back and regrettably watched the kind man enter his house and was about to turn the horse onto the road when a rifle shot rebounded through the windows. She jumped back off the horse and ran onto the porch but knew from the door that there was nothing she could do.

She hung her head sadly and said, "That is the damn shame."

The brothers pulled into Cheyenne with little gas to spare.

"Let's find a place to stash the truck and we will ride from here," Darien said. "We may be able to pick the truck up on the way back and find enough gas somewhere to get it home."

They parked the truck just off the road inside a grove of trees and unloaded the horses.

Warrick couldn't help grinning as he holstered his revolver then slid his rifle into the scabbard.

"Like I said," Darien said to Dylan as he pointed at Warrick and laughed. "Born in the wrong century weren't you Billy."

Warrick didn't respond. He just kept on grinning. He swung onto his horse and headed east at a gallop.

Dylan smoothed his shirt and dusted off his boots. He picked up his hat and looked into the mirror at his hair and scowled as he pulled it on his head. "Hat hair!" he huffed then mounted his horse and pushed him into a gallop following his brother.

Darien shook his head and smiled to himself, "I'm going on a dangerous, two month long mission with Billy the kid and Johnny Bravo. What could go wrong?"

Connor couldn't believe he was stuck here! He was going crazy. He had been holed up in this motel for what seemed like days trying to figure out what to do. The staff hadn't been showing up for work and there wasn't any food left. He paced the floor again and decided, enough was enough. He was going to walk back to the Rockies.

The city had grown tense as the supplies ran short. People had started breaking into stores and fighting in the streets. It wouldn't be long before it would be too dangerous to even be in the city.

He picked up his luggage and sorted through it, dressing in his field clothes. He strapped on his holster and put on his boots. Anything that didn't fit into his duffle bag was left. He headed out the door planning to stop at the sporting goods store that he'd seen on the edge of town. He would definitely need better supplies for the long journey ahead of him.

Outside, the streets were worse than he'd thought they would be. People were stealing stereos and gas out of the stalled cars in the streets in broad daylight. Small fires were burning everywhere and there was no sign of police anywhere. He picked his way to the outskirts of town and was relieved to find it a little quieter out here. He spotted the sporting goods store and knelt down behind a parked car to scope it out.

He was about a block away making sure that no one was around when he saw a woman sneaking around to the back alley entrance of the store. He stood up curiously and followed her around the building. He watched as she picked up a rock and broke out the window in the back door and with a quick glance behind her, slid inside.

'What the hell is she up to?' he thought to himself then followed her inside.

Rebel rode quietly up to the bank of the Ohio River and was amazed at how big it was. It kind of reminded her of parts of the Snake River back in Idaho. She quickly realized that the only way to cross the river from here was over a freeway overpass in the city of Parkersburg. She edged upriver toward the city and got as close as she dared without being seen. Her horses needed rest and she needed supplies. She would have to go into the city. She looked around until she found an empty building tucked way off the road then dismounted and led the horses inside.

"Not real comfy Jake," she said to the animal as she unsaddled him. He didn't seem to mind as he stood quietly.

She hid the rifle behind a stack of crates just in case someone did come inside. She didn't want to lose the horses and her weapon. She took off the coat and vest and stashed her duffle bag. "Okay, I'll be back soon. Just sit tight," she said then headed into town on foot.

The outskirts of the city were semi quiet. She had imagined it to be much worse. She breathed a sigh of relief when she spotted a sporting goods store a couple blocks up the road. She crept around to the back alley hoping to get inside easily. She picked up a rock and broke out the window in the back door then paused for a moment feeling as if someone was watching her. She glanced back but couldn't see anyone so she stepped inside and hid behind a very large safe. She pulled out the mighty .22 and waited.

Fuck! She was right, someone was following her inside. 'It's probably the cops,' she thought to herself. Looting was a big deal in situations like this. She held her breath as a man walked quietly past her into the store then stealthily stalked up behind him and pushed the barrel of her gun into the back of his head.

"Why are you following me?" she demanded.

The man froze and slowly raised his hands up. He was dressed in black from his shirt to his boots and carried only a duffle bag. She glanced across his wide shoulders and noticed a holster that more than likely held a firearm.

"Hold on there," he said calmly. "I was on my way in here same as you. You were just first in line that's all. I wasn't following you, I just needed a few supplies."

"Hand over your weapon!" she said pushing her gun a little harder.

He surprisingly complied, setting the revolver on a shelf next to her.

Rebel lowered her gun, but kept it in her hand. She picked up his gun wondering what the hell she was going to do now. He had just as much right to be here as she did. Fair was fair. After all, it wasn't her store.

Conner turned around to check out the woman who had assaulted him. He looked her up and down pleasantly surprised. To her credit, she just stood there glaring back at him, but didn't move. She was dressed in a t-shirt, jeans and boots and didn't look to be all that threatening. She wasn't tall, but wasn't short either. She was very trim, athletically built and looked to be in very good physical shape. She wasn't a raving beauty but was subtly good looking with hazel eyes and medium length brown-blond hair.

Rebel studied the man standing in front of her trying to decide if he was a threat. He was ruggedly handsome and stood with a confidence that comes from being able to handle yourself in a fight. His arms were thick and his chest was enticingly wide. She browsed downward and took in his thick thighs and long legs.

After moments of scrutiny, he pointedly asked, "What in the hell is someone like you doing looting a place like this?"

Rebel vaguely heard the question and tried to focus on the words but was distracted by the sudden fire shooting through her veins. "I'm just passing through," she mumbled after she released the breath she had been holding. She forced herself to turn away from him and fought to calm her racing pulse. Her heart was pounding and it wasn't because she was afraid. Her body was tense and she was suddenly aware that she hadn't cleaned up in awhile. Her stomach was doing some kind of butterfly dance and she felt warm all over. 'What the hell is this shit about?' she asked herself, aggravated by her physical reaction to him.

She hadn't thought about a man that way in a long time let alone physically responded to one checking her out. But there was something about those sharp blue green eyes that seemed to burn through her clothes and melt her skin as he looked over every inch of her body.

'What an ass hole!' she thought, suddenly angry. 'How dare he eyeball her like that?' She strode quickly into the store trying to put some space between them. She was so flustered that she bumped into a barrel full of fishing poles and it crashed to the ground.

"Jesus Christ!" she grumbled under her breath, trying to gain control of the heat that still traced the length of her veins. "You don't have time for this shit, Rebel!"

She stomped over to the gun counter and broke the glass out of the case with more force than necessary. It did make her feel a little better to break something though. Her body felt flushed and she still wasn't breathing right. Her mind drifted to his tousled hair. It was dark blond and made him look terribly handsome as it curled over the top of his ears. He was about six inches taller than her and extremely physically fit.

Her stomach tightened again as her mind flashed a vision of his bulging arms and strong thighs. She couldn't help thinking about how his pecks moved under his tight black shirt. His face was tan and his hands were big and calloused telling her that he didn't work behind a desk. 'For Christ sake!' she thought. 'She had been checking him out too!'

"God damn it!" she exclaimed out loud. Then closed her eyes and thought, 'Fuck! Get a hold of yourself!' She forced herself to focus as she set his revolver down and reached into the glass cabinet and pulled out a Colt .45 caliber semi-automatic pistol. She smiled, admiring the handgun for a moment then turned to the weapons lined up on the wall behind her and picked out a nice 12-gage shotgun. She grabbed a bag and filled it with ammunition and extra clips for her growing collection of weapons.

The man had slipped from her mind for a moment as she armed herself but when she turned to find a holster, she caught his eye. He was casually leaning against the wall about six feet away with his arms crossed across his wide chest watching her. Her pulse jumped and her breath caught in her throat.

"What?" she practically yelled at him and couldn't help watching his biceps ripple as he pushed himself to his full height.

"Nothin, I was just wondering why a woman like you would be alone in a place like this. You obviously know weapons and I can see that you're arming yourself for a reason," he responded.

Rebel was so flustered at herself that she didn't dare answer him. She shook her head in frustration as she strapped on the duel holster and slid the Colt into one side and the Ruger into the other. She found another bag and started stuffing it with supplies.

He followed her around picking up supplies for himself as she shopped for lighters, candles, water purification tablets and a boy scout style aluminum mess kit. She picked up a towel and some soap, a lantern and a bottle of propane. She threw in several more knives, a water bottle, a large first aid kit, and picked up a Steelers 'ball cap. His presence seemed to fill the space between them and for a brief second, almost seemed comforting. She had been alone for a long time.

Conner laughed as she pulled the hat on her head then glared at him. 'Wow,' he thought to himself. 'She doesn't like me at all.' What a weird situation and what a strange woman. From what he could see, she knew what she came into this store for and it wasn't for gathering supplies to guard her home from looters. 'What is your story?' he pondered to himself watching her closely. Curiosity was going to get the best of him today.

Rebel couldn't help once again feeling like she was in a movie. It was pretty symbolic to go into a gun shop and strap on a holster, load up with weapons then go kick some zombie ass. Too bad this was real and it was gonna get ugly. She looked up at the very good-looking man standing in front of her grinning. 'Too bad I couldn't let you distract me for a few days,' she thought to herself then blushed when he looked back at her as if he could read her mind.

She forced herself to turn away from those piercing eyes and looked around the store. 'Keep your mind on business,' she reprimanded herself again and picked up a small tent, a sleeping bag and a nice pair of binoculars. She grabbed a couple t-shirts and another pair of jeans She spied a camp style coffee pot and threw in a couple bags of coffee. When she felt she had everything that she needed, she turned to go.

"Aren't you going to give me some kind of an answer?" Conner asked urgently. Why he cared so much he didn't know. His job made it impossible to have a relationship let alone have a family and he hadn't been with a woman in awhile. Women didn't understand his need for freedom and he certainly didn't need the hassle of explaining it to one right now. But there was definitely something about this tough little thing that made his blood heat up.

"I did answer you!" Rebel said, again too harshly then mentally calmed herself so that she could at least answer him civilly. "I'm just passing through, on my way west."

This caught his attention and he stiffened, looking at her intently. "You're traveling west on foot? How far are you going?"

Rebel felt her knees soften under the weight of his stare and couldn't seem to tear her eyes away this time. She couldn't help but feel as if he were looking into her soul. 'What the hell was it about him that made her respond like this?' she wondered. She was very perplexed and shook her head and smiled at herself in dismay. 'You are unbelievable Rebel! Just get over it and move on.'

Conner's heart fluttered a little when her face softened and she actually smiled a little. 'Why was he so affected by her?' he wondered curiously?

"I don't know you. Why would I tell you where I'm going?" Rebel asked regaining some strength. "You could be some handsome stalker that kills women after he charms them into telling him everything about themselves."

"Handsome? Did you just say that I'm handsome?" he asked her and laughed at the vexed look on her face.

"I don't have time for this!" Rebel said trying to pull herself together. But she stammered when she said, "I have to go."

"Wait," he said and caught her arm. "I'm not a stocker. I am handsome, but not dangerous." He smiled down at her knowing instinctively that he had affected her somehow.

Oh my God! When he smiled he had just the slightest tease of a dimple. She could barely breathe and her heart was now pounding so hard she was sure he would hear it. He was standing so close that she could feel those pecks that she had intently noticed earlier. She shifted her weight and his extremely muscular thigh brushed up against hers. The touch greatly tested the last of her reserve and she almost moaned out loud.

Conner felt the heat flash that exploded like a bomb between them and his body responded violently. Standing this close, he could sense her sleek muscles and almost feel her breasts heave with each breath she took. He tensed and unconsciously leaned into the weapons that she had strapped to her nicely formed hips.

Rebel jumped at his touch, breaking the spell that had drawn them together for a brief moment. She closed her eyes tightly and brought herself back to reality. This was a distraction that she could not afford right now. Her logical side took over and she stepped away from him, her heart still pounding.

"I really have to go," she breathed. It took all of her strength to pick up the bags and disappear the same way she came in.

Conner just stood there breathing heavily, trying to decipher what had just happened. He was not the type to fall for just any woman so the obvious physical connection that had seared them both a moment ago left him stunned. He watched as she disappeared out the door and suddenly ached for another encounter with this fiery little mystery woman. He decided then and there that he would follow her. He couldn't let this go without further exploration.

He quickly grabbed his revolver that she had left on the counter and the bag of supplies he'd gathered up. He looked around and couldn't pass up the breakdown recurve bow and a handful of arrows. He picked out a shotgun and a rifle, grabbed some ammunition and followed her out the door.

Rebel cursed herself as she stomped back to where she had left Jake and the mare. She was so riled up that she wasn't being cautious and cursed herself again. "What the hell just happened," she said out loud. It was not like her to get all twitterpated over just anyone. "I am not some high school girl that swoons at any gorgeous guy that happens to brush up against me!" she ranted as she opened the door to the building.

Jake perked his ears up and blew at her nervously. "It's just me Jake," she said soothingly and he instantly calmed at the sound of her voice.

As she saddled the horse, she intentionally forced that intoxicating man out of her head. She had to focus on getting through the city and across the bridge without being assaulted by bands of rioters or gangs. It wasn't going to be easy. She couldn't afford to be emotionally vulnerable right now. There was no room in her world for friends, boyfriends, attraction, or love. Especially not love. It would make her lose focus and right now she needed to be at her best to get to Jade.

She put the vest back on and filled the saddlebags with some of the supplies she'd picked up and strapped the rest of it in the duffle bags across the mare's wide shoulders. She led the horses out of the building, mounted and headed toward the overpass

She kept to the trees as she neared the freeway and dismounted to let the horses graze as she waited for the cover of darkness. Her nerves were shot. This was dangerous and she couldn't keep that man out of her mind. Images of him were competing with thoughts of loading weapons and dodging bullets.

Suddenly she felt as if someone was watching her again. Jake noticed at the same time she did and lifted his head to stare into the distance with his ears pointed forward. He blew softly and Rebel gently soothed him by rubbing his muzzle. She pulled out the colt and stood behind him.

She looked into the clearing and saw a man walking toward them. Jake started stomping his front foot in response to her sudden tension. She slid the safety off and racked the weapon. The man recognized the distinct sound immediately and stopped.

"It's me," he said flatly.

Rebel couldn't tell if she was scared, relieved, or pissed off. "What the fuck are you doing?" she yelled. "I would have shot you! You are following me! Who the hell are you anyway?"

The tirade of emotions swept through her one at a time. First she was scared then pissed and still, somehow she felt a sense of relief.

"I'm sorry, I didn't mean to scare you. I was just, uh, worried about you." Now it was his turn to be flustered. She certainly didn't seem to be the type that needed someone to worry about her. She was looking at him as if he were insane and still hadn't lowered the weapon that was dialed in on his chest. The thought crossed his mind for a second that she might actually shoot him. This had been a foolish quest on his part. Why would she trust a stranger? God, he suddenly felt nervous.

"My name is Conner," he went on trying to calm her. "I am heading west as well. My family is in Montana. I was working out here but was stranded when my car wouldn't start. I had decided to walk home and went to the store to get supplies for my trip and saw you go in first. We are really just traveling on the same path. I promise again, I'm not dangerous."

Rebel relaxed a little seeing the sheepish look on his face. He seemed sincere. She holstered the colt and stepped around Jake. "Are you asking if you can travel with me?" she asked as she walked up to him. That was a big mistake. She instantly felt a tingling spark of heat vibrate through her as if she were holding a lightning rod into a storm. She immediately stepped back toward her horse.

He grinned at her as if he could read her thoughts and replied, "Well, ya, I guess I am. We are both heading in the same direction and I can offer you some protection."

Rebel looked him over feeling her abdomen tighten in an erotic jolt then quickly turned away, "You can't protect me from this fucking turn on," she said under her breath and idly tightened the cinch on the saddle.

He walked up behind her and she froze as her muscles tensed in anticipation.

"Or maybe you can protect me," he whispered softly.

She spun around and pushed him back. "Fine! You can follow me but keep up and keep your distance."

"Fine," he said smiling at her conflicting words.

His smile told her that he was enjoying this little game of fire and ice. He knew exactly what she was feeling.

When she just glared at him, he stepped back and put his hands up in mock submission. "Ok, ok," he said then turned serious. "Nice horse. I thought you said you were on foot."

"No, you said I was on foot. He was a gift from a very nice man," Rebel explained, fondly remembering the man who had been so kind to her.

Conner suddenly felt like he had been kicked in the stomach by that horse. 'Jealousy? Over a woman you've known for five whole minutes?' he asked himself shaking his head in dismay. 'Why wouldn't she have a man in her life you idiot?' He had to change the subject. He didn't like this feeling at all. "So do you know what the hell is going on with the power outage and the cars quitting and shit? No one seems to know anything about it."

"Ya, I know what's going on, but first we need to cross this god dammed river without being seen. Do you know the area?"

"Not really, but I know the only way to cross is the overpass. That part shouldn't be hard but getting there unseen will be a trick. People are crazy out there."

"I know,' she said solemnly. "Since I left D.C. I've had to shoot people, save people, escape gang fights. All of a sudden just because there are no police, men think that it's open season on women." She shook her head angrily. "At least I made a few of them pay a price."

Conner raised his eyebrow and crossed his arms over his chest. "Maybe you are the dangerous one, not me. Maybe I should be afraid of you."

Rebel looked him up and down and laughed. "I don't picture you as the type to be afraid of much. Besides, I didn't kill them. They will survive if they can find medical attention." She inhaled deeply and admitted, "I just couldn't walk away while she was screaming."

Conner's gut wrenched at the thought and he couldn't help feeling admiration for her mixed in with his dismay.

She glanced up at him seeing his apprehension and lied with a smile, "It's not like I brandished a fully automatic machine gun and went on a shooting spree."

Conner could sense that she was lying and tried to hide his emotions. He smiled back, "See then? You can protect me."

'God, please don't smile at me,' Rebel thought trying to control her traitorous body.

"Here, take the mare, it's dark enough to go," she said trying to ignore the fire that had been ignited in her soul. Silently they led the horses toward freeway overpass.

Chapter 3

Shane, Cayden and Jade searched until they found a little privately owned store a few blocks from the motel. The owner had locked the door and was guarding it with a scowl and a shotgun. Shane finally convinced the man that they weren't dangerous and Jade had showed him the money so he let them in.

They quickly picked out the supplies that they would need and prepared to leave.

"Thank you for helping us," Cayden said to the storeowner as he paid him.

Shane peeked out the door and said, "The problem now is trying to get this stuff back to the motel without getting mugged."

Jade was visibly nervous and it must have made the little man feel bad because he offered to sell them a shotgun.

Cayden thanked him again and they headed up the road.

They were almost to the motel when a string of National Guard Hummers drove by.

"They have declared Martial Law," Shane said. "This could be both good and bad. Rebel told me stories about concentration camps that the government has built all over the U.S. There are thousands of them. She said that once the shit came down, the government would not be able to control the population, so they will put any troublemakers in the camps. Hopefully just the trouble makers."

"Ya," Cayden said, "we are going to have to stay out of sight until the brothers get here. Thank God we found enough supplies to get us by."

"We need to remember that once they declare Martial Law we do not have the right to bear arms. If they see the shotgun, they will take it. I think we should hide it and most of this stuff just in case someone does show up," Shane said opening the door to their little apartment.

Inside, they figured out a way to hide the supplies in

one of the closets in the bedroom behind a large armoire.

"That will do, I guess," Cayden said when everything was stashed away.

While Shane started dinner on the barbeque just out the back door, Jade asked the boys, "Do you really think that we will see a geomagnetic pole shift? I've seen projection maps of what earth will look like afterward and there is ocean all the way into Idaho. Most of the east coast is under water. The entire Midwest is flooded from the Mississippi to the Missouri."

"I believe that it's possible. I heard that Einstein was extremely interested in the theory and believed it was inevitable. Some people think that it could happen in a matter of hours or days," Cayden replied as he picked up three water bottles.

"Some scientists say that the earth will actually slow down and stop then start spinning in the opposite direction. If earth is spinning at a rate of one thousand miles per hour, what would happen to us if it slowed down even just a little?" Jade said moving uneasily in her chair.

Cayden opened the water and said, "We would be thrown to the ground. Everything would be. Even the bible talks about three days of darkness. You could interpret that as the earth stopping during our night and staying still and dark for a few days until it started turning again." He sat down and continued, "The Islam's talk about the sun rising in the west. If you put all of that together, I think it adds up to a geological pole shift."

"Have you seen the books that mom used to collect and sort her research? There were a lot of them. She always told me that something just told her to research it. Even though some of it made sense, I didn't think it would happen. I didn't believe her," Jade said thinking about her mother.

"Even Rebel wasn't sure if it would happen," Shane said to ease her mind. "She believes that we should be prepared for anything. Even if just one of these events takes place, we will be ready."

"Ya, but now we are all separated and it is my fault.

I'm the one who had to break the plan up," Jade cried out suddenly.

"Jade, Rebel didn't make all of those plans for when it happened. She made the plans for after it happened. This is just a bump in the road to her. She wanted to ensure that we would survive after all of the chaos was over. This is just the beginning. If she is right, we will need her plan for next year and the year after that. We will all be home safe by then," Cayden soothed

"Now let's eat and stop worrying," Shane instructed, handing Jade a plate.

"I'm really glad you guys know how to cook. I can, but I don't like to."

"All of the brothers can cook. Probably because they are all bachelors. That includes us too. They may have close relationships with women but they aren't the marrying kind I guess," Shane laughed.

"Well, they work a lot, and they to travel to work so it's hard to have a family," Cayden defended. "Just look at us. I wanted to meet girls here but I haven't had time."

The three continued talking well into the evening then headed off to bed.

Shane waited until he was sure the other two were sleeping then snuck out the door into the night. He needed to find a better weapon and wanted see what was going on outside. It was a huge risk though, with so many military personnel guarding the streets. He wondered if they would be able to keep control or if the city would eventually fall to the large gangs that marauded through it. Either way, he needed more protection for Cayden and Jade. Besides, he didn't trust the military and wondered if they may be the second largest threat that they would face.

He looked back at the little motel worriedly. If shit came down, they would be trapped between the city of Omaha and the river. As he neared the city center he could see fires burning and heard gunshots ring out periodically. The gangs were already fighting the restrictions of marshal law and engaging the military.

He turned into a quiet alley and noticed candlelight flickering through the window in an abandoned building half way down the block. He peeked through the window and saw a circle of about eight men standing around a table. Every one of them held an AK47.

"God, I would like to get my hands on one of those weapons," he mumbled out loud.

His thoughts were interrupted when he heard someone coming down the alley. He quickly slipped behind a dumpster and held his breath. Two well-armed men walked toward him dragging a gagged woman with them. Her hands were bound and she was fighting them with every step.

'What the Fuck?' he breathed to himself.

The woman had obviously been crying and even in the darkness he could see bruises on her face. Chivalry ran deep in his family and Shane knew he wouldn't be able to walk away now.

"What are you going to do with her?" one of the men asked the other. "Frank is going to shoot you for bringing her here."

"Fuck Frank, I can have a little fun if I want to," the man spat back.

Shane held his breath trying to figure out how he was going to free the woman. He wasn't afraid of a fight and could definitely hold his own. He stood about six foot two and was built like a football player. On the other hand, he was used to having back up from one of his brothers but this time he knew he was on his own and it was going to be tough.

The man holding her stopped by the door and pulled her up close to his large body then licked his tongue across her entire face. She shrieked with terror and desperately fought her captor.

That was all it took for Shane to launch from behind the dumpster and pound his fist into the closest man's face. The impact knocked the man into the wall with such force that his head bounced off of the brick knocking him unconscious. The other man shoved the woman away from him and turned to face his attacker.

Shane recovered quickly from round one and spun around landing his fist into the other man's jaw, sending him reeling backwards. The man lifted his weapon and would have gotten a shot off if Shane hadn't kicked the gun out of his hand. Shane pulled a knife out of his belt and sliced it across the man's chest, spilling blood onto his hand.

Suddenly a shot rang out causing both men to freeze. They both looked in amazement at the small woman standing about five feet away holding the gun. Then the man slumped to the ground.

Shane's reaction was lightning fast. He knew that the men in the building would have heard the shot and come running. He grabbed the weapon and the woman and yelled, "Run!" They bolted down the alley just as the door flew open and eight men exploded out of the door.

Shane searched for a place to hide because the woman couldn't keep up the pace and the men were right behind them. He kicked the door open to an empty building and pushed her through it then kept moving, dragging her behind him and out the front door. The main street was being guarded by the military so maybe the men wouldn't follow them. He pulled her into the next building and pushed her behind the counter.

The eight men burst out into the street just as a military hummer rounded the corner. A blazing battle erupted as the men took on the military boys. Shane held his breath hoping that they hadn't seen him and the woman enter the building. After a moment, all eight men were dead. Shane took the woman by the arm and headed to the back of the building and out the back door into the alley. They snuck quietly down the street until they were several blocks away from the action.

Finally Shane stopped and turned his attention to the pretty young woman he had just saved. He gently removed the gag and the rope binding her hands. She was trembling and sobbing silently.

"It's ok," he soothed. "You're safe now."

"Thank you," she breathed barely able to speak.

"Come with me, I can take you to a safe place," he gently urged her and quickly got them back to the motel.

The brothers stopped to rest their horses on a ridge at the Nebraska state line.

"What the fuck is that?" Warrick asked handing the binoculars to Dylan.

"It looks like the train derailed. But look at the military vehicles. It must have been carrying something important. And how the hell are they driving around," Dylan replied.

"I told you, military hummers and some tanks are designed to withstand an EMP bomb. That is where the plans came from for the truck I built," Warrick said proudly.

Darien dismounted and looked around. "We will have to go around them."

Suddenly one of the trucks started heading toward them. "Fuck, they spotted us. What are the chances that they turn us back?" Darien asked passing the binoculars back to Warrick.

"Well, I guess that depends on the cargo on that train," Dylan replied.

"Oh my god! It looks like a big generator. Like the ones used to circulate coolant in a nuclear plant," Warrick said.

"That either means that they didn't get one of the plants shut down or that they store spent rods somewhere close that still need to be cooled. If the generators are damaged, we could be looking at a nuclear catastrophe," Dylan said.

"I say we find out what's going on. We don't want to look suspicious though so let's stash our weapons and go down to them," Darien said taking the visible weapons from the others and stuffing them in a hole in the rocks. He covered them with brush and mounted his horse.

The three rode down the ridge a ways and met the hummer coming across the rough terrain.

"Colonel," Darien said, greeting one of the men getting out of the hummer. He had done his time in the military as a marine and knew what the stripes meant. These guys weren't just grunts. Something serious was going on here.

"This area has been closed to the public," the Colonel stated, looking them over. "What is your destination?"

Again, Darien took the lead. "We were just checking some livestock over the ridge. We heard that there were cattle thieves about," he lied calmly. "We are heading back to Sidney."

The colonel took his time responding, which made Warrick uneasy and he started to fidget. Warrick wasn't comfortable around authority, having pulled a few stints in jail for fighting. He was a self-proclaimed nonconformist and didn't like being told what to do.

Dylan could read his brother like a book and felt the tension building inside him. He moved his horse a little closer to him, trying to distract him from his uneasiness.

"Are they having problems with a nuclear plant somewhere?" Darien asked.

"I am unable to discuss that," the man said.

Warrick rolled his eyes drawing the colonel's attention. Warrick just looked right back not giving him the submission that he was obviously looking for.

Tension filled the space between the five men until Darien stepped in and said, "Well, we will be on our way then."

He didn't wait for the colonel to respond he just turned to Warrick and said firmly, "Let's go!"

Warrick gave the man a fuck you kind of nod and turned his horse up the ridge.

To their surprise, they let them ride away.

"Fuck, Warrick," Dylan railed. "Do you have to confront every man that looks at you?"

"What!" Warrick said. "He was the one challenging me!"

"You trigger happy sun of a bitch. Like I said, Billy the kid," Darien said with a grin.

"I'm worried. There are two active nuclear plants in the vicinity of the kids. We need to hurry and get them out of there," Dylan said urgently. "Come on let's get moving."

The brothers rode out making good time over the next several hours. Their horses were well build and in excellent condition. They could easily cover up to fifty miles a day or more if they were fed and watered properly. They were all accomplished riders having been raised around livestock. If this hadn't been such a dangerous situation for the entire family, it may have been and exciting adventure for them.

Rebel and Conner made it across the Ohio River safely. She sighed with relief as they walked silently in the dark into Ohio.

Conner turned to Rebel and said, "So, what is it exactly, that's turning this country upside down?"

Rebel paused and thought, 'This is where I always lose them.'

She looked into his inquisitive eyes and before her body could betray her again, just started talking, replaying the broken record. "Well, a huge filament on the sun erupted and ejected a billion ton cloud of electrically charged plasma out of the sun. The shock wave and the radiation from the coronal mass ejection wiped out the orbiting satellites and stripped our magnetosphere back so that when the body of the solar storm hit, it slammed us like a bolt of lightning and ripped through the ground into our electrical system. The big transformers couldn't take the punch and overloaded, wiping out the entire grid. A CME basically brings the suns magnetic field with it and if its polarity is a certain way, it will destroy all electronics. This one acted like an EMP bomb and smacked us with a massive electromagnetic pulse."

"Oh, is that all?" he laughed.

She smiled nervously.

He looked at her seriously and said, "All electronics? And what about the cars? I didn't think a CME could take out a car."

Rebel nodded. "You're right, even a large CME

would leave most cars on the road, but this one wasn't typical. Right now our sun is in its solar maximum. It has been theorized that this solar max will be more extreme than any we have ever seen before. I've studied the plausible causes online and some believe the reason for its severity is because our solar system is presently moving through the Galactic Equator. There is a very large amount of gravitational pull and magnetic disturbances in this space emanating from the large black hole at the center of our galaxy."

Rebel glanced at Conner wondering if she sounded as crazy to him as most people took her but he kept walking silently so she continued.

"The theory is that this disturbance has aggravated the sun and helped create those massive sunspots and filaments that are responsible for the recent earthquakes and the reason this coronal mass ejection a few days ago was so extremely large. Add this to the fact that the CME's magnetic field lines were opposite that of earths, and you end up with an geomagnetic solar storm like never before seen on earth."

Conner glanced at her then shook his head trying to sort through the information.

"Our sun has a twenty two year cycle and it erupts with intense solar activity every eleven years when its magnetic poles flip. Some believe that the last time the sun was this disturbed, it discharged so much energy when its poles flipped that it launched Venus upside down and that is why she rotates backwards today," Rebel added.

Conner glanced at her but kept walking in silence.

"Aren't you going to call me a 2012 junkie or a conspiracy freak, because believe me, I've heard it all," she said then held her breath hoping he didn't think she was a weirdo.

"Well, maybe later in the story, but it sounds logical so far," he smiled.

"Ya, but it gets worse. We are set to cross the galactic equator this coming winter solstice. Some scientists say that the magnetic pull added to intense gravity generated from the black hole in the center of the galaxy will cause the earth to suffer a pole shift," she paused glancing up at him. "Are we still ok?"

Conner laughed, "Ya, I'm with you so far."

She smiled and took a deep breath before she continued. "Some theorize that the magnetic field lines spin in the opposite direction on the northern hemisphere of the galaxy. You know, like how water in a bathtub drains opposite in the northern hemisphere than the southern here on earth? They believe that when we cross over the galactic equator into the northern hemisphere of the galaxy, everything will rotate the opposite way. It could potentially make the earth stop and start rotating in the opposite direction. At best, it would force everything on earth to reverse directions. The jet stream and oceanic currents would slam into each other and the entire crust of the earth would shift. "

At that, he stopped and stood quietly facing forward for a moment then looked at her and said, "You're not just talking about the north and south poles switching places?"

She shook her head no.

"Are you talking about three days of darkness and the sun rising in the west and all that shit?" he asked looking at her intently.

"Yes, I am. A geomagnetic pole shift," she said and kept walking. "A shift of the entire mantle of the earth. Most scientists believe that the poles can't flip unless the earth stops rotating or at least slows down. This would reduce, if not eliminate our magnetosphere for some time. The magnetic field is already at the lowest point ever recorded. If the earth stops rotating or possibly starts rotating in the opposite direction, very few of us will live through it. We wouldn't survive the volcanic eruptions and earthquakes let alone the extreme gamma rays. It would be Book of Revelations stuff. Apocalypse. Armageddon."

Connor stopped again. "I need a fire, let's make camp," he said and walked off into the darkness toward a stand of trees.

'Great,' Rebel thought, 'he thinks I'm a freak.' She shook her head and followed him. Humans were supposed to be intelligent creatures but most of them weren't able to embrace the fact that this kind of disaster is possible.

Rebel unsaddled Jake and just let him wander off to graze.

"Aren't you afraid that he will run away?" Conner asked.

Rebel looked fondly toward the horse and said, "No, he and I have bonded."

"Lucky him," Conner said under his breath as he lit the fire.

Rebel couldn't help but smile at the innuendo but frowned when her stomach did another flutter dance.

After a moment he said, "K, I think I'm ready for more now, please go on."

Rebel sat down next to him by the fire and went on with her story. "Do you watch the stars much?" She looked up into the sky when he shook his head no. "See Orion there? See that star to the bottom left?"

Conner knew how to take advantage of the opening that she had unwittingly given him and scooted closer and leaned into her as he looked up at the stars.

"That star wasn't there a few years ago. I believe that it is The Destroyer, sometimes called Nemesis or Planet X and also referred to as Nibiru."

Rebel paused, enveloped by the heat smoldering between them. She closed her eyes and let those long dormant feelings pulse through her entire body. He was like a major solar flare ejecting delicious searing electrified particles at her. She had to admit that his company was nice and relaxed for the first time in a long time. She knew that if anyone approached, Jake would let her know. She breathed in his intoxicating smell and allowed herself to actually enjoy being next to him.

He looked down at her waiting for her to continue but when he looked into her eyes, he instinctively knew what she was thinking and his eyes flashed as his body convulsed in reaction to the temptation she was trying to hide from him.

Rebel quickly turned away and went on with a slight tremor in her voice, "The Destroyer is said to be our sun's binary twin." She took a deep shaky breath. "Some believe that it has its own little solar system of planets and that Nibiru is one of them. It is said to be on an elliptical orbit around our sun and every thirty six hundred years, it crosses paths with our solar system."

"Binary twin?" he asked somewhat confused.

She sighed and continued, "Most stars out there are a part of a binary system. If our star is alone, it is in the minority."

Rebel paused and looked into the fire watching the flames dance in the darkness. She hated talking about this shit but continued, "The other theory is that it is a planet that belongs in our solar system and is dragging several moons behind it. Either way, if it's projected orbit is correct, it has already blown through the ort cloud like a bull out of a chute and has sent thousands of rocks into the inner solar system, straight toward us."

She had his complete attention and was surprised at how easy he was accepting what she was saying. "Some believe that during one of its visits into our solar system, it crashed into a planet that used to reside between Mars and Jupiter smashing it into pieces and that is where we got the asteroid belt. That's why some call it the twelvth planet. This planet or sun, whichever you believe, is also responsible for the melting of the polar ice caps on Mars, the gas planets becoming more luminous and global warming on earth."

Rebel paused, feeling his eyes burn into her. "Do you think I'm crazy yet?"

When he didn't answer her, she looked back at him and had to focus to make sure she was breathing as she was once again taken by those intensely sharp eyes. He just held her gaze locked in his.

Rebel inhaled sharply reminding herself that a distraction like him was dangerous and she was on a mission to get Jade home. She suddenly stood up, pacing around the fire agitated as she pictured a metaphoric red angel on one shoulder and a white angel on the other. The white one was logic and the red one was mayhem. Mayhem was constantly trying to override logic and had gotten her in trouble before.

Logic was telling her that she couldn't allow herself to lose focus. Here she was explaining the end of the world as they knew it and yet she was all butterflies and rainbows when she looked at him. He didn't even know her name, and he certainly didn't know that she had a daughter. She shook her head with resignation and stomped over to her saddle and laid it down John Wayne style beside the fire. She rolled out her sleeping bag and sprawled onto it pulling her coat up over her shoulders, huffing in frustration.

"Why do you do that?" Conner asked her. "Why do you keep yourself so locked up? What in the hell happened to you anyway?"

"Nothing happened to me! We don't know anything about each other!" Rebel replied. "I have things to do and I can't be distracted right now! I have a daughter that is stuck in Omaha of all places. She is in danger and waiting for me to come get her." Rebel paused, then looked straight at him and said, "You don't even know my name! I don't have time for this…, this whatever it is going on between us!"

Conner looked deep into her eyes and said, "Look, I know that you're on a mission, and I want to help you, not distract you." He got up and rolled his sleeping bag out by the fire and stretched out on it. He intentionally put his head about a foot away from hers then propped himself up on his big wide shoulders and asked, "So, what is your name pretty lady?"

God, why does her stomach tighten and her pulse race every time he speaks to her? She scowled, angry with herself. Angry at her physiological betrayal, angry at the desire that was building inside her like magma in a chamber under a volcano and angry that she had to deny herself this ruggedly handsome man lying next to her. She looked back at him and inhaled deeply, "My name is Rebecca. Everyone calls me Rebel."

Conner started laughing. "How fitting. It had to be something like that."

"Why, what kind of person do you think I am?" she asked defensively.

He reached out and touched her face then looked into her eyes and said, "I think you are a rebel." He felt her tense at his touch and dropped his hand away. He didn't want to push his luck with this feisty little fireball. He turned up toward the stars and said, "What's your daughter's name?"

She was surprised when he didn't push her. If she was a rebel then he was a saint because she wasn't sure if she would stop him again. She rolled over and looked again into the brightly starlit sky. "Her name is Jade," she told him. "I flew to D.C. to get her when I learned about the big solar flare erupting and a couple of hours later, a big quake hit in Washington. I knew then that something big was on its way because D.C. rarely has earthquakes."

Rebel shivered when she described what the apartment complex looked like when she had driven up to it. "Thank God she got out before it collapsed. The only flight out of D.C. was to Omaha where my youngest brothers are working so I put her on a plane and here I am."

'That explains her unwillingness to relax', he thought and reached out and squeezed her hand. "I'll help you get to her, Rebel," he said sincerely.

She hadn't really leaned on anyone emotionally since Jade's dad left sixteen years ago. If she needed muscle, she called the brothers. Kira and Jade were her only focus. She hadn't been interested in getting close to anyone else in all these years and wondered curiously how Conner had awakened all of those buried feelings. And why now? Maybe it was because she was out here alone facing life threatening danger and feeling so anxious about getting home. She knew better though and told herself that she needed to be careful. She could genuinely fall for this guy.

Conner read the silence and simply asked, "So tell me more about this Armageddon stuff."

"Well, the Maya people believed that there were five

life cycles or ages. Each of the first four ended in utter catastrophe. Their calendar marks the end of the fifth age or world, on December 21, 2012. They say it will end in earthquake. Coincidentally, in the same timeline, our solar system is passing through the galactic plane, the earth completes its wobble, Planet X is due to pass through our solar system, the poles are trying to shift weakening our magnetosphere and the sun is entering into the most intense solar max ever. The numbers tell me that something is bound to happen on earth and although I don't know exactly what it will be, I have been preparing for it for years."

"What do you mean preparing for it? Don't tell me you bought one of those underground bunkers."

Rebel laughed. "No, we don't have that kind of money and I don't think I could handle living underground. Besides, I think they may be flooded. I will have to survive in one of nature's bunkers. My family and I bought a piece of property in the mountains of Idaho that has a large cave and a flowing spring. We stocked it with food and supplies. We planted a huge garden with seeds that are fertile and filled the valley with livestock."

"I would definitely say that you're prepared," Conner nodded somewhat surprised. The only time he had thought about the end of the world was when his sister in law told him about an ancient cave in the mountains of Montana that had some kind of Native American survival history.

"Well, there is one downfall," she added. "Our property is located only a couple hundred miles from Yellowstone and I can't prepare for the eruption of a super volcano. But if it goes off, we will all die anyway."

"So how do you enjoy life with all of this shit in your head?" Conner asked curiously knowing she wouldn't answer him. After a moment he braced himself up on his elbows again and looked at her. "So, is your husband in Idaho waiting for you?" He held his breath then reprimanded himself for caring so much about the answer.

Rebel rolled over onto her stomach laughing then

tried not to stare at his wide chest that rippled under the weight of his muscular shoulders. "No, I'm not attached to anyone. I've been busy."

Relief flooded through him. 'God damn,' he thought, 'why had he let her get to him so bad?' He laid back down trying to slow his racing blood. He needed to change the subject. "Have you noticed how dark it is now? It's not just dark, it's black."

"I have noticed. I'm a little nervous in the dark. I don't like being unable to see what's coming. Now, without any kind of background light, it is terrifyingly dark."

Conner laughed and asked curiously, "How were you handling traveling alone at night if you're afraid of the dark?"

"I just stay by Jake. I trust him to let me know if anything is out there," she smiled. "Speaking of dark, look at how bright the fireflies are. I've only seen them once before and they weren't this bright."

Conner smiled and picked up one of the nasty looking bugs. He looked around and suddenly climbed to his feet. "Look," he said pointing.

Rebel sat up and stared in awe at the millions of light bugs around them. Every tree branch, limb, and bush was covered with little glowing balls of light. "They look like Christmas lights," she laughed.

They talked well into the night before both falling into a peaceful sleep.

The next morning, Rebel was up early and ready to go. She whistled for Jake who came bounding out of the meadow toward her.

Conner watched her saddle the horse with knowing precision. He was particularly interested in watching the tight muscles in her butt and thighs as she swung the saddle onto his back. She turned toward him suddenly and he jerked his head up and flushed like a teenage boy.

"I guess you can ride the mare. You can ride a horse can't you?" she asked.

"I can ride a horse but it's not my favorite thing to ride," he said distractedly.

She looked at him fiercely crossing her arms over her chest and lifting an eyebrow.

"That's not what I meant, I mean, what did you think I meant?" he stammered obviously flustered, but continued. "I mean I would rather ride motor bikes or 4-wheelers, you know, stuff like that. But I can ride a horse." He exhaled sharply at the vision that filtered through his mind from that little mishap.

Rebel shook her head and smiled. "We need to find you a saddle. Let's get going."

Conner swung easily onto the stout mare's back and followed her at a gallop.

Jade walked into the front room rubbing sleep out of her eyes and nearly screamed when she spied the woman sleeping on the couch.

'The poor thing,' she thought after she had recovered. The woman was bruised and battered and obviously exhausted.

Shane walked up behind her and looked sadly at the woman then waved her into the kitchen.

Cayden looked up from the grill where he was making breakfast and said, "So what's going on Shane?"

Shane sat down at the table and told them about the events that had happened the previous night.

"Don't ever go out by yourself again!" Jade reprimanded just as the woman walked into the room.

"Sorry," Jade said to her. "Did we wake you up? I'm Jade and this is Cayden. Obviously you've already met Shane."

The woman looked at Shane and said, "My name is Lynn. You took a huge risk last night and I am eternally grateful."

Lynn shuttered and Cayden jumped to get her a chair. "Here sit down and I'll get you something to eat," he said with concern. Then he started acting a little strange, hovering over her and waiting on her hand and foot.

Jade and Shane looked at each other curiously. Jade

shrugged and Shane grinned. Cayden didn't even notice because he was so absorbed in the young woman.

Finally Shane said, "I don't mean to pry but how is it that those men got their hands on you?"

"I'm a little embarrassed to say this but my brother sold drugs for them." She hung her head down. "I tried to get him to quit dealing but after our parents were killed, he turned to it for an income. I was in school and he was determined that I finish. It is my fault that he was killed." Tears ran down her face but she continued, "He must have owed them money or something because they came to the house and shot him and took me."

Jade rushed to her and give her a hug. "I'm so sorry," she said holding her.

"I don't know what they would have done with me if Shane hadn't been there. Now I have nowhere to go because they burned the house down," she sobbed.

"You can stay with us." Cayden jumped in. "Can't she Jade?" He didn't look at Shane who may have objected.

"Of course she can," Jade answered looking directly at Shane who wouldn't have dared deny her.

Shane just sighed and didn't respond. Saving someone was completely different than taking responsibility for them with too few supplies. But he wouldn't have turned her away either.

"Come with me," Jade said after Lynn had picked through her food for a while. "I have some water and toiletries. Let's get you cleaned up. That cut on your arm needs to be cleaned and bandaged."

Lynn gratefully followed Jade into the bathroom leaving the boys to ponder their new situation.

The brothers met up with the river after riding hard through the night and were well on their way to North Platte. After a few hours of sleep they were saddling their horses laughing and kidding each other with the usual jibes about women and recent fights. Warrick usually caught the worst of it because he was the worst womanizer among them. They were enjoying the camaraderie and preparing for the road when the horses started snorting and pawing the ground.

"Calm down, god damn it!" Darien growled.

Suddenly the ground started shaking. The earthquake was a bad one, lasting a good two minutes and throwing water out of the river up onto the banks.

"Fuck!" Dylan said as his horse reared into the air. He dodged the pawing hooves and struggled to control the large animal. "Easy there Ace. It's all over," he soothed the upset animal.

"That would have taken out some bridges," Darien said worriedly. He knew that crossing the Platte River was going to be complicated. It was going to be bad enough getting through the blockades that the National Guard would have inevitably put in place.

"Let's get a move on," Warrick said suddenly in a hurry.

They mounted and headed out at a gallop allowing the animals to work out their nervousness on the move.

Their path led them into a dangerous position between the North and South Platte Rivers. The rivers paralleled each other for quite a few miles and there wasn't much room between them to maneuver if they ran into trouble.

Darien took the lead coming up a ridge but at the top he held his hand up for them to stop. Warrick and Dylan reined in and came up beside him. Down below they could see a large farmhouse on fire.

"What the hell?" Dylan asked as he watched four men push a small herd of cattle into the tree line about a mile away from the house.

"Not sure if we want to get involved," Darien said.

"Fuck that!" Warrick responded. "Thievin bastards. They may have killed someone, I'm going down."

The three made their way down to the farmhouse but knew that if anyone was inside the structure, they were dead.

Warrick looked in the direction of the men. "I think

we should follow them and see where they go."

"Fine, but remember that we are in a hurry to get to Omaha," Darien warned.

They followed the men pushing the slow moving herd for about an hour keeping out of sight. When the thieves stopped to rest, the brothers dismounted and crept closer to their makeshift camp. One of the men walked toward them leaving the safety of the others. Warrick slipped up behind him and put a chokehold around his neck dragging him back to their hiding place where Dylan put the barrel of his revolver to the man's head.

"Don't even breath," Dylan said quietly.

The man nodded in compliance and Warrick released his hold.

"Were people in that house you torched?" Darien asked lifting his handgun to the man's head as well.

The man nodded yes.

"So you're murdering cattle thieves?" Warrick exploded, landing his big fist in the man ribs.

Dylan heard the bones break and the man cried out as he dropped to his knees.

"You fucking punk!" Warrick said in a deadly quiet voice.

The brothers knew that Warrick was tough as nails and did his share of being a renegade. But he was honest and had a great big heart. He always stood up for the underdog and couldn't stand cruelty.

"I think we should string 'em up!" he said angrily.

"Calm down Warrick," Dylan said then looked at Darien. "But I agree. They should be punished. Tie him."

Warrick laughed unable to tell if the man paled from the pain or the threat.

After the man was affectively bound, they went after the others. One by one they were all tied and gagged.

"You ever read about how the Native Americans got their justice back in the day?" Warrick yelled at them unsheathing his hunting knife. "They left it to nature!" He walked to the closest man and pointedly sliced a gash across his cheek.

After each of them was bleeding, the brothers gathered up the men's weapons and unsaddled their horses and let them loose.

"Look at this," Darien said as he pulled a huge bag of cash out of a pack on one of the saddles. "It's hundred dollar bills. Must be thousands here."

"That's why they killed them. It was for money," Dylan said disgustedly.

"We will put it to good use," Warrick said, tucking it in his saddlebags. He looked back at the bleeding men and yelled, "I guess we are back to western justice, boys. You fuckers deserve worse. We should have hung you!" With that he pushed his horse into gallop and rode east.

Darien and Dylan followed, still surprised that Warrick hadn't killed them just for good measure.

Rebel leaned over a rock holding her binoculars. "I don't see anyone around," she said to Conner. "Why would they abandon this place?"

The house sat tucked between a large shop and an even larger horse barn. Livestock wondered aimlessly across the lawn as if someone had intentionally left the gates open.

"Wait here Rebel, I will go down and check it out," Conner said. When she started to object, he added, "I need you to cover me with the rifle."

She smiled to herself knowing he was playing her. "Fine, I'll wait. And cover you."

He winked at her and started down the slope.

Rebel felt butterflies tickle her stomach again. She had become familiar with the sensation because it happened so often. In fact, it happened all the time. All he had to do was look at her and all the cliché shit happened. 'Now would be a good time to write a love song', she thought. 'Knees go weak, butterflies and shit. Fuck, what a girl. Here I am in the middle of a global meltdown and all I can think about is piercing eyes and bulging muscles. I'm a danger to myself!' She shook her head, struggling to focus her attention through the scope. If someone was hiding down there,

Conner could be in danger.

"I found the reason," he yelled up at her. "There is a dead man in the house."

Rebel shuttered as she made her way down to him and looked into the house. "I don't see any wounds. Would the EMP from the CME have taken out his pacemaker?" she mumbled sadly. "He looks pretty old."

"I don't know. It's too bad," Conner said. "Come on, let's find the tack room and get going."

Conner poked around the barn and found tack and a saddle that would fit him. He had told Rebel that he could ride but had understated his skill. He quickly bridled a large gilding then saddled him. He strapped his rifle and supplies onto the horse and haltered the feisty little filly.

His experience was clear when he swung easily onto the animal. Rebel just shook her head at his apparent deception and mounted Jake.

They pushed the horses at a gallop for miles. Rebel was relieved to finally be well on their way.

Several hours later, they pulled up to rest the animals.

"This highway will take us strait into Cincinnati. We need to make a plan to go around. It will be out of our way, but that city will be exceptionally dangerous," Conner said.

"I agree. We need to avoid people as much as possible. That will be hard right here though, because it's heavily populated all the way north to Dayton and the Ohio River is south. Maybe we should just follow the river through and save the time," Rebel pondered.

"I don't think it will be worth the risk and I don't think we will get the horse through the docks. We also need to consider the National Guard being there in full force," Conner argued.

Rebel nodded in agreement. "Let's head northeast then."

They rode hard for several more hours pushing the animals hard.

Rebel reined in pointing to the sky. "Look at those clouds building."

Conner looked into the brewing storm and noticed that the sky was a weird orange-green color. "You ever see color like that? I've seen a lot of storms in my day but that is weird."

"I've never seen that before either," Rebel said. "We better make camp before it rains.

They found a secluded camp site just outside of Hillsboro and unsaddled. Conner staked his gilding and the packhorses, not trusting them as Rebel did Jake.

While he fussed with the horses, Rebel built a fire. She felt all jittery at the thought of facing another night alone with him. This whole situation had her on edge. They had both intentionally kept their distance from each other recognizing that the smoldering fire between them was hot would only need a small spark for ignition. The impending firestorm would be unstoppable.

"Did I see you pick up a tent?" Conner asked.

Rebel jumped not realizing that he was standing so close to her and looked up into the raindrops wishing that they would just douse the fire inside her once and for all. The tent. Fuck, it was tiny. She trembled at the thought of sleeping next to him in such a small space.

"It's right there," she said pointing to her pack, hoping he wouldn't know what she was thinking.

He quickly had the tent standing and both of their sleeping bags in it.

Rebel stood quietly looking at the tent and must have been wearing her emotions on her face when Conner walked over to stand beside her.

He looked at her then the tent then back at her. Realization came over him and he quickly said, "I will sleep out here." Then moved to get his sleeping bag.

"No!" Rebel caught his arm. "I wouldn't let you sleep in the rain. We are both adults here."

He gently withdrew his arm from her grasp and tilted her face up to him. "Look, I feel it too and I understand that you aren't willing to pursue this... this connection between us, so I won't either, k? I'll stay clear," he said with a genuine smile.

She nodded, frozen in those gentle eyes. "K," she mumbled then thought, 'It's not you that I'm worried about,' as she turned into the tent and scurried into her sleeping bag.

The rain continued throughout the night keeping her awake. The rain, and the steady breathing coming from the man lying next to her. He had kept his word though and hadn't even spoken to her when he came inside. He just climbed into his sleeping bag and went to sleep.

'Would it be so bad?' Mayhem asked her and Logic answered, 'Yes, it would be dangerous.' Rebel knew that love made you vulnerable and vulnerability made you less affective in circumstances like this. She wouldn't allow herself to be distracted from her family especially until she knew Jade was safe. Finally, she fell asleep with blue green eyes dancing in her dreams.

The next afternoon they were picking their way through the suburbs just north of Cincinnati and south of Middleton. The rain continued to drizzle and heavy clouds blocked out the sun. The ominous weird color in the clouds made her nervous and the fact that they had to come in close proximity to the city and the people wasn't helping her anxiety.

They had chosen a small road to follow so that they wouldn't be stopped by fences and were doing their best not to cause a disturbance but they looked out of place and caught a lot of attention. There was no way to avoid riding through the suburbs and the many people who were struggling to maintain their lives in this traumatic time.

As they rode past the houses, Rebel noticed that some of the people had instinctively gathered in groups, probably to share supplies and give each other protection. She glanced up at what looked like a family sitting on the front porch of one of the houses and waved back at a young boy who was watching them curiously.

They rode toward a retail area with a convenience store and gas station. There was a large group of men gathered in the doorway drinking and laughing.

Jake responded to the sudden tension Rebel felt as they neared them and was dancing sideways and tossing his head. The mare was reacting to Jake, pulling on her lead rope.

Rebel looked at Conner nervously and he gave her an encouraging nod.

"We will be fine Rebel, just keep moving."

She nodded back appreciating the fact that he understood and relieved that he was here with her. Suddenly Conner reined in the gilding and focused intently on the group.

Jake stomped his foot, objecting to the hold up so she spoke soothingly to him and rubbed his neck.

"What's wrong?" she asked.

"Those guys are armed and they are going to be trouble. Here take the filly and stay behind me," he ordered then eased the gilding into a walk and continued forward unsheathing his rifle.

Rebel unholstered the colt and followed.

"Well, well, what have we here?" one of the men asked standing up and walking toward them. He was dirty and unkept and obviously intoxicated. He held a gun loosely in his hand and waved it in the air.

Conner didn't hesitate. He pointed the rifle at the man and said threateningly, "Nothing you want to mess with friend."

"Oh? Well, I wouldn't call that pretty little thing nothin," he tormented practically slobbering at Rebel. The other men laughed and cheered him on.

Conner stopped in front of the group and motioned for her to keep going. She rode past them a bit then turned in her saddle and pointed her handgun into the group of men.

"She ain't nothin to you," Conner countered staring the man down.

The tension between them sparked and the others grew quiet. Rebel's heart was pounding and her palm was sweating all over the weapon. 'God,' she thought, 'what if he shot Conner?'

After what seemed like forever, the man raised his hands and said, "Ya, alright. Whatever."

Conner nudged the gilding forward never taking his eyes or his rifle off of the man.

Rebel let out a sigh of relief. 'Jesus, what a fucking nightmare,' she thought. She held the colt on the men until Conner was next to her and out of their range then they pushed the horses into a fast run. They continued the pace for several miles before they slowed up to give the horses a breather.

"I think we should ride into the night. They may follow us," Conner said. "That man does not like to lose."

Rebel shivered thinking about how creepy they were. "That is the reason I wanted to avoid people. All the freaks come out of the woodwork and run rampid, uncontrolled."

Conner sensed her growing discomfort and reined his gilding closer to Jake. He reached over and put his hand on her thigh. Even this benign touch created delicious sparks of heat between them. He looked down at his hand as if it were on fire and regretfully pulled it away.

They rode into the night until they reached the Indiana state line. Rebel was exhausted when they finally unrolled their sleeping bags so they didn't bother with the tent or a fire even though it was still drizzling.

Just before dawn, Rebel was awakened by a loud thump. She bolted upright just as a man slammed the back of a gun onto Conner's head. Before she could scream, she fell to the same fate.

Conner became conscious to the sun peeking through the clouds. He launched to his feet and instantly dropped back down to his knees from the pain in his head. It was pounding and covered in blood. He looked at Rebel's empty sleeping bag and roared with rage, "I will kill you fuckers this time!"

He ignored the pain in his head as he put his saddle on Jake. He was sure that the bond between Rebel and her horse would lead him to her. He tied the other horses and headed out giving Jake his head.

The rage that roared through his veins awakened a deadly monster that normally lay dormant. He sometimes had to struggle to keep the beast at bay but when he was angry, he couldn't contain it at all and the beast broke through its barrier, unleashing brutal destruction on the enemy.

He rode for some time before Jake turned north and Conner prayed he'd been right about the horse's instincts. If those men touched her he would break every bone in their bodies before he killed them. He was going to go insane thinking about what they may be doing to her. He had to find her. 'How could I let this happen?' he cursed himself then said out loud, "Find her for me Jake."

Rebel woke up in a sitting position with her hands tethered to a tree behind her back and was instantly consumed by intense terror. She suffered from claustrophobia and closed her eyes tightly to hold back the scream of panic that welled in her throat. It took a moment for her to calm down and think about getting her knife out of her boot. Thank god she had slept fully clothed last night.

She almost lost it again before she could get the knife free and cut the rope. Finally she was loose but she sat still for a moment trying to calm herself. She could hear the voices of several men and recognized them immediately.

'God damn it, they did follow them,' she thought, knowing she was in danger. Even if Conner was alive, there was no way that he would find her. She didn't want to even imagine what they had done to him after they knocked her unconscious.

One of the men stood up and walked toward her. It was the same man that had confronted Conner yesterday.

"Well, well," he slobbered, still clearly intoxicated. "Not so tough without your big man to save you, huh."

"Untie me and let's find out," Rebel challenged him hoping he would take her up on the offer. She loved to fight and looked forward to bashing him in the head.

He arrogantly underestimated her and walked closer unaware that she was no longer bound to the tree.

From a sitting position she kicked him hard right between his legs.

The man doubled over and screamed, "You bitch!"

His agony got the attention of the other three men who came to investigate.

Rebel scrambled to her feet and punched the man in the face before he could recover from the kick, the impact sending him sprawling to the ground.

The others realized what had happened and laughed and jeered at him. One of them turned toward her, motioning for her to take a shot at him.

She gladly accepted the offer and spun around with a kick to his head before he lifted his arms. He landed on the ground next to his friend.

The other two tried to cover their surprise as they advanced on her.

"One at a time boys," she said teasingly. "Fair is fair. But don't worry, you'll both get a turn."

They looked at each other and grinned then one of them stepped in with his fists up.

She raised her fists to imitate him and stepped in, snapping his head back with a quick right to his chin.

He was so consumed with shock that he stopped short and looked at his friend clearly stunned.

She smiled and slammed her fist into his temple and watched him slump to the ground. She turned to the last man standing and said, "Don't underestimate me like your friend here did."

The man nodded, confidently stepping toward her. He swung at her and she easily ducked past his fist, slamming her elbow into his eye.

He screamed in pain and stepped back covering his face with both hands.

The first man recovered and stood up behind her. He grabbed her hair and jerked her head back. She spun around and couldn't resist herself. She kneed him in the nuts again, this time adding a perfectly aimed head butt to his temple. The man went down again.

"You guys are pathetic," she said then turned and bolted into the trees. She easily outran them taking the high ground and crouched down behind some brush about half way up the side hill. She looked down into the little valley and watched them search for her.

Conner knew that Jake had found her. He was walking faster with his ears pointed forward and was pulling on the bit in anticipation.

Suddenly he heard someone yell, "Where the fuck is she? I'm going to kill that bitch when I find her."

He pulled Jake to a stop and listened. Rebel must have gotten away and they can't find her. Relief flooded through him but it didn't calm the rage roaring for revenge. He dismounted and tied Jake behind a tree then crept forward focusing on the closest man to him.

Rebel watched in surprise as Conner silently stalked into the clearing with his bow in his hand. Thank god he was alive. How the hell had he found her? Then she noticed his stance and realized what he was about to do to the men searching for her. They had no idea he was there.

Conner was an avid archery hunter and had perfect aim. The rain from the night before had softened the leaves under his feet giving him the silence required for his sneak attack. He knocked an arrow in his bow and took aim knowing exactly how to calm the natural adrenaline that rushed through him before the shot and felt no regret as he watched the silent broadhead pass cleanly through the man's chest. The man crumpled to the ground as Conner knocked another arrow. He repeated the act two more times, the silent weapon never giving his position away. He saved the leader for last so that he could look into the man's eyes when the scum drew his last breath. He traded his bow for a hunting knife and crept up behind the distracted man.

The man froze and sobered the instant he heard a deadly voice ask, "Are you looking for me?" He spun around in disbelief and knew instinctively that he was going to die.

Conner didn't waste a moment, he just put the filthy man out of his misery with a deep slice across his throat, the fear in the man's eyes as his blood drained enough revenge.

He stood over the body trying to tame the raging monster inside of him. He looked down at himself covered in blood and wondered what Rebel would think about the death he had been responsible for here. "I hope you don't hate me when you find out what I'm capable of," he said out loud then looked around wondering where she would hide. "Rebel!" he yelled loudly. No response.

Rebel heard her name and she suddenly became aware that she had been holding her breath. Conner had just silently, precisely executed those four men.

"Rebel," he yelled again.

"I'm here!" she answered finally coming out of her trance and starting down the hill.

Conner ran to her and wrapped his big arms around her holding her in a tight hug that lasted for a sweet eternity. Finally he said without letting her go, "Is this why Rebel? Is this why you keep this distance between us? I was out of my mind thinking about what they might do to you. Oh my God, I was so worried. I'm sorry I let them take you." He just stood there holding her with his face buried in her hair.

Rebel was stunned by his emotion. She could feel his heart pound against her chest and the tension in his arms. 'He cares this much about me?' she thought. They had only known each other for a few days.

He pulled away and looked deep in her eyes then leaned down and kissed her.

Her breath left her and her body exploded in response. She leaned into him stealing strength and comfort from his embrace.

Finally, he pulled away and led her to Jake, gently lifting her onto his back. He swung up behind her holding her tightly. They rode together in silence each taking comfort in the closeness that riding double provided. Jake handled the weight easily and quickly carried them away from the slaughter.

Back at camp, Conner became silent and brooding. It always took several hours to confine the beast back in its cage and now that he had calmed down and was certain that those men hadn't hurt her, he was feeling like an animal. What would she think if she knew that he had killed those men? Slaughtered them. She would probably think he was a monster and leave.

Rebel watched him prepare the horses and wondered what was going through his mind. He wore a scowl that she hadn't seen before and wouldn't look at her. She knew that he didn't know that she'd been watching him in the clearing.

Before they mounted up, she stopped him and said, "What? What are you thinking? I told you that I am fine."

Conner looked down at her knowing that this could be the end but decided to put it on the line. "Before we continue on," he said nervously, "you should know that I killed those men. All of them." He stood silently and waited for her to respond. She would either accept him or hate him. He couldn't look at her and didn't dare breathe. God, how could she accept a monster?

Rebel reached up and turned his face to her. She looked deep into his eyes and said softly, "I know. And I know that you killed them for me. Thank you." She pulled his head down and kissed him.

She felt the tension leave his body and could feel him relax in her acceptance. She understood then that he hadn't been sure how she would react to his violent side. To her though, he was a knight in shining armor. He had charged to her rescue on her trusted steed and triumphed even though he had been outnumbered. He was truly a hero in her mind. An absolutely handsome, sexy hero.

Chapter 4

Kira sat on the front porch of her new little home sipping coffee and thinking about the days to come. She was worried about Rebel and Jade but knew that the brothers would find them and bring them home.

Evie sat next to her worrying in her own way. Evie didn't have any family other than her friends up here. The brothers had helped take care of her for the past few years and she had grown very attached to them. Kira and Evie looked after each other whenever the brothers were away working.

Each day, more and more family and friends showed up at the camp. Several months ago, Rebel had sent out mass texts and emails warning their friends and family to be prepared for disaster and letting them know that they had a safe place if anyone needed it.

It turns out that Idaho was more dangerous than anyone had thought. The National Guard was stretched very thin and people had banded together stealing supplies and just taking whatever they wanted. As homes became unsafe, and supplies were taken, people headed up the mountain to Kira's place.

Today, she would have to establish a small army of her own and prepare to guard the camp and everyone and everything in it. The small population had grown into one quite large one and establishing some kind of routine would make it all run more smoothly. Kira had called a meeting for everyone to attend after dinner tonight.

After they all ate and while the kids were cleaning up dinner, Kira headed up the big meeting. "Its time to turn this humble little hideaway into a full fledge compound. We have quite a large population here and we need to establish some ground rules and organize a community type living structure," she said to everyone. "We are all going to have to pitch in and work together. First of all, I need a volunteer for secretary. I would like to keep track of the people and events that happen up here."

A young woman that Kira didn't recognize raised

her hand and said, "My name is Aden. I have a degree in information science which I may never use again and am willing to trade in my computer for a notepad and pen."

"Perfect," Kira said and handed her a pen and paper. "I need a head count so that we can plan our meals. I also want documentation of every person in this camp. I want spouse's names, children's names and ages and information about where they came from. Add in any kind of genealogy that they may know."

Kira turned back to the large crowd and said, "Before you leave tonight, check in with Aden and be prepared to answer some questions. But before we get to that, I need occupations. Is there anyone trained in medicine or dentistry?" Two hands went up. "You are very important and I am going to ask that you take precautions. Don't help in the kitchen or chop wood or anything that might damage your hands. We will create a medical clinic in one of the rooms in the bunkhouse for you to use. Next, there are a number of children who will need to continue their education. Are there any teachers among you?" Once again a couple of hands went up.

Kira went on down the list of professions getting names and asking for their help. Then she said, "If you haven't volunteered for a previous position, raise your hand if you have your own weapon and have experience hunting wild game." Several men stood up. "Neil will organize and plan hunting expeditions with you. I will also need fishermen to fish the lower creek. Everyone else will be put in a rotation to help cook meals and clean up. One more thing, Nicholas will need experienced marksmen to ride the border of our community and keep watch. If you have any questions, be sure to ask. Thank you for your help."

"Well, "Evie said as everyone stood to leave, "that turned out well I think."

Kira smiled happily and both women walked back to the main house.

Jade and Shane sat in the front room curiously

watching Cayden and Lynn talking and laughing in the kitchen. Jade looked at Shane and said, "This is very odd. I don't remember him being so open with women."

"Me either," Shane agreed. "He is definitely acting very strange."

They both looked back at the pair lost in thought when they suddenly heard shouting and gunfire erupt outside.

Lynn jumped to her feet in alarm.

"It's ok," Cayden soothed. "We should be safe in here."

Shane stood up and said, "You guys stay here. I will check it out." Strangely, neither Jade nor Cayden argued with him as he slipped out the door.

Cayden peered out the window and said, "Turn out the lights Jade."

Shane looked over the fence that bordered the street in front of the little apartment and was amazed at the obvious war playing out in front of him. National Guard personnel were lined up trying to push back crowds of fighting men. Shane knew that there were two very large opposing gangs in this city and it looked like they had finally collided. The military force looked to be out manned when you added the bodies from both gangs.

The crazed people were overturning cars and breaking windows out of the buildings. They were stealing anything they could carry and fighting with each other.

He scanned the horizon and watched the fires enveloping all of the buildings in front of him grow out of control. "Oh my God," he said out loud suddenly horrified as he realized that it was going to engulf the motel.

He bolted back through the door almost landing Cayden on his ass. "Pack as many supplies as we can carry!" he ordered. "The motel is in the path of a firestorm."

Jade jumped into action. She knew better than to question this one. All four of them scurried to load food and water into their duffle bags. Shane grabbed the AK47 that Lynn had lifted from the man in the alley and threw the shotgun to Cayden.

"We will wait till the last minute, but be prepared to run and stick together no matter what!" he said to them. Then he whispered to Cayden, "Bro, the gangs are fighting and the National Guard may lose this one. We are walking out into the middle of a war."

Cayden looked at Jade and Lynn and shook his head. "How will we protect them from this?" he asked softly.

"Here it comes. Follow me!" Shane yelled leading them through the back gate and down the alley. They could hear the undeniable sounds of the war just yards away. When they reached the crossroad onto the main street, bullets sliced the air past their heads.

"Fuck!" Shane yelled. "Get down." Where was he going to take them and how in the hell were they going to get there. Fear coupled with the need to protect his family gave him an adrenalin rush from hell. He waved for them to follow and stepped out into the brightly lit night. Ash rained down on them as the firestorm consumed every building in its path. Men screamed and yelled around them and the gunfire never paused.

The small group skidded to a stop as a hummer flew across their path. A man in uniform yelled out to them, "Find cover!"

"What do you think I'm trying to do?" Shane mumbled then jerked his head around and watched the vehicle drive down the street. He turned to the others and actually smiled.

Cayden looked at him like he was crazy.

Shane led the group to a dark corner and said, "Wait here!" Then he turned and disappeared down the smoke filled street.

"What is he doing?" Jade yelled at Cayden.

A moment later a hummer screeched to a halt in front of them and Shane jumped out. "Hurry, get in!" he yelled.

"Are you crazy?" Jade screamed as she climbed into the stolen vehicle. "We are all going to end up in prison camps."

Shane ignored her and sped off down the street.

He turned the vehicle north and drove along the Missouri river until they were out of the city. He would have kept going but just his luck, the vehicle was out of fuel. He found an old abandoned barn about five miles off the main road and pulled the rig inside.

Jade climbed out and threw her bag onto the ground. She turned and faced Shane with fire in her eyes. "They could have shot you for stealing this truck! Don't you ever risk your life like that again!" Then she wrapped her arms around him and started sobbing.

"Jade," he said soothingly, "I had to. I am going to protect you no matter the cost. We wouldn't have survived back there. I saw dead people all over the streets. I had to get us out of the city. We are better off out here."

"I know," she sobbed, "but they wouldn't have hesitated to cut you down. It was a big risk. What if we'd lost you?"

Shane just held her allowing her to cry out her fear. He looked at Cayden who was still shaking his head and gave him a sheepish grin.

"Let's figure out some kind of beds for the night. Tomorrow we will regroup and go from there, K?"

Jade nodded and turned to find somewhere to sleep.

There was a weird silence between Conner and Rebel as they rode throughout the day. The fact that Rebel didn't really know the man next to her had never been more clear. She had no way of knowing what to read from his dark mood. She missed the joking smiling guy that she had seen up until now.

"So tell me, what's really got you so uptight?" she inquired breaking the silence.

Conner shrugged and looked away. He just couldn't believe that his murderous rampage this morning hadn't freaked her out. He didn't regret what he'd done and he knew that he would do it again. But that was the problem wasn't it? How much violence would a genuinely kind person like Rebel be able to deal with. This is exactly why he stayed away from women. His job had made him a barbarian. Or, maybe he was a barbarian that liked his job.

He continued to reflect on himself wondering if maybe they should just part ways. She shouldn't be subjected to the dark beast that always lay in wait inside him. But the thought of leaving her made his heart physically ache.

Rebel sensed that he regretted her knowing that he was capable of murder but also knew that she would do the same thing if she had to so why wouldn't he believe her that she was ok with it? His insecurity made her upset.

"Conner, look," she said, "I have always relied on myself. I've never really needed anyone else. But believe me, I've never been alone or without protection. Not until I was stranded back here. My brothers have always had my back no matter what I did."

He didn't respond.

"Stop god damn it and look at me!"

He stopped and faced her with a frown.

"The reason I am ok with what happened is because I could bet my life on the fact that any one of my brothers would have done the same thing. Shit, they will probably slap a metal on your chest when they find out. And I wouldn't hesitate to kill if I had to either."

Conner just shook his head. "Self defense is different than what I did back there. That was murder and I would do it again," he said pointedly. "My only regret is knowing that you know."

"You might have to do it again!" she exclaimed in frustration. "We were just thrust back into the 1800's. Don't you think that it would benefit me to have a man at my side that was willing to kill for me? I mean after all, that is what I'm used to."

The logic made him feel a little better. He peered down at her not trusting the words. He needed to look in her eyes and see the truth for himself. He started to relax a bit seeing that she was sincere. Then it dawned on him. Who were her brother's? With that kind of back up, no wonder she was so confident. A new anxiety started building inside him. Did she compare him to them? What were they like? Would he have to fight them to date their sister?

Rebel watched the different emotions cross his face. She wished again that she knew him better so she could read him. But he seemed to relax and accept what she was saying so she nudged her horse forward and couldn't help saying as she grinned back at him, "Did I forget to mention that my brothers are all mean sons 'a bitches and if you fuck with me, they will kick your ass!" She pushed Jake into a run leaving him sitting there to contemplate that small detail.

Conner just shook his head still not knowing how to take this complicated fiery mystery woman. He nudged his horse into a run and matched her speed.

By nightfall they were contemplating a path that would flank Indianapolis, another very large dangerous city directly in their way.

"Should we risk riding at night and running into rioting gangs or riding in daylight and being seen by crazy people?" Rebel asked. "I vote we keep going."

"I don't know Rebel, we pushed the horses pretty hard today and neither of us got much sleep last night."

"I'd rather ride at night to avoid people," she argued.

"Shh. Did you hear that?" he asked as their quiet conversation was interrupted by voices coming through the darkness.

Rebel pulled out the colt and Conner palmed his revolver. Jake danced underneath her responding to the sudden tension. They eased the horses forward in the darkness out of the path of the oncoming voices.

"They are following us!" a young man whispered nervously. "They'll kill us for what we saw!"

"We shouldn't have went back in there," a second young man agreed.

The little filly started to fidget and stomped her foot, catching the attention of the two young men.

"Who's there?" one of them yelled absolutely terrified.

"We are friendly," Conner answered riding into their line of sight. "We are just passing through. Who is following you?"

Both young men sucked in their breath and eyed him suspiciously.

"We are well armed, maybe we can help," Conner encouraged.

"We don't know who they are. There is about ten of them. We were…," the young man paused, embarrassed.

"We were robbing houses," the other guy continued. "But only the empty ones. We went into this one house to get the food and heard people down stairs so we ran out the door and was gonna leave." The young man stopped clearly emotional.

The other boy took over. "We heard a girl scream so we decided to go back in."

"They killed her!" the first young man exclaimed and covered his face in grief. Then in a wavering voice said, "Right there in front of me. He just sliced her throat wide open. She was young!" He ducked his head down to hide his tears.

Conner visibly stiffened. The beast started moving inside him again forcing his blood to heat up. His eyes narrowed and the pulse in his neck started pounding.

"Rebel, hide the horses," he ordered as he pulled out his rifle and bow.

'Here we go again,' she thought as she tied the animals inside a thick stand of trees. She grabbed the shotgun and the rifle and headed back to the men. She handed one of the boys the shotgun and said, "You got five shots, four in the magazine and one in the chamber. You won't have time to reload so don't miss. My guess is about a thirty-yard range max or he will return fire. What is your name?"

"My name is Mason and he's Colton," he answered pointing to his friend.

Conner handed his rifle to Colton and the other shotgun to Rebel then said, "Get behind those rocks and stay put. If they show up, wait till they are in range then fire. Rebel will take lead."

Then he disappeared into the night.

Conner had no intention of letting those murdering bastards anywhere near Rebel and the boys. He had nine arrows left and six rounds in the revolver. He headed in the direction the boys had pointed, anticipating the confrontation.

He walked silently in the darkness until his well-trained ear picked up footsteps. 'Easier than hunting elk,' he smiled to himself then circled around behind the group and went to work.

When he returned, both boys were sleeping while Rebel kept watch. She stiffened when she heard him and he quietly said, "It's me."

Though she wore questions on her expression, she didn't ask them out loud. He was grateful that she just let it go. They silently bedded the horses and rolled out their bags then went to sleep without any words spoken.

The next morning Rebel woke up and knew that Conner wasn't in camp. The boys stumbled out from behind the big boulder that they had used for cover the night before.

"What happened?" Mason asked.

"Don't worry, those men won't hurt anyone again. Conner had them arrested last night," Rebel lied just as Conner entered camp leading the horses.

He stopped in midstride surprised then smiled at her appreciatively, silently thanking her for the lie.

She smiled back and winked at him. "So, where are you boys going?" she asked turning her attention back to the two young men.

"Can't we stay with you? We don't have anywhere to go." Colton asked pleadingly.

"What about your family? Don't you want to go home?" Rebel asked.

"Colton hates his dad. He hasn't talked to him since last year when he came back to school beat half to death," Mason volunteered.

"Shut up!" Colton reprimanded

"You shut up. I wouldn't say it if it weren't true," Mason defended then added, "My mom lives in St. Louis. We were students at U of I. But now, there is no school."

Rebel looked at Conner who shrugged. 'It would be nice to have some company to relieve the ever building sexual tension between them,' she thought to herself. Then replied, "Well, I don't see why you can't hang with us for awhile. St. Louis is sort of on our way. Can you ride bareback?"

"Ya, Mason rides pretty good. He took me a couple times when we visited his house for break," Colton said.

"K, let's get on our way then," she smiled and turned to repack their dwindling supplies so that the boys could ride the mare and the filly.

Conner rode in silence listening to Rebel chatting with their new companions. He had been surprised that she'd lied for him. She was probably trying to protect the boys but still, he felt like she was protecting him. And when she winked at him, he thought his knees would go out from under him. She made him feel like a teenage boy living his first crush. Every day it became harder to stop himself from taking her into the tent and never coming out. He wanted her and it was making him crazy. He thought about last night and was glad that there had been a physical distraction.

"Today is going to be really tense Rebel," Conner said after a few miles. It was the first time he had spoken since he'd left them the night before. "It is a densely populated area and there are a few rivers to cross. There is a military base south of Indianapolis that is sure to be fully manned."

Rebel nodded wondering how the hell they were going to get through with their weapons. Her apprehension grew as they neared the city. She looked around trying to see an alternate route but there was no way without riding for days.

They neared a freeway at the edge of the city and crossed under the overpass without being seen, much to their relief. The horses grew skittish at the sound of their hooves echoing around them and reared when they reached the other side and were instantly surrounded by military personnel.

"Fuck!" Conner said under his breath and instinctively edged closer to Rebel.

"Martial Law is in effect in this city. What is your destination?" a very stiff private asked them.

"We are just passing through on our way to the Rockies," Conner answered.

"Step off the horses and hand over your weapons," he requested.

"Fuck!" Conner again out loud this time.

Colton slid off the filly and strode up to the private. "Let us pass!" he ordered. "They are escorting my friend and I home to St. Louis."

The private didn't budge.

Colton leaned in close the man's ear and said, "I am Colton Steelman. If you don't let me pass I will call my dad and have your ass. You know my dad, Sergeant Steelman?"

The private stiffened and looked at his gunner nervously.

Colton reached over and swiped the private's radio. He put it up to his mouth and engaged the key.

"Let them pass!" the private yelled. "Let them pass!"

"Thank you private," Colton said with an arrogant salute. Then tucked the 2-way radio back into the man's belt and give it a haughty pat.

He swung back onto the filly and led the group past the hummers.

"What the fuck was that about you little devil?" Conner asked with a grin.

"His dad is a big dog on the base," Mason volunteered.

Colton just shrugged, "They hate him as bad as I do."

By nightfall they were safely past what Rebel considered the hardest part of their journey. Now it would be easier to stay away from the cities and people. She felt some hope replacing the constant feeling of dread that never left her. She was really proud of Colton for standing up for them. She wouldn't have guessed his background, which made more sense now.

They came upon a small river and dismounted. The boys scurried off to find wood for a fire and Rebel silently unsaddled Jake.

Conner finished staking the other three horses and glanced over to Rebel who was just standing there holding the bridle watching Jake graze. As if by their own power, his legs walked him up behind her. He stopped close enough for the usual electro static vibration to start burning into him but not close enough to make her edgy.

She felt the friction emanating from him as he stood behind her. Her pulse quickened and her entire body warmed. 'How does he do that to her even at a distance?' she wondered.

Mason and Colton split the electrifying tension when they came into view with their arms full of driftwood. Conner sighed and moved to help them build a fire.

He sat down with the boys and listened to their conversation about girls. Mason was telling a story about a recent date and he laughed as the young man exaggerated the girls' breast size.

Rebel listened to that deep, sexy laugh and frowned. She was in a weird frame of mind. The tension between them was deepening to the point where she rationalized that it was affecting her worse than giving in to him would. 'Would it really be so bad?' Mayhem asked again. "Shut the fuck up logic," Rebel said out loud before she could stop herself.

Conner looked up at her questioningly.

"Nothin" she said to him shrugging sheepishly.

'God she is beautiful,' he thought to himself as he watched her fuss around in her bag. He no longer tried to control his physical response to her, partially because it had become impossible.

"Are you guys married?" Colton asked innocently.

"Don't I wish!" Conner breathed loudly.

This brought Rebel's head up and her piercing eyes straight to his. He just stared right back at her, daring her to respond.

Both boys laughed until Rebel leveled her gaze onto them.

"Mason is dating an older woman too," Colton said casually.

Another look from Rebel brought a grin to Conner's face. "Older woman huh," he said teasingly still holding her gaze. "They are fiery. You better be careful boy."

Rebels eyes flashed.

The boys didn't notice the interaction this time and Colton went on, "He says older women are more fun but I say that younger women are more fun."

"Let's ask Rebel what she thinks," Mason said excitedly.

"Ya, let's ask Rebel," Conner encouraged laughing but never letting her eyes drop from his.

"What do you think Rebel. Is it better for us to date older women or younger women," Colton asked expectantly.

"Well," Rebel hesitated. She wasn't their mother. How would she know? She noticed that Conner seemed more interested in her answer than the boys were so she decided to tease him. "Well, see that filly over there?"

All three of them looked at the pretty little horse grazing by Jake then looked back at her.

"She is young, sleek and trim, beautiful. Its very exciting to ride her because she is fast and full of fire."

Both boys nodded but Conner was looking at her with the strangest expression on his face.

"But along with that fire, is inexperience. She is fidgety, impatient and flighty. At any moment a bird could fly up and she would spin right out from under you leaving you sitting on your ass in the dirt. You would have to chase her and if caught her again you would have to keep an eye on her because she would always be looking out for greener pastures."

Conner leaned forward anxious for more of her

analogy.

"Now, see that mare over there?"

Again, all three of them looked toward the horses.

"She is a little fuller. Not quite as sleek. She isn't what you would call beautiful but she is a good looking animal. She is steady and strong. She may not be as exciting to ride but she is just as fast because she just knows how to pace herself. She knows how to control the fire. She doesn't fidget when you ride her because she has experience. She has seen the birds fly up so they don't scare her. You don't have to watch her because she knows where she is and is satisfied with the path in front of her. She knows what the greener grass tastes like so she doesn't seek it out."

Rebel looked at her captive audience and said, "The choice is yours boys. Do you want the flighty filly or the steady mare?"

Rebel knew that the boys didn't get as much out of her story as Conner did. He just sat there with that dumb expression on his face. The boys looked at each other and started laughing again.

Rebel smiled at them and stood up. "I'm going to take a dip in the river."

Their camp was only about thirty yards from the small river so she hiked up the bank a little ways before undressing and sliding into the cold water. The moon was shining overhead in an otherwise unusually dark cloudless sky. Its light illuminated the ripples in the water around her.

She lathered soap in her hair and washed her face then leaned back, floating on top of the water looking at the stars that sparkled brightly above her, defying the full moon with their light.

Conner sat by the fire pondering the 'steady and strong' part of her story. 'Knows how to control the fire'. 'Happy where she is'. 'Was she directing that to him?' he wondered then shook his head telling himself to grow up. He looked over and noticed that she had left her rifle leaning against her saddle. He thought about the men who had kidnapped her a few days ago and quickly talked himself into following her to make sure she was safe.

Silently he walked upriver intending to just stand guard but froze when he saw her floating on top of the water with the moonlight reflecting off of every curve of her well defined, muscular body. His eyes traveled over her creamy white breasts, across her tanned flat stomach and down to her distinct bikini line.

He almost groaned out loud and cursed himself for the self-inflicted torture he had just subjected himself to. He ducked down feeling like a stalker as she swam to the bank and stood up. White fluffy bubbles from her shampoo gently slid down her breasts and flat abdomen enticing him into a moan. He clamped his mouth shut tightly and watched her pick up her soap and slowly wash then dive back into the water.

He had to get out of here. This was not going to help their situation. But he couldn't tear his eyes away when she stepped out of the river to her towel.

'Move now!' he told himself and somehow managed to creep away from the water's edge. He hurried back to camp and climbed into his sleeping bag hoping the boys wouldn't tell her he had followed her.

He listened to her walk into camp and climb into her tent then slowly faded off to sleep with the mare in his dreams.

The brothers rode into the city of North Platte planning to cross the river on the overpass. As they rode closer to the bridge, it was clear that the earthquake had indeed dampened their progress.

"Fuck me! The god damned bridge is out!" Warrick cursed.

They all looked across the fast moving water apprehensively.

"That is a long way for horses to swim," Darien pondered out loud.

"Ya, and my boots and guns will get wet!" Warrick cursed again.

Dylan dismounted and walked to the waters edge.

He looked down river wondering if it narrowed at all anywhere close. "We're gonna to have to swim it," he stated.

They knew that their horses could swim well but it was very dangerous. If a rider went off, he was at risk of being killed by the strong churning hooves or even being pulled underneath the animal and drown.

They dismounted and loosened the cinches on their saddles so that the horses had more room to breathe.

"All right then, slow and easy. And for God's sake don't go off!" Darien said.

The three nudged their mounts into the water, each sucking in their breathe as the icy wetness settled around their thighs.

"Fuck! This was a good idea!" Warrick bellowed sarcastically.

Though the animals were fresh and strong, the current was rapidly taking them downriver. Their progress was slow against the fast current and the horses were getting more nervous as they went.

"God, don't panic Ace," Dylan soothed his gilding.

Half way across the river, Darien's horse started thrashing and trying to turn back. "God damn it!" he yelled gently pushing the animals head toward the bank.

"Almost there," Warrick encouraged them.

After what seemed an eternity, the horses found footing under the water and they climbed up the bank on the other side. Both man and horse just stood there panting.

"Jesus Christ! I don't want to do that again," Warrick said when he caught his breath. "Let's make a fire and dry our shit. We'll let the horses rest for awhile before we continue on."

Dylan nodded in agreement.

After a couple of hours, their cloths were dry and the horses were rested.

"Let's head out," Dylan urged them.

They rode cross-country northeast so that they could stay above the Big Platte River as they neared Omaha.

"There aren't any roads that straight shot in our

direction," Dylan pointed out. "That means no bridges. We may have to swim few more rivers," he teased his brother.

Warrick looked at him and said, "Don't think I won't shoot you."

Dylan grinned and pushed his horse into a gallop.

They rode fast until they came into a state park that opened into a large reservoir.

"Maybe I'll catch us a fish for dinner," Darien said. He enjoyed fishing and loved trout.

Warrick was about to invite himself when fifty guys in leather jackets strolled out from behind the trees startling the horses. His gilding reared and spun around trying to break into a run. "Knock it off!" he yelled at the animal using his large arms to bring the horse up.

Darien's big horse was prancing around pawing the ground.

"Hello there," Dylan offered to the group of men. "Didn't mean to bother you. We were just looking for a bed and fish to fry."

The brothers waited silently for their reaction.

"Biker dudes," Dylan said under his breath to Warrick who was already puffing up. "You think you can take them all on?" he taunted.

Before Warrick could answer the smart-ass remark, the group of men moved toward them. All three brothers tensed. They were tough but they weren't stupid.

"Bunch of cowboys, huh?" the leader of the group asked.

"Only when we have to be," Darien calmly replied. "We are on our way to Omaha to extract our brothers and niece. They were stranded there when the shit came down."

"Do you always have to sound so military?" Warrick barked. "Extract! What kind of word is that?"

"Do you always have to sound like such a fucking redneck?" Darien shot back.

The brothers glowered at each other.

The lead guy laughed at the exchange and said, "We can respect that. Blood is blood. Come join our fire."

The tension lifted and the brothers dismounted.

Dylan took the horses while Warrick and Darien shook hands with some of the men.

After they were settled in and everything was calm, Darien took out his collapsible fishing rod and went down to the reservoir. Several hours later he returned with about thirty fish. "Dinner is on me," he said handing them over to the hungry men.

The evening was enjoyable with lots of conversation and jokes. The brothers felt right at home with these roughnecks.

Chapter 5

Conner woke up the next morning with Rebels tanned flat abs in his mind. He lay still for a moment trying to figure out how he was going to act normal around her now with this overwhelming sexual tension even more severe than it had been. He stood up and rolled his sleeping bag then noticed that she was already up and had put her saddle on the filly.

"What are you doing?" he asked a little confused.

"Wait and watch," Rebel said.

The boys came walking up to them and Connor instantly knew what she was talking about. Poor Colton could hardly walk.

Conner laughed and asked, "Saddle sore? The filly too much for you Colton?"

Colton blushed.

"Leave him alone, Conner. I'd like to see how you walked after a night bareback on a fiery filly," she shot at him.

Connor flushed as an erotic image shot through his head.

"I've put my saddle on her for you," Rebel said turning to Colton. "I will handle riding bareback better than you did." She gave his hair a brotherly tousle.

Conner bristled at the intimate gesture but quickly recovered when Rebel looked at him fiercely. She cocked an eyebrow at him then stalked over to Jake and swung easily onto his back. "Let's move," she said, and pushed her horse into a lope.

Mason coughed in a distinctly fake manner and grinned as he mounted his horse.

Colton didn't look at Connor or say anything, just followed Mason.

Conner swung onto his gilding feeling a little jilted. He had definitely just been put in his place.

Rebel kept the pace well into the morning, wanting to reach the Wabash River by nightfall. When she finally reined in to rest the horses, she fell back in step with

Conner's gilding.

Though she'd been angry at his response to her innocent interaction with Colton this morning, she'd relished in the obvious jealousy. He had tried to cover up his reaction but she'd felt it. 'He was really falling for her,' she thought smiling. She made a mental note to be a little more cautious interacting with the opposite sex from now on. She would never intentionally provoke jealously but in her defense, she hadn't had to worry about that for a long time.

They continued riding side by side lost in their own thoughts. The boys were behind them talking and laughing.

Suddenly Conner reined in his gilding bringing their attention to him. He heard horses coming, many horses. Then he heard one whiney, which meant that they knew they were there.

"Get off the road, now!" he said in a quiet urgent voice.

Rebel motioned the boys to follow her into a small group of trees just off the road. "Not very good cover," she whispered turning to Conner. But he hadn't followed them. What was he doing? Jake perked his ears up telling her that there were other horses out there and she watched as twenty mounted men rode at a full gallop around the bend in the road just ahead of where Conner was standing.

They all stopped in front of him, their dancing horses lathered and dripping sweat. The men were well armed and from the looks of them, were itching for an excuse to use their weapons. Two of the men each held a woman in front of them. The poor creatures were tied and gagged with wild eyes portraying their terror.

The boys stiffened and looked at her nervously. She held her finger to her lips telling them to be quiet and prayed that the horses wouldn't whinny at each other. This was a bad deal. Her worst fear. Why men turn on each other in times of tribulation, she would never know. But it had always been the reality.

The conversation between Conner and a very large man grew heated and Rebel watched in horror as the men pointed his gun at Conner. She jumped and nearly screamed when the shot rang out and Conner slumped off his horse. Tears ran down her face as she put one hand over her mouth and held the boys silent with the other.

The man dismounted and caught Conner's gilding that had jumped out of the way. He and another man picked Conner's body up and flung him across the saddle and bound him onto the dancing animal. Then they simply got on their horses and rode on down the road.

When they were out of sight, Rebel let out the sob she had been holding in. The boys rushed over to her and caught her as she slumped to the ground overtaken with grief.

"He's not dead," Colton insisted. "He was conscious when they put him on the horse."

Rebel grabbed his arm and looked into his eyes asking hopefully, "Are you sure?"

He nodded with certainty. "Come on, we have to follow them," he said leading her to Jake.

The three quickly but cautiously followed the sound of pounding hooves.

Rebel's mind was racing. How badly was he injured? Where were they taking him? How in the hell was she going to save him? What could have provoked them to shoot him? And why would they take him with them?

The large group rode south until dusk then stopped and made camp in a small tree covered valley.

Rebel and the boys tied the horses far enough away that they wouldn't betray their position and snuck closer to get a better look. Rebel looked through her binoculars from the top of a small ridge. Relief slammed through her when she spotted Conner slumped over in front of a tree. Her relief faded quickly though, when she saw the amount of blood that covered his chest and spilled down his side. He raised his head a little when one of the men walked by and kicked his boot.

"He's alive," she told the boys.

"I knew it," Colton breathed.

"K, we will wait till dark, then I will sneak down and

untie him," Rebel said. "You guys will cover me from here with the rifle. The shotgun won't be much help at this range."

Both boys objected at the same time. "We have to save the girls. What if Conner can't walk and you have to carry him? What if they catch you sneaking in?"

"All right guys," Rebel soothed. "Calm down." But she knew they were right. He may be too injured to walk and she had been so preoccupied thinking about Conner that she hadn't considered the two women.

"We are going to get Conner out first then we will figure out how to get the girls. Agreed?"

They both nodded.

"Who is the best shot with the rifle?" she asked them.

Colton raised his hand timidly. "My dad took me to the training field all the time when I was younger."

"Alright, you stay here and cover us with the rifle. Mason, you come down closer with the shotgun. I will take the handgun. Remember, Mason, thirty yards max for a kill but you can pepper 'em pretty good up to fifty yards. I will find Conner's horse and get him out on the gilding. We will have to wait until they are asleep."

The boys nodded again.

Rebel ground her teeth, impatiently listening to the men partying well into the night. 'Where were the National Guard when you needed them?' she fumed. This is how she had pictured it to be when the shit came down. Lawlessness, plundering, rioting, theft, rape and murder. What she hadn't envisioned was falling in love and being exposed to an emotional threat outside of her own family. She had prepared for their safety and had planned on defending them. But this, this new love hadn't been in the scenario.

She closed her eyes tightly fighting the hysteria threatening to explode inside her mind. 'It's going to get nothing but worse,' she thought knowing that this was only the beginning.

Finally the camp grew quiet and Rebel pushed the

negative thoughts aside. She focused on the present and nodded to the boys who moved into action. They each took their positions while Rebel stealthily flanked the campsite. She found the gilding still saddled. "Fucking pigs!" she raged under her breath, "Can't even take care of the animals." She led the horse as close to where Conner lay as she dared then crept into the camp.

The night was especially dark thanks to a thick heavy cloud cover and she could barely see her feet. Thunder clapped loudly and a flash of lightning lit the camp for a split second. Carefully she felt her way to the tree that Conner was tied to and knelt down beside him. He moaned when she cut his hands free.

"Quiet," she whispered stroking his face gently. Her rage deepened when she felt the aftermath of fists on his skin. 'They had beaten a wounded man! Mother Fuckers!'

He opened his eyes and tried to focus.

"Can you walk?" she asked urgently in his ear. He nodded his head slightly and tried to stand. She braced herself underneath his shoulder and heaved him to his feet. She staggered under his weight, sheer determination the only thing keeping them upright. Slowly they hobbled through the trees to where she'd left the gilding. It took every bit of strength they had left to heft him onto the horse. She climbed on behind him hoping she could keep him from falling back off and nudged the animal quietly away from the camp.

She didn't dare move fast even though they were out of hearing distance because Conner was barely able to hang on and moaned at every step the horse took.

The boys met up with her in the grove where they'd left their horses and silently mounted, worry and concern written clearly on their faces.

They rode in the darkness until Conner lost consciousness and almost tumbled off the horse. The boys scrambled to dismount and help her lower him to the ground. They drug him into a dense thicket of trees and laid him beside a patch of boulders that would shelter him from the rain that threatened to fall at any moment.

Rebel turned to the boys and said, "Hand me the first aid kid then find a place to hide the horses."

They silently did her bidding.

She turned her attention to the gunshot wound just below his collarbone. The wound was still bleeding and tears ran down her face as she cut off his blood soaked shirt. She rolled him to his side to see if there was an exit wound. 'Thank God,' she thought. 'It went all the way through.' The man had fired at close range and the gaping hole was huge. She feverishly worked to stop the bleeding, praying he hadn't lost too much blood.

He moaned and lifted his hand to her face, wiping her tears with his thumb then slipped back into darkness, unconscious again.

"I've slowed the bleeding," she told the boys when they returned. "Those fuckers beat him when they got to camp."

Anger flickered across their faces and they both shook their heads.

"Stay here with him Rebel," Colton said. "We are going for the girls. We'll take them in the opposite direction so that if they catch our trail, it won't lead them to you. We're going on foot so we can hide easier."

Worry and regret weighed heavily upon her as she handed the boys the colt and Conner's revolver. She handed each of them a hunting knife and said, "Be very careful you guys. These men will kill you if they catch you."

"Try to get some rest. You are well hidden here," Mason said. "We will meet back up with you later." Then two boys headed out on a manly mission.

Rebel draped the tent like a tarp over the large boulders covering Conner's makeshift bed and pulled the sleeping bags over his trembling body. She lay down beside him and dozed off listening to the rain keeping pace with his heartbeat.

The boys arrived back at the men's camp just before dawn. They decided to stay together and save one of the women at a time. It had taken them several minutes of searching to find them. The first woman they found lay confined in the massive arms of her captor. The man had separated them slightly from the group, which made the rescue a little easier. Colton picked up a large rock and brought in down on the sleeping man's head as hard as he could. It made a loud thud and the man moaned at the impact.

They both held their breath watching for the other men to stir. The woman, still gagged, stared at them with wild hopeful eyes. Mason gave her a reassuring nod and unwrapped the unconscious man from around her and helped her to her feet.

Colton looked at the bloody, badly beaten woman and couldn't help himself. He pulled the large blade from his boot and drove it deep in the chest of the unconscious man.

"What the fuck?" Mason mouthed angrily.

Colton just shrugged and led the woman out of camp.

"Thank God," the woman whispered tearfully when they removed the gag. "Thank God, thank you so much." She grabbed Mason and hugged him.

"We have to go back for the other girl," he told her pulling away. "Stay here and don't move. We will come back and get you."

The trembling woman just nodded in agreement.

They found the second woman in the same general position as the first. Colton picked up another large rock and bashed it across the big man holding her. Mason pulled the girl to her feet.

When Colton pulled out the blade, Mason moved to stop him. Colton shoved him back and sliced the man's throat wide spilling blood across his hand then silently stalked back to where the first woman waited.

Mason turned on Colton. "What the fuck? Now you are a murderer?" he whispered loudly.

"Look at them! Look at what they did to them!" Colton loudly whispered back.

Mason didn't like the look in Colton's eyes. He had

known him for several years and the two were inseparable. He knew that Colton had a dark side but hadn't realized that his best friend was capable of taking another man's life. He just turned and led the two women away looking for a hiding place far away from the band of plunderers.

Conner became conscious with Rebel curled up next to him, sleeping. Even in his battered condition his body responded to her. He moaned at the residual pain that the uncontrolled movement of his body caused and mentally willed himself to relax so he could enjoy being close to her.

Rebel stirred, caught in that delicious sleepy, half dreamy state, selfishly lingering in comfort and desire. She felt fingers rubbing her back and pictured Conner's seductive face above her. As reality crept in stealing away the fantasy her mind had created, she realized that it was Conner gently caressing her. Now fully awake, she hesitated to shatter the moment, wondering why she had denied his touch for so long.

She knew the answer though. She had been trying to protect herself from the agony that she had endured watching him fall from the horse presumed dead. 'Thank God he had survived,' she thought and looked up into his eyes.

His face was swollen and marred with gashes and cuts. Both of his eyes were blackened and his lips were swollen and split. He had a very pronounced bulge on his left temple and another just behind his ear that was covered in blood. A deep purple bruise covered a large portion of his chest and side, hiding several broken ribs and the hole gouged out from the bullet was still seeping blood. She took it all in knowing that these were just the visible wounds.

He tried to smile at her and winced in pain.

"What did they do to you?" she whispered softly, once again threatened by tears. She stood up and angrily wiped them away. She rarely cried. In fact, couldn't remember the last time she had. Then she thought about the day she couldn't reach Jade on the phone and had left for

D.C. She had cried then.

"Why didn't you follow us off the road?" she said turning on him. "Why were you arguing with them? What in the hell did they want?" she raged finally reacting to the fear and frustration that had built up inside her.

Conner calmly waited for her to finish knowing that she needed the release. It didn't take long and she crouched back down beside him and said, "I thought you were dead. That shot ripped my heart out Conner!"

She stood up again and started pacing in the small space under the tarp. "I'm not supposed to fall in love with you. I am supposed to be a cold hearted, gun slingin, bad ass, ready and prepared for this nightmare that I knew was coming. Instead, I am a teary eyed, love sick, twitterpaited weenie with butterflies in my stomach and love songs in my head! And I hate to cry!" she yelled at him stomping her foot.

Conner just grinned that typically sexy maddening grin then winced again at the simple gesture. 'She loved him,' he thought and smiled again then groaned at the pain.

"God, hold still you ass," she reprimanded kneeling down with concern. She looked into his captivating eyes, consumed by emotions.

"They knew someone was there, Rebel. But they didn't know how many. I had to keep you safe," he said slowly through battered lips.

Realization crossed her face as she sorted through the moments before she had left the road. He had stayed in sight because they had known someone was there and if they had rounded the corner and found no one, they would have searched for them. She sighed sadly and lay down beside him holding him carefully. He had just saved all their lives and paid a heavy price to do it.

Colton found shelter for the small group on the bank of a creek under an old covered bridge. The rain was pounding down above them but the structure kept them dry. The women were exhausted and slept soundly holding on to each other. Mason was dozing a few feet away still holding the colt in his hand protectively.

Colton couldn't sleep. He was wrestling with a newfound excitement from the blood lust that had just awakened inside him. He wanted more. All of those years of being under his father's fist had made him numb but tonight he felt a vicious, murderous, demon awaken inside him, burning for revenge. He felt alive.

He walked over to Mason and stood over his best friend's sleeping form. He was saddened at the realization that Mason would never accept the dark side of him that he had shown him tonight. His life would be very different from now on.

Colton left Mason and the women sleeping and crept back toward the camp. The sky was angry and thunder rumbled, slapping lightning into ground around him. The rain turned to hail and he looked up into the green tinted sky, instantly recognizing the pre tornado weather.

The men in the camp were enraged as they prepared to brave the storm to hunt for their stolen fugitives. Colton watched from a safe distance as they pointed to the two dead men and yelled at each other. A bolt of lightning hit the ground in front of him with such magnitude that it made the morning light seem dim.

The bright light dissipated and that was when he seen it, a massive twister that touched down just yards from their camp. The preoccupied men saw it too late and were wiped out by flying debris and full trees that were flung through the camp by the immense winds of the writhing tornado. Horses scattered and men screamed as nature's justice was unleashed upon them.

The newly awakened evil tingled inside Colton's body as he eagerly watched the destruction. "You fuckers are lucky it got to you first!" he yelled into the blinding rain and wind.

Mason was pacing under the bridge hours later when Colton rode up to him leading three horses. He flinched inside when he looked at his friend and read the worry and confusion on his face.

"I went back to steal some horses so that we could get away" he lied. "But before I got there, a tornado ripped through their camp and killed most of them," he explained. He didn't mention the fact that he'd finished off the few survivors. "We better go check on Conner and Rebel."

The brothers were well rested after their night of eating and drinking with the biker guys but the morning sky was cloudy and rain threatened to fall. They pulled out their rain gear and braved the storm riding hard.

Darien reined his horse in from the fast pace they'd kept for most of the morning with a curse. "My horse threw a shoe."

"God damn it. It was bound to happen sooner or later," Dylan said coming up beside him. "We'll have to walk until we find someone who might have one."

"They might have something," Warrick said from the top of a small ridge in front of them. "Looks like they have some livestock."

They rode down to the little farmhouse and dismounted.

"Anyone home?" Darien asked loudly.

A man came out the door packing a shotgun. "What you want?"

"My horse threw a shoe," Darien stated. "We seen your stock and wondered if you might have one?"

The man glowered at them suspiciously.

"We'd be glad to compensate you," Dylan added.

The man smiled greedily and yelled, "Bev, bring the boys somethin ta drink." Then he looked at the brothers and said, "You'll find what you need in the barn."

A pretty young woman came out the door and set a tray with some glasses on a table on the porch. "This here is my niece," the man introduced her with a sneer.

All three of the brothers removed their hats and said, "Nice to meet you, ma'am."

"No need to ma'am her," he growled. "Her daddy was piece of crap and so is she! Just left her here before he got arrested!"

Dylan stiffened as the young woman flushed at the disrespectful comment and slunk back into the house. Warrick looked at Darien and Dylan glared at the filthy man.

"Dylan, why don't you wait here? Warrick and I will tend to the horse," Darien said.

Dylan tied the other two horses to the fence and walked up to the porch. "Nice to have family to help out," he said stiffly, eyeing the man.

"Maybe if she did anything around here!" he huffed then yelled toward the door. "Bring my sandwich out here!"

Dylan clenched his fist trying to remain calm.

"Want something to eat?" the man asked as Bev came back out holding a plate of food. The uncle scowled at her and she was so unnerved that she dropped the plate as she tried to hand it to her uncle.

"God damn it! You think this shit is free?" he screamed roaring to his feet. Then he backhanded her in the face sending her flying back against the house.

In one swift move Dylan was off his feet and had the man against the house next to her with his fingers wrapped tightly around his throat. "Go on back into the house little lady," he said to the girl with such calmness that the uncle's eyes widened in fear.

"Don't take kindly to men hittin women," Dylan growled into the uncle's ear as the young woman scurried through the door.

In a show of strength, the uncle said, "This is my place, don't come here and tell me what to do with what's mine."

Dylan slammed a big fist into the man's nose without removing his other hand from his throat.

"Fuck you!" the obstinate man said glaring at him through the blood running down his face.

Dylan lost the control he'd managed to keep until then. He beat the man damn near unconscious then he stepped back, leaned over him and said, "I'm coming back here in a few days and if she even has one red spot on that pretty face, I will bury you in the barn."

Darien and Warrick stepped up on the porch.

"Dylan?" Darien said worriedly.

Dylan picked up the man's shotgun and emptied the shells from the weapon. He stuffed a wad of cash into the chamber and slammed it into the man's chest. He looked him in the eye and said, "Not a mark!" Then he stalked to his horse without another word. He mounted the gilding and turned him east.

A sudden gunshot rang out bringing his attention back to the porch. The woman stood in front of her uncle's dead body with a pistol in her hand.

Dylan cursed under his breath and dismounted again. He walked toward her and said, "Bev?"

She jumped and whipped the gun around on him.

"Easy there, Bev," he said calmly. "I'll take it from here, k?"

The woman was so rattled that she dropped the weapon and stood trembling in shock.

Dylan waved his brothers over and said, "We better help her bury him."

They both nodded and went to the barn for a shovel.

The rain had subsided so Rebel took down the tarp and helped Conner into a sitting position. He leaned back against the boulder to rest from the effort. He had slept most of the day, trying to regain some strength. Rebel built a fire to dry their tack and bags then looked up into the cranky evening sky and watched the lightning ripple horizontally through the thick black clouds. 'Amazing,' she thought.

The sight made her think of Jade and she wished she were here to see the beautiful electromagnetic storm. Jade loved lightning and spent hours with her camera trying to catch the perfect shot. Saddened by the thought, she prayed silently that Jade and her younger brothers were safe.

She wondered how far along her older brothers had gotten since they'd left mom in the mountain camp. Hopefully they were close and would be able to find the kids quickly. The injuries Conner had suffered at the hands of those land pirates would slow them down and she cursed the bad luck.

Her thoughts went to Mason and Colton. 'God, what if they had been caught and killed,' she worried, thinking that she should go after them then jumped at the sound of hooves galloping toward them.

"It's just us," Mason yelled out so that she wouldn't panic.

Mason and Colton rode into camp followed by two very disheveled women.

"Thank God you're alright. I was just thinking I should go look for you," Rebel said as they dismounted. Colton hadn't said anything and she caught a sense that something was wrong as she stepped closer. "What's wrong? Are you injured?" she asked looking from him to Mason.

Colton forced a smile for her and without looking at Mason said, "We are fine Rebel. In fact, I have a story to tell. How is Conner?"

"I'm fine," Conner answered for himself weakly. He had caught a strange tension between the two boys as well.

"K," Rebel said looking back and forth at them. She turned to the two women and said, "Come on, let's get you cleaned up and fed." With a glance back to the boys, she followed them to the fire.

The boys silently unsaddled the horses and staked them for the night.

Rebel kept busy bandaging a deep gash on one of the women. The tension in the air grew as the boys sat down next to each other by the fire. Rebel and Conner exchanged glances both wondering what the hell was going on.

"Mason, would you introduce the ladies to us please?" Rebel asked breaking the silence.

Relieved, Mason said, "This is Abby and this is Steph."

"Sorry to meet you under these circumstances," Rebel said giving them a welcome smile. Then she turned to Colton, "So... do you want to tell us what happened?"

"We snuck into the camp and got the girls. Then we

hid under a bridge. I decided to go back and steal some horses. But before I could, a tornado ripped through the camp and killed all those men," he said hurriedly. "Can you believe it? It was huge and they were screaming and the horses were running. It was really cool." He paused then went on, "After the tornado did it's thing I caught the horses and went back for these guys. I found us our own guns too."

Rebel looked at him suspiciously knowing that there was more, but she let it go and said, "Good, I'm glad it went well. At least you have a saddle now."

"Thank god," he laughed, relaxing a little. "My ass still hurts."

Even Mason broke into a smile.

Lightning flashed through the sky again turning the dusk to daylight. Rebel looked up and said, "So this weather is the aftermath of a tornado. I've never experienced this before."

"Not the aftermath," Mason broke in. "It's the making. We will see more tornadoes tonight. We need to find cover."

"I'm not willing to move Conner yet. I don't want his wounds to start bleeding again."

"Stop talking about me like I'm a child," he objected. "The boys are right we can't stay out here in the open."

"You aren't moving!" Rebel stated flatly.

Conner just huffed and looked away.

They built the fire up big and bedded down around it. The girls huddled together under one of the sleeping bags and the boys put an unusually large space between them, crashing on the ground. Rebel climbed under her sleeping bag next to Conner. They all lay awake in silence watching the beautiful display of light that nature had provided them.

The clinic that Kira had set up in the mountain camp was busy this morning. One of the kids had sliced his finger open whittling on a stick and one of the men walked in with a fishing hook buried deep in his hand.

The only person with medical training was a licensed

practical nurse named Jerry. She was doing great, easily keeping up with the minor injuries that they had seen so far and Marv, the young dentist was trying his best to help her.

She and Evie were sipping coffee on the porch watching the smooth running little system that they had established with Aden sitting beside them writing in her precious notebook. She was eagerly keeping track of everything that happened in the camp.

Kira tilted her head sideways, suddenly realizing that the chickens were all in the henhouse. Curiously she looked over at the horses that were mulling around impatiently. The dogs jumped up and started howling. Kira set her cup down and stood up. "Earthquake coming," she said just as the ground started shaking.

The horses reared and the dogs yelped. The small group of children playing in the creek down in the meadow screamed and their mothers ran toward them.

The ground shook for several minutes knocking her cup off the table. Everyone ran out of the tents nervously looking around.

Then she heard it. The very distinct rumble of hooves. Kira recognized it immediately and yelled, "Stampede! Get the kids out of there!" She bolted off the porch running toward the meadow. "Get behind the trees!" she screamed at the women gathering up the kids.

The women grabbed the small hands, dragging the children into the tree line just as the sixty head of crazed cattle thundered over the hill, heading straight for them. The herd sought cover in the trees and shot past them flinging dirt into the air with each step. The ground shook again as their thrashing hooves ground into the soil.

Kira glanced over and saw one of the women lose her grip a frightened boy. The kid stepped back, leaving the cover of the tree and was instantly enveloped by the herd of stampeding animals. Kira launched herself at the boy, landing on top of him, covering him with her body. She instinctively covered his head and curled into a ball. She could feel hooves land on her back and taste dirt and blood in her mouth. She knew they would be lucky to take another breath. Oddly, she thought about the Johnny Cash song, 'Ghost riders in the sky'.

"Their brands were still on fire and their hooves were made of steel," she sang to herself. "Their horns were black and shiny and their hot breath he could feel. A bolt of fear went through him as they thundered through the sky…" Then she faded into unconsciousness.

After the herd had passed, thirty people gathered around Kira and the boy. "Oh, my god," someone said then they silently carried her back to the little cabin.

Nick strode through the door and was instantly overcome by the sight of his sister. "God damn it!" he roared.

"She's going to recover," the young nurse soothed, patting him on the shoulder. "She will be ok."

Conner woke up the next morning to a clear sky and pulled himself to his feet, clenching his jaw against the pain. He knew that Rebel was in a hurry to get to Jade and refused to stand in her way. He tried to steady himself, nearly toppling over from dizziness. He regained his balance and took a step, breathing hard.

"What are you doing?" Rebel jumped up. "Conner, it's too soon. You'll start bleeding again."

"We are moving on!" he said, stubbornly echoing her flat tone from the night before.

"Please Conner," she pleaded knowing she would lose this fight.

His expression softened as he looked down at her and tried to smile. "I'm fine Rebel. Look, no hands." He spread his arms wide for her to see.

Rebel sucked in her breath and tried to focus on his words but was instantly consumed by the sight in front of her. She couldn't take her eyes off of him, finding herself acutely entranced by his deeply tanned, bare chest. The muscles that had laid at rest while she had doctored his wounds were now rippling seductively inches from her face. She forced herself to breath as her entire body tightened with tantalizing intensity. Her blood pounded through her heart, making her dizzy as her gaze slid slowly down his ribs, raking over the well-defined six-pack he wore in his abdomen. A light trail of hair dipped enticingly down into his jeans.

Conner stiffened under the intense scrutiny, his own breath catching in his throat. His body reacted violently to her provocative exploration of his anatomy and a convulsion ripped through him, the pain almost dropping him to his knees.

Their eyes met and clashed like two bolts of lightning colliding. The magnetism was so strong that neither could break the binding force that held time still.

The vision of her floating in the river crossed his mind and he swayed from the intense tightening of his badly bruised muscles, the pain once again threatening to bring him down.

The movement jolted Rebel out of her trance and she reached out to stabilize him. Fiery hot flames licked down her loins at the touch of his bare skin and the shock of his perfectly toned abs contracting under her palms.

He swayed again and slipped out of her grasp, dropping to his knees. She reached out to him again and he exclaimed harshly, breathing heavily, "No! Don't touch me! God damn, woman, what are you doing to me?"

She stood over him trying to calm her racing pulse. She had never felt this kind of searing passion before. Her heartbeat pounded through her, refusing to slow down.

After a moment, Conner hefted himself back to his feet, the gaping hole in his chest oozing blood. When she moved to help him again, he held up his hand. "If you don't want me to take you back into that tent right now, then don't touch me!" he said firmly then strode away from her.

The boys stirred and she tucked her head to hide the flush that covered her entire body. She walked to the fire to cook breakfast and tried to ignore the unyielding fire that still raged nearly out of control.

An hour later, the six of them saddled and packed

the eight horses. Rebel looked worriedly toward Conner and could see a red blotch staining his clean shirt.

"You shouldn't be riding," she said to no avail.

Conner just swung onto the gilding and pointed him northwest.

Rebel looked around trying to figure out where they were. Conner's captives had ridden south for almost an entire day blowing her projected road map to Omaha all to hell.

Conner was still unapproachable so she allowed Jake to fall in step next to Abby and Steph. They chatted casually for a while then the subject turned to the boys and their rescue.

"Something happened between them last night and neither one of them will volunteer anything. Will you guys fill me in?" Rebel asked.

"All I know is that Mason was pissed that Colton killed the man that was holding me," Steph volunteered.

"He killed the man that held me too," Abby added somewhat surprised.

"In self defense? Were they fighting?" Rebel asked.

"No," Abby answered. "First he knocked him out with a rock then after I was out of his grasp, he stabbed him with a big knife right in the chest."

"Same with the man that held me," Steph added. "Except, he didn't stab him, he sliced his throat wide open."

Rebel was deeply upset by this information. This was much bigger than she had anticipated. She thanked the girls and moved Jake up in pace with Conner's gilding. She rode beside him in silence contemplating what the girls had told her.

By early afternoon they met up with the Wabash River. It was big, fast and wide. Rebel insisted they stop so that she could replace the bandage on Conner's gunshot wound and try to stop the bleeding again.

The boys helped him dismount then volunteered to ride ahead and look for a way to cross. On their way, they would drop the girls in the first town they came upon and try to get the National Guard to return them to Indianapolis.

"We will move upriver till we meet back up with you," Rebel said and waved goodbye.

She turned her attention to the stubborn man slumped over beside her. "Take your shirt off," she ordered.

"Not that again," he teased but complied when she glared at him. He tried to anticipate her touch but couldn't help flinching when her fingers brushed across his bare chest.

"Goddamn it Conner, we can't continue acting like a couple of sixteen year olds."

Fire flashed in his eyes. "Well maybe if you didn't turn me on so fucking bad I wouldn't be acting like a sixteen year old!" he exploded.

Rebel clenched her jaw at the unfair statement, barely able to contain her anger. If he hadn't had so many bruises on his face she would have slapped him. "I'm going to chalk that up to pain induced delirium," she spat back at him and ripped the tape and gauze off of his wound, taking hair with it.

"Fuck!" he roared as pain shot through him.

"Turned on now?" she growled and stomped over to her saddlebag.

Conner sulked as she silently finished dressing the hole in his chest. When she was finished and had put several feet between them, said, "Colton killed two of those men when they went after the girls."

This brought Conner's head up. "How did he kill them?"

"He knocked them out to get the girls away from them and then while they were unconscious, he stabbed one in the chest and sliced the other guys throat open."

Conner just looked at her not knowing what to say.

"I think that is why there is so much tension between them. Obviously Mason didn't agree with the violence. Maybe you could talk to him or something."

"It won't do much good Rebel. You are either capable of killing or you're not. He will be fine. He's a good kid." He slowly stood up and said, "We might as well get going."

They rode upriver in silence until Conner said, "I'm sorry Rebel. I shouldn't have said that to you. Obviously I was irrational, it's not your fault."

She glanced sideways at him.

"I don't know what the hell is going on," he admitted, shaking his head. "I've never felt like this before. I feel like I'm a lightning rod and you are lightning and whenever you are near, my whole body starts to vibrate and sparks fly and shit."

Rebel laughed at the analogy because she had been thinking the very same thing. Her body warmed even now at the thought that he wanted her with such passion.

"Look, Conner, I... I just can't allow myself to be swept up into some kind of love story in a romance novel. I've spent the last five years preparing for this hell and everything that has happened so far is just the cartoon before the movie. I'm not sure if you understand that we have a one in a million chance of being alive in a year. Look at you, we may not survive the trip home," she said solemnly.

"I do understand Rebel," Conner said softly. "But I'm still alive and besides, you can't stop living now or all of the preparation is for nothing."

Rebel jerked her horse to a stop and her eyes flew to his. 'That was exactly what Jade had said to her when she'd left for D.C.,' she thought to herself suddenly becoming agitated. Jake danced underneath her so she let him have his head.

'He's right,' Mayhem said from her shoulder, 'and Jade would agree with him.'

'You want him too,' Logic added, joining forces with the other side. 'You can't deny it anymore.'

The boys rode up to them distracting her from the inner conflict.

"There is an overpass in a town called Hutsonville just up the river but there are a lot of people camping on the other side. Looks like some kind of tent city," Colton said.

"The people are leaving the cities," Rebel

murmured. "Either they are running out of supplies, or the cities are too dangerous."

"Maybe there is a doctor there," Mason said worriedly looking at Conner's ashen face.

They continued on until they met the overpass and rode easily across the river but were met on the other side by about ten armed men.

"We are looking for a doctor," Rebel said to the group just as Conner swayed, almost toppling off his horse.

One of the men, obviously a sheriff, walked closer eyeing them suspiciously. He looked at Conner and said, "We don't want no trouble here."

"We won't be any trouble, sheriff," Conner ground out through the dizziness that had taken hold of him.

The sheriff stepped back and waved them forward. "We have a doctor. I'll send for him. You can set up camp over there for the night."

Rebel thanked him and moved her companions to the pointed location.

The boys helped Conner dismount and leaned him against a tree, his wound bleeding freely now.

An older gentleman walked over to him and paled when he saw the severity of Conner injuries. He sat his bag down beside him and removed his blood drenched shirt and dressing.

Rebel uneasily watched the doctor work on him, sensing from the concern on his face that the injury was life threatening. She stood up and walked away unable to contemplate the implication.

After the doctor had successfully stopped the bleeding again and had Conner resting comfortably he walked over to where Rebel was quietly talking to the Sheriff. "How did this happen?" he asked out of habit then pointed out, "He's been beaten and shot."

"A band of twenty men rode past us and tried to take his horse and weapons. When he refused, they shot him and took him to their camp where they beat him. The boys and I rescued him in the night," Rebel explained visibly upset by the memory.

The sheriff stiffened beside her and instinctively moved his hand to his weapon. "Where are they now?" he asked protectively.

Colton stiffened beside her.

"They were caught in a tornado," Rebel continued. "I don't know how many survived."

Colton flushed and stalked off leaving Mason looking after him in confusion.

"He needs a hospital," the doctor said looking at Conner. "He has lost way too much blood and will need a transfusion and surgery as soon as the power comes back on. If he makes it that long."

Rebel looked at Conner and bit her lip to keep it from trembling. 'If he makes it that long.' The words played over and over in her mind. She closed her eyes and pushed the thought out of her head. She looked at the sheriff, then at the doctor and said quietly, "The power isn't coming back on."

They both looked at her sharply.

"What do you mean its not coming back on?" the sheriff asked.

"A coronal mass ejection wiped out the entire electrical system. The transformers are fried and we don't have backups. The power isn't coming back on for years," she said and strode away trying to keep the thought of losing Conner out of her head.

The next morning, Rebel lay beside Conner watching him sleep as the sun came up into another much-appreciated clear sky. The pain medication he'd taken was allowing him a deep slumber. His determination to continue on despite his condition had made her heart hurt. He needed weeks to recover, time she just didn't have.

The doctor had told her that with the amount of blood he'd lost, he was lucky to be alive and would surely die if he lost any more. She knew by now how stubborn he was and also knew that he would never ask her to wait. With a heavy heart, she decided that she would continue on without him, leaving him here in the doctor's care. 'It's the only way he'll survive,' she told herself with sagging regret then quickly dressed and eased silently out of the tent.

The boys would be separating from them today as well, heading southwest toward St. Louis.

Her mood was sullen and dark as she packed her stuff on the mare. The thought of riding alone threatened to make her change her mind. But she could see no alternative. She was saddling Jake when she felt him walk up behind her.

"After everything we've been through, you would just leave me?" he asked, angrily taking in the distinct separation of their supplies. "I'm too much of a burden now? Slow you down too much?" he added irrationally.

She could hear the hurt in his voice but knew she had to do this. The only way he would survive is if she hurt him more. "Yup," she said stiffly without turning around.

"Fuck!" he roared.

"Everything ok?" Mason asked as the boys walked up.

"Fuck no!" Conner raged on. "Suddenly I'm a fucking drag on her whole 'save the world plan' and she's leaving! Alone! I'm nothing more than a stray dog that's just in the way now! She was probably using me this whole time! And definitely teasing me this whole time!"

Rebel spun around in a flash and slammed her fist squarely into his still swollen lips as hard as she could swing.

Conner staggered backward and both boys inhaled sharply.

"Fuck you Conner!" she raged at him. "Watching you die out in the middle of nowhere is definitely not in my 'save the world plan', you stubborn son of a bitch!"

Conner recovered his balance and stood glaring at her, wiping the blood from the new gash on his mouth. 'Fuck!' he thought with angry admiration. She had just punched him as hard as any man he'd fought.

Sparks ignited the air with tension as they faced off. The boys squirmed, watching the silent battle of wills being fought in front of them.

Finally Colton broke the silence saying, "I'm leaving

too." He forced himself to look way from Mason knowing that his friend wouldn't react well to his unforeseen decision.

All three of them looked at him curiously.

"What?" Mason asked so softly that they barely heard him.

"I wanted to make sure you got home safe before I left but you can handle it from here," he said refusing to look at his friend.

"You can't leave me!" Mason cried out. "I thought we decided to go to St. Louis?" Desperation seeped into him when Colton turned away. "I thought you were going to marry my sister and we'd be brothers." Tears threatened to spill from his eyes as reality sank in and he angrily rubbed them away.

Colton finally looked at him and gently explained, "I've changed Mason. I'm not a good person. I wouldn't subject your sister to the darkness I feel inside me. She is too sweet and kind to love someone like me." He hung his head and added, "And you shouldn't be hanging around me either!"

He turned and walked toward his horse.

"She told me that she was in love with you," Mason said desperately trying to play any card that would change his mind.

Colton stopped, encouraging him to continue.

"She needs you Colton! Look around! She needs you to protect her." Mason held his breath, then breathed softly, "So do I."

Colton swung around and their eyes locked.

"Please don't abandon me," Mason pleaded. "I don't care what you've done. You are my friend. No matter what!"

Colton caved realizing that Mason was forgiving him and would never again judge him. He walked over and wrapped his only friend in a huge bear hug.

Moments passed before Mason pulled back and said, "Come on, let's get riding." He wanted to leave before Colton changed mind.

The boys thanked Rebel and Conner and said sad goodbyes then rode south.

Rebel took the two extra horses that the rescued girls had ridden and handed the doctor the reins. "Thanks for your help," she told him and turned to mount Jake.

She didn't look at Conner as she rode out of camp. She didn't want him to see the tears that ran freely down her face. A piece of her heart broke with each stride the big gilding took until she felt an empty hole in her chest.

Shane impatiently paced the large space in the empty barn. Cayden didn't notice because he was completely immersed with Lynn. The two sat high up on a beam in the loft swinging their legs into the air and chatting like lovebirds. Shane looked up at them shaking his head then continued on, wearing a distinct path in the dirt floor.

"Hold still Shane!" Jade ordered. She was trying to catch a wild kitten that resided in the back corner of the structure.

Shane couldn't hold still. Because of the mad dash out of their little fort, their food supply was short and they were going to run out of water very soon. He wasn't sure how long it would really take for the brothers to get here or if they would even find them.

He turned and pounded his fist into the wall beside him in frustration causing everyone else to jump at the sudden explosion.

"What the fuck bro?" Cayden yelled down glaring at him for the interruption.

"Sorry," Shane mumbled. "I'm just worried that they won't find us now that we've moved," he said defensively.

Cayden helped Lynn down off their perch and came over to stand beside him.

"I need to go into town and find more supplies but the hummer is out of gas," he said dejectedly.

"Why don't you steal a horse and ride into town?" Jade said softly from across the room where she crouched, staring at the kitten mere inches from her face.

Both brothers looked at her completely shocked by the uncharacteristic comment. Jade just wasn't the stealing kind and neither of them could grasp the change of heart.

The kitten dashed away and Jade stood up stomping her foot. "Shit!" she exclaimed. She looked at her uncles who were still staring at her with blank expressions and said innocently, "What?"

Shane looked at Cayden and said, "It's a good idea."

"I'll go with you!" Cadyen said excitedly.

The boys prepared to leave telling the girls to stay put no matter what. They said goodbye and headed south along the river.

"That is a big river," Cayden said looking across the swollen body. The recent rain that had accompanied the severe tornadoes was still draining into it.

Shane glanced over distractedly. He was searching the rural country in front of them for livestock. "Over there!" he said spying about five head of horses grazing in front of a little house and barn.

Cayden grew nervous. These farmers were grumpy and might shoot them. "Ya know, horse stealin is still a hangin offense in Idaho," he said. "In fact, there is still a law in the books that says you get a horse and a gun when you get out of jail."

"God, Warrick would have a whole herd by now," Shane said and they both laughed thinking fondly of their brother.

The boys snuck closer to the empty farmhouse and looked cautiously around. The place was completely abandoned. The door hung open, and a curtain fluttered through a broken window.

"No one's here" Shane said, pointing out the obvious. They crept forward and stepped through the door. It was empty. "They've moved and took all their stuff."

"Why would they leave the livestock?" Cayden asked, confused.

"The gate is open. They probably thought that the animals would fend for themselves. It's too bad cause they would have starved. Domestic horses normally won't leave their familiar place."

They walked out to the barn and found a tack room

then caught and saddled four of the horses. "This guy will probably follow, so just put a halter on him," Shane said pointing to the other horse.

They were getting ready to mount when Cayden heard a whimper. "Did you hear that?" he asked listening intently. He walked over to the back porch and knelt down. Peeking out at him from under the step was a five or six month old Labrador puppy. "Come here," he encouraged. The frightened, hungry animal crawled out wagging his tail submissively.

Cayden looked up at Shane who was about to object. "It's better than that cat Jade is trying to catch," he said picking up the animal. He strode to the horse and mounted still holding the dog.

They returned to the barn where they'd left the girls.

"Jade, I have something for you," Cayden called out. She came out the door as he stepped off the horse and let the puppy run to her.

"Oh my god! He is so cute."

Lynn came out and the girls both swooned at the wriggly little dog letting him lick their faces and laughing at his typical puppy behavior.

It was nice to see such girly happiness and Shane nodded approval at his brother.

"Come on, let's find him something to eat," Cayden said leading the girls inside.

"Cayden," Shane said stopping him. "I'm going to ride into town and check it out. Between the tornados, the fire storm and the gang war, I bet the city is razed to the ground but I want to see if the motel is still standing."

"I don't think that's a good idea Shane," Cayden objected. "It is too dangerous."

"I don't want you to go either," Jade agreed with Cayden.

"We are going to need supplies. I'll just take a peek and be right back. I promise, I won't be gone long," he said and rode off leaving them staring after him.

Shane rode into the city and was amazed at how

much it had changed. Most of the buildings had burned and the streets were black with soot. The abandoned cars had been torched and fires still smoldered everywhere. But there were no people. No one was shopping, no one was rushing to work or waving down taxis. He just couldn't believe how much life had changed so suddenly.

He needed to either get to the motel or find a store and get some supplies. He headed south toward the their old fort, his horses' hooves making clacking sounds on the sidewalk which echoed loudly throughout the empty windowless buildings.

The sound of a shotgun shell being loaded into the chamber brought him to a stop. He turned into the doorway he was passing and looked into the eyes behind the gun.

"Just passin through friend, didn't mean to bother you," he said calmly.

"Give me the horse and your gun!" the voice said hoarsely.

Shane raised his automatic weapon up to the man behind the shotgun and said harshly, "Don't think so friend. Now set that shotgun down."

The man complied knowing he was outgunned.

Shane rode forward turning in the saddle to keep his weapon pointed into the door. Sure enough, the man ran out after him and fired the shotgun. Shane returned fire and kicked his horse into a run.

He rounded a corner and skidded to a stop in front of tens of National Guard rifles pointed at his chest. Shane put his hands in the air. "Fuck!" he said loudly.

"Drop the weapon and step off!" one of the men yelled.

Shane did what he was told and thought, 'The brothers are gonna be pissed.'

He kept his tongue while he was handcuffed and stuffed into a military vehicle. He thought about Cayden and Jade. 'Now what will they do?' He turned to the driver and asked, "Where are you taking me?"

"You will be held in the temporary prison north of the city," the private answered. "You are charged with possession and discharge of an illegal firearm."

Chapter 6

Conner angrily watched Rebel ride away feeling completely rejected. He had truly thought that she might have loved him but she just left him standing there without a goodbye. The pain medication was wearing off and his entire body ached. His ribs stabbed him with each breath and his head was muddy from the three concussions he'd suffered. The hole in his chest throbbed continuously and his lip stung from the new wound he'd received from Rebel's fist.

'What a pathetic fool!' he thought to himself. She didn't need him. He'd allowed her to be kidnapped and almost raped and killed. He'd been taken captive, forcing her to risk her life in a dangerous rescue. He'd been the recipient of proof that she could hit as well as any man. No wonder she left him. All he'd done since she'd met him was slow her down.

Conner continued wallowing in self-pity for several hours, pacing until he was dizzy then sitting, then pacing some more. His mind drifted to her muscular, tanned body. God, she was so sexy. He laid his head back on the blanket they'd shared the night before and inhaled her scent from it. It wasn't really a smell. It was more like a ...., he couldn't explain it. It was just ... her. He thought about the well defined biceps that formed her upper arms and the flat abs that did nothing to help hold up the holster that always hung from her shapely hips. The image of her floating in the water with the moon highlighting her every curve, filtered through his mind.

His body betrayed his anger at her, stiffening hard and flinging piercing hot sparks of desire throughout his abdomen. He bolted to his feet then reminded himself to move slowly when dizziness almost brought him back down again. He thought about the tender way she had cleaned the blood from his chest and her tears when she whispered 'please don't die on me' into his semi conscious ear.

He couldn't let her go! It wasn't simple sexual attraction that produced this searing heat between them. It was love. He had fallen deeply in love with this tough little spitfire and he was sure that she loved him back.

Conner walked outside and packed his gear then saddled the horses. He shook hands with the sheriff and ignored the disproval of the doctor then headed out to find Rebel. He didn't care if he bled to death in the middle of nowhere. He had to find her and make her his own.

Rebel slowed Jake to a walk and watched the sun set. She had pushed him hard trying to outrun her broken heart. It hadn't worked though and a heavy sadness rested mercilessly on her narrow shoulders.

"It was the only way to save his stubborn life," she said to Jake defensively. He flickered his ears at her voice as if he understood.

She made camp just as darkness swallowed her in a lonely silence. She lay by the fire scanning the stars unable to sleep and watched as the familiar purple, red and green swirls of the aurora began to dance in the sky above her. 'Another coronal mass ejection,' she thought as she watched nature's beautiful display then fell asleep with visions of Conner's deeply tanned rippling muscles moving under her hands.

Several hours later, she was suddenly jolted awake by the distinct, unmistakable guttural growl of a mountain lion. The mare snorted and reared, stomping her feet and pulling on the lead that tied her. Rebel felt for the rifle next her and found it a half second too late and as if in a nightmare she watched in disbelief as massive cat appeared out of the darkness in full flight above her.

She rolled quickly just as he landed where she'd slept a moment before. He swiped a huge paw at her catching her shoulder in his long claws, dragging her toward him. She grabbed up the knife that lay next to her rifle and started swinging.

The cat screamed at her as she sunk the blade deep into his shoulder. He swung again raking his claws along her rib cage, shredding cloth and flesh. Rebel shrieked in pain and sliced the blade through the darkness finding a target in the animal's neck. She felt his blood mix with hers as they wrestled in a mortal death match.

Again, she drew back and swung with every ounce of strength she had, burying the knife deep in the animal's throat, opening it wide. The cat screamed again moving much slower, giving her enough time to grab the .22. She screamed as he grabbed her shoulder in his huge mouth but she ignored the pain and brought the weapon up between them and emptied the clip into the animal's chest.

Conner knew he was close to Rebel. He had counted on the big gilding finding Jake and the animal had just picked up his pace and pointed his ears forward with a fond whinny.

He was feeling a little nervous about seeing her and was pondering what he would say when he heard the hair raising scream of a wounded, frightened horse echo into the night. The sound made his stomach jolt and his heart jumped out of his chest. He let the filly go and raced forward into the darkness. He pulled the rifle to his shoulder as the mare came into view with a two hundred pound mountain lion astride her with all ten claws embedded deep in her shoulders. He aimed and fired the same instant that he heard Rebel scream.

Rebel heard the rifle shot just before as she pulled the trigger on the .22. The animal collapsed on top of her and bled out right there on her chest. She struggled to remove the two hundred pound carcass that engulfed her significantly smaller body.

The mare was stomping and snorting as she walked over to try and calm her. She was bleeding badly from each shoulder and had a gaping rip across the back of her neck from the lion's teeth. She turned to look at the dead cat laying a few feet away just as Conner's gilding walked through the darkness toward her.

"Conner!" she screamed fearing that one of the cats had gotten him too. She searched in the predawn darkness yelling his name for several minutes before she found him in a heap, completely unconscious.

The sun appeared over the hilltop exposing the

deadly, bloody scene. Rebel bled from the gashes in her shoulder and rib cage and the cat's blood blanketed her like a cloak in a horror movie.

She looked down at Conner, whose shirt was shrouded in blood as well. She pictured the gunshot and imagined the recoil from the rifle that must have slammed him hard in the shoulder, almost impacting the hole in his chest strait on.

When Conner opened his eyes his heart instantly contracted from the sight of the blood-drenched woman sitting in front of him. "Jesus Christ, Rebel!" he said and sat up grabbing her into his arms. "Are you ok?" he pushed her back and looked her over.

"I think so," she answered softly still a little stunned from the grisly event.

He pulled her back to his chest and held her tightly. "God Rebel, I'm always late coming to your rescue. Come on."

He pulled himself to his feet and helped her stand then they slowly walked back to her camp.

Conner froze in his tracks and stared when he saw the huge dead cat sprawled on her sleeping bag. "You killed that thing?" he asked incredulously, shaking his head in disbelief.

'Fucking warrior princess!' he thought to himself, once again admiring her strength.

"It was him or me," she shrugged taking no pride in her accomplishment.

"Jesus, you are something." He hung his head and said, "No wonder you left me. I've done nothing but hold you back and you are obviously capable of taking care of yourself."

"Conner, you jack ass!" Rebel ground out, suddenly angry again. "I didn't leave you because I didn't need you. I left you because of this!" She stomped over and poked him in the chest drawing back a bloody finger. "You shouldn't even be on your feet let alone riding obviously all day and night to catch up to me." She swung away from him overcome with fear and frustration. She sucked in her breath and shakily said, "I don't want to see you die out here. The doctor couldn't believe you were still alive after losing so much blood. Now here you are, bleeding worse than that cat over there."

He wrapped his arms around her and she sunk into his chest. "I won't let you leave me for that reason Rebel," he said firmly then whispered into her hair, "and I'm not going to die out here. But you might if we don't stop your bleeding."

He sat her down and inspected her wounds. She had deep scratches across both arms where she had fended off the cat. One of the massive paws had lain open her jeans and left five perfect slices through the muscle of her thigh. But the worst wounds were those on her shoulder and rib cage.

"We need to stitch some of these gashes," he said sadly. "I have nothing to deaden the pain and it's gonna hurt."

Rebel just shrugged and didn't look at him until he told her to take off her shirt. Fire exploded through her at the words and the pain was forgotten for a moment. It was his voice, that deep unintentionally sexy voice saying that to her. She shot a glance at him and couldn't hide the combustion that flashed in her eyes.

As usual, his entire body reacted to the searing electricity that sparked between them. This time though, he harshly squelched the flame inside him and turned his back to her, waiting.

She pulled her t-shirt over her head and said sarcastically, "Ok, Dr. Jekyll, patch me back together."

He smiled and turned around without allowing himself even a glance past the deep open gouges along her ribs. Concern lowered his brow as he looked closer and could see bone inside each of the gaping wounds. He cursed under his breath.

'This is not good. Thank God she had a fully stocked first aid kit,' he thought to himself as he worked as gently as he could. 'But why wouldn't she? She had pretty much been prepared for everything that had happened so far. Except him,' he remembered her saying.

Rebel was silent as he carefully stitched her wounds. She winced once in awhile but never cried out. His heart hurt for her each time he pushed the needle into her soft flesh.

"What a pair we are," he said absently.

After what seemed like hours, he was finally finished. Rebel was weak from the pain of so many sutures. She turned around to face him and fear streaked through her at the sight of his ashen face. The long ride, the impact from the rifle, the fall from the horse and the hours he'd just spent stitching her wounds had taken a toll. He looked like he was going to pass out again.

He was so weak he could hardly move himself as she helped him lean back against a rock. She went to the gilding that was grazing a few yards away and retrieved his sleeping bag. She gently covered him and turned to check on the mare. She finished caring for the horses then lay down exhausted beside him and fell instantly asleep.

Kira opened her eyes to the sound of quiet voices around her. She listened to her brother and best friend chatting and noticed that their usual small talk had changed, sounding a little more intimate. Then her thoughts flew to the boy and she asked urgently, "Is the boy ok?"

Nick and Evie rushed to the bed, clearly concerned.

"He's going to be fine Kira," Nick answered reassuringly.

"Thank god," she said trying to sit up. Pain shot through her ribs making her cry out.

"Don't move silly," Nick said. "You have a concussion and some broken ribs."

"Ya, I got the broken ribs part," she spunkily replied. "Get me some coffee, would ya?"

Evie grinned as she poured the coffee relieved that her friend was ok. She turned and handed the coffee over to Nick for delivery, accidentally brushing her hand against his.

Kira raised her eyebrow as her brother tensed at the

touch. Curious. They had been around each other before, both attending Thanksgiving dinners and family parties. What had changed she wondered?

She accepted the coffee from her brother quizzically searching his expression. Evie fussed nervously with the bedding and Nick was suddenly very interested in the lantern on the end table.

"What's going on!" she demanded.

They both jumped and looked at each other.

"Nothin!" Nick defended reaching for his hat. "Glad you're ok sis. We were worried." Then he strode to the door and left the house.

Kira looked at Evie who was sheepishly looking at the door he'd just exited then blushed at Kira's sly grin.

That afternoon, the little boy that Kira had saved came to see her and said, "I'm sorry you got hurt."

Kira smiled into his sweet face and said, "I'm so glad you didn't."

She waved goodbye carefully and relaxed back into the pillows. She listened as the successful hunting party returned and were congratulated on their kill. She heard Nick on the front porch receiving news that grounds were safe. She heard hammers pounding nails, repairing the fence damaged by the earthquake. She smelled dinner cooking in the big barbeque pit. Everything seemed fine.

After several hours of just lying there, Kira grew frustrated. She had never been one to just sit around. "I'm going outside!" she suddenly exclaimed and waved off the numerous objections that erupted around her.

Her friends quickly realized that she meant business and scurried around to prepare her a soft chair on the porch.

"Ah, that's better," Kira said settling back to watch the sunset. 'Peaceful and calm,' she thought to herself. But her thoughts quickly turned to the carnage that was inevitably materializing across the nation and wondered about the months ahead. Would the crust of the earth shift setting off the volcanoes? Would a meteor impact earth, destroying all life?

She thought of Rebel and the brothers. Would they

find each other? Would they return at all?

Her dark brooding thoughts were interrupted when Nick strolled up leading a pretty little paint mare. Kira smiled, her gloom lifting instantly as she spied the newborn, wobbly little filly hiding behind her mother.

"She's beautiful!" Kira exclaimed finding hope again in the new life.

"She foaled last night. I thought you'd like to see her," Nick said fondly. Then he smiled at Evie, who blushed.

Kira giggled and the color deepened.

Nick bowed his goodbye. "Lady's," he smiled again and practically skipped away.

"That's it!" Kira said. "What the hell is going on with you two?"

"We were so worried about you last night that we sat up watching over you till late," Evie shrugged then paused and said bashfully. "We fell asleep on the couch and I woke up in his arms," she shrugged again, the color swiftly returning to her cheeks.

Kira erupted in laughter. "Well, go for it Evie, take him by the horns," she said then laughed again when Evie clicked her tongue and waved the words away.

The two women sat together light heartedly while twilight settled into the camp.

Rebel awoke several hours later and instantly felt the burn of Conner's stare. She didn't know how long he'd been lying there propped up on his elbow watching her sleep. Some of the color had returned to his face and there was definitely a spark in his eyes.

She shifted and groaned as her sore muscles objected to the movement. She glanced down to peak at his handiwork with the needle and was mortified to find she hadn't replaced her shirt.

Conner grinned as the realization crossed her face making her heart nearly catapult out of her chest. He was amazingly handsome with that seductive glow in those blue green eyes and the rugged growth of beard that did little to hide that hint of a dimple in his cheek. Even though swollen, his appealing lips just begged to be kissed. She licked her own lips and let her eyes drift down his physic.

She felt small against his powerfully broad chest and wide shoulders. His arms were long and thick with muscles that antagonized her as they rippled at the slightest movement. She could feel the skiff of hair on his solid, tanned chest brush her arm and she had to close her eyes tightly to gather her strength. She knew she had to either get up or lose herself to the desire that cascaded through her like a raging river.

She gritted her teeth against the pain and stood up. She could feel him watching her as she dug through her bag for another t-shirt. Finally, fully clothed, she faced him. "You look a little better today," she said pointedly, still trying to regain control of her heart rate.

"You look very good today," he teased still wearing a lustful grin.

Rebel shook her head and turned away from his captivating gaze. "The mare's wounds are pretty bad," she said to change the subject. "If you hadn't gotten here when you did, she would have fallen to the attack." She shuttered and glanced over at the dead animal still lying a few yards away.

Conner followed her gaze and shuttered himself wondering how the hell she had killed the massive cat. "I should have been here. That god damned thing could have killed you. You are something Rebel," he said pushing himself to his feet.

'You are something too,' she thought to herself as she intently watched the muscles quiver across the golden brown length of his lean v-shaped back. 'Fucking erotic sun god is what you are,' she mused then turned and whistled for Jake.

Her muscles were so sore from the deadly wresting match the night before that she could barely swing onto the horse. Her stitches stretched with the maneuver causing her to cry out in pain.

Conner looked at her worriedly.

"I'll be fine," she assured him and nudged Jake into a slow lope.

They rode northwest all day. That afternoon, huge dark clouds started rolling in. The strange orange glow reappeared causing the horizon to look like in was doused in blood.

Rebel reined her horse to a walk and said, "It's going to rain again."

Conner looked up and nodded in agreement. "How are you doing Rebel? Are you ok?"

He heard the strain in her voice when she answered, "Fine, I'm fine."

'She is lying,' he thought to himself as he noticed the huge red stain that covered her t-shirt and her jeans wore a fresh dark patch over her thigh.

All of a sudden the little filly reared straight in the air, yanking her lead rope out of his preoccupied hands. Jake jumped sideways almost unseating Rebel and the mare took advantage of her unsteadiness and jerked out of her grasp. The two horses raced away making Conner's horse bolt, trying to follow.

Rebel regained her balance and settled Jake with some calming words.

"Do you hear that?" Conner asked, trying to control his dancing gilding. "It sounds like a freight train."

The words had barely left his mouth when the ground started shaking powerfully. Both horses reared and spun around launching out from under them, landing them both hard on the ground. The earth seemed to ripple and roll in front of them. They both just sat there riding out the wavelike motion. Trees tumbled over and boulders seemed to grow legs and move around. The hillside seemed to jolt back and forth as if it weren't attached to the ground.

"Move!" Conner yelled yanking Rebel to her feet just before the earth underneath her opened into a massive crevice. They stood watching in stunned silence as the earth split for hundreds of yards. The shaking continued for many minutes before falling still beneath their feet.

"Where are we?" Rebel asked quietly pondering the severity of the quake.

"Somewhere in the middle of Illinois."

"Then that was the New Madrid seismic zone moving just south of here. It meets up with the Wabash Valley Fault and has been really active for the last couple years."

Conner tilted his head sideways expectantly.

"Haven't you ever...? No, you wouldn't have. The New Madrid is responsible for one of the largest earthquakes in the Midwest. In 1811 and 12, it produced some huge earthquakes that killed hundreds of people and leveled cities. At one point, it shook so hard that they say it made the Mississippi River flowed backwards for time," she explained. "It created a very large lake and it's rumored that they felt it all the way to Washington D.C. Some predict that it was over a nine on the Richter scale."

Conner shook his head wondering how she knew so much about this shit.

"Some researchers have linked the earthquakes here on earth to the sun. We just had another solar storm yesterday so there is probably a very large sunspot or coronal hole facing earth."

Suddenly she turned to him and said worriedly, "There is a nuclear power plant just south of here. If that quake damaged the circulation system, we are going to get radiated. We need to get the hell out of here."

Conner looked around him then back at Rebel still curious about her knowledge.

"That would have taken out roads and bridges. How the fuck are we going to cross the Mississippi now?" she continued looking off in the distance.

But he had stopped listening. He was staring at the blood dripping off her holster. "Jesus Christ, Rebel!" he exclaimed grabbing her and pulling up her blood-drenched shirt. "We are camping here," he said fearfully. "You aren't riding one more step!"

She yanked her shirt from his grasp and yelled, "Oh! Now you are worried about me riding with a bleeding wound!"

"The fall ripped out the stitches!" he argued angrily, anticipating her rebellion.

"To fucking bad! We're moving on!" she glowered at him.

"Goddamn it!" he roared. "You are the most stubborn woman I have ever met! We're making camp!" Fire flashed in his eyes as he her dared her to argue further.

She glared at him for a moment. "Fine!" she huffed, then turned and stomped away to find the horses.

Relief flooded through him when she surprisingly submitted. He watched her walk away, his eyes following the drops of blood that splattered on the ground at her feet. He was worried. She needed a doctor.

Shane hadn't returned by nightfall so Cayden saddled one of the horses and said, "I'm going to find him."

Jade wanted to argue but she was so worried that she kept her silence.

"Here Jade," Cayden said handing her a waki taki. "We are supposed to turn it on at sunset every night for ten minutes until the brothers get here. I want you to take over starting tonight. I may not be back by then, so...." He paused for a moment. "If you hear from them, give them directions to here." He pointed out their location on a map. "I love you. Take care of Lynn for me."

Jade watched him ride away, upset by the way he'd said goodbye. She took up pacing on Shane's old path giving it another good work over.

Cayden rode into town and observed the damage from the storms and the fire. It looked like a nuclear bomb had gone off. Nothing was undamaged. He rode south staying at the edge of the city. 'Where the hell would he have gone?' he wondered.

He picked his way through the dark street unit he came upon a large city park. His horse perked his ears and whinnied. He looked into the darkness and saw the horse Shane had been riding grazing on the big lawn. He easily rode up to the animal and took up his reins. 'Weird,' he thought then continued on heading south. He topped the hillside and stopped surprised by the huge camp that had been erected in the valley. He couldn't count the number of fires burning and it looked like it housed a large group of rough looking people.

Cayden dismounted wondering if Shane had run into them. He took out his binoculars and scanned the camp. No sign of Shane that he could see. 'Fuck! Where is he?' he thought again as climbed back on his horse and headed back to the northern part of the city.

The sun was just about to rise as he approached the outskirts of what looked like a temporary military prison. He dismounted again and hid the horses behind an empty gas station. He crept up to the thick barbed wire boundary and pulled the fencing pliers out of his belt and cut the wire.

He slipped through the small hole in the fence just as a big spotlight circled around toward him. "Shit!" he cursed and crouched down. The light passed without focusing on him so he continued into the compound.

He snuck down a row of small wire cages that each contained a sleeping human. 'This is no better than a dog kennel!' Cayden thought, disgusted at the sight. Then he found him. His brother was curled up on a very uncomfortable looking cot.

"Shane! Wake up!" he whispered loudly.

Shane woke up and fear instantly gripped him. "What are you doing? Get out of here before you get caught too."

"God damn it Shane! I told you not to go!" Cayden said. He was pissed off that his brother hadn't listened. Typical though.

Suddenly, two uniformed men rounded the corner in the row of cages across from them.

"Here take this! Channel nine," he said handing Shane the second waki, then snuck back to the hole in the fence.

Cayden hated leaving him in there but he couldn't risk getting caught and leaving the girls to fend for themselves. 'At least now I can communicate with him,' he thought as he rode back to the barn where he'd left Jade.

Rebel sat watching the dancing flames of the fire as she munched on the venison Conner had brought back earlier. Even the slight movement of eating shot pain through her overextended muscles. Wrestling something twice your size was not a good idea especially if it had five-inch claws and huge teeth. The deep puncture wounds in her shoulder burned like a fresh brand and the gouges in her side wouldn't stop bleeding. She had packed it with gauze to hide the sight from Conner. Her jeans aggravated the deep slices in her thigh because the bandage wouldn't stay on. She was in way worse shape than she was letting on to him.

Conner glanced over at her every once in awhile as she sat there trying to hide her pain from him. He knew she was lying to him about how bad she was hurting. He had spent enough time with her now that he could read her pretty well.

Though he wouldn't admit it, he understood how she must have felt watching the lifeblood drain from him. He also understood her reasoning for leaving him behind at the river. She had wanted him to stay still until he had healed a little. Now, he wanted the same for her. He unrolled his bag and intentionally placed it on the opposite side of the fire. He didn't want anything to make her wounds bleed more than they already were.

Silence hung heavily in the air the next morning as Rebel prepared to saddle Jake. But when she tried to lift the saddle, searing pain ripped through the holes in her shoulder making her groan loudly.

Conner was by her side in a split second. He took the saddle and threw it onto the big gilding's back. "Let me look at it," he requested and gently pulled up her shirt

"Fuck!" he said under his breath. "It's infected Rebel. We need to find you a doctor."

She didn't answer, just finished saddling the horse and climbed on. Antibiotics were going to be hard to come by now. She knew that after this long without power, food, and water, people would have started hoarding certain supplies and antibiotics would be one of them.

She thought about the death that had no doubt devastated the population by now. They had pointedly stayed out of the cities and away from people as much as possible so they hadn't seen it yet. It was hard to visualize the affects of a major blackout in an industrialized nation like this one. There had been no new food supplies trucked in, no medications delivered, no communication or travel. The water supply would have been shut down and hospitals would be like morgues.

By now, she imagined, people would be in a frenzy to survive their unthinkable plight. She pictured them as zombies in a movie, desperately scurrying around to find food. She thought about the chaos in the aftermath of hurricane Katrina years ago, and pictured it a hundred times worse, and enveloping every city in the country. Her stomach convulsed from nausea and she quickly jumped off Jake and puked behind a tree.

Conner silently walked up to her, concern weighing heavily on his face.

"I don't want to see the cities, the destruction, the death," she said as she leaned into her arm against a tree. "Millions of people would have died by now. I can't even imagine the suffering." She heaved again from the thought.

Conner waited patiently beside her.

When she finally had control of her stomach, and had cleared her mind of the maddening sadness, she stepped back and apologized, "Sorry, I guess the reality just hit me suddenly. I've been so absorbed in my quest to get to Jade, that I hadn't allowed myself to think about what was happening around us."

Conner listened quietly.

"I tried to tell people, a lot of us tried, but they wouldn't listen. No one believed this would happen."

Conner took her in his arms and fear instantly wrenched his gut when he touched her and felt the temperature of her skin. She was burning up from fever.

"We have to find a doctor right now," he said urgently pulling her back to her horse.

Conner pushed them hard in desperation. She wouldn't survive this infection if he didn't find antibiotics soon. He thought about losing her and almost cried out with grief.

Finally they came upon the outskirts of a small town. He reined in and searched for a place to hide Rebel and the horses. He didn't want to risk taking her into danger in her weakened condition.

He lifted her off Jake, the fever so bad now she was delirious. She mumbled something he couldn't understand as he propped her up and laid her rifle across her lap. "I will be back Rebel, just hang on."

He raced the big gilding into town and was amazed at the destruction. The quake had leveled the entire city. He rushed through the debris searching for a hospital or drug store and finally spotted a grocery store with a pharmacy. He slid the horse to a stop about a block away from it and leaving the gilding in the alley, crept closer. No one was around so he hurried to the back of the building and entered the barely standing structure.

He went straight to the pharmacy area and quickly realized that someone had already raided the place. Fearfully he searched through the bottles littering the floor trying to remember the name of an antibiotic. Nothing! He spied a box of syringes scattered across a table and paused wondering if there was a refrigerator somewhere. He broke through the door to the little office and was elated to find one that had toppled from the counter onto the floor. Frantically, he opened the door and there it was. Penicillin. He grabbed a bag and stuffed it full of the medication.

Rebel was sleeping when he returned. Her body glistened from sweat and he could see the fever burning her face red before he reached her. His hands were shaking as he shoved the syringe into the bottle and injected the medication into the muscle of her shoulder. He sat down and pulled her into his arms rocking her gently, desperately praying that she would be ok.

It was a full day later before Rebel opened her eyes. She was snuggled comfortably under Conner's arm. She could hear his heart thumping in her ear and feel his chest rise and fall as he breathed. God, he felt so good she didn't want to move. He opened his eyes as if he felt her looking at him and smiled down at her.

"It feels like your fever is gone. I was worried about you."

She sat up and stretched. "How long have we been here?"

"Two days. You were out the entire time."

"Thanks for taking care of me," she said, suddenly realizing the extent of the care she'd needed.

He smiled and said, "I'm just glad you feel better." He stood up and made a fire to make her some coffee and cook her something to eat. He fussed around trying to feed her, then trying to get her to drink more water. Eventually she grew impatient with his hovering and reprimanded him.

"I'm feeling better now Conner, stop pestering me."

He laughed at the comment, relieved that she was back to herself.

Rain was pouring down outside helping him convince her to stay one more night but the next morning, she was up and ready to leave.

The much-needed rest had done them both good. Conner's wound had stopped bleeding and the gashes across Rebel's ribs had started to close. The redness around the puncture wounds on her shoulder had lightened telling him that the infection was under control. But Conner's mood was dismal and quiet. He still couldn't shake the thought that he could have lost her. He looked over at her as she swung onto her horse reassuring himself that she would be fine.

"I want to ride back into town," Conner announced quietly. "I saw a veterinarian's sign and I think we should leave the mare with him if he's still there. Her wounds are healing some but I don't think she should travel."

Rebel nodded sadly. She'd gotten attached to the solid little horse.

They rode back into town and up to the door marked Dr. Gladys Bell, DVM.

Conner dismounted and knocked, waiting patiently for the woman to answer.

"We seen your sign," Conner said. "We have a wounded mare in need of a vet's care."

The woman stepped out the door, instantly going to the horse. Worry riddled her face as she gently inspected the deep gash on the animal's neck and puncture wounds on her shoulders. "Mountain lion," the woman half asked, half stated. "I'll try to help, but I don't have a lot of supplies."

"Ma'am, if you would just keep her and do your best, we would be in your debt," Conner said handing her the lead rope.

The woman accepted the offer and nodded to them as they rode away.

The brothers made camp on the outskirts of Omaha under a heavily cloud covered sky that held the smoke from the burning city low to the ground. They could tell even at this distance that something bad had taken place.

"My god!" Dylan said. "We gotta find them."

"We will," Darien said. "They probably moved to the outskirts. I'm sure the boys handled it ok." He took a deep breath trying to convince himself and pulled their waki's out of their protective box and turned them on.

Warrick walked up and said, "Maybe we should go in tonight and have a look."

Darien looked at the military vehicles moving around and noticed the barbed wire enclosure that marked their temporary base. "I guess we could leave our horses and most of the weapons here and walk in. I wouldn't mind getting an idea of what we are facing tomorrow."

They secured their camp and left on foot toward the smoking city of Omaha each of them packing only their handguns and a knife.

They skirted the military boundary and slipped between two buildings on the north side of town. The city had definitely undergone massive devastation. Most of the buildings had either been leveled from the tornado, or burned down from what looked to have been a firestorm from hell. Large fires still burned and ash covered the street under their feet.

"There has to be thousands of people displaced from this. Homeless. Where are they?" Dylan asked.

"Ya, and what about the nuclear plants? I hope they still have control of them," Warrick added.

"I bet they can answer that," Darien said, pointing to a military vehicle closing in on them.

"Warrick don't you say a fucking thing! Don't glare at them either!" Dylan commanded.

"No one is allowed on the streets after ten, that gives you exactly fifteen minutes to get back home," one of the guys said.

"Yes sir, we understand. What happened here?" Darien asked them looking around.

"Gang war. We were engaged in battle for days. The fires that started from the tornado were increased by human hand and there was no water to put it out so the ensuing firestorm engulfed the entire city," the private explained.

"Where are all the people? I'm sure there are a lot of homeless," Darien pushed on.

"We have commandeered any standing motels and put some of them there and created large tent cities out by the Air Force Base. Many of them left the city. But the two gangs that were fighting have reestablished themselves just outside our boundary. One, south of the city and the other one just across the river to the east. They are dangerous. My advice to you is stay to the north and don't cross the river," he said.

"Do you know anything about the nuclear plants? Were they safely shut down?" Dylan asked.

The private stiffened. "As far as I know, everything is fine." Then he got in the vehicle and left.

"Fuck!" Warrick bellowed. "Rebel is coming in from the East. If she doesn't see that gang, she could ride right into their camp."

"Ya, we need to find the kids fast and warn her somehow. She is at least two days out. Come on, let's get out of here," Dylan said.

Conner and Rebel had ridden day and night barely stopping until they reached the banks of the big Mississippi River.

"My god," she said when she looked at the destruction from the big earthquake. The roads had cracked apart and the overpasses were impassable. Water spilled over the banks of the river turning the landscape into an ocean.

"We'll just keep riding north," Connor said trying to ease her disappointment. "It may not be as bad upriver."

Rebel nodded and nervously rode through the eighteen inches of water that flooded their path. The ground was invisible for miles and trees stood out in front of her as if they were floating.

"I've seen pictures of floods like this but didn't realize that they impacted such a large area. Where are the people?"

"I'm sure they were safely moved away from the flood," Conner said gently. "This has happened here before."

They continued on for many miles before finally coming upon a large highway overpass that had withstood the earthquake. Water covered the road on both sides but at least they could get across.

As they splashed onto the pavement, a big man stepped out from behind one of the stalled trucks on the highway, spooking the horses.

"This here is my road," he drawled, "an there's a price fer crossin my bridge."

"All right," Conner replied bristling at the confrontation. "What's the price?"

"We'll be havin the lady there," he sneered just as two men surrounded Jake, one grabbing his reins, the other pulling Rebel off the animal.

Conner growled and leaped from the gilding landing

on top of the man, pounding his fist into his face in a rage. The sound of the colt being cocked froze him in mid swing. He jerked his head toward Rebel who was being held tightly with a hand over her mouth and her gun pointed at her temple.

Conner half raised his arms in submission and said as calmly as he could, "Gentlemen, I'm sure we can work out a deal here. No sense anyone getting hurt."

"We already told ya the deal," the man said walking up to him and planting a big fist into Conner's already broken ribs, dropping him to his knees.

Rage ripped through Rebel as she watched pain flash across Conner's face. She kicked the man that was holding her as hard as she could in the shin and slammed her head backward smashing him in the chin. He bellowed in surprise and pain, losing his grip on her and lowering the weapon from her head. In one quick motion she spun around, whipped up the .22 and emptied the clip into his chest. The man looked at her, his eyes wide with surprise as he dropped the colt and fell to the ground.

The man facing Conner was clearly stunned as he watched his friend fall. Conner leapt into action using the distraction to his advantage and landed a big fist into the man's face knocking him cold.

Rebel and the third man leapt for the colt at the exact same time but Rebel was quicker. She dove into the water grabbing the weapon.

The other man was trying to wrench the gun from her grasp when Conner landed in front of him, his inner beast fully awake and ready for blood.

The man shoved Rebel hard into a nearby car and faced Conner. The men clashed in battle, each landing blow after blow, blood showering the water around them, turning it red.

Rebel's head glanced off the car igniting sparks in front of her eyes. She fought to stay conscious and fumbled around trying to find the weapon but couldn't see clearly through the water.

Conner's eyes were black with rage as he pummeled

the much larger man with his fists, the taste of blood feeding the savage beast inside him. Even though Conner was injured, he had the advantage. He was in much better shape and the bigger man was wearing down fast. He moved in for the kill landing a solid hit on the big man's jaw and the guy went down like a slaughtered bull.

Conner whipped out his knife plunging into the man's heart. But the beast wasn't done and he stalked over to the other man and opened an artery. He stood over him as he bled out, trying to cage the rampaging beast that had once again escaped and overtaken him.

Slowly, his senses returned. He glanced around for Rebel and found her sitting by the car watching him. He instantly flushed, embarrassed that she'd seen him in that uncontrolled deadly state.

She got up and stumbled over to him, wrapping her arms around his waist. She held him tightly until his breathing became normal. She stepped back and quietly led him to where the horses had instinctively gathered together. Without a word, she handed him the gildings reins, picked up the filly's lead rope and swung onto Jake.

They crossed the overpass in silence, neither knowing what to say, then made camp somewhere in the north west corner of Missouri. Rebel built a fire and sat down next to Conner whose mood was once again very dark.

She hesitantly reached out to wash the blood from his face. He waved her hand away scowling. She tried again, same reaction. This time she caught his wrist in her firm grip, which brought his eyes to hers. He submitted to the demand in her eyes, lowering his arm and looking away.

Gently, she wiped the blood from the new gashes and bruises that once again marred his handsome face.

She'd been fascinated by the calculated, deadly way that he'd fought. Every deliberate movement precise and disciplined, each lethal, cunning impact skillfully executed. The raging power of his muscular body pointedly controlled by sheer will.

Rebel took up his big powerful fist and wiped his

still bleeding knuckles. She raised them to her lips and kissed them.

Conner inhaled sharply his eyes bolting to hers.

"There you are," she said softly.

He visibly relaxed at her words, finally allowing the dark tension to fall away.

She leaned her head on his shoulder and sat quietly watching the flames in the fire, absently stroking the inside of his forearm.

After awhile, Conner sighed and said regretfully, "I never wanted you to see me like that. See the brutal beast that I really am."

"I love you Conner, all of you. Including the beast."

His heart swelled at her admission and wholehearted acceptance.

Rebel woke up with an excited urgency. She knew that they were close to Omaha and Jade. She looked over at Conner and wondered what Jade would think of him. He looked up at her as if he felt her watching him and smiled in his usual ruggedly handsome way.

"You seem to be feeling well this morning," he said.

"I finally feel like we are getting close. We still have to cross the Missouri River, but then we will find the kids and it will be easy going till we get home. I'm going to unpack the waki. I bet my brothers are close."

Conner watched her closely as she unwrapped several layers of foil and plastic from a box and pulled out the radio. "I don't get it," he said curiously.

"It's called a faraday cage," Rebel explained. "It keeps the destructive EMP pulse that a nuclear bomb produces from frying the delicate electronics. In our case, the electromagnetic pulse from a solar storm. Hopefully it worked." She flipped the switch and smiled when the radio turned on.

"I remember hearing something about that, but only related it to military," Conner said thoughtfully.

"I will turn it on at sunset each night for a few minutes until we meet up with my brothers. Shane and

Cayden should have one too." She turned the radio off to save the battery and tucked it into her bags. "The problem is, the range is short, maybe three miles max. Finding them isn't going to be easy."

Conner swung onto his gilding and asked, "Are you ready?"

Rebels wounds were extremely painful, a reminder her of her dance with death, as she slowly climbed onto Jake. She thankfully patted his neck for patiently standing still as she mounted. As the gilding started forward, she mumbled, "God, I wish I had better pain meds. Maybe we should stop in one of the smaller towns and restock the first aid kit. I could use some new clothes. All my stuff is either shredded or stained from blood."

"K, but I don't dare take the animals and weapons in. I doubt if the military is in control of the smaller towns so we should be able to find something."

"Now if only I could find a hot shower," she said laughing.

As they rode upon the outskirts of a small town Conner said, "Let's hide the animals over there and walk from here."

They tethered the animals and walked the short distance in a peaceful silence. The small town was silent and looked to be completely empty. The wind seemed to whistle through the buildings giving it a distinct ghost town feel.

They cautiously approached the main street from a side alley to avoid being seen. Conner stepped out onto the sidewalk and looked around then waved to her to follow him to the back of a type of general store.

Suddenly Conner stiffened, feeling someone watching them out the window. He pulled out his handgun and whispered, "Someone is there. Hello," he called out. "We've come to purchase some supplies."

The curtain swayed and a moment later a man opened the back door and looked them over nervously. "Haven't had many customers lately. Mostly just thieves."

"Ya," Conner said encouragingly, "we've ran into

some bad ones ourselves."

The man thought for a moment then said, "Well, I guess you can do some shopping. I haven't opened since the power went out."

"Thank you," Rebel said, quickly going to the med section and filling a bag with first aid supplies. She walked over to a rack of t-shirts and pulled a few from their hangers. "They don't have any jeans," she mumbled, then spotted a shelf with military camo pants. "Ah, that will work." Next she picked up a pair of gray sweat pants.

"I used to spend all day Sunday in my sweats watching football with my brothers," she smiled, looking up at Conner.

Conner smiled back at her and thought about lounging around with her in their pajamas without a worry in the world except whether or not their team won. That was a far cry from the life they were living now.

He turned to finish picking out his cloths and spied the beer cooler. That was too much to resist. He picked up a twelve pack and a bag of chips. Rebel was staring intently at the toothpaste so he stuck them in a bag without her knowing. He gathered up some canned food then asked Rebel if she was ready.

"Yup," she answered and handed the shopkeeper several hundred-dollar bills.

The man smiled and said, "Nice doing business."

Slowly they walked back to the horses and packed their stuff in the bags. "Today has been a good day so far," Rebel said. "It's nice to see a decent person for once."

"They are out there Rebel, there are good people out there," he encouraged then mounted the gilding.

Lightning flashed brightly startling the horses and thunder clapped behind them. Rebel cursed and pulled her hat down on her face. "I'm sick of rain. I hate this kind of weather.

Conner laughed and said, "Welcome to the Midwest in the spring time." He turned the gilding onto the road and pushed him into a gallop.

Later that evening, Conner noticed a gas station and

a little motel on the road ahead of them.

"Move into the trees and wait for me," he instructed then rode ahead to check it out.

The place was completely abandoned. The station door was locked up and no one was in the motel office. He looked around then smiled to himself as he grabbed a key from the wall. He walked outside and opened the door to room one and looked inside.

'A real bed,' he thought then rushed to get Rebel.

She dismounted in front of the door and pushed it open. She spied the bed and flung herself on it excitedly. "Oh, my god! I'm in heaven!"

Conner grinned enjoying the big smile on her face. "I'll go tend to the horses if you want to find us something to eat."

He tied the horses behind the building on an overgrown lawn that bordered a little creek and as he was walking back, noticed a fire pit and a stack of wood. He thought about Rebel's comment this morning about a shower. He looked at the water then at the wood and once again smiled at himself. He built a fire and found a couple big pots and started heating water.

When he returned to the room with the hot water, he said, "I have a surprise for you." He walked into the bathroom and poured the water into the tub.

"No!" Rebel exclaimed, her face lighting up. "A bed and a hot bath in one day! Thank you, I'm so tired of bathing in the cold rivers."

Conner flushed and spun around exiting the room, suddenly needing to jump into a cold river himself as the image of her floating in the water wafted through his memory once again.

While he slowly filled the tub, they sat down to eat. He pulled out the beer and handed her one. "I chilled these in the creek for awhile, hope its cold enough."

She raised her eyebrow at him and smiled. "You are just full of surprises tonight."

He smiled back then stood to get the last pan of hot

water.

Rebel felt like a little girl as she found her new cloths and skipped into the bathroom, grinning in anticipation.

'Finally!' he thought. 'I can give her something normal.'

Rebel lounged in the tub reveling in the hot water. Something so simple that she had taken for granted before. She found the hotel shampoo and washed her hair. She washed her wounds and scrubbed her face then toweled off and dressed in her new sweats and t-shirt.

She exited the bathroom and laughed when Conner jumped up and said, "My turn."

She picked up another beer and lit some candles to dispel the darkness. She munched on some chips and drank enjoying the relaxation. The moment was perfect. That is…, until Conner stepped from the bathroom with only a towel wrapped around his waist.

The peaceful calm that she was enjoying erupted like a massive volcano spewing fire and molten lava throughout her entire body. His hair was wet and water dripped down his thick chest. Her eyes followed a droplet as it seductively slithered slowly down his tight abs to the towel draped low on his hips. The candlelight flickered across the wet sheen on his deeply tanned skin stopping her heart from beating and her lungs from breathing. Time stood still and she couldn't tear her eyes away from the half naked sun god standing in front of her.

"Jesus," she finally breathed feeling her heart go from zero to two hundred in a split second. Her knees went weak and wouldn't hold her body up. She stumbled back a step, bracing herself against the wall.

Conner watched again as Rebel did a thorough up and down of his anatomy. The physical reaction that always accompanied it was nothing compared to how his body responded this time. The jolting explosion was exquisitely painful as desire spiraled through him. He strode toward her as if she were a magnet pulling him in and placed his hand on the wall above her leaning into her, demanding her lips.

There was no stopping the firestorm now.

She eagerly returned his kiss, responding to the maddening hunger that flowed down her abdomen. She breathed him in, her senses leaving her. His damp chest tantalized her as her hands traced his defined muscles then moved across his powerful shoulders. Her entire body tingled as she explored every muscular detail of his body.

He leaned against her, deepening his kiss and moaned with anticipation as she allowed her hands to explore his long muscular back and trail down his thick thighs. He slid his hands down her small waist and cupped her butt, lifting her up to him. She wrapped her legs around him as he carried her to the bed and tenderly laid her down. He gently dropped on top her reminding himself that she was injured. He forced himself to move slowly as he passionately made love to her.

Chapter 7

The sun woke Rebel out of a gratifyingly satisfied sleep. She gently unwrapped herself from his long thick arms and wriggled her leg from between his thighs. Her mind replayed images from the night before and her body tightened again. She looked down at the gorgeous man beside her and knew that she had fallen for him body and soul. 'Fate has a way, don't it?' she thought as he opened his eyes and looked up at her.

"Good morning beautiful," he said smiling.

"Morning," she echoed. It had been a very long time since she woke up with a man in her bed and she couldn't help questioning the timing.

"Don't do that," Conner said gently, understanding her insecurity. "Just let it be what it is."

"I will," she smiled. "I just never imagined my journey home would include this. Include you. Do you believe in fate?"

"Yes, I do, and this morning I am grateful that fate handed me you."

She smiled down at him again then regretfully climbed out of his comfortable bed. 'I just hope we live long enough to enjoy it,' she thought as she dressed and packed her stuff.

Conner sighed and climbed out of bed dressing quickly. He went to his bag and turned to her. "I made you something."

She looked at him curiously.

He held out his hand and placed a beautifully braided leather necklace in her palm.

"I made it with the claws from the cat you killed. I thought you would like a souvenir of our journey."

Rebel was sincerely touched by the gesture. "Thank you Conner. Its beautiful."

He turned toward the door then paused looking back at her. "Rebel, I've fallen in love with you." Then he stepped outside.

Rebel looked at the door and said, "I've fallen in

love with you too."

Cayden rode into the barn and Jade instantly leaped into his arms.

"Where is he? Did you find him?" she asked worriedly.

"Yes, he got himself arrested. He's in a temporary prison set up north of the city," Cayden said angrily. "We told him not to go."

"What are we going to do?"

"Turn on the radio. I gave him mine so at least we can communicate." Cayden reached for the radio that she handed to him and turned it on. "I don't dare call him in case someone is nearby so we will have to wait till he calls us. Thank god I got extra batteries."

"Try the brothers since it's on," Jade advised.

"Dylan, you copy?" Cayden said into the radio. He looked at Jade anxiously waiting for a reply

Nothing.

The brothers broke camp as the sun entered the sky. Everyone was uneasy and the horses were skittish.

"K, the airport is here and the motel they were staying at is here," Dylan said pointing to the map. "We will have to ride north around the city and back down along the river."

"If they had to move, they would have went north knowing that we would come in that way, so it's possible that we will find them on the way," Darien pointed out.

"Good, let's ride," Warrick said mounting the big gilding. "We should check the waki, maybe the kids will turn it on early."

Darien dug it out of his pack and turned it on. He keyed the mic and said, "Cayden, Shane, you on?

Cayden and Jade both jumped when the waki started talking and they recognized the familiar voice.

"They're here!" Jade squealed in excited relief.

Cayden whipped up the radio and said, "Darien, I'm

172

so glad you're here."

"Hey little brother, where are you?" Darien asked.

Cayden gave them directions to their location and grinned at Jade. "They aren't very far away from us."

Jade was so relieved. Now they could go find her mother. She had been so worried about her, not knowing if she ended up on a plane somewhere or was trying to walk all the way from D.C. Just having her uncle's here made her feel like everything would be ok.

When the brothers rode into the barn, Jade spooked the horses with her excitement.

"Good to see you too sweetie," Darien said. They all hugged her fondly.

"Where is Shane?" Warrick interrupted the greeting.

"Well, he got himself arrested when he went for supplies," Cayden sighed. "He is in the military compound. I cut the fence and found him last night."

"Son of a Bitch!" Dylan said.

"I slipped him my waki but we are either out of range or he hasn't been alone to call us," Cayden said regretfully.

"Wow, Cayden," Darien said. "That was dangerous, but good thinking."

"We will have to get him out tonight," Dylan said. "But we need to make a plan first because we will have to get out of town as soon as we break him out. We need to cross the river to meet up with Rebel."

"There is a gang camped out on the south side of the city," Cayden said worriedly.

"Ya, and another just across the river," Warrick reminded them.

"Are there other bridges we can cross?" Jade asked.

"We could ride way north but it would take time. The best way is Plattsmouth but we can't ride through the city. We'd never make it past the National Guard," Dylan said half to himself.

"We could swim the river," Cayden said.

"Oh, no!" Warrick interrupted. "I've had enough of that shit!"

Darien spoke up saying, "I say we ride north then cross into Iowa. We will go all the way out around the base and the gang camped out there then drop south."

"That puts us underneath the Platte River for the ride home," Warrick said unhappily.

"Cayden, you will take the girls and ride north. We will cross on the highway 30 overpass. Wait for us on this side of the river. We will get Shane and meet you. Don't unsaddle cause we will have to ride fast," Dylan said.

Cayden nodded.

"Cayden, good job," Dylan said slapping him on the back. "I'm proud of you guys. You kept Jade safe and you've acquired horses. You did great."

Cayden smiled. "Wait till we tell on Shane! Getting arrested wasn't the only thing he did."

Jade giggled and nodded.

"Well, let's eat and you can tell us while we wait for dark," Dylan laughed and they sat down together at last.

Rebel and Conner rode across the Iowa state line that afternoon. She figured that they only had about a two-day ride to reach Omaha. She had been feeling anxious all morning. Maybe it was because they were so close to the kids or maybe because she wasn't sure what to say to Conner.

They hadn't really spoken to each other since this morning but it was a comfortable silence. She thought about last night and her stomach coiled enticingly. She glanced over at him. God, he was so sexy.

Conner was scanning the road ahead of them. He was a little tense, his intuition telling him that something was up there. He had learned to tune into his intuition and trust it. He couldn't see anything though and glanced at Rebel who was looking at him. "Let's rest a bit," he said smiling at her.

They dismounted and walked off the road leading the horses toward some brush. Conner turned to Rebel and said, "Something is not right up ahead. I have a weird feeling right now."

"I do too. I've been agitated all morning." She smiled and added, "I thought it was just anxiety from last night."

Conner felt his body respond to the images that slithered into his mind. "I'm feeling something close to anxiety when I think about last night too," he said lifting her chin up for a kiss.

The gentle touch of his lips sent shivering spirals of desire through her and she instinctively leaned into him, returning his kiss.

Gunfire rang out, shocking them from their intimate embrace. They both spun around and watched in horror as a group of five men opened fire on three women who were running across a field next to the road. They dropped instantly, causing Rebel to cry out in horror

Conner grabbed his rifle and bolted into the brush, stealthily closing the gap between him and the armed men.

Rebel pulled out her rifle and followed but before she reached his side, he had fired four rounds so quickly that the men didn't have time to run. The last man standing dropped his weapon and raised his hands in submission.

Conner angrily strode up to him and bashed him in the face with the stock of his rifle, knocking him cold.

Rebel ran back to the field where the women were shot and checked their pulse. "One of them is alive," she yelled to Conner then bent over her to inspect her wounds.

"They kill everyone in their path," the woman whispered. "There are over a hundred of them."

"Why are they killing everyone?" Rebel asked.

"They said there are too many people on the planet. That's why all this is happening," she said so softly that Rebel could barely hear her. "They are holding my friends. They'll kill them too."

Rebel took her hand trying to give her some kind of comfort, sadly knowing that she wouldn't live. She helplessly looked at Conner taking comfort in his gentle eyes.

He knelt down beside her and felt for a pulse but found nothing. "Come on Rebel, we can't do anything for them."

"No, but we can help their friends. Those men are holding them somewhere. She said that they kill everyone to reduce the population. Fucking psychos."

"Rebel, we should ride on," he encouraged. "We are only two guns and they are a hundred strong."

"We have to at least see if we can help. I want to check it out," she insisted.

He sighed and said, "Ok, but I don't want you to get your hopes up. We may be helpless in this situation."

She nodded and climbed on Jake. "Bring that piece of shit with us," she said pointing to the unconscious man lying on the ground.

Conner picked up the dead men's weapons and packed them on the filly then threw the man across his saddle in front of him. Silently they rode toward the murdering gang.

"There they are," Rebel said pointing at a large herd of horses on the outskirts of a small town. They must be staying in that town. Let's hide the horses and walk in."

Conner dropped the man off of his horse and jumped down beside him. "Get up you fucker," he said angrily.

Rebel tied the horses and grabbed her rifle then followed them to the edge of the town. "Look, the sheriff's office is right there. Let's go see if anyone is in there."

He nodded.

She covered the door while Conner swung it open.

He looked inside then waved at her to follow. He sat the man down and said, "Guard him. I'm going to check the back." He walked down the hall toward the jail cells and cautiously looked around the corner. He could see two men in one of the cells but no one else so he walked to the cell door and was surprised to see that they were in uniform.

"Are you the sheriff?" he asked.

"Yes, your not with them?" he returned.

"No, in fact I just witnessed them murder three women. I killed four of them trying to save them but couldn't," he admitted.

"Between you and me, I'd like to kill every one of those murdering bastards," the sheriff said.

"How do I open the door?"

"Out at the front desk, you'll see the panel."

Conner walked back to the front office and pushed the lock to open. He turned to the door as the sheriff and his deputy walked into the room. He held out his hand and said, "I'm Conner, this is Rebel. And this little fucker is one of the five men who murdered three women just down the road."

The deputy handcuffed the man and drug him back to one of the cells.

"I'm glad you came by but you are in danger here. They have almost wiped out the entire town," the sheriff said.

"One of the women told Rebel that these men were holding some of their friends. We wanted to at least attempt to help them."

"We will help you. I think I know where they are holding them. Follow me."

Conner looked at Rebel nervously and said, "Wait here, the sheriff and I will handle this."

"Not on your life Conner. I'm going with you," she said and followed the sheriff and deputy out the door.

He led them down the road to the hospital and stopped. "They wanted the drugs and the beds."

Rebel inhaled sharply at the thought of those murdering bastards terrorizing the injured and ill people here. "Let's find a quiet entrance," she said walking toward the back of the building.

"Over here," Conner said then turned to the others. "Let me go in alone. I just might go unnoticed. You three will stand out like a sore thumb."

The sheriff nodded in agreement but Rebel didn't respond.

"Rebel, this is what I do. What I'm trained for. Trust me. Just be ready to get them to safety if I can get them out." He kissed her and entered the building.

She tried to contain the fear that consumed her and

turned to the sheriff, "You are going to need a way to get out of here."

"I'm thinking that we will hide out until they're gone. From what I understand, they're like locusts. They move in, eat everything, kill everyone, then they blow out. I have the perfect place to hide," he explained.

Rebel grew anxious as she waited impatiently for Conner to return. What if something happened? She was just about to go find him when he burst through the door with two women.

"We have to move," he said urgently leading them away from the building. When they were safely away, he turned to the sheriff and said disgustedly, "There was no one else alive in there besides the gang. It's like a morgue."

The sheriff nodded sadly and said, "We will take it from here then. Thank you."

Rebel shook his hand and smiled encouragingly at the women then followed Conner back to the horses. Rebel swung onto Jake and was turning him onto the road when she heard Conner say, "Drop your weapons." She spun around to the three men he was talking to, surprised that she hadn't heard them.

One of the men challenged him by pointing his rifle straight at him.

Rebel slowly pulled out her shotgun and the unmistakable sound of the shell slamming into the chamber made him jerk his head toward her.

"Do what he said," she ordered.

"You don't want to mess with us mister. We got a lot of friends," one of the men said.

"Don't threaten me you little fucker!" Conner growled, walking toward them. "Drop those weapons!" After they complied, he said, "Now go back the way you came."

They all took off running toward the town. Conner turned to Rebel and said, "We need to get the hell out of here. I beat the group leader damn near to death and they will be coming for me."

Rebel looked at Conner and said, "I guess your intuition was right on."

"Ya, I hate when that happens," he shrugged.

"Come on, let's ride then."

They rode hard until it was dark then slowed to a walk but kept moving.

"This was always my worst fear," Rebel said dejectedly. "The people turning on each other like this. Scumbags running around unrestrained. I can deal with no power and hunting to eat, but I can't deal with the people, they are crazy."

"Shit, I thought people were crazy before this happened. Now they are much worse," Conner agreed. "Rebel, those guys are going to follow us. There are more than a hundred of them. We are in serious danger."

Just as Rebel was going to answer, Jake stumbled and started limping. "Shit, Jake just threw a shoe or something." She jumped off and picked up his foot. "It didn't come off clean."

"It looks like the nail took off a corner of his hoof," Conner agreed.

"Oh, Jake!" Rebel said clearly upset. She stood by him stroking his neck for a minute then removed her saddle and put it on the filly. She took off his bridle and let him go.

Sadly, she mounted the little horse and they silently went on with Jake following at his own pace.

"He will be fine Rebel," Conner soothed. "He will keep up without any weight on him. We will find somewhere to get shoes for him and he'll be good as new."

Rebel just nodded and silently rode into the night.

The brothers were enjoying their dinner with Cayden and Jade listening to the stories about Shane. Cayden was explaining the puppy when the waki crackled to life.

"Cayden, Cayden, you there?"

"It's Shane!" Cayden said with relief.

Dylan picked up the radio and said, "Brother, its Dylan. Glad to hear from you."

"I'm glad you're here. I'm still in the same place and

I have a pretty good schedule of the guards," Shane said.

"K, we will be there just after dark. Be ready," Dylan said.

Darien stood and said, "Mount up everyone. Cayden, take the girls north and we will meet you there."

Jade mounted and called the puppy to follow. "See you soon," she said to the brothers.

The brothers rode to the military camp and hid the horses behind a half burned building about fifty yards away. They crept to the area where Cayden said he'd cut the fence.

"You guys cover the boundary fence, I'll go inside and get him out," Warrick volunteered.

Dylan and Darien found cover just out of reach of the spot light but close enough to the fence that they could cover Warrick when they came out.

Warrick silently crept to the cage where Shane was being held and quickly cut the wire. Shane followed him back to the hole in the boundary fence.

"The spotlight is coming," Warrick whispered.

They both crouched down and held still until it passed.

"Come on," Warrick said, squeezing through the hole.

They quickly moved away from the compound to the horses and finally relaxed a little as they joined the others and headed north.

"I expect you to break me out of jail the next time I'm in," Warrick said to Shane. "Fair is fair."

Shane laughed and said, "Thanks man, it's good to be out. Where is Cayden and Jade?"

"They went on ahead. We'll meet them at the river," Dylan said.

"I have some disturbing news. There are two gangs hanging out somewhere out there," Shane said worriedly.

"Ya, we know where they are approximately," Darien said.

"Good. There is also a band of assassins marauding across the Midwest. They are murderers, killing anyone they come up on. They have some kind of population reduction theory going on. The National Guard is tracking them but they are so overwhelmed that they haven't gone after them yet," Shane told them.

"Did they say where they are now?" Darien asked.

"They said that they are coming in from the east toward Omaha but they avoid the large cities where the National Guard is located so they may drop south," Shane said worriedly.

"They are on the same path as Rebel!" Warrick said. "I hope she hasn't run into them."

"If they get to close, they will run into the gang that is camped across the river in Iowa," Dylan said.

Suddenly a loud siren went off shattering the night silence. "They've found out your gone! Let's move!" Darien yelled urging his horse into a full out run.

They rode hard barely resting the horses until they reached the closest bridge across the big Missouri river about twenty miles north of Omaha. Dylan pulled out the radio to call for Cayden.

Cayden and the girls were waiting close to the bridge so they all quickly crossed the overpass.

"We have to go out around the area where the gang is camped and try not to run into this murdering bunch of bastards coming in from the east and try to find Rebel all at the same time," Dylan said.

"Ya, and keep ahead of the National Guard who will be hunting us, and go around the tent cities bordering the base," Warrick added.

"I think we should find a place to hide the kids, then go find Rebel," Darien said.

"What if we can't get back north to get them?" Dylan asked.

"We want to stay with you," Cayden objected. "We can hide the girls along the way if we have to."

"Fine but you and Shane are in charge of taking them to a safe spot if we run into trouble," Dylan agreed. "Warrick, you take the lead and scout a little bit ahead. Rebel will be coming in on highway thirty four so we need to be on it as soon as possible so we don't miss her."

They headed southeast moving slowly with Warrick riding ahead about a half mile to keep an eye out.

That evening, Conner and Rebel rode into yet another small city.

"We need to find someone to warn about those men," Conner said as he looked for the police station.

Rebel nodded in agreement then pulled out her map. "We are almost to highway thirty four. That is where Dylan will be looking for me. Once we get there, we will follow the road west."

"That puts our assailants right on our ass," Conner pointed out. "If they ride fast, they might come up on us from behind." He dismounted in front of the police station. "Wait here, I will see if anyone is in there."

Rebel looked around as he disappeared inside the building. The town looked empty just like all of the other smaller towns they had gone through. She thought about how quickly order turned to chaos when there was no communication or power. Without grocery stores and vehicles, people were forced out into the open where they could find water and hunt for food.

A woman walked across the street toward her and asked, "Are you traveling? Is the power on anywhere?"

"No, it's a global blackout," she answered. "How many people are in this town?"

She looked around and said, "Maybe five hundred or so. Used to be about five thousand but we are out of supplies so they left."

Rebel nodded sadly. "It's the same everywhere. Try to find a water source and wild game."

The woman tried to smile but failed so she just waved as she continued across the street.

Conner returned and said, "The sheriff is still in control here. He had no idea that they were facing that kind of danger."

"People who are unarmed are the first to fall. They

have no protection from the evil out there. It makes me sick thinking about how our population became so completely dependent upon the government. If they would have had their way, no one would own weapons," Rebel said sadly.

"No one but the criminals. You can damn sure bet they would be armed no matter what. All it would have done was put the wrong people in control," Conner agreed. "On a lighter note, the sheriff told me about a ferrier that lives about ten miles up the road."

"Oh good," Rebel said smiling. "Thank you."

"Come on, let's get your horse fixed up," Conner said mounting the gilding.

They rode through the gate of the ferrier's house and a man came out to meet them. He held a rifle in his hand but greeted them calmly.

"The local sheriff told us that you may be able to replace a shoe on our horse," Conner said to the man.

"Sure, come on out to the barn," the man answered. He took a look at Jake then looked at the filly and gilding. "It may not hurt to shoe all of 'em."

"Regrettably, we don't have the time," Conner said. "I'll just have you do the buckskin."

The man nodded and went to work. Conner proceeded to warn him of the band of marauders that were on their way toward him. "All we know is that there are a lot of them and they kill anyone in their path," he said.

"I'm grateful for the information," he said as he finished his task. He looked at Rebel and said pointing to Jake, "I would give him a couple days before you ride him but his hoof will be fine."

Rebel thanked him and handed him some money.

"Oh no, not necessary," he responded to the gesture. "I have money. Maybe you could spare a rifle."

Rebel handed him one of the spare weapons and thanked him again as they mounted and headed out.

They rode into the evening not stopping until they reached the highway. Rebel spent a few minutes checking Jake's shoe. "He did a good job. I think it will heal completely," she said to Conner. When he didn't answer, she looked up at him.

Conner was looking to the east listening intently to something Rebel couldn't hear and she could tell he was worried.

"What is it?" she asked nervously.

"They are close, I can hear them," Conner breathed. "Maybe we should continue on. I don't want them to catch up to us."

"K, let's ride," Rebel agreed.

Warrick rode back to the brothers and said, "We have a problem. The gang is on the move. They are moving east and we will run into them if we keep moving in this direction.

"We have no choice but to keep moving. Can you keep us out of their path?"

"I'll try but they are moving fast. They are going to pass us and reach the city before we do," Warrick said.

Jade listened anxiously. She could tell that the brothers were nervous and they weren't afraid of anything. She glanced at Cayden and said, "Are we going to be ok?"

"Yes, we will be fine," he said convincingly. He glanced at Lynn who was completely terrified. "Just stay close, we will protect you."

Lynn tried to smile. Jade moved her horse closer to hers for moral support and the two girls rode quietly beside each other.

Shane glanced at Cayden then nodded reassuringly at the girls. "He's right ladies, we will be fine."

Jade tried to let his words comfort her but she knew that Rebel was riding blindly into this gang and no one could warn her. "Shane, what will they do if they catch her, or us?"

"I don't know Jade. They may not do anything. But from what I overheard the National Guard saying, they aren't friendly to anyone outside their group. They are pissed off about losing their territory and are looking for a new place to control."

They rode quietly well into night before Dylan

reigned in and said, "Let's get some sleep and rest the horses. We will reach the city by tomorrow evening."

They found a thick grove of trees by a small creek and made camp for the night.

Conner and Rebel took turns sleeping for a couple of hours before they broke camp just as the sun was coming up. Rebel wanted to make it to the city of Red Oak by nightfall.

Conner was edgy and hadn't slept well at all, feeling something big coming. He checked and rechecked his weapons and sharpened his knife. He glanced at Rebel and wondered if they would actually make it home.

"Rebel, I.. I," he paused unable to get the words out.

Rebel looked at him expectantly.

He walked over to her and continued, "I wanted you to know that I was serious when I said that I have fallen in love with you. The night we spent together was…," he paused again.

Rebel wrapped her arms around him and said, "I've fallen in love with you too." She pulled his head down to hers and kissed him, tracing his lips with her tongue.

Conner held her, reveling in the sweet touch of her mouth.

She pulled back regretfully and said, "I wish we had time to…"

"Me too," he finished for her, "but I feel something in the air again. We need to move out. Come on." He led her to her horse and boosted her up. He looked up at her and said, "I can't wait till this is all over and we can relax together."

She smiled down at him and said, "Me too."

They rode west at a full gallop. Conner was worried that the gang behind them would be moving fast too and possibly catch them.

Finally that afternoon, he reined in to allow the horses to rest. Jake had taken the fast pace well and didn't show any kind of limp.

Rebel was relieved because the filly was significantly

smaller and wasn't handling the weight very well.

"I'm going to leave the radio on now. If everything went well, the brothers should be getting close," she said.

"The city is a few more miles. Let's keep moving."

There is the city," Dylan said. "Warrick, find us a safe place to hide the kids and I will try Rebel on the radio."

Jade waited anxiously for her mother to answer and tried to hide her disappointment when she didn't.

"Don't worry Jade, she has to be within a few miles to hear it. That doesn't mean she isn't there," Darien reassured her. "We'll find her."

Jade nodded trying to find comfort in his words.

Warrick waved them to a safe campsite. "We should be able to see all around us from here," he said then motioned for Darien to follow him.

"Any word from Rebel?" Warrick asked making sure that they were out of hearing distance from Jade.

"Not yet," Darien said regretfully. "Jade is getting pretty upset."

"I'm sure she will get here. Dylan laid out the road for her before we left." He sighed glancing at the girls. "I just hope we can keep the kids safe in this nightmare."

"I want to leave the kids and ride into the city to look for her. We can't risk her riding unknowing right into the middle of that gang," Darien said. He turned to Jade and said, "I want you guys to stay here. Jade, you keep checking for Rebel on the radio. We are going to ride ahead and look for her. Keep the horses saddled."

The brothers rode south toward the city.

Conner and Rebel looked at the small city up ahead. Conner glanced behind them and said, "They are right behind us. Let's get to higher ground, maybe we will be able see them from there."

They rode quietly onto the main street. Cars littered the roads and the buildings down town had obviously been looted. Windows were broken out and trash littered the sidewalks. It was a fairly small city, one that would be easily overtaken by the murdering gang behind them.

Conner reined in his gilding and pointed to five young men in the street ahead who turned and ran as soon as they seen them. "Did you see their tattoos?" he asked her.

"Ya, maybe some guys from an Omaha gang," she answered.

They eased forward cautiously.

"There he is!" someone yelled from behind them.

Conner and Rebel instinctively kicked their horses into a run and raced down two blocks then turned a corner around a building. They both slid to a stop right in front of a hundred men standing in a park area that spanned a full city clock in front of the city office building. Conner palmed the revolver and started his horse toward the right.

"Don't move!" one of the men said stopping him.

"Look friend," he said, "there are over a hundred men behind us and they don't look like they belong with you."

The man nervously glanced at the guy beside him just as the mounted men came barreling around the corner, hooves sliding to a stop on the pavement. There was a slight pause and an eerie silence before all hell broke loose. Both the gang and the band of murderers let loose with bullets with Rebel and Conner caught right in the line of fire. The filly reared and spun around, and Conner's gilding jumped sideways.

The brothers rode around the city building and looked in horror at the scene in front of them. They were just in time to see their sister caught in the middle of a gang war. Gunfire split the air around her and her horse was rearing. Fear for her drove them into action and all three of them started firing.

The filly reared again and Rebel fought to stay astride the animal. She looked to her right and watched as if in slow motion, a man raise an automatic weapon and open fire in a spray across the line of men directly behind her. She knew she was going to die. She felt a bullet slam into her thigh as the weapon cut a straight line of artillery across the filly that was still up on two legs. The animal screamed then just dropped from underneath her.

She faintly heard four men scream her name and she tried to focus on her surroundings but total chaos unleashed around her. Men were fighting and shooting and yelling above her. She couldn't move because her leg was solidly pinned beneath nine hundred pound horse. Piercing pain shot through her leg as she tried to push the animal off of her.

Conner watched the filly drop and his heart stopped. Time just stood still as the horse went down with Rebel on its back. He flew off the gilding and ran toward her but the front lines of the fight clashed in battle right over the top of her. He pushed and fought his way to her side. "Rebel!" he yelled, fear wrenching his gut. 'God, please be alive,' his mind kept saying.

Finally he reached her and heaved her from beneath the fallen horse.

"Conner," she said softly.

"Thank god, Rebel," he cried as he lifted her into his arms and pushed his way to the side of the street against a building.

Three big men instantly surrounded them asking if she was ok.

"I'm fine," she said through clenched teeth.

"This way!" Warrick yelled above the roar of the fight.

Conner followed him carrying Rebel with Dylan and Darien guarding their backs.

They found their way around the corner and along a quieter street. Darien kicked the door of a building open and they took Rebel inside and leaned her against a wall on the carpet.

All four of them asked in unison, "Rebel, are you ok?"

She smiled at them and said, "Yes, I'm hit but I'm fine. Now give me hugs, I missed you guys so much."

After she had gotten sufficient hugs from her

brothers she looked up at Conner who was standing back watching the reunion. "This is Conner," she said to the brothers.

They all three turned on him, looking him over.

"We've traveled together from West Virginia," she said

Darien offered his hand and said, "I'm Darien, this is Dylan and Warrick. Nice to meet you." Dylan and Warrick took turns shaking his hand.

Rebel suddenly tried to stand up. "Where is Jake?" she asked Conner worriedly.

"Don't stand yet Rebel. I will go see if I can find him," Conner smiled at her then walked toward the door.

"Who is Jake?" Dylan asked.

"He's my horse. Thank god I wasn't riding him today," Rebel answered sadly.

Darien went to work trying to secure the wound in her leg so that they could move her. "So, what's up with you and Conner? Looks like he's more than a friend," he said teasingly.

"Ya," Warrick added with a laugh, "a little out of character for you isn't it?"

Dylan grinned and said, "He charged in after you like a bull. I didn't know who he was but I knew he was worried about you."

She blushed then smiled, "He is a good guy. We have gotten close over the past few weeks."

"We can see that," Darien teased again.

"I missed you guys. Great timing by the way," she laughed feeling a little better about life.

Darien finished bandaging her wound and said in a serious tone, "We need to get you out of the city. Warrick find the horses."

Conner looked around the building where the filly lay in the middle of the road among many dead men. The fight had migrated down the block so he sadly walked up to the fallen animal and stood over her trembling. Rebel could have been killed so easily. The thought of losing her again made him weak. He shuttered once more then whistled for

Jake who appeared from the opposite direction.

Warrick walked up behind him and said, "Too damn close wasn't it?"

Conner just nodded then collected Rebels saddle and bridle. Jake stood quietly as Conner saddled him. "I'm glad it wasn't Jake," he said sincerely.

"She does tend to get attached to her animals," Warrick agreed fondly.

They led the horses back to Rebel and helped her hobble out to the street. She sadly glanced at the corner where the filly had fallen then mounted Jake. "Take me to Jade, k?"

The three brothers nodded and headed north away from the fighting gangs.

"So tell me about your venture so far," Darien said to change the subject as they rode out of the city.

"Well," Rebel said not knowing where to start, "I was stranded in the middle of the city when the truck went down. As I was walking through I had to shoot some guys because they were trying to rape a woman in the alley. Then I was caught in the middle of a gang war like this one but was pulled to safety by some guy that yanked me into a building. Then we seen them grab a woman and take her into the alley so I stole an automatic weapon and shot them and saved her." She paused as Conner stiffened. He hadn't heard that part before. "Then I met Conner. We both broke into a sporting goods store at the same time. Pretty ironic I guess. He was heading west too, so we joined forces." She smiled at him remembering their first encounter.

The brothers looked at each other but didn't say anything. They waited patiently for her to continue.

"Then we met up with a couple of boys who rode with us for awhile. Conner saved them from being killed by a group of murderers. Then Conner got shot."

"Shot?" Warrick said, "Now your both shot?"

"Yes, he almost bled to death by the time I rescued him from about twenty men," she added. "Then, I was attacked by a mountain lion and almost lost one of the horses to a second cat but Conner shot it. Then some men tried to mug us when we crossed the Mississippi and I killed one of them with the .22 and Conner killed the other two."

"My god Rebel!" Warrick exclaimed. "One of us should have been with you! We should have never let you go to D.C. by yourself."

"Well you're with me now," she smiled at him. "You know you can't be with me every minute. Now tell me about your ride."

"We certainly haven't had as much excitement as you," Dylan said. "Warrick almost strung up some cattle thieves and confiscated $500,000 that they had stolen from a rancher that they killed."

"That's a lot of money," Rebel said.

Dylan nodded and said, "Then we had a run in with some military guys protecting something in a train wreck just inside Nebraska, but the best news is that we had to break Shane out of a National Guard prison."

"What?" she breathed surprised.

The brothers all laughed. "Oh ya, and Dylan beat up an abusive uncle giving the girl the courage to shoot the guy," Warrick added.

"And Warrick cried like a baby when we had to swim the river," Dylan laughed.

"I didn't cry you fucker, I just didn't like getting my revolver wet," Warrick sulked.

Rebel laughed and glanced at Conner who was grinning. 'God he is so handsome,' she thought.

"Rebel, we are close enough for you to call Jade on the radio," Darien said.

Rebel grabbed the waki out of her bag and keyed the mic. "Jade, it's your mommy."

"Mom? Is it really you?" Jade answered instantly.

"Yes, we are almost to camp. I can't wait to see you," Rebel said with relief.

She looked at her brothers and said, "Thanks for getting here so fast and finding the kids."

The brothers just smiled at her.

At camp they helped her dismount and sat her by

the fire. Jade landed beside her with a big hug. "Mom, I'm so glad you're finally here. I was so worried about you." She hugged Rebel tightly again then looked down at her leg and yelled, "Oh my god, you've been shot. Are you ok?"

"I will be fine Jade. You can help me change some of my bandages later."

Dylan turned to her and said a little fiercely, "What other bandages?"

"Well, I wrestled with the cat before I killed him," she said softly.

The entire camp went silent. "Let's see!" Warrick ordered worriedly.

Rebel showed them the gashes across her ribs and the wounds on her shoulder. "I also have five pretty slices across my thigh," she admitted. "Which you will see when you dig the bullet out of my leg."

"Fuck! You could have been killed," Warrick roared. "No wonder Conner was so pale when the horse went down. It wasn't your first close encounter."

Conner, who had been quiet up until now, nodded in agreement, "She scares the shit out of me almost daily."

Jade looked at Conner then back at Rebel quizzically.

"I'm sorry Jade, this is Conner. He's helped me survive this journey so far," Rebel said somewhat nervously.

Jade stood and walked over to Conner looking him up and down then held out her hand and said, "I'm Jade."

"I've heard a lot about you Jade. Your mother was frantic to get to you," he said shaking her hand.

Jade turned and introduced him to Shane and Cayden. "They took really good care of me while we were stuck in Omaha. Cayden gave me a puppy," she said with admiration. She whistled at the dog that came bounding into camp. "This is Lucky."

Everyone laughed at the dog.

"Cayden who is your friend?" Rebel asked seeing that he hadn't left the girls side since they had arrived.

"This is Lynn. Shane saved her from some guys in

Omaha," Cayden said.

"Nice to meet you Lynn," Rebel smiled. "So, come here guys, sit down and tell me about the last few weeks."

Cayden led Lynn to the fire and sat down beside her and said, "We found a cool place to hide up in and Jade had money in her emergency bag so we bought supplies. Shane went out one night and come back with Lynn. Everything was good for a while until the gang war started. Then the fires that were burning erupted into a firestorm that took out the entire city. We had to get out of there so we took as much stuff as we could. But out on the street, the gangs were fighting and we were stuck. So Shane stole a hummer and whisked us out of town."

Everyone looked at Shane who shrugged sheepishly.

"We holed up in a barn until our supplies ran short then Shane and I confiscated some abandoned horses. Then he decided to go into the city to get some supplies and have a look around and got arrested," Cayden said.

Everyone looked at Shane again.

"You little devil," Rebel smiled.

"Then the brothers showed up and broke him out and here we are," he finished.

"So where do we go from here?" Rebel asked Dylan.

"Well, I don't exactly now. We have the National Guard looking for us to the north, there is another gang camped to the southwest and we have this shit to the south. We are still in a dangerous spot here," Dylan sighed. "And that don't include the gang that's across the river."

"Let's get some sleep and head out in the morning. I'll keep watch tonight," Warrick said standing up and picking up his rifle.

Conner grabbed the sleeping bags and laid them out next to Rebel. He picked up the first aid kit and looked at her. "We need to get that bullet out of your leg," he said regretfully. "Good thing we restocked the medical supplies."

"I have a bottle of whiskey in my bag," Darien offered. "We can get her good and drunk first."

Everybody laughed as he poured some whiskey into a coffee cup.

"Mom, I have some shorts you can wear," Jade said.

Rebel changed and drank a few shots then settled down on one of the sleeping bags. "Ok, Dr. Jekyll, patch me up again," she smiled at Conner.

Conner, Dylan and Darien looked at the hole in her leg and shook their heads.

"God, Rebel, that bullet is in there and it's gonna hurt comin out," Darien said as he pulled out his knife and sterilized it.

Rebel looked at the three uptight men and said encouragingly, "I'm fine guys, just get it out and we will go from there, k?"

They nodded and grudgingly started the grisly task. Dylan pinched the skin on her leg capturing the bullet between his fingers while Darien sliced the blade through her flesh straight at the metal. Rebel inhaled and tensed. Conner grabbed her hand and held it tight.

"K, I felt the tip of the knife touch the bullet. It should come out…," he said twisting the blade slightly and pulling both the knife and the bullet out at the same time.

Rebel leaned her head back and for the sake of the three men working on her, fought to stay conscious through the familiar stars that once again fluttered in front of her vision. 'Just breath through it,' she told herself.

Finally, she calmed a little and opened her eyes then laughed out loud at the sight of the men holding their breath above her. "God, you guys, I'm not going to disappear in a cloud of dust."

All three of them exhaled and started talking at once. Conner pushed gauze into the holes on both sides of the wound to stop the bleeding and wrapped more around her thigh.

Dylan inspected the five gashes from the cat and Darien poured more whiskey in her cup. Finally they were satisfied with their work and Conner moved up to the wounds on her rib cage.

"Jesus Rebel," Dylan said softly. "This is way worse than I thought."

After her bandages were all replaced, she looked at Dylan and asked, "Will you change the bandage on Conner's shoulder?" She patted the ground silently asking him to sit beside her.

He complied and took off his shirt.

"Dude, that's a bad hole too," Dylan said.

Darien nodded in agreement.

Rebel looked at the wound and shuttered again at the thought of almost losing him. She leaned back to rest with Jade on one side of her and Conner on the other and for the first time in weeks was at peace.

Chapter 8

The next morning Rebel woke up tucked under Conner's arm with her head nuzzled against his wide chest. God, it felt so good to be close to him.

Jade was sprawled out next to her with her arm slung across her waist sleeping soundly. Rebel smiled down at her thankful that they were all safe for the moment. At least now they were together.

Conner moved under her and she looked up into his smiling face.

"I love you," he whispered in her ear.

"I'm thinking that I love you too," she smiled up to him then slipped out from under Jade and tried to stand. Pain shot through her leg and she swayed.

Conner leapt to his feet and balanced her. He looked down at her wound as fresh blood spilled down her thigh. "You can't ride Rebel, or we will never get the bleeding stopped."

"We have to move on," she said defiantly.

"Ya, well now I have backup and me and your brothers will win the fight against your stubbornness," he said with a mock smile.

Warrick handed her a cup of coffee and said, "You can't ride Rebel." Then he gave Conner a high five across the fire.

"I'm sure your gallantry has no end but we can't just sit here and wait for them to find us," she said haughtily.

"She's right," Darien said taking her side. "We are sitting ducks here."

Rebel imitated Conner's mock smile right back at him.

"You're all right," Dylan broke in. "We have to move but we can wait till later."

Rebel looked at the worried looks on their faces. They were obviously torn between the danger here and the danger of her bleeding to death. "Ok, look guys. Jake is smooth, he's calm and rarely jumps. We can wrap the wound tight and I will ride in shorts so you can all keep your eye on the bleeding." She looked at Conner pleadingly, "I don't want to put the kids in more danger."

"Fine, but if the bleeding gets worse, we stop," Conner said looking to the brothers for agreement.

They all nodded.

Conner went to saddle the horses. He picked up her saddle and shuttered again at the sight of the blood that saturated the leather. He took it to the creek and washed it off then saddled Jake. He picked up his hoof to check the injury then set it down satisfied that he was healing well enough to be ridden. "Be careful with her Jake," he said to the horse.

"I'll ask you the same thing," Warrick said startling Conner who was so deep in thought that he hadn't heard him walk up. "She hasn't allowed a man to get close to her since Jade's dad left so you are kind of a surprise to us."

Conner looked at Warrick and said, "Don't worry, I would never hurt her. She surprised me too, just kind of snuck into my heart and took it over."

Warrick smiled and slapped Conner on the back. "I believe in fate and never second guess it."

"She is so stubborn though," Conner thought out loud. "I'm worried about her wounds. She got a bad infection after she killed the cat and I had to find antibiotics. We holed up for a day or so but she insisted we move on. Maybe now that she is with Jade, she will ease up a little."

"I doubt it. We will keep a close eye on her Conner. If she gets weak, we will make her stop," Warrick encouraged.

"What's up?" Dylan asked walking up to them.

"We were discussing your sister's stubborn streak," Warrick smiled at Conner. "She is very tenacious."

"Ya, I'll help you keep an eye on her," Dylan said as he saddled Ace.

After the horses were saddled and packed, Dylan pulled out his map. "We have to go south far enough to miss the other gang across the river. But somehow we have to sneak through the gang camped below us to the west. The only way to cross the river is down toward Nebraska City."

"We will just have to scout ahead and pick our way through. I'll ride ahead with a radio and guide you," Warrick said. "We need to arm the kids."

Conner pulled out the two extra rifles and handed one to Shane and the other to Cayden. He handed Jade and Lynn the extra handguns.

"K, I'll stay within talking distance of the waki. Keep an eye on that leg," Warrick said heading out.

They rode slowly to minimize the movement of Rebels wound. Jade watched the blood drip from the hole and looked at Conner worriedly. He smiled at her reassuringly trying to cover his own concern.

Rebel rode ahead to talk to Dylan and Darien leaving Jade beside Conner.

"So, you really like my mom? How did you meet her?" she asked him.

"Ya, I really like your mom," he smiled. "We met when we both needed supplies and broke into the same store. She didn't take to me very easily."

"She don't trust people," Jade said shrugging. "But I can tell she likes you, which is weird because I don't remember her getting close to anyone since my dad left."

"Do you see your dad much?" he asked curiously.

"No, he left us both. He sends me birthday cards and I send him school pictures. That's about it. But I have my uncles," she said fondly. "I'm glad you were with her these past weeks. I was so worried about her. She made me get on the plane but I didn't want to leave her alone."

"She talked about you the entire way here. I feel like I know you already. She couldn't wait to get to you," Conner told her.

"Me and grandma have always been her whole world. I tried to get her to do other things, you know go out and stuff but she wouldn't. Then she started researching this 2012 thing and that was it. She didn't think about anything else. She said that something just told her it was real. I didn't believe in it all though," Jade said regretfully. "If I would have believed her, we wouldn't be here right now."

"Don't think like that, Jade," Conner soothed. "She wanted you to live your life. Besides, if she hadn't come after you, I wouldn't have met her."

Jade laughed, "I'm glad something good came from it then."

Conner smiled and glanced at Rebel who looked back at them. She smiled back then turned her attention back to Dylan.

"It's a little weird to see my mom smile. Not that she wasn't happy, but she always seemed lonely," Jade said softly so Rebel wouldn't hear her.

"That is a shame, she has a beautiful smile," Conner said still looking at Rebel.

Jade laughed again.

"Is she always this tough, this determined," he asked.

"Yes, always. She wouldn't let up till the property in the mountains was completely prepared and stocked. She works out at the gym every day. I mean every day. She studies martial arts and boxing and though she would never say it, she loves to fight."

"She loves to fight?" he asked surprised.

"Yes, she says it's the only thing that clears her head. But that's only part of her. She has a Bachelors degree in psychology but doesn't practice because she hates being indoors. She works in the construction field with my uncles. She coaches girls basketball, she is an EMT and she helps rescue animals for the shelter."

Conner nodded in surprise, realizing that he barely knew this woman.

They had ridden for about an hour when Warrick's voice broke the radio silence, "There is something going on up here. Hold back and wait for me."

They rode into some trees and dismounted. "Shit!" Darien said. "We are right between the city and the gangs camp."

Shane and Cayden stiffened and Jade and Lynn both

cringed.

Darien rode out to meet Warrick who came in at a run. "They are still fighting and they seem to be circling around each other. We are right in the middle of it."

"Let's keep moving slowly and keep to any cover we can find," Darien said. "Cayden, pick up that dog and see if he will ride, we don't want him to give up our position."

They mounted and slowly rode on with the girls in the middle and the men on the outside and behind them. Everyone carried their rifles in their hand.

After about a mile, Warrick stopped his horse. "Something is up, and I don't like it."

Darien nodded in agreement and said, "It's too quiet. I'll ride ahead this time."

They followed him for a bit then came upon his horse, but no Darien.

"Fuck!" Warrick said. "Where is he?"

"He's right here," a voice said from behind them.

"You fucker!" Warrick roared when caught sight of his bloody unconscious brother.

The voice stopped him from dismounting when it said, "Don't move, we have fifty rifles pointed at you."

"Liar! If they are there they better show themselves or I'm gonna kill you!" he yelled, beyond pissed now.

Slowly fifty men appeared from behind the trees with guns drawn.

"Son of a bitch!"

"Now, drop your weapons!" the man said.

Rebel gripped her rifle tightly. She wouldn't be able to protect Jade without a gun.

"Now! Or we start shooting!"

They all looked at each other realizing that they had no choice and dropped the rifles.

"What do you want?" Rebel asked angrily.

A second man stepped closer. He wore a black bandana and sleeveless shirt. "Don't you remember us? I told you we had friends and not to fuck with us."

"God damn it!" Conner said, instantly recognizing

the men and realizing that they were after revenge.

"What do you want?" Rebel asked again eyeing the man in the bandana.

"We want what you took from us. Weapons and women," he sneered then stepped closer to Jade. Suddenly he reached up and yanked her off of her horse.

Rebel launched off of Jake and landed on the ground in front of the man holding her daughter.

He quickly pointed a handgun at Jade's head and drug her back a step. "I'll take her dead if I have to."

Rebel stopped and stood glaring at him trying to calm her anger and think rationally. She looked around at the tens of rifles pointed at them. There was no way they would win in a gun battle. She looked at Conner and her brothers and knew that they would fight to the death trying to save them and would certainly be killed because they were so outnumbered.

She looked back at the man holding her daughter and took in the fact that he had a small build and was probably not athletic at all. He didn't look to be much of a fighter so she said, "I'll make you a deal tuff guy. I'll fight you for her."

Conner and all of her brothers yelled, "No!" simultaneously.

But Rebel could see no other option She had to try to get them out of this situation without using the weapons and she was betting on the fact that the man would be to embarrassed to say no in front of his buddies who were watching in amusement.

She turned to them and said, "Is he afraid?" She looked back at the man, trying to force him into accepting her challenge. "Are you afraid to fight a woman? A wounded woman?"

She unholstered the colt and pointed it past Jade into the man's head. "Do you even have enough honor to keep the bargain if I won? Or should I risk it all and take you out right now?"

Conner held his breath. He never imagined that she had balls this big. My god, she was baiting him into a fight and he and the brothers would not be able to help her.

The man looked at the colt and the expression on her face. He squirmed, realizing that she was deadly serious. He turned to the expectant faces of his so called friends and knew they would never let him live this down if he said no. "Alright, I'll fight you for her you psycho bitch!" he said putting on a show.

"If I win, you let us all go, with the weapons," Rebel insisted.

"Fine!" he said releasing Jade and shoving her back toward her horse.

Rebel walked over to Jade and handed her the colt, "If he reneges on our deal, you shoot him in the head."

Jade nodded, glaring at the man nervously.

"This fight is to the death, Tim. If you can't beat her, you don't ride with us!" a blonde guy yelled, excitedly getting into the action.

Again Conner sucked in his breath. He looked at the brothers who weren't nearly as worried as he was. Warrick almost wore a grin. 'Is she that good?' he wondered.

The man facing Rebel, Tim, looked at the blonde guy in disbelief. "Fuck you, Stew! You don't make the rules. Damien would still be the boss if he wouldn't have killed him!" he said glaring at Conner.

Rebel followed his gaze to Conner who shifted uneasily on his horse.

Stew swung the rifle on Tim angrily, "Well I'm making the rules now. And I will make sure this deal is honored."

That was all Rebel needed to hear. She moved in quickly, swinging her fist, hitting Tim hard in the chin, sending him reeling backwards. She followed with a kick to the side of his head that plowed him to the ground. His crowd cheered, smelling the blood like animals.

"Wait! No fair! I wasn't ready, god damn it!"

"You fucking pussy!" Rebel spat back at him. "Stand up!"

The man got to his feet and squared for battle.

Rebel closed in again with a left then a right hand to his face.

He swung back, landing a blow to her cheek.

"You hit like a girl!" she laughed trying to keep him upset and off balance. She swung again and landed another good one to his chin.

"You bitch!" he screamed coming at her on a run.

She ducked under him and grabbed him around the back of his head and using his own momentum, flung him over her back and slammed him into the ground again. Her leg was throbbing and she wasn't able to move very quickly as she spun around to face him.

Tim landed hard and looked up at her in surprise. Then he spied the blood running down her thigh and kicked her as hard as he could from the ground, hitting her wound dead on with his boot.

Rebel crumbled to the ground next to him in agony and moaned loudly when he stood up and kicked her in the abdomen.

Conner moved to dismount and help her but Warrick put his hand on his arm stopping him, his expression telling him that she would pull this off.

Rebel gritted through the pain and swung her leg, kicking his legs out from under him then grabbed one of them and rolled on it, twisting over his knee then heaved her body weight onto the unusually placed joint.

"Fuck!" Tim screamed in pain.

Rebel stood up and kicked him in the face breaking his nose. She swayed again from the pain in her thigh.

"To the death!" Stew yelled, lifting his rifle again.

Tim climbed to his feet unsteadily and swayed as he faced her.

Rebel stepped in and swung with every ounce of strength she had, backing it with all of her body weight, and slammed her fist into his broken nose, sending the bone into his brain. He sagged to his knees then toppled forward and didn't move.

Rebel dropped to her knees now barely able to breathe through the pain.

Conner let out the breath that he had unconsciously been holding throughout the entire fight. If he hadn't been so worried about her, he would have been totally amazed by her fighting skills and precision. "My god!" he said out loud.

He looked again at Warrick and Dylan who weren't surprised at all but noticed that they were both holding their handguns just in case.

Stew waited for one of his men to check Tim's pulse and when he shook his head no, yelled, "Lower your weapons and for God's sake buy this woman a drink!" He turned to Rebel and grinned, "I'm impressed. He wasn't our best fighter but you kicked his ass good."

Rebel forced herself to her feet and hobbled to Jade, taking back the colt. She guarded her until she was on her horse then gutted through the agony as she climbed slowly onto Jake. She motioned for Shane and Cayden to get the weapons then get Darien. With Warrick, Conner and Dylan covering their back, they moved away from the large group of men.

Warrick was grinning as they rode away.

Dylan glanced at her and said, "Good fight Rebel."

Cayden and Shane just kept looking at her in amazement.

Conner hadn't said anything and didn't know what to think. He had been on the receiving end of one of those fists and knew she could hit but would have never guessed the amount of skill she possessed. Jade had told him that she loved to fight but she hadn't mentioned that she fought well.

Darien was pissed that he had been ambushed and huffed in frustration.

Jade and Lynn were quiet.

They rode as fast as they dared until they felt it was safe to stop.

"We will hole up here until she stops bleeding," Dylan said as they rode up to the face of a bluff. "I want all of you up front here with the weapons. Don't let anyone close."

Conner and Dylan helped Rebel off the horse while

Warrick and Darien helped the kids set up the front line.

"God damn it!" Conner said looking at the blood running down her leg. He could tell the pain was excruciating from the look on her face. The gashes across her ribs were wide open and bleeding from the kick to her side and the five slices across her thigh had reopened oozing blood, but the hole in her leg was pouring red.

Conner grabbed the first aid kit and pulled out the rest of the gauze. He looked up at Dylan who glanced back at him worriedly.

"Stop it!" Rebel snapped at them. "I'll be fine. Just cover the wounds so Jade don't get upset." She leaned her head back and tried to calm the adrenaline that was making her heart pound the blood out of the hole faster. "I didn't see any other choice. Did you?"

"No," Dylan agreed. "You saved all our asses back there. But now we get to save yours so no more bitching. We say when we ride and it may be awhile!" he added a scowl to make his point.

Rebel smiled weakly at him. "Fine!" she huffed teasingly.

Conner just shook his head as he bandaged the wounds. "Try to sleep, it will slow the bleeding," he said kissing her on the forehead then followed Dylan to the horses.

"We need a place to hole up," Dylan said. "Some kind of fortress. They are still out there and I don't trust them. She will need a couple of days minimum."

Conner nodded in agreement. "I am going to see if I can find some venison. I will keep my eye out for something while I hunt." He mounted the gilding and rode out of the camp, needing some time to think.

He still couldn't believe how skillfully Rebel had fought especially with a huge gaping bullet hole in her leg. He really didn't know her very well. The brothers had obviously known that she could hold her own in a fight but she had killed the man without a second thought, with her bare hands! He was completely utterly impressed.

He spied a deer and dismounted then stealthily crept

toward the animal knocking an arrow. The blade passed cleanly through the lung dropping it where it stood. Conner thought of all of the men he had killed the exact same way.

Rebel hadn't been upset about the deaths he was responsible for because she knew that she would kill if she had to. She had tried to tell him but he hadn't taken her seriously back then. She had killed the man who grabbed her at the river but that was with a weapon and in self-defense. But this, killing a man with her bare hands in a fight was beyond what he thought she was capable of.

He quickly prepared the deer for transport and tied it across his saddle then turned to find his arrow. He needed to find more supplies soon. He had retrieved the arrows twice before and the blades were getting dull. The first aid kit was running low because of all of the injuries they had received and he was running low on ammunition. He pondered all of this as he led the horse back toward camp. He glanced around him and noticed a stone structure in front of a tall rock faced ridge. It was surrounded by a clearing and had good visuals all around it.

He returned to camp and hung the deer. "Shane would you start skinning this while I check on Rebel?"

"Sure thing," he said and called Cayden to help him.

Conner walked over to Rebel who smiled up at him. Her face was pale and she was weak but alert.

"Couldn't sleep?" he asked, knowing she didn't like to be babied.

"No, I was worried about Jade. She just witnessed her mother kill someone right in front of her," she said frowning regretfully.

Conner glanced at Jade who didn't seem visibly upset. "I'm sure she understands Rebel. It was kind of a life or death situation."

"Ya, but still, it's not an everyday event. I guess this is how you felt about me knowing you killed all those men," she said then added softly, "I should tell you that I watched you kill my captors that day, from my hiding place on the ridge."

Conner was surprised. He stared deep into her eyes. "Why didn't you tell me?"

"I'm sorry, you were just so upset about me even knowing that I didn't want you to know that I witnessed the actual act. I didn't mean to lie to you."

"It's ok," he said sitting down beside her. "I was pretty freaked out and I know I didn't react well. I was afraid you wouldn't want to be around someone capable of that. Of course, I didn't know then that you could have helped me. I mean, I didn't know I was tagging along with a hell cat," he teased.

Rebel grinned. "You know what they say about lions protecting their young. When he grabbed Jade …" She shivered then continued, "I could tell he wasn't going to be a good fighter. It wouldn't have been that easy otherwise with this leg slowing me down. Back home, I used fighting to keep in shape cause I spent so much time in front of the computer researching. But I never really knew then how important it would be and never thought I would use my skills to kill someone."

"Your brothers weren't surprised. Did they know?" he asked.

"That I would kill him? Not really, they just know me. I don't do things half assed. I used them as sparing partners so they knew I could fight but I could tell they were worried about my leg," she said fondly looking over at them.

"Well, I'm impressed by your skill." He rubbed his lip and grinned saying, "Although, I already knew you could fight too."

Rebel smiled at the memory of her fist landing on his mouth. "I never did say sorry about that. I shouldn't have hit you while you were injured."

"Don't be, I shouldn't have said that shit to you. I understand why you left me there and I feel like an ass for starting that argument," he sighed. "Since we are confessing, I should tell you that I spied on you bathing in the river. I was just worried and wanted to make sure you were safe, but I got too close. That's why I couldn't keep control of myself. Why I was so irrational."

She laughed. "I guess you did deserved my fist in your face then."

He nodded with a grin.

Dylan walked over to them eyeing Rebel, "It's nice to hear you laugh Rebel." He glanced at Conner and said, "Thanks for dinner man."

"No problem. Hey, I found a rock structure in front of ridge not far from here. It may provide some protection from the rain that is coming. I think we can guard it pretty easy," he offered.

Dylan looked up to the sky and nodded. "K, how you feelin Rebel? Can you ride for a bit?"

"Yes, I'm feeling much better. I think the bleeding has slowed for the most part."

Dylan turned to the others and said, "Let's pack it up. Conner found us a shelter that we can hole up in."

They rode slowly toward the rock ridge under a thick blanket of dark clouds. Lightning flashed randomly all around them and thunder rumbled threateningly in the distance. Soon they were building a fire in front of the stone structure. They had the horses tied so they could graze and had made Rebel a bed inside.

"I want to sit by the fire for awhile before it rains," she said and eased down to the ground propping herself against the stone wall. She smiled as she watched the boys cook the venison on the fire. It was so nice to be with her family again. She thought about Kira and wondered how life at the ranch was going.

She looked at Jade and Lynn who were chatting with Conner and smiled when Jade laughed at something he said. She was glad they were getting along so well.

Shane handed her some of the meat and sat down beside her. "I knew you could fight Rebel but I didn't know you could fight like that," he said with admiration.

"I'm just sorry you had to see that whole deal, Shane. I hope it doesn't make you think differently of me."

"Oh I think differently about you alright. I think you are a total bad ass!" he smiled and hugged her tightly then went back to help Cayden.

Darien wondered over to her and sat down. "I like him," he said tilting his head toward Conner. "Jade seems to like him too."

They both looked at the three of them talking and laughing together. "I'm glad, it means a lot to me," Rebel said. "I really like him too."

"I'm sorry that you had to kill that man today. It's never an easy thing to deal with no matter how many times you do it," he said softly.

"I just kept thinking about him holding Jade and knowing what he would have done to her. Men like that deserve their fate," she assured him. "I have no regret."

"K, but if you need to talk about it, come see me. How is the leg?"

"Good, I want to move out in the morning," she said hopefully.

"Don't count on it sis," he laughed and stood to take his turn on watch.

After dinner, they prepared for bed. Rebel and the girls slept on one of the sleeping bags and Shane and Cayden slept on the other. The brothers and Conner slept outside each one taking a turn watching over the camp. It started to rain and didn't stop all night.

Kira and Evie sat next to Aden on the big front porch watching the clouds build into a storm above them. They had been documenting the earthquakes that seemed to grow in number each day.

"Don't forget to write down the meteor shower last night," she said to the young woman. "We want to document everything that is happening because it's the only way to predict future events now that we don't have Internet."

Evie jumped as thunder clapped loudly and lightning flashed in the valley in front of them.

Nick walked onto the porch and sat next to her feeling her anxiety. "It's just a thunder storm Evie. We will be just fine."

She nodded and slid closer to him.

Kira smiled, finding their newfound love comforting. They had both been alone for a long time and she was glad that they had each other in this trying time.

"How goes the journals?" he asked.

"I don't know if we will ever need them but something just told me to write it down. Rebel seems to have a way of putting it all together so maybe it will help somehow," she smiled.

"I agree. I sure can't wait until they get home."

The next morning Rebel was still very weak and the pain in her leg kept her from moving much. She hobbled outside and leaned her rifle against the structure and found her seat next to the stone wall. The rain had stopped and the sun was warming up the camp.

Conner and Warrick had taken the horses to drink in a small creek not far away. Darien and Dylan were saddling up to scout around and see if anyone was close by. Shane and Cayden were preparing for their turn on watch and the girls were braiding each other's hair.

Rebel felt grumpy. She hated to hold still and was not happy about staying one more day. She glanced down at her leg and cursed the bad luck.

Dylan came over to her with a cup of coffee and said, "I know you want to move out but you can't so just drink your coffee and keep your scowl to yourself." He smiled affectionately at her and added, "I love you, grumpy face." Then turned to leave.

"I love you too, butt hole!" she glowered at his back.

He just laughed and galloped off with Darien.

Conner caught the exchange as he came back into camp and shook his head. 'These guys are something else,' he thought. He was starting to understand the reason she was so sure they would come for her. They all loved each other like nothing he had ever seen. There wasn't anything short of death that would keep them from protecting each other.

"Mom, you want me to braid your hair?" Jade asked.

"No, just bring me my hat," Rebel answered.

Jade stepped inside and got the hat. She dropped it on Rebels lap. "Your weird," she said then went back inside.

Conner laughed at the accusation and Rebel glared at him.

"Wow," he said, "you are just like a caged tiger. Don't worry, we will most likely leave in the morning."

No response.

"Do you want more coffee?"

She looked up at him trying not to be cranky and nodded yes.

He filled her cup then sat next to her but kept quiet thinking that she would talk to him if she wanted to.

After a while, she said, "I wish we could find another motel room."

The comment was so random and unexpected that Conner's body exploded like a nuclear bomb. He stiffened and clenched his fist trying to control the firestorm threatening to escape his control. He looked at her sharply, the raging fire dancing in his eyes.

She looked back at him, her eyes mirroring the passion.

He leaned into her ear and whispered seductively, "I'll make sure of it!"

She smiled as she felt her stomach tighten and her entire body warm.

Shane walked up to them and said, "Conner, the horses are acting weird. They keep pulling on the lead and stomping around."

Rebel quickly stood and yelled, "Jade, you and Lynn get out here. Hurry!" She turned to Conner and said, "Earthquake."

"Mom, the puppy won't come out!" Jade yelled.

"Cayden get the dog," Rebel ordered. "Where is Warrick?"

Warrick appeared just as the ground started shaking and Cayden staggered out the door holding the dog.

"Get back away from the rock wall!" Rebel yelled trying to keep her footing. "It's a bad one."

Conner took her hand to help steady her. Boulders tumbled down the rock bluff behind the structure. The horses raced past them in a panic having broken their lead. Trees swayed pushing the limits of their strength. The earth buckled and rolled under their feet forcing the stone structure to topple onto itself in a roar and a cloud of dust.

A ghostly silence enveloped them as the ground grew quiet beneath their feet.

Warrick was the first to speak as he threw down the venison he'd managed to hold on to through the quake. "If that took out the bridge, we will have to swim the fucking river!"

Dylan and Darien rode into the damaged camp and looked around. "Is everyone ok?" Dylan asked.

"Ya, but Warrick is crying about swimming the river again," Shane laughed making everyone join in the humor.

Warrick scowled then flipped his brother his middle finger, striding off to find the horses.

"There are signs that a tornado blew through over the hill last night," Darien said. "They are getting worse by the day."

"Rebel, I think you are going to get your wish. That band of men are camped not far from here and I don't want to risk them changing their minds about us," Dylan said then added, "But we are going to move slow and stop often."

Rebel nodded in agreement as Warrick returned with the jittery animals. "We lost one of the horses," he said softly. "Broke his leg."

Jade and Lynn both inhaled sharply and looked at Rebel.

"Girls, I'm sorry, but you know that things like this happen some times," Rebel said reassuringly.

"I'll put Jade's saddle on the extra horse," Warrick said.

They both nodded then turned to ready their stuff.

"We need more horses and more supplies," Rebel

said to Darien. "And we need to get them before that gang of locusts blows through the next city."

"I agree and the people in that town will need to be warned that they are coming," Darien said.

Everyone saddled and packed except Rebel. Conner insisted that she stay still as long as possible. "No unneeded movement!" he had said as he prepared her horse.

When he had finished, he helped her mount.

Rebel smiled when his hand lingered on her butt as he boosted her up. She looked down into his eyes and he smiled devilishly back at her.

"Go easy, k?"

She nodded then followed Darien around the bluff.

They rode all afternoon before coming to the edge of a small little town. There was severe visible earthquake damage to all of the buildings and roads. Debris covered the sidewalks and abandoned cars littered the roads.

They looked around not seeing anyone.

"Too quiet," Darien thought out loud. "Hello!" he yelled as they rode down the street.

A police officer walked around the corner ahead of them carrying a shotgun.

"We are looking to buy some supplies if anyone has them for sale," Darien said to him.

"Most of the population left the city," he said. "The earthquake this morning leveled most of the buildings and homes. There was no reason for them to stay."

"We also wanted to warn you that there is a large band of murdering thieves coming this way. They kill everyone in their path," Rebel said.

The officer looked behind them with concern.

"It may be safer for you to gather everyone and take them to Lincoln City. At least then they would be protected by the National Guard," she added.

"Maybe so," the officer said thoughtfully. "We are still looking for survivors in some of the damaged buildings. But I will have some of the men round everyone up.

"We will help you look and organize the move," Darien offered.

"I would appreciate that if you can spare the time. I am the only official that stayed," he admitted. "Mr. Stevens owned the general store there. He was killed and has no family. You can get whatever supplies you need there if you want."

"Rebel, if you will appropriate and arrange the supplies, we will help the officer," Darien said, then followed the other men around the corner.

Rebel waved to Jade and Lynn to follow her and headed to the store. She stepped into the barely standing structure and looked around. Shelves were overturned and ceiling tile littered the floor. Glass shards crunched underneath her feet and the smell of rotting food filled her nose. She bent over and picked up several backpacks from a display that had tipped over.

"Each of you get a pack and fill it with canned food. Grab an extra set of cloths and extra socks. Be sure to pack a bag full of bathroom stuff. When your bag is full put it by the door and get another one. We can carry two or three per horse. Be careful guys, this building could come down."

As the girls went to work on the food, Rebel focused on the extremely small first aid section. She grabbed all the gauze, tape and ointment that she could find. She stuffed in rubbing alcohol, cotton balls and pain medication then found a rack of bandanas and threw them in. As she walked past the fishing supplies she thought about her stitches and threw in some fishing line and grabbed a sewing kit full of needles.

They placed their packs by the door and headed for the clothing. "Jade, both of you get a hat so you don't get so sunburned," Rebel said as she picked out some sunglasses.

After she had the supplies ready, she turned to the girls, "Why don't you guys eat here while we wait for the men. I'm going up the road to that doctors office."

She picked up an empty backpack and walked up the street to the badly damaged office building. The waist high window had been broken out so she climbed through it and walked down the hall to the supply room. She opened the cabinet and smiled as she stuffed the bag full of supplies.

Conner and the brothers returned a little later and joined the girls in their feast, which included potato chips and warm pop.

Rebel stashed her bag by the door as she entered and laughed at the boys who were stuffing candy bars in their mouths.

"Sugar is good for you," Cayden said sheepishly.

"I better have one then," she laughed opening the wrapper. "So did you find everyone? Are they leaving?"

"The officer thinks everyone is accounted for. Everyone in the city left, but there are a lot of people who live in the rural areas outside of town that don't want to leave their homes," Dylan said sadly. "Hopefully they can defend themselves."

"The officer gave us directions to a ranch just west of town. He said that the man there will sell us some horses," Darien said.

"K, let's move out," Warrick said. "Rebel, how is the leg?"

"I'm good," she said. "Ready to ride."

"Good, I want to reach the river tonight and try to find a standing bridge," Warrick said then scowled daring anyone to make a swimming joke.

Dylan just grinned and led the group toward the horse ranch.

Rows of white fences told them that they were nearing the ranch. Almost a hundred head of horses scattered the pastures. Jade and Lynn gasped and pointed at several of the animals. They rode up to the main house and dismounted.

A distinguished looking older gentleman stepped outside and looked at them suspiciously.

"Officer Watts sent us. He said you might sell us a couple horses," Darien said to ease the man's stress.

"I see," the relieved man said as he walked toward them. "As you can see, I have more than I can deal with right now. I have some nice ranch stock that you can choose from if your needing that sort. Right this way."

Darien followed the man and picked out five nice gildings that were well broke and looked physically fit. He saddled one of them and helped Jade mount.

"How much do we owe you?" Rebel asked.

"No, I don't need the money," the man said. "And I certainly don't need the horses."

Darien thanked him and told him about the danger on its way toward him then waved goodbye.

That evening, they reached the banks of the Missouri River and made camp. Rebel was relieved to have gotten new supplies and the kids were enjoying another meal that didn't include venison. She smiled at them as they joked with each other, enjoying each other's company.

She walked up the bank of the river and stood staring at the swollen body of water. The familiar buzz of electricity engulfed her as Conner walked up behind her and put his arms around her. She leaned back into his thick solid chest and said, "It's flooding. The quake must have taken out the dams upriver."

"Tomorrow we will ride until we find a bridge or overpass. We can't swim it, its too dangerous for the girls," he said.

"Come on, let's eat and get some fresh bandages on our wounds," she said leading him back to camp.

The next morning, they rode south looking for a way to cross the swollen river. The current was fast and the water was muddy.

Warrick kept glancing over the bank. "We might have to ride clean into Kansas before we find a bridge. That quake was bad."

"There is a bridge just ahead. It may be standing," Darien soothed looking through his scope.

As they rode closer Dylan laughed at the tension on Warrick's face. "It's just a wooden bridge but it looks to be intact," he said.

Rebel dismounted and walked to the first plank. She looked back at Dylan. "It's not stable. It must have been rattled pretty good." She stepped out over the water and jumped a couple of time. "But I say it's worth the risk."

"I'll go first," Darien volunteered as he rode past her. He reached the other side and yelled back, "Warrick bring one of the pack horses."

Warrick crossed followed by Dylan and the other pack animal.

"K, Jade you go, then Lynn," Rebel directed feeling a little nervous.

Cayden and Shane took their turns and waited expectantly for Rebel.

Rebel nervously watched the violent water churning below her as she crossed. The planks under Jake's feet creaked and shuttered with each step. She hated water and was relieved to reach the other side of the river.

"Are you ok?" Conner asked as he reached her from the other side.

"Ya, I have some pretty horrid phobias and water is one of them," she admitted.

"I wouldn't have guessed. I know you're afraid of the dark, what are the others?" he asked curiously as the group headed west.

"She's afraid of heights," Jade said lightheartedly.

"God, so am I," Dylan laughed. "I always said, if I ever fall off of a cliff or building, I hope I have an air hose or an extension cord in my hand."

Lynn looked at him strangely and said, "Why, I don't get it."

All three brothers laughed again and said in unison, "Because one of them will get caught on something."

Rebel laughed with everyone then explained to Lynn who was still confused, "You would have to be a construction guy to get that one. Hoses and cords are always hanging up on shit while your working."

Conner smiled and looked back at Rebel. "Are there more?"

"Yes, I'm extremely claustrophobic. Not the small room shit, it's my hands being held or tied. I can't take it. So if I ever get arrested again, just shoot me," she said seriously.

Conner laughed and said, "You've been arrested?"

"It's a long story."

He could tell she didn't want to talk about it so he said, "Well, you hide your fears well. I would have never guessed you had any vulnerability as tough as you are."

"Just don't tell anyone or I'll have to kill you," Rebel teased. "When those men hit me over the head and took me, I woke up tied to a tree. I about flipped out. The only reason I made it through is because I had a knife in my boot and was able to cut the rope. I was so pissed off about it, I beat the crap out of them."

Conner inhaled sharply remembering the blood on the men before he killed them. "I wondered why they were bleeding but I was so caught up in the moment, it slipped my mind. I can't believe you took on all four of them."

Rebel just shrugged with a grin and said, "They were a bunch of pussy's."

"God, now I'm even more upset about it."

"Hold up!" Warrick barked. "Did you hear that?"

"What was it?" Dylan asked. "We should be well south of the other gang."

"No, it wasn't human," Warrick said looking around.

"Keep moving," Darien urged. "Warrick fall behind and make sure nothing is following us."

Jade rode closer to Rebel and Lynn eased up next to Cayden and Shane as they rode forward up the side of a small mountain.

When they got to the top, Dylan and Darien dismounted to wait for Warrick who was still in the clearing a half-mile below them.

Warrick's gilding suddenly reared and spun around. He reared again, this time going over backwards and landing on top of him.

The brothers both grabbed their rifles and dropped behind a rock prepared to cover him.

The horse staggered to its feet just as eight huge gray wolves launched toward him. Warrick scrambled to his feet and ran toward the hill with the snarling animals right on his ass.

"Fuck!" Darien yelled as he looked through his scope and fired dropping the closest attacker.

Dylan followed suite taking out a second animal.

Conner grabbed his rifle to help and shot still astride his horse.

"Don't hit me you fuckers!" Warrick yelled still running as fast as he could toward them.

One by one the three men killed the vicious wolves. Warrick walked the last few yards to the top of the ridge and stood panting, desperately trying to catch his breath.

"I don't think I've ever seen you run that fast, or that far," Cayden laughed then turned to Shane. "Have you?"

"No, I've never seen him run at all," Shane laughed with him.

"Shut up you little bastards!" Warrick said finally able to breathe. "Now go get my horse!"

The boys headed back down the mountain still laughing.

"They must have come from the Omaha zoo," Rebel said. "That place was huge. There could be other dangerous animals on the loose. We need to keep an eye out."

Jade looked around nervously and said, "Ya, like tigers, lions and gorillas."

"They had grizzlies too, every kind of bear you can imagine, but I think I would be most afraid of the gorillas," Rebel agreed then saw the blood running down Conner's shirt. "God damn it Conner! No more rifle for you!"

Conner just shrugged and slid his rifle in the scabbard.

"Let's get going," Dylan said as the boys returned with Warrick's horse.

"I don't understand why zoo animals would attack someone. Aren't they used to people?" Lynn asked as they rode west.

"I'm sure that some of them are more aggressive

and mean than others but remember that they are all wild animals and should never be taken for granted. Just like that horse your riding. Never turn your back on him or you could be injured," Darien explained. "Wolves are naturally pack hunters so both their hunger and their instincts fed the urge to attack."

Lynn nodded in understanding.

They rode for several miles chatting about the animals when Darien suddenly reined his horse to a stop and held up his hand, "I hear gunfire."

Dylan nodded in agreement then looked back at the kids. "We either go around or we leave the kids and go check it out."

"I think we should know what we are facing," Warrick said. "There was a little house back there, we could hide the kids there."

"Rebel," Darien said, "you take the kids back to the house and wait with them until we come back."

Rebel scowled and turned her horse back down the road. "Come on guys, let's get out of sight."

The brothers and Conner headed south toward the gunfire. "It's just up ahead," Warrick pointed out. "Let's top that ridge and scope it out from there."

Conner pushed his gilding up the hillside and dismounted. He pulled out his rifle and looked through the scope into the valley below. "Jesus!" he exclaimed when he saw the bloody battle unfolding through the lens.

"I'm guessing the men to the north is that other gang from Omaha. But that other group look like militia," Darien said.

"The gang is going to flank them," Warrick said. "Whose side are we on here?"

"I'm sure as hell not with the gang!" Darien answered. "Those militia guys are probably retired or ex military. They could be the good guys."

"There is no way of knowing until we can talk to them but we do know that the gang isn't good so I say we back the militia," Dylan reasoned.

"I agree," Warrick said. "What do you think Conner?"

"I'd go with the militia guys here," he answered. "We can at least make it a fair fight with the rifles from here."

Darien picked a large boulder and leaned his rifle across it. Everyone followed his lead and took cover pointing their rifles into the group of men advancing on the weak side of the militia. They all fired at the same time dropping four men. Then fired again.

A man who seemed to be leading the gang pointed at them and yelled something inaudible in the gunfire.

"If we can't hold them back, we will have to get to the horses," Warrick yelled.

Thirty men from the gang broke from the main group and headed their way. "Here they come!" Darien said firing again followed by the other three.

"Look, the militia is sending some of their guys this way too," Warrick said. "I hope they realize we're on their side."

"They are going to set up below us. Fire over their heads," Dylan said.

"Damn!" Conner added as he fired again. "That gang is almost a hundred strong. How many on the other side?'

"I'm guessing a little over a hundred. I hope our ammo holds up or we will have to go hand to hand," Warrick said.

"I hear Conner is pretty good with a bow," Darien grinned.

"And a knife!" Warrick added squeezing the trigger.

"Ya, well I hear you guys are pretty good yourselves," Conner returned.

"Fuck!" I'm out of ammo," Dylan yelled.

"Here take Rebels rifle," Conner offered. "She insisted I take it."

"She's something ain't she?" Dylan said.

"Yes, she is," Conner laughed.

"The gang is retreating!" Darien exclaimed. "Now

maybe we will find out how this all came down."

Conner and the brothers mounted and rode down to the small group of men below them.

Chapter 9

Rebel and the kids tied the horses and went into the house.

"Let's see if they left any canned food," Shane said as they made themselves at home.

"Hey look! The cabinets are full!" Cayden yelled after following Shane into the kitchen. "These people must have left in a hurry."

"We will find a bag and pack it up," Jade said looking at Lynn who nodded.

Rebel was pacing by the window. She didn't like waiting around wondering if one of the brothers or Conner were in danger. She listened to the kids talking and knew that she needed to stay here and protect them.

She looked out the window again just as a man ran down the road in front of the house. "Shane, come here! A man just ran down the road."

Shane peered out the window. "Look! There are men chasing him! What should we do?"

"You stay here. I will follow them on the horse and see what's up. If something happens go find the brothers," she instructed. "I'm taking your rifle."

She rushed outside, mounted Jake and followed the men. She stayed off the road, edging forward in the cover of brush and trees. The man being chased wasn't wearing shoes and he was bleeding profusely from his nose. He was battered and bruised and looked like he would fall at any moment. Rebel wasn't sure at this point if he deserved this treatment, but she knew she had to find out.

There were five men chasing him, each holding a knife. She couldn't make out any other weapons. They didn't seem to be from a gang so maybe they were just some local men from a nearby town.

The five men stopped and hunched over to catch their breath giving the bloody man the same opportunity. Rebel moved in and pointed the colt at them saying, "What's this about gentlemen?"

All five men spun around in surprise. "This ain't

none of your business lady," one of them said.

"Maybe, maybe not. Why are you chasing this man?' she asked.

"He raped my sister! And I'm going to kill him!" a very young man exclaimed.

Rebel turned to the barefoot bleeding man and asked, "Is this true?"

"No! She loves me. Tom is her ex boyfriend and talked these guys into beating me," he yelled scowling.

"Murder is still against the law," Rebel said turning back to the five men in front of her. "Just because the police are busy, doesn't mean you will get away with this kind of aggression."

"What are you going to do about it?" Tom asked. "We haven't seen the police for weeks."

Rebel nudged Jake up close to the man and looked down at him past the gun. "The National Guard is well equipped to come down here and take you back to Omaha. And believe me, I think it would be well worth my time to ride up there and inform them of this situation."

Tom looked at his buddies for backup. Receiving no input from them, he hung his head.

"Now turn around and walk away. I will be informing the authorities to keep an eye on you," Rebel threatened.

The five men sulked back down the road. The bloody man walked up to Rebel and said, "Thank you. I think they would have killed me if you hadn't stopped them."

"They still might if you go back there. The fact is that there aren't many police officers left out here so you are still in danger," Rebel said regretfully.

The bloody man shrugged, "I'll just have to be careful. Thanks for your help." He turned and followed the five men back down the road.

Rebel looked around trying to figure out where she was. She thought she had followed the men about a mile north but she wasn't sure. Suddenly she heard gunfire ring out and screaming from the direction the men just went.

She urged Jake off the road taking cover. 'What the fuck?' she wondered as she eased her horse around the corner and peeked past the trees. The six men she had just talked to hadn't been carrying guns.

'Oh my God!' Rebel breathed. It was the men she who tried to kidnap Jade. She almost panicked when she caught a glimpse of the six dead bodies lying in the middle of the road. 'Murdering bastards!' she thought.

She waited hoping that they would ride north. "Please don't come this way," she prayed but no such luck. They mounted and started in her direction.

"Fuck!" she breathed knowing that their path would take them way to close to the house where the kids were. This was bad, how the hell was she going to protect them?

She rode ahead of them, just out of sight knowing that if they got too close to the kid's hideout she would have to show herself and lead them away from it. 'And what will I do then?' she thought trying to control the panic exploding through her again.

She turned Jake back the way she came careful to stay out of sight. She could hear them riding behind her talking and laughing loudly. She held her breath hoping they would turn but luck just wasn't on her side. They turned onto the road that would lead them straight for the kids. "Son of a bitch!" she cursed under her breath.

This was it. She would have to show herself. She waited until she came to a crossroad then eased Jake into the middle of the road and waited. She didn't have to wait long though before a scout seen her and signaled his discovery to the entire group of almost a hundred men.

She kicked Jake into a full out run followed closely by the large band of savages. She knew she was in trouble. The brothers were miles away and the kids had no idea where she was. She also knew that if she hadn't followed those six men, this band of murderers would have rode straight to the house they were hiding in and probably killed them all.

Rebel could feel Jake weaken and knew he was

getting tired as she raced on with the men right behind her. She hoped that the brothers were west of her position. She was well south of the house where the kids were so she turned Jake west on the next cross road still pushing him hard.

The brothers and Conner rode down the hill toward the eight men riding toward them.

Darien looked at Dylan and said, "We were right, looks like military. Could be friend or enemy, still hard to tell."

"Hello," he said as they reached the riders.

The lead man of the group wore a camo ball cap and jacket. He had several tattoos on his forearms and a scar across his cheek. "Hello," he said back. "Appreciate your help. Are you guys local or passin through?"

"We are passing through on our way to Idaho. We heard the ruckus and noticed you were about to be flanked so we decided to make the odds a little more even. And you?" Darien asked.

"Neither. We heard that there is a large group of men terrorizing towns across the Midwest. We came up from Kansas City to stop them but we ran into this gang this morning and they engaged us in the gunfight. I guess you know the rest," the scarred man said.

"We've run into those men your talking about several times in the last few days. They are deadly," Dylan said.

"We would appreciate any information about their location," a second man stated. He wore a black hunting vest and a pair of pistols around his hips.

"They are almost a hundred strong, mounted and well armed. Why would you boys risk your lives to take them on let alone this gang?" Warrick asked. "You look militaryish, are you doing this for a military reason or is it personal?"

"We are retired and ex military and some in our militia were once police. We are over a hundred strong as well and are just wanting to help people until the government can regain control in the rural areas," the scarred man said.

"Well then, first we should let you know that there is another large gang from Omaha just over the river into Iowa. That is where we met up with the band of ravagers the first time. They rode straight into the gang and their numbers were significantly decreased in the ensuing gunfight. One of our people was shot in the battle," Darien explained.

"We barely escaped the second run in, and had to fight our way out," Warrick added.

"Sounds like you were lucky," the man in the black vest said. "We aim to take them all out."

"Yesterday we helped a local cop evacuate a small town in their path," Dylan said. "We would help you further today but we need to protect our family here."

"We understand. We will be able to handle them. By the way, we have a young man with us who was stranded in Kansas and needs to get to Wyoming. You willing to let him ride with you?" the scarred man asked.

"Sure, if he's a good boy," Warrick answered.

"He is, I will speak for him," the man in the black vest said.

"We will ride east with you for a bit. There are zoo animals scattered between here and the river so keep an eye out. We took out eight wolves that attacked us. There is a bridge to cross the river due east of here but I don't know if it will handle a hundred horses. It's badly damaged. You will run into the men you seek just across the river if they aren't closer by now," Darien said.

"We appreciate the info," the scared man said.

The large force of men rode east several miles before entering a large clearing. Conner eased into a position at the outside of the group. He was feeling something and anxiously scoured the edge of the meadow across from them. His big gilding perked his ears up and pulled on the bit. Conner followed the animals gaze and nearly cried out as Jake and Rebel suddenly burst out of the trees at a dead run on the other side of the meadow with a hundred mounted men right on her ass.

Rebel came through the trees and straight into the face of another large group of men. She kept riding though, knowing that nothing was more dangerous than what followed her. She blew through the front line of riders barely catching a glimpse of Darien with a look of amazement on his face.

'The brothers are with them. Thank god!' she thought as she slowed Jake to a walk smack in the middle of the very large army of men.

She turned him around and watched as the bastards that chased her skidded their horses to a stop a mere hundred yards in front of her brothers and their new friends.

An ominous silence emanated through the meadow lasting almost a full minute, then total hell broke loose. Over two hundred guns fired in a single blast that thundered through the trees rebounding around them in a circular pattern.

Men yelled, horses screamed and rifles exploded in a deafening roar transforming the silent meadow instantly into a war zone.

Jake was still heaving so Rebel kept him moving at a slow walk. "Easy big boy," she soothed worriedly. "That was a long run for you, wasn't it." He twitched his ears at her voice as his breathing settled somewhat. He wouldn't have made it much further. It was sheer luck that she came into the same meadow that the brothers and their friends had been in. She eased Jake to the side of the meadow and deep into the thick grove of trees. It would not be good for him to have to run again right now.

Conner rode up to her and asked, "Are you ok? What happened?"

"I watched them murder six unarmed men about a mile away from the house. They were on a path heading straight for us. I had no choice Conner, I had to get them to chase me away from the kids," Rebel explained.

"You were lucky Rebel. If we hadn't been here they

would have caught you. Jake wouldn't have made it much further," he said worriedly.

"I know, but they would have had us trapped," she defended.

"I want you to stay here. This militia group traveled all the way here from Kansas City just to take them out so this will be a battle to the death," Conner said. "And the brothers have committed to help them."

"Be careful," she said frowning as he rode back into the carnage. She looked at the fight and had no intention of sitting it out. Those men would have killed the kids and she was feeling a little vengeful. She led Jake closer to the edge of the clearing looking for cover. She came across a scatter of large boulders at the edge of the tree line and tucked Jake behind them. She climbed up into the rock formation and leveled her rifle toward the mayhem.

Her position was just to the side of the militia's front line and it didn't surprise her that Conner and all three of her brothers were right up there in the lead. She looked through the scope of her rifle and put the crosshairs on the chest of a man preparing to shoot at one of their new friends. She squeezed the trigger and watched the man fall from his horse. She pulled off four more shots and replaced the clip with the last of her ammo. She cursed herself under her breath for only grabbing one extra clip.

Some of the militia guys were running out of ammunition too and were abandoning their horses for hand-to-hand combat. Conner traded his rifle for his bow and shot from his horse dropping the man riding toward him. He launched off of the gilding and pulled off another kill on the run. Rebel held her breath when another rider turned his attention on him. She didn't hesitate and shot the man before he reached him.

Conner whipped his head around to her and smiled a thank you, then turned back to the fight. God, even in the middle of death and gun smoke, her body flared at the connection between them.

She shrugged off her emotions and aimed at a mounted man riding toward a dark haired young man who had just ran out of ammo in his pistol and panicked. She fired just as the rider came into pistol range of him. The rider toppled off of his horse and rolled to poor kids feet. He looked toward her in surprise then grabbed the dead man's gun and went back to work.

Everyone was off their horses now and most were fighting with knives and fists because they didn't have time to reload their weapons. Rebel had three more shots and was keeping an eye on Conner and her brothers. Dylan was fighting a large man and Rebel noticed that a second man was on his way to help his murdering friend. She pulled the trigger, dropping him to keep the fight fair.

Two hundred horses were loose and frightened. They screamed and bolted in every direction. Twenty head stampeded past her into the trees. The sound of men fighting, men shooting, and men dying infiltrated her ears making her want to cover them. Jake was stomping and blowing nervously behind her.

She tried to overlook the dead bodies littering the meadow and focus on keeping her men safe. She looked through the scope and located all of her brothers but couldn't see Conner. 'Where are you?' she thought.

She pointed the glass back at Warrick who was fighting two men at the same time. "Son of a Bitch! Typical, Warrick." she said out loud. She looked to his right and saw a third man rushing toward him. She fired, dropping the stunned man about ten feet away from the unfair fight.

'One more shot,' she thought trying to focus. She scanned the scene again and came upon Darien just as a bloody man slammed a knife into his chest. "Darien!" she screamed, watching him fall then pulled the rifle to her shoulder and shot the man as he raised the knife for another blow. She threw down the rifle and scurried down the face of the boulder hurrying through the battlefield to reach her brother.

"Darien!" she yelled as she reached his side. "Oh, thank god, you're alive!"

Darien looked down at the knife wound and smiled.

"I'm good," he said lightheartedly.

She smiled down at her brother and said, "Let's get you out of here." She helped him stand and led him back to the boulders she had hidden in, propping him up behind the shelter of a big rock. She scurried around to Jake and retrieved her shotgun. "Here, take this," she said and turned to check on the others.

She could see Dylan and Warrick still fighting but Conner was not in the meadow. The militia had almost eradicated the murdering band of men and the finality of death was weighing heavily in the air. The smell from the mixture of gunpowder and blood threatened to overcome her. She fought to keep herself together so she could find Conner.

She pulled the colt from her side and walked along the tree line searching. Nothing. She spied his big gilding standing just inside the brush and took up his reins looking around again then mounted the animal. After searching the entire outer edge of the meadow, she looked into the bloody field of death and tried to calm her racing pulse as panic settled in. It was the only place she hadn't looked.

She rode back to Darien and asked in a quivering voice, "Did you see Conner?"

"No sis, I didn't. We'll find him," he said solemnly, waving Warrick and Dylan over.

"God damn, you guys!" Rebel said when they got closer and she could see that they were covered in blood. She quickly made sure the wounds weren't life threatening then looked in the clearing and said, "I don't see Conner."

Warrick and Dylan looked at each other, then followed her gaze with concern. "I'm sure he's fine Rebel," Dylan said. "You stay here with Darien, we will take a look around." They walked into the meadow talking quietly.

Rebel turned her attention to the knife wound on Darien's chest. She helped him out of his shirt and examined the damage. The hole was just above his collarbone on the right side. "It's deep," she observed. "It seems to have missed the artery by a fraction of an inch. It is almost the same place Conner was shot." She cleaned the bleeding hole and pushed his shirt into it. "We need to keep pressure on it."

"Thanks sis, for getting him for me. I don't think he would have missed my heart the second time," Darien said seriously.

Rebel smiled at her oldest brother and squeezed his hand.

He looked past her and smiled. "They found him."

Rebel turned as Warrick and Dylan helped Conner walk toward them. "Thank God."

"We found him laying there all crumpled up. I thought he was dead. Scared the shit out of me. But he was just unconscious," Warrick said.

Conner's face was ashen and his bullet wound was bleeding badly. "Here set him by Darien. Conner? Are you ok?" Rebel asked as the brothers helped him lean back against a rock.

"Yes," he said obviously in serious pain. "My wound started bleeding from the pressure of the bow. I had only shot once since I was injured. After my arrows were gone, I went hand to hand with a guy who happened to notice the blood and gun butted me square in the old wound then he punched me in the ribs. I managed to slit his throat before I blacked out."

The militia's leader walked toward them leading their horses. "I sure appreciate you helping out. We are going to make camp a couple of miles from here, you are welcome to hang with us for the night if you'd like." He turned to Rebel, reaching out his hand. "I'm Dave, I hear you helped us too little lady. Danny there," he said pointing to the dark haired young man, "Danny said that you saved his life and he is sure grateful."

Rebel smiled at Danny then looked at Dave and replied, "I'm sorry that I surprised you with a hundred men like that. You all saved my life too."

"You just helped us fulfill our mission faster than we had anticipated. I'm glad to have been in the right place at the right time," he laughed. "We have a doctor riding with us, so after he has treated the more severe injuries, we will have him stitch you guys up. See you at camp." Then he left to help transport his men.

Rebel stood up and said, "I'll go get the kids and meet you at camp. Dylan, can I ride Ace? I don't want to ride Jake anymore today," Rebel asked.

"Rebel, you can't ride anymore today either," Dylan answered looking at blood running down her thigh. "I want the doc to look at your leg too. I'll go get the kids." He turned and mounted the gilding before Rebel could argue.

She turned to Darien and Conner then looked at Warrick's bloody body. "Well, aren't we a sight."

"Can you two ride?" Warrick asked.

They both nodded yes and stood up. Rebel helped Conner mount and Warrick helped Darien. She retrieved Jake from behind the boulders and climbed on wincing at the pain in her leg then followed the guys to the campsite.

The fires were already burning and the cook had made a delicious stew with some beefsteaks on the side.

The doc had made his rounds and was now working on Darien's knife wound with concern. "I'm worried about infection in a wound this deep. You never know where that knife could have been."

"We have some antibiotic if he needs it," Rebel said.

"Good cause I'm guessing you will," the Doc replied. "I've got you bandaged up good and the bleeding has lessened but I don't want you to move very much for the next few days. Who is next?"

"Rebel is next!" Warrick said firmly. "She was shot in the thigh a couple days ago and the wound is bleeding badly again."

The Doc looked at her leg then looked around at the camp full of men. "These are good guys, but we shouldn't look at your wound out here in the open."

"I'll set up her tent," Warrick agreed. "Take a look at Conner while I work."

Rebel knelt down beside Conner sensing that he was in severe pain. His face was now almost blue and she bit her lip as she helped him remove his shirt so the doc could take a look.

The doctor knelt down beside her and listened to his heart rate then turned to Rebel. "His pulse is weak and his blood pressure is low. This man should be in a hospital. He shouldn't be moving let alone riding into a fight like that one."

Connor felt Rebel stiffen at the news and smiled at her weakly.

"So, you've both been shot. You guys have been busy," the Doc added as he looked closely at the bullet wound. "Yes, it was healing good until it was reopened. All we can do is keep you still and stop the bleeding. It doesn't look infected. He glanced down at Conner's ribs and said, "I assume that bruise hides a few broken ribs. They don't look like they are healing correctly, or maybe," he mumbled to himself feeling the bones with his fingers, "ya, they aren't just broken, they are shattered. At least four of them. No wonder you are in such pain. When you lose the structure of your ribs, your heart and lungs are dangerously at risk. This could kill you. I'm amazed you're breathing at all."

"I have the tent standing Doc, whenever you are ready," Warrick interrupted.

"Thank you Warrick," Rebel said as she followed the Doc inside.

Conner watched her walk inside and grinned as Warrick stood guard at the door in a very protective stance. "I find your family quite intriguing," he said to Darien. "I didn't really get it until I seen you guys interact together."

"We are lucky," Darien agreed. "Unconditional love is a hard thing to come by. It runs deep with us. Blood is blood, is what we always say." He paused then said, "She saved my life today and I will be there to save hers tomorrow."

Conner nodded, "She saved mine today, too."

They both looked up as Rebel followed the Doc out of the tent.

"What's the deal?" Conner asked, "Are her wounds going to heal ok?"

The Doc glanced back at Rebel and asked, "Did she really kill that cat or is she pulling my leg?"

Conner, Darien and Warrick started laughing. "No, Doc, she isn't pulling your leg. She killed the cat practically with her bare hands. You'd just have to know her."

The Doc shook his head then said, "The wounds from the cat are going to heal fine but the leg is badly damaged inside from the gunshot. Watch it close for infection. It's not healing right and I can't do anything for it in the field. My suggestion is she doesn't move at all for at least two weeks and especially don't ride until you can find a hospital."

Rebel looked at Conner then at Darien. They stubbornly looked back at her daring her to argue. She turned to Warrick who crossed his big arms across his chest and glared at her defiantly.

"God damn it! Fuck all you all!" she said stomping over to Jake to unsaddle him.

Dylan rode up interrupting the three men staring after Rebel. "What? What did she do?" he asked very amused.

"She just told us all to fuck off!" Darien said with a grin. "Doc says she can't move for two weeks and you know how she feels about that."

Jade smiled knowing how her mother could rattle her uncle's. She dismounted and followed her to give her a hug.

"Well," the Doc said trying to cover his surprise. "Let's get you two stitched up. Warrick that gash on your arm looks pretty bad."

After the doctor had fixed them all up and the kids had gotten dinner, Rebel helped the girls roll out their sleeping bags in the tent.

"I will sleep in the tent with the girls," Rebel announced and waved good night. She hadn't taken the doctors warning about the large group of men lightly and though she knew that Conner and her brothers would protect them, there was no reason to test the theory.

Conner and the brothers retrieved their blankets and

each took a spot around the fire. Conner looked at the tent and sighed. Rebel was angry with all of them but together they might be able to keep her down for a few days.

Rebel lay in bed for several hours thinking about the ride home. She knew that it was going to be rough with the injuries that they had all suffered. She thought about how easily Conner had fit in with her brothers and was now taking their side against her. She couldn't blame them though. She knew her wound wasn't healing right and really did need the time to recover.

She and the girls slept in late the next morning feeling safe with over a hundred men guarding them. Conner and the brothers were sitting around the fire still drinking coffee when she finally poked her head out of the tent.

"I'm glad you finally got some sleep Rebel. How are you feeling this morning?" Conner asked.

She hobbled over to a log by the fire and sat down. "I'm fine. I guess I didn't realize how tired I was."

Dylan pushed a cup of coffee into her hand with a smile.

"The young man that you saved yesterday, Danny, is going to ride with us to Wyoming. Is that cool?" Darien asked.

"Of course, where is everybody?" she asked suddenly noticing that a large number of men weren't in camp.

"They went to bury the dead," Warrick said solemnly.

"The cook saved you and the girls some breakfast," Dylan said pointing to a pan by the fire. "He said you are a brave lady and you need to eat."

Rebel looked toward the main fire and waved a thank you at the cook.

"The militia is moving on as soon as they get back," Darien said. "We need to find a place to hole up again cause I really don't want Rebel riding at all."

"Ya, and Conner shouldn't ride with those broken ribs," Warrick added. "And Darien will be a worthless shot until his arm is better."

"Fuck you, I can shoot left handed," Darien said clearly offended.

"I've seen you shoot left handed and like I said, worthless," Warrick shot back laughing.

Darien flipped him the bird and said, "Dave said that there is a town southwest of here that is pretty much abandoned. Maybe we can find a motel or something to stay in for awhile."

Conner shot a devilish grin at Rebel whose body responded in an explosion making her spill her coffee down her shirt.

"God damn it!" she yelled, then blushed when all the brothers looked at her curiously. She glared at Conner who just kept grinning.

"It will be much safer to travel now," Shane pointed out.

"I agree," Darien nodded. "We will head out as soon as the girls wake up. Dave said we should reach our destination by nightfall."

Warrick and Dylan both stood.

"We will saddle the horses. You guys just stay still as long as you can," Dylan said as they strode away.

A few minutes later, the girls poked their heads out of the tent.

"Sorry, we didn't mean to sleep so late," Jade said sheepishly.

"I'm glad you did, you needed the rest," Darien said fondly. "Come eat cause we will be leaving soon."

Shane and Cayden folded the tents and repacked the horses.

Rebel decided to ride one of the new horses and let Jake rest after his very long sprint yesterday.

Warrick gathered up several of the dead men's horses to add to their growing herd of pack animals as well as bags of extra rifles and hand guns.

"Are you ready?" he asked the girls who nodded.

Darien said goodbye to Dave and waved to the large group of men then introduced the dark haired young man to the kids. "This is Danny, he will be riding with us to Wyoming."

Rebel raised her eyebrow at Jade who tensed in her saddle and blushed.

Conner caught the exchange and smiled. Then grimaced in pain as he mounted his horse. It was going to be a long afternoon.

Danny, Shane, Cayden and Lynn talked and laughed as they rode side by side down the road. Jade was abnormally quiet and rode next to Rebel.

"Is everything ok?" Rebel asked her.

"Yes, I just really need a shower," Jade sulked.

"We are going to try to find a motel or something to stay in for awhile. If we do and we can find water, we will be able to take a hot bath," Rebel soothed.

"Really? That would be awesome," Jade said excitedly.

'Ya, awesome,' Rebel thought to herself. She looked at Conner anticipating the sweet anxiety of her body's response to the thought. As usual, he looked back at her as if he could feel her eyes on him. 'That is so curious,' she thought.

Later that evening, they rode into the small town that Dave had told them about. It was quiet and like all the other towns had abandoned cars in the streets and earthquake damaged buildings. The horses hooves clipped loudly on the sidewalk, echoing off the empty structures.

"I don't see a motel," Darien said. "Maybe it's outside of town."

"We need to get some ammo, I'm going to see if anyone is around," Dylan said. He dismounted and walked across the street to a storefront and pounded on the door.

Warrick rode around the block and yelled back, "Hey, they have a hardware store with guns." He dismounted and looked through the door. "No one is here, I say we break in."

"I will stand guard with the ladies. Dylan, Warrick, take the boys in from the back and get the ammo," Darien instructed.

"I should go in and see if I can find arrows for my bow," Conner said sliding painfully off his horse.

Rebel and Darien led the girls and the horses to the side of the building and waited. Rebel noticed a newspaper vending machine by the door. She walked over and kicked the glass out of the front of the box and took out a paper.

"That's old news," Jade laughed.

Rebel smiled at her joke then flipped through the pages looking for an advertisement for the local motel. There it was. She walked over to Darien and said, "Can we find that address?"

Darien looked at the street signs then back to Rebel. "It looks like it's just down the main road on the outside of town," he said excitedly.

The boys came back handing each of the girls a soda and a candy bar. Conner was smiling and inspecting a handful of arrows and Warrick and Dylan loaded two large duffle bags full of ammo onto the packhorses.

"Follow me," Darien said leading them toward the motel.

"I hope there is water. Maybe a creek nearby," Conner said innocently teasing Rebel.

"Me too," Rebel said softly to antagonize him. It worked because she heard him inhale sharply in response, which almost made her giggle out loud.

"There it is," Darien said pointing to an L shaped structure with ten rooms and an office. "There is smoke coming out of the chimney in the kitchen area. Someone is there. I'll check it out."

Darien opened the office door and went inside. "Hello," he yelled throughout the building. "Is anyone here?" He turned toward the kitchen and was stopped short by the barrel of a shotgun pointed into his chest.

"Hello!" a woman said from behind the gun.

"Hello, ma'am, are you the owner here? We would like to rent some rooms from you for a week or so," he said calmly trying to reassure her.

Her only response was a thorough up and down of

the man in front of her.

"Ma'am, is that a possibility?" Darien gently urged.

The woman held tight to the shotgun obviously afraid, "I haven't rented the rooms since the power went out."

"I assure you, you will be safe. I am here with my sister and four brothers and several friends. Some of them are injured and need to heal before we continue our journey to Idaho," he said trying to ease her anxiety. "I'll bring them in to meet you. Is that ok?"

The woman slowly lowered the weapon. She looked out the window and said, "Yes, that would be fine."

Darien waved to the others to come inside and introduced them to the woman by name. "And this is…." he looked at the woman expectantly.

"I…, I am Richelle, my friends call me Ric," she said. "Back when I had friends anyway."

Darien unconsciously leaned forward wanting to comfort her. "What happened here? Why has everyone left town?" he asked.

Ric sighed and said, "This was a very poor town. No one had money and when the power went out and people couldn't take care of themselves, they went to Lincoln City where the government would feed them."

"Why did you stay? Are you alone here?" Dylan asked.

"I've run this motel for ten years. I got it in my divorce. I have a large food storage in the kitchen, and nowhere to go. So here I am," she said.

"We would like to rent seven or eight rooms for about a week," Dylan said. "We can pay you well."

Ric looked at Darien for a moment then walked behind the desk and pulled out the keys to all of the rooms. She handed them to him and said, "You are welcome to stay as long as you want. I would enjoy the company. There are ten rooms."

"Is there water around here close?" Jade asked, thinking about a hot bath.

Ric smiled and said, "Actually yes. I have a well with a hand pump. It takes a little sweat but it flows good."

Conner ducked his head and smiled. Rebel turned and walked out the door before the electricity blasting through her veins erupted into a visible bolt of lightning. She looked up into the building clouds that seemed to mirror the storm brewing inside her. She walked to the back of the building looking for a place to corral the twenty head of horses that they had acquired. There was a forty acre fenced pasture to the right of the motel. She mounted her horse to ride the fence line.

The fence was acceptable so she returned to the office where everyone was still talking. "Can we pasture the horses in the field next door?" she asked Ric.

"Yes, my neighbor left and took the ten head of cattle he had there. You will have to pack water though, it is a dry piece of ground," Ric answered. "You are welcome to put your tack in the mower shed out back."

"Thanks Ric, for everything," Rebel said sincerely. "Let's get the horses bedded down before we settle in."

"We will handle the horses Rebel, you aren't supposed to be moving remember?" Shane said stopping her from going out the door.

"Not you too!" Rebel cried.

"Yes, us too!" Cayden said laughing as he followed Danny and Shane outside to take care of the animals.

Dylan laughed at her frustration and handed her a key. "Go get your stuff in your room. And then you are down for a week!"

"Ric, if you would show me the kitchen, I will start heating water so everyone can get cleaned up. Then I would be glad to cook us all dinner," Darien said.

Ric smiled at him and said, "Sure thing, follow me. Its right through that door."

Rebel looked at Jade and Lynn, "You two want to bunk up or have your own rooms?"

"We can share a room," Jade answered laughing. "But I get the first bath."

Lynn laughed with her then followed her out the

door.

Warrick and Dylan left to help the boys with the horses leaving Rebel and Conner alone to ponder the electrostatic bolts bouncing between them.

"I'll help you get your stuff to your room," Conner said. "It's right next to mine," he grinned.

Rebel smiled at him, relishing the clash of sparks that once again threatened to ignite the raging fire in her soul.

"Rebel!" Cayden yelled from outside. "Here's your stuff."

"Thank you," she answered still looking into Conner's eyes. "Come on, let's get settled in before it rains."

Conner's smiled turned devilish as he followed her out to Cayden who handed them her bags.

"I put your stuff by your door," Cayden said to Conner.

"Thanks bro. I appreciate your help," Conner said slapping him on the back. "Can I do anything for you guys?"

"No, Darien has us on water packing duty. We are going to fill the girls tub first," Cayden answered heading toward the kitchen.

Darien handed him a large pan of hot water as soon as he walked through the door, then followed him to Jade's room with a second one.

"It's really hot Jade," he said as they entered. "It will cool while the rest of it is heating."

Jade hugged her uncle and said, "Thank you uncle Darien. I can't wait."

Darien returned to the kitchen and placed more water on the antique cook stove that Ric had piped into the chimney. "You seem to be set up pretty good here. I see why you stayed. Where did you get this antique cook stove?"

She returned his smile and answered, "I bought it at an antique store for decoration. I didn't pipe it in until I realized that the power wasn't coming back on. I was lucky that it was complete and in working order."

They continued to make small talk as pan after pan

of water was heated and transported to the bathtubs.

Rain poured down outside and lightning flashed through the windows.

One by one, everyone filtered into the kitchen feeling refreshed from their hot baths.

"Smells good," Warrick said. "What are you cooking?"

"Fried chicken and fried potatoes. I also have some canned fruit and veggie's," Ric answered. "And Darien helped me bake a pie."

"Pie!" Cayden and Shane exclaimed at the same time.

"Way to go Ric," Warrick grinned.

Jade smiled at Rebel finally relaxing a little around Danny who sat across from her. Rebel had noticed that Danny was a little shy around Jade too.

Everyone ate dinner and talked enjoying a tranquility that they hadn't felt for awhile. It was nice to be safe and among friends and family with enough to eat and no weapons in their hands.

After they had eaten the pie, Darien's stood up and said, "Ladies, I don't mean to pull a gender thing here but if you would help Ric clean up, the boys and I will clean and reload the weapons. I want to sort out the ammo and make sure everyone is rearmed.

Jade and Lynn jumped up.

"Thanks for cooking dinner Ric and uncle Darien. We don't mind cleaning up at all," Jade assured him. "And thanks for the hot bath."

Rebel and Ric stood to help the girls while the men gathered up the weapons and ammo. The room was filled with laughter and small talk as everyone worked.

A massive bolt of lightning crashed into the ground nearby and thunder rumbled then clapped so hard the dishes rattled.

Jade stepped closer to Rebel saying, "Bad storm, huh."

"I'm going to take a look outside," Dylan said. "That does look pretty bad." He stepped outside as another bolt of lightning flashed through the window. He quickly stepped back in the door. "Do you have a shelter just in case?" he asked as calmly as he could.

"No," Ric answered. "But we can go into the basement if we need to."

"Ya, we better keep an eye out. It looks like this storm could produce a tornado," he said.

Rebel could see the fear in Jade's eyes as she dried the dishes and put them away. "It will be fine Jade. The chance of a tornado hitting the motel is pretty slim," she soothed.

Jade nodded and kept working.

"Hey girls, I still have some fuel left in the generator if you want to watch a movie when we are done," Ric offered trying to help Rebel ease their distress. "My T.V. is very small and old but it works."

Rebel laughed at their excitement and nodded her appreciation to Ric. The four women finished their chore then headed to the lobby area where Ric kept the television. "I spend most of my time in here because I was open twenty four hours a day. My apartment is just through there," she pointed to a door. "This room should be big enough for all of us to hang out."

"Mom, why does Ric's TV work? I thought everything electronic was fried," Jade asked.

"Well, it depends on how the current from electromagnetic pulse interacts with the ground and any other conductor it can find. This TV is pretty old so the connections may have been a little stronger that those in a new one and the fact that this building has metal siding may have something to do with it. It could have acted like a faraday cage," Rebel explained. "There could be a lot of things that may have survived."

"It was in the basement and it wasn't plugged in. Maybe that helped," Ric added.

Rebel nodded and stepped onto the patio outside the back door to start the generator while Ric showed the girls her selection of movies. Soon the girls were settled on the couch enjoying some normalcy.

"I'll go make a pot of coffee," Ric said to Rebel, "and let the boys know the movie is on."

"Sound great," Rebel said getting comfortable in a love seat.

Cayden, Shane and Danny burst into the room a few moments later. "What are you watching Jade?" Cayden asked. "It seems like forever since I seen a T.V."

"We picked out Twilight," Jade giggled.

All three boys groaned and laughed at the girls.

Conner walked in and handed Rebel a cup of coffee. "Ric is hanging out with Darien, so I am the delivery boy."

"Thanks," she smiled accepting the cup. "Want to watch vampires and ware wolves?"

Conner sat next to Rebel and leaned back carefully. His ribs were throbbing and the new bruise across his bullet wound was aching horribly.

"Are you ok? Do you want some pain meds?" Rebel asked with concern.

"I just took some, but thanks. I'll be fine. I am sick of being injured though," he grumbled.

"Me too," Rebel agreed. "I hate that we are stuck sitting here just to heal. How is Darien? Is he showing signs of infection?"

"He is being a little stubborn about letting anyone look at his wound. You will probably have to put a ring in his nose to get him to cooperate," Conner laughed.

"Oh, I'll get him to cooperate alright!' she said firmly.

Conner laughed and pulled her against his chest. "My little spit fire!"

Rebel curled up in his lap loving the closeness and feeling completely at peace. Jade was safe and her brothers where here to look after them and Conner was holding her tight. She didn't want the feeling to end and fell asleep in Conner's arms dreaming that the world was back to normal.

An hour later, Conner waved goodnight to the kids and carried the still sleeping Rebel to her room. He gently laid her on the bed and stood over her watching the peaceful expression on her face.

The storm raged outside and lightning lit the room as bright as day. Thunder clapped loudly causing Rebel to jump up.

"It's ok," Conner soothed sitting next to her. "The storm is moving off for the most part."

"I didn't mean to fall asleep. Did the kids enjoy their movie?" she asked.

"Yes, they are all tucked in and Dylan hog tied Darien and changed his bandage. The wound is showing signs of infection, so he started him on the penicillin," Conner explained.

Rebel scowled remembering her brush with death when she had her infection. "I'm glad we have it."

"You might need it again too Rebel. That doctor was worried about your leg."

"I can tell something is wrong. I was hoping that the pain is because I got kicked and it is bruised. It will be fine," she smiled then pulled him down beside her. "Are you sleeping in my room tonight?"

His answer was a deep passionate kiss.

Chapter 10

Rebel woke up late again the next morning and wondered into the kitchen looking for coffee. The storm had calmed some but lightning still illuminated the cloud cover once in awhile.

"Good morning," Conner smiled when she walked in. He handed her coffee and sat down beside her.

"Good morning" she answered. "Have you been watching the storm this morning? I'm worried because that lightning could be caused by an extreme geomagnetic storm. If that is true, we could be getting some major doses of gamma rays."

"Is that bad?" Ric asked.

"Gamma rays are a form of radiation. Solar wind carries these particles toward us all the time but our magnetosphere usually protects us from them. Right now though, our magnetosphere is very weak and has a hole in it. It won't be able to stop it if it's very bad. Large amounts of this kind radiation at one time can have very negative effects on humans and animal life," Rebel explained. "Without any kind of communication, we will have no idea if that is the cause or not."

"Can we protect ourselves from these gamma rays?" Ric asked, very interested in Rebel's explanation.

"If we were at home we could go into the cave and be safe because I had the inner walls lined with a lead mesh, which is the only thing it can't penetrate. But out here, we are very vulnerable," Rebel said seriously.

"Is there another explanation? I mean, maybe it's not a solar storm creating the lightning," Ric pushed for more information.

"The other explanation is that we are getting closer to the galactic plane and the electromagnetic disturbances are coming from the black hole in the center of the galaxy. That is a much worse scenario because some scientists theorize that the amount of gamma rays coming from the center of the galaxy will be five trillion times the amount coming from the sun."

"Well, I guess I'll hope for a solar storm then," Ric huffed and sat down at the table. "Darien kind of filled me in on this end of the world shit but he didn't really go into detail."

Conner looked at her seriously and said, "That's because he doesn't want to scare you. If you want details, Rebel has them."

"Why is the magnetosphere weak right now?" she asked.

"The theory is that we are beginning to experience a geomagnetic pole shift. Some say that our magnetic field will actually drop to zero right before it happens."

"Why would it go to zero?"

"Well, the crust of the earth and the core of the earth rotate in opposite directions and that creates earth's magnetic field or magnetosphere. If the earth's rotation slows down then it would reduce the magnetic field strength."

Ric nodded and asked, "So what does that have to do with the black hole?"

"The black hole at the center of our galaxy is massive and spins with such force that it flattens the galaxy into a disc. Our solar system is currently passing up through this disc and our magnetosphere is our only protection from getting the full brunt of the energy emanating from the black hole. And it seems to be sleeping on the job."

"Wow, that makes me fairly nervous," she admitted.

"Me too," Rebel smiled. "Are the girls still sleeping?"

"Yes," Conner answered. "So are the boys. The brothers rode into town to check it out and see if they could get more fuel. The kids have requested another movie. Boys choice tonight."

"I see. So why the hell does Darien think he can just go riding off when he is supposed to be healing and may have an infection?" Rebel asked no one in particular.

"He is quite a man," Ric commented to the room.

Conner grinned and said, "Yes, they all are. Rebel is

the only person I've seen so far that can even half way control them."

"I wish!" Rebel snorted. "There is no controlling them what so ever. They are a bunch of hoodlums."

"Who are hoodlums?" Dylan said walking into the room. "You wouldn't be talking about us now, would ya?"

"Ya, we ain't hoodlums," Warrick added.

"Well, I'm a hoodlum," Darien said laughing as he sat down beside Ric.

Rebel and Ric laughed at the admission. "How is your shoulder?" Rebel asked. "I heard it may be infected. Let me see it."

Darien hesitated looking a little defiant.

"Just take off your damn shirt!" Rebel demanded.

"She is just worried about you," Ric encouraged.

Darien looked back and forth between the two women deciding he was outnumbered and grudgingly took off his shirt.

Rebel heard Ric inhale sharply at the sight of her brother's bare chest as she leaned in to get a better look. She smiled to herself then removed the bandage and focused on the wound, poking and prodding the reddish skin around the hole. "It's definitely infected. Take the penicillin twice a day. Promise?" she pleaded.

"Yes ma'am. I will follow your orders," Darien said sarcastically.

Rebel eyed him not believing his words. "I mean it Darien. We need you to be well so you can get us home, k?"

Darien smiled at her and said, "Rebel, I will take my medicine. I promise."

She went to the coffee pot and filled her cup. "So what did you find in town?"

"Warrick siphoned some gas out of an abandoned car so the kids can watch their movie," Dylan said. "And we picked up our own ferriers tools so we can shoe the horses. Those rednecks rode their animals barefoot."

"I grabbed more scabbards to so it will be easier to pack the extra rifles," Warrick added.

"And I brought this!" Darien said as he held up two

bottles of Jack Daniels.

Everyone laughed.

"I've got warm coke," Ric volunteered.

"Good, it's a date then, after dinner," Darien laughed.

"Darien, did you take a look at that lightning?" Rebel asked sitting back down beside him. "I'm a little concerned that it's not just a storm."

Darien turned serious and said, "I did get a weird feeling about it this morning. We better all wear hats and sunglasses because we have no way of knowing what's going on."

"We will be on our way soon enough. Everyone will be healed and ready to ride hard then we will get home and into the shelter," Dylan said warding off the bad atmosphere settling in the room.

Jade and Lynn trailed into the kitchen interrupting their thoughts. "Good morning," Jade said.

"More like good afternoon," Dylan teased.

"Funny! I thought we were supposed to rest while we were here," she teased back.

"We made pancakes this morning. They are on the stove," Ric offered. "I wish we had a microwave to warm them though."

"Thanks Ric. They will be fine just like they are," Jade said. "Come on Lynn, let's eat."

Cayden, Shane and Danny entered the room as Jade and Lynn sat down. Danny smiled at Jade who smiled back then ducked her head. Lynn giggled and caught an elbow to the arm for her humor.

"What!" Lynn exclaimed.

Jade glared at her over her glass.

"Cold pancakes on the stove." Ric said again this time to the boys.

"So, what movie are you guys picking tonight?" Rebel asked to distract attention off of Danny and Jade.

"We were thinking Armageddon," Shane said enthusiastically.

"Oh, that's fitting," Rebel laughed then fell silent when someone knocked on the front office door.

Darien looked at Ric who stood and hesitantly started toward the office. He stood with her and followed, stopping in the doorway between the office and the kitchen.

Everyone but the girls followed his lead staying silent but palming their handguns.

Ric opened the door and said, "I don't have any vacancies, sorry."

"We just need a couple rooms," a gruff voice said.

Darien turned to the brothers holding up four fingers meaning there were four men.

"I said that I am full for the next week," Ric explained.

"I don't see anybody. Are you lying to us?" the gravelly voice asked.

"Why would I lie?" Ric asked getting nervous.

Dylan bobbed his head toward the back door sending Conner and Warrick out the back to cover from the side of the building. Rebel pointed to the big window instructing the younger boys to cover from there. She traded her colt for a shotgun and waited beside Darien.

"I think maybe you just don't want us staying in your high falutin hotel," a second man said sneering.

Ric was scared now and tried to shut the door. The gruff man kicked it back open and strode into the room.

Darien nodded at Rebel who pumped the shotgun, the intimidating sound stopped the man in mid stride. He shot his head toward the door and looked straight down the barrel of Darien's revolver. He paused then looked at Rebel who had leveled the shotgun at his chest. Dylan was right behind her with a rifle pointed at his head.

"Well now, maybe you were telling the truth. I'll just be finding a room somewhere else," he said to Ric trying to back out of the room.

Darien advanced on the man following him out the door surprising his friends who reached for their weapons.

"I wouldn't do that if I were you," Warrick growled from behind them, shoving his rifle into their backs. Conner pointed his at the man next to him.

Rebel and Dylan followed them out the door and finished surrounding the four men. The younger boys guarded Ric just inside the door.

"Easy now," the gruff man said. "We don't want no trouble here."

"Really? And what was it you were going to do to her when you kicked her door in. It looked like trouble to me!" Darien said in a deadly voice.

"Just let us on our way," one of the other men pleaded. "We will leave and never come back."

"Do you really think that I would let you leave and find someone else to terrorize?" Darien ground out. "You are dangerous and shouldn't be interacting with decent people. Tie them Warrick!"

Warrick stepped forward and jerked the first man's hands behind his back and bound them together with a leather shoestring from his pocket. Dylan handed him another tie keeping his weapon pointed to the man's head.

After they were disarmed and tied Rebel went into the office to check on Ric who was standing in the same place trembling. "Ric?" she said. "Are you ok?"

Ric nodded her head, tears streaming down her cheeks.

"Come on, let's get you some coffee," Rebel said leading her back into the kitchen where Jade and Lynn quickly sat beside her reassuringly.

"I'm sorry that happened to you Ric. I was abducted back in Omaha. I was so scared, but Shane saved me," Lynn said trying to calm her. "I have found that if you are with these guys, you are as safe as you can get."

Rebel smiled at the comment as she poured Ric a cup of coffee. She handed it to her and sat down across the table. "It's true, the brothers are pretty protective when it comes to their family or friends."

"Thank God for that. But what if you hadn't happened by yesterday and I was alone here today. I'm alone in a lawless world and when you're gone, will have no protection," Ric said sadly.

"Come with us then," Jade said encouragingly. "You can come home with us!"

"I'm sure Darien would love that idea," Lynn laughed. "I think he is infatuated by you."

Ric blushed then looked at Jade. "That is very nice of you, but..."

"But what?" Rebel asked. "You just said you were alone here. Idaho isn't the best state to live in but you would be safe and among friends."

Ric started crying. "I haven't had friends for a long time. I'm so lucky you guys came here. I would love to go to Idaho with you."

Darien entered the kitchen and strode to Ric who was still sobbing.

"Ric, I'm sorry that happened. Are you ok?" he asked very concerned.

"She is going with us to Idaho," Jade informed him. "She doesn't want to stay here alone."

"That's great. We would love to have you join us," he said trying to hide his excitement.

Lynn giggled and Jade elbowed her again.

"I wish we had a way to take her supplies. It's a shame to leave her stuff behind," Rebel thought out loud.

"What are we taking?" Dylan asked as he and Warrick walked into the kitchen.

"Ric is going with us to Idaho," Jade said again.

"Good, I was worried about leaving you here alone, Ric," Dylan said. "We have plenty of pack animals for whatever you said we were taking."

Rick looked at them and started sobbing again. "Thank you."

Conner hobbled into the room obviously in pain and quickly found a chair staying silent.

"What the hell happened?" Rebel demanded.

Warrick ducked his head and Dylan looked out the window. Conner looked away and said, "Nothing. Nothing happened."

"Don't you dare lie to me! What happened!" she

demanded again.

"One of the men head butted him in the ribs!" Warrick exclaimed caving in to her unwavering demand.

"Rebel, I just didn't want to worry you," Conner defended.

Rebel looked around the room. She glared at Conner then said through gritted teeth, "I want to leave here as soon as possible. If we can't leave until we have all healed then this is how it is going to go. Darien will take his medicine and not go into town on a joyride! Conner will not handle the prisoners! Dylan and Warrick will not remove their stitches until I say, and no one else will be injured! Does everybody understand?" she turned and stomped out the door.

The room was silent after she left, everyone looking at the door.

Jade sighed and said, "We all know how bad she hates standing still. She isn't mad at anyone in particular. Let's all just do as she says and get healed and rested. We will be on our way in a few days."

"Jade is right, and Rebel is right too. We need to take better care of ourselves," Darien said softly. "We need to be prepared to protect the ladies and to do that we need to be healthy." He paused then added, "But before we reform ourselves, I say we drink that whiskey!"

Everyone laughed. Ric got up to get the coke and Jade grabbed some glasses. They handed everyone a drink then sat down.

Jade sat by Conner and gave him a reassuring smile. "She won't stay mad long. Don't worry," she assured him. "I'll take her a drink and bring her back for dinner."

Conner smiled back at her. "Maybe I better take her a drink. You go watch your movie and finish your drink." He picked up his glass and headed for Rebel's room.

He knocked hesitantly on her door. "Rebel, I'm sorry. I didn't mean to lie to you. I just think you have enough to worry about and my stupidity shouldn't be in the equation," he said knocking again. "Please let me in."

Rebel opened the door and looked into his pleading eyes. He lifted the glass offering her the drink. She stepped back and accepted the glass then followed him to the bed and sat beside him.

"I seem to have these fits of fury and yell at everyone I care about," she said softly. "It's just really hard to watch you guys fight and get hurt." She took a drink from the glass then sighed and said, "I searched for you in that field of dead bodies and I would have died myself if I'd found you dead out there."

Once again, Conner found himself sitting quietly listening to her vent her frustration.

"And I watched that man plunge his knife into Darien's chest through my scope. I thought I'd witnessed his death. I'm just not dealing well with all of these near misses," she admitted.

"We understand that Rebel and only ask that you remember that you put yourself at risk along with us. We worry just as much or more about you," Conner said tilting her chin up so she was looking at him. "I almost died when the gang shot the filly out from under you. I thought you were dead too. I understand how you feel Rebel, we all do. It's going to be ok. We will make it home. All of us."

She wrapped her arms around him and kissed his soft lips then tugged him to her bed.

Several hours later, Rebel got up and pulled her jeans on. "We better go eat dinner. They will be expecting us."

Conner smiled as he watched her dress. "Yes, they will definitely be expecting us." He got up and dressed then led her to the kitchen and opened the door.

Every male in the kitchen stood as Rebel walked into the room.

"Rebel, we are sorry. We have committed to taking better care of ourselves," Darien said looking at the others who nodded in agreement.

"I'm sorry too. I shouldn't have yelled at you, it's not your fault," Rebel explained. "It's just that in the last couple weeks, I've watched Conner get shot off his horse,

Jade ripped from hers and held at gunpoint, Darien being stabbed right in front of me and Conner lying in a field of dead bodies and I guess it all just overwhelmed me. I'm sorry I took it out on you guys."

"Rebel, you know we understand. Now come in here and eat something cause Darien is just itching to finish that whiskey," Dylan said.

Everyone laughed and started dishing up their plates. Conner and Rebel sat down and joined them.

"I hope you don't mind chicken again," Ric said. "I figured we should eat them cause we can't take them with us."

"We haven't eaten anything but canned food or venison for weeks," Shane answered. "I miss chicken."

"Me too," Cayden agreed.

"I wanted to formally thank all of you for inviting me to tag along with you to Idaho. I appreciate your friendship and promise not to be a burden," Ric said sincerely.

"You won't be a burden with this cooking," Warrick teased getting roar of laughter.

"I should thank you formally as well then," Lynn said.

"Me too," Danny added nodding his head.

Darien stood and raised his glass of whiskey. "Too our new friends. And too our family."

They all toasted and cheered.

The next few days were spent sorting through Ric's food storage and acquiring supplies from the town. Each of them repacked their gear and bedrolls that they prepared from the blankets in the motel.

Dylan and Warrick took each one of them into town to get new boots, jeans, jackets and tents. Rebel made sure that everyone got a hat and sunglasses and insisted that the girls and the younger guys had sunscreen.

Ric packed her small tent and sleeping bag and was sorting through her personal belongings when Rebel knocked on the door of her small apartment.

"How is it going? It must be hard to leave most of you stuff behind," Rebel said. "I didn't have time to pack mine before I left for D.C. and I don't know if it is still there."

"Not really," Ric replied. "I'm mostly going to take some pictures of my parents and some pieces of jewelry that are sentimental. The rest of it is either useless or replaceable."

"Well, let me know if you need anything. I'm going to check on the girls. They seem more interested in the boys than packing their stuff," Rebel said smiling.

She went out the back door to the yard behind the motel where Warrick and Dylan were shoeing some of the horse. "I'm just making sure that Darien is sitting this out," she teased.

"I'm sittin clean over hear. Not even close to the action," he teased back.

"Are we ready to leave in the morning then?" she asked him.

"I think so, I'm pretty much on the road to being healed up and Conner said he was feeling much better too. How is your leg?" he asked.

"It still hurts pretty bad and is still seeping blood," Rebel informed him then shrugged. "It will be fine. I'll take the stitches out of Warrick and Dylan tonight."

"I know it was hard to stop for this long but I think we will be better for it," Darien said. "But if you need more time Rebel, we aren't in a hurry."

She shook her head no. "We are going to make one more big breakfast before we leave in the morning. The boys have requested more pancakes. What are you going to do with those four guys down in the basement?"

"I'll let them go once we are on our way. They really didn't break any laws, not that they wouldn't have if we hadn't stopped them," he said solemnly. "I just wanted to give them a little piece of humble pie."

Rebel smiled. "K, I'll see you at dinner." She stood and disappeared into the lobby.

Conner was pacing the kitchen window when Rebel walked in. "What's wrong?" she asked.

"I guess I'm just a little anxious to be on our way," he said. "Are you all packed?"

"Yes, I'm ready. I checked on Jake and he looks good after a week off," she said. "The girls and I are going to get in one more hot bath tonight so I'm going to start heating water."

"I'll help you," he said. "I'm all packed up and bored."

"Maybe I can help you with that later," Rebel said enticingly.

Fire lit his eyes as he responded to her invitation. "Can't wait," he said huskily.

"Rebel! Come look at this!" Darien yelled through the door.

Rebel raced outside and looked up into the sky where Darien was pointing. She sucked in her breath at the sight of the yellowish brown dust cloud overtaking the evening sky.

"What is it?" Ric asked nervously coming out the patio door.

"Volcano!" Darien and Rebel said in unison.

"Oh my God! What if it was Yellowstone acting up?" Rebel said fearfully.

"Come on Rebel, there are a number of volcano's that are large enough to do that. I think if it were Yellowstone we would see a lot more ash," Darien soothed.

Rebel put her hand over her mouth and watched the sunlight dim behind the grayish yellow brown cloud filtering throughout the atmosphere.

"I'm sorry, but I don't get it. What about Yellowstone?" Ric said anxiously.

Rebel turned to her and explained. "It is one of eight super volcano's visible on earth and there are many more under the oceans. Most scientists agree that if one of them erupts, it would eject so much dirt, ash and steam into the atmosphere that it would block the suns rays and send us into an ice age. If it went off, the ash would cover much of the continents surface making it almost impossible to grow crops for many years. The ash is sterile and nothing can grow in it."

"It would eventually put down six feet of ash right here where stand," Darien agreed. "It's one of the hardest scenarios to plan for. We would see acid rain, poisoned water. It would be bad."

Rebel looked at Conner who took her hand reassuringly. "Thousands more will die from this eruption. The ash is like tiny shards of glass and the poisonous gas will kill you if you breathe it," she said helplessly.

Conner took her into his arms and held her tight as the realization filtered across the faces of the others.

Ric edged closer to Darien fearfully. "We aren't going to make it are we?"

"Yes we will, won't we Rebel. We are going to be fine," he assured them all.

Rebel lifted her head and agreed, "He's right, we will be fine. We are prepared for the worst."

"Let's get you ladies some hot water, then we will eat the last of those chickens," Conner said to lighten the mood. "We can't do anything about the weather."

"He's right. Let's enjoy our last night in luxury before we hit the trail," Dylan agreed.

The next morning Rebel woke up wrapped in Conner's big comforting arms. She would definitely miss the bed and the privacy that they had enjoyed for the last week. She watched his bare chest rise and fall as he breathed peacefully and couldn't help reaching out to caress his well-formed muscles.

He opened his eyes at her touch and smiled at the invitation on her face.

Some time later, they entered the kitchen together and sat down across from Darien and Ric. Dylan handed them both a cup of coffee and Warrick flipped pancakes on the stove. The room was quiet, each of them lost in their own thoughts.

Laughter erupted outside the door as the boys

caught up with the girls and raced them to the kitchen. They flew through the door, the girls the obvious winner of their little game.

"I'm glad to see you are happy and rearing to get on with the day," Dylan said.

"Pancakes on," Warrick informed them. "Let's eat and hit on the road."

"You guys talk funny," Lynn said. "Why do you say hit the road?"

Rebel laughed and said, "He talks like that because he's a redneck."

Warrick smiled and bowed making the girls laugh.

"I'm gonna miss this place," Ric said absently. "Maybe I'll be able to come back one day."

"I'm sure you will," Darien agreed as he poured syrup over his breakfast. "Maybe I'll come with you."

"You would do that?" she asked excitedly.

"Of course, if you want me to," he said.

Ric smiled and couldn't help watching him as he sipped his coffee. "I'm a little nervous venturing away from everything I've ever known. But I'm glad I will be with you guys."

"Our camp at home is really cool. You will love it. I can't wait for you to meet my grandma," Jade said to Ric and Lynn. "She is just the coolest person. I miss her!"

"She is quite a lady," Dylan agreed. "I'm sure she is running that camp with an iron hand."

"Ya, I'll bet she is," Warrick agreed laughing.

Cayden and Shane shoveled the last of their food into their mouths and stood up.

"We will go get the horses," Shane offered. "Come on Danny."

"Is everyone ready to go?" Dylan asked.

Everyone nodded and stood up. "I'm going to lock everything up," Ric said. "No sense leaving it wide open."

Rebel and Conner followed the brothers outside to saddle the horses. Ric joined them and they mounted for the long journey home.

"It sure is dim out here," Jade said looking into the sky as they rode onto the road. "I can literally look right into the sun."

"Ya, well don't," Rebel reprimanded, "and put on your shades."

Both girls dug for their sunglasses.

"I'm not looking very good in this hat!" Jade pouted.

"I think you look just fine in the hat," Danny said softly, making her blush.

Lynn giggled and shoved the sunglasses onto her face.

Conner eased up to the lead with Warrick and Rebel fell back in step with Ric. The kids brought up the rear of their little posse as they started down the road.

"Let's move!" Warrick yelled back urging them to match his speed at a fast gallop.

Rebel felt a rush of pain envelop her entire thigh as she eased Jake into the faster pace. 'Not good,' she thought to herself. 'Something is seriously wrong.' It had been hurting all week but now that she was on the horse, it was unbearable. She tried not to think about it as they rode hard into the afternoon but was relieved when Darien reined in to rest the horses and get something to eat.

Conner walked over to Rebel and instantly knew something was wrong. "Are you ok?" he asked softly so he didn't involve the brothers in the conversation.

"Yes, but my leg hurts pretty bad," she answered echoing the volume. "It kinda took me by surprise. I'll take some pain meds, it'll be fine. How are you doing?"

"My ribs are aching but my chest wound is good," he assured her.

Ric slowly walked toward them. "Damn! It's been a long time since I was on a horse. I'm gonna be a sore puppy by the end of the day."

Rebel laughed handing her the bottle of pain pills. "Hopefully Darien still has some whiskey to help us sleep tonight."

Shane offered everyone a piece of the cold chicken

that they had packed for lunch. "I guess we are back to venison after this," he said sadly.

"I'm sure we can find something besides deer, Shane. I'll get you a rabbit if you like," Conner said grinning. "I heard Darien is quite a fisherman."

"Ya, but Ric cooks a mean piece of bird," he smiled.

"Thank you, Shane," Ric said. "But Conner is right. We will run into another bird, maybe a wild turkey. There are dove, duck, pheasant, and geese around here. I won't let you go hungry."

"Let's get going," Warrick said.

Darien stopped beside Ric and asked. "Is everyone good so far?"

"I'm going to be saddle sore tonight," Ric laughed. "But other than that, I'm fine."

"Alright, let's ride," he smiled.

"Where are we?" Cayden asked.

"The bottom of Nebraska. We will head northwest until we hit Interstate eighty then follow it to Cheyenne," Dylan said as he mounted his horse.

They rode fast until dusk when Dylan waved them to a halt. "We will take care of the horses, you guys find some wood and start a fire," he said to the boys.

The campsite was bordered by trees and just off the road. Rebel helped the girls erect their tent and get settled in. She looked toward Ric and laughed as her friend fought with the poles.

"Need some help?" she asked grabbing one end.

"I was never much for camping," Ric admitted. "But I am determined to pull my weight and not be a pain in the ass."

"We will help you Ric. Don't be so uptight about it. We won't judge you," Rebel assured her.

Shane, Cayden and Danny ran over and took the tent out of their hands.

"Ladies, may we be of service?" Shane asked grinning.

"Thanks, guys. We will get you something to eat for

your trouble," Rebel laughed.

"They are great boys," Ric said as they walked to the fire. "I've never seen such commitment and love between siblings."

"Some people think we are weird," Rebel said. "But I think I am a lucky woman."

"I think you are too," Ric laughed as she pulled a couple cans out of a pack.

"They were typical siblings and fought a lot when they were younger but always managed to work it out," Rebel laughed.

Warrick walked over and prepared a pot of coffee then stuffed it into the fire. "It's nice to have tents but I'm sure gonna miss that bed," he scowled into the flames.

"Oh Warrick, we should only have about three weeks ride. Then we will be home in our own beds," Rebel encouraged.

He grunted and poked the fire with a stick.

"What's wrong with happy?" Dylan asked pointing his thumb at his brother as he sat down on a rock.

"He's homesick," Rebel teased getting a middle finger in response.

Dylan and Ric laughed as Rebel returned the gesture.

Lucky preceded Lynn and Jade to the fire, going straight to Warrick and giving his face a thorough licking.

"You little bastard!" Warrick growled, petting the top of the dog's head affectionately.

Rebel looked up and noticed Conner standing on the road looking into the field. She stood up and walked closer followed by Warrick and Dylan.

"What is it?" she whispered from behind him.

"I don't know, I thought I heard something," he whispered back.

Suddenly the puppy ran into the field barking.

"Oh shit!" Warrick said as he saw the look of horror on Jade's face. "I'll get him," he assured her.

Warrick and Conner advanced into the field following the barking dog.

Jade took Rebels hand and strained to hear what was going on.

"It's ok!" Conner yelled back. "It's another dog."

Everyone released the breath they were holding as the two men walked back into their line of sight followed by the puppy and a big Sheppard.

"It looks like we have a new friend," Conner said petting the animal.

"Shit!" Warrick yelled and ran toward the fire. "I'm burning the coffee."

Rebel laughed bending down to get acquainted with the dog. "I wonder if he has a home or if he was abandoned."

"Don't know. I guess he can choose if he wants to follow us or not," Conner replied. "Let's eat. Come on boy."

"At least he is friendly with the puppy," Jade said as she followed them back to camp.

They gathered around the fire and ate and drank coffee watching the puppy try to entice the Sheppard into playing with it.

"Boys, I found some marshmallows. Would you cut us some willows to roast them with?" Ric asked.

The boys jumped up excitedly and disappeared into the trees.

Rebel poured some whiskey into her coffee hoping that it would help take the edge of the pain in her leg. Conner raised his eyebrow at her questioningly as she chased it with four Excedrin.

"I'm going to bed," she announced and stood up to go to her tent.

"Are you ok sis?" Darien asked concerned.

"Yes, my leg is just tired, that's all," she said. "I'll be fine." She walked away stiffly.

Darien looked at Conner expectantly.

"Either we didn't wait long enough or something is wrong with it," he said. "We need to find another doctor and have it looked at."

"Maybe it is getting infected. Should we start her on

antibiotics?" Dylan asked.

"I'll go take a closer look at it and see if I can see anything," Conner said following her to the tent with the Sheppard right on his heels.

But before he reached the tent, the ground began to shake violently. Jade and Lynn both squealed and the boys came rushing out of the trees. The puppy started howling and the horses snorted and stomped their feet. Warrick grabbed the coffee pot before it toppled over into the fire.

After about sixty seconds of shaking the ground grew quiet. Rebel limped out of the tent and stood beside Conner.

"Is there a fault line or subduction zone out here?" Dylan asked.

"We are close to the mid-continental rift and the Humboldt fault line starts near here and runs south but this area isn't famous for any large quakes that I know of," Rebel said. "But I've heard them say that on this side of the Rockies, there are so many fault lines that they just can't find them all. They are everywhere."

"I'll check the horses," Warrick said setting the coffee down.

"Come on Rebel, I want to have a look at that leg," Conner said.

"Girls," Rebel said, "there could be an aftershock but don't be afraid. We should be fairly safe here ok?" She waited for them to nod then followed Conner into the tent.

"Drop em!" Conner said very concerned. "I'm really worried Rebel."

Rebel obeyed without argument and they both peered at the nasty wound on her thigh. "It doesn't look infected. I don't get it," she said.

"Sit down," he said and followed her down to the sleeping bag. He looked closely, poking the skin around the wound. "It looks fine to me too but I want a second opinion k? Dylan, come in here will ya?" he yelled.

"I don't see anything weird. Take a look," Conner said as Dylan walked into the tent.

Dylan crouched down and studied the wound as

Conner had. "I don't see signs of infection either. The bullet was intact when we cut it out so it can't be shrapnel."

"What about strands from my jeans?" Rebel asked.

The two men looked at each other and nodded. "It's possible that a piece of denim is in there," Dylan agreed. "It would definitely cause an infection, but wouldn't we be able to see signs on the outside?"

"Maybe not, and she has been sleeping a lot lately," Conner said.

"Darien, we need your opinion!" Dylan yelled.

"What's up?" he asked stepping into the now crowded tent.

"We are discussing the possibility of an infection deep in Rebels leg. Is it possible that we wouldn't see the infection on the outside? What do you think?" Dylan asked looking back at the wound. "Conner pointed out the fact that she's been sleeping a lot lately."

"I think it's completely plausible. I vote we start her on the antibiotic just in case," Darien said.

"I agree. Thanks guys," Conner said digging out her first aid bag. He pulled out the vile of penicillin and filled a syringe. "Sorry Rebel. We are back to this again." He injected the medication into her shoulder.

The two brothers exited the tent and Rebel laid back into the sleeping bag. "I'm not stopping again, just so you know," she said firmly.

"I'm not the one you have to convince now," Conner grinned and lay down beside her. "We are going to seek out another doctor though, just so you know."

"This whole siding with my brothers thing isn't fair," she said turning on him.

"How can you blame me? You are so god damned stubborn. I'll take all the help I can get," he laughed then pulled her into a kiss before she could argue.

Rebel climbed out of the tent the next morning and looked into the sunrise. The sky was a weird color and it seemed dusty and dim.

"I'm thinking that geomagnetic pole shift theory is about to be proven," Darien said handing her coffee as she walked to the fire.

"Rebel you started telling me about the pole shift. Why is it so bad?" Ric asked.

"There are two different theories behind a pole shift. The first one is simply that the north and south poles flip like we talked about the other day. The only way that would affect us is if we lose our magnetosphere completely during the event and are impacted by the radiation in the solar wind. But the theory behind a geomagnetic pole shift is that the entire crust of the earth would shift when the poles move. Some claim that the earth would actually slow or stop its rotation and possibly even start turning in the opposite direction. Either way, every volcano on earth would erupt and we would see major earthquakes as the tectonic plates adjusted to compensate for the rotation changes," Rebel explained. "I just hope we get home first or we will be in a world of hurt."

"Don't worry Rebel, we will get home in time," Darien assured her. "How is the leg this morning?"

"It is still painful but we are moving on, k? I don't want to stop again," she insisted.

"Let's just take one day at a time, we'll just see how it goes," Darien said not really committing either way.

Conner stepped past her grinning with an 'I told you so' look on his face.

"Fuck you Conner!" she spat at him.

"Good morning to you too, Rebel," he said laughing.

They ate breakfast then packed and saddled the horses. Conner helped Rebel onto Jake and mounted his gilding. He looked down at the Sheppard as the little posse started down the road and said, "Well, are you coming or not?"

The dog barked at him as if he understood and trotted toward him. "I guess if your gonna hang around, we better find you a name. What do you think Rebel. Any ideas?"

Rebel looked at the dog and said, "I'm terrible at naming my animals. I once had a dog that was named Little Boy because I never found him a real name."

Darien laughed and said, "That is a true story. I remember that dog."

"And I once named a cat 'Bum Show'," she continued.

Everyone laughed at that one.

"What about Tucker?" Jade asked.

"I think we could live with that," Conner agreed. "What do you think, Tucker?"

The dog barked at him again and trotted along beside his horse.

"Rebel, can you handle a run?" Darien yelled back.

"Yes, I'll be fine," she answered then pushed Jake into a fast gallop.

After about an hour at that speed, Darien waved them to a walk then pointed ahead. "There is a small city up there. I think we should ride through and see if there is a doctor."

"I don't think we should take our supplies in just in case," Dylan said. "You and Conner take Rebel into the city and Warrick and I will continue on." He pulled out his map and searched for a meeting place. He pointed to a spot and showed Darien.

"Take care of Jade for me Dylan," Rebel said quietly to her brother.

"Don't you worry, Rebel. I hope you find a doctor there," he said with concern.

Darien, Conner and Rebel rode into the small city followed by Tucker. They scanned the streets for a hospital or doctor. "I don't see anyone," Rebel said.

"Ya, I'm not understanding why all of the little towns are abandoned," Conner added.

"I'm thinking the people moved to larger cities to get help after their supplies ran out," Darien offered. "Or they have moved way into the mountains so they could hunt and find water."

"Look, there is someone in the Police station," Rebel said.

Darien dismounted at the front door and went inside. "Officer, we are in need of a doctor. My sister is injured and I'm worried that her injury is life threatening," he said urgently.

"We have established an emergency shelter and stocked all of our supplies at the local hospital. We have several doctors still on staff there," the man said.

"Thank you. Where is the hospital?"

"It is down one block and to the right two," he instructed.

Darien came out the door excitedly and swung onto his horse saying, "They have doctors on staff." He led them to the hospital around the corner and tied the horses while Conner helped Rebel inside.

"Stay here Tucker." Conner said to the dog as they walked into the hospital doors.

A nurse came toward them asking, "Can I help you?"

"Yes, this is Rebel and she received a gunshot wound over a week ago. We believe that it is infected. We started her on penicillin yesterday," Conner explained.

"Right this way," the woman said directing them into a room down the hall. "Put on this gown and I'll have the doctor come in."

Rebel sat down in a chair and prepared for a long wait but the doctor surprisingly entered the room moments later.

"Gunshot huh? I've seen way too many of them recently," the doctor said as he entered the room. "Jump up on the table and let's have a look."

Rebel climbed onto the table and flipped the gown off of her thigh.

"We had to cut out the bullet doc, but it came out in one piece," Conner said.

"I'd say that it is definitely infected," the doctor agreed. "Maybe the bullet nicked the bone. The only way I would be able to tell without an x-ray is to cut it open."

Rebel shot a shocked look at Conner who nodded encouragingly.

"Surgery without power is quite a trick as you can imagine, but I think it is the only thing we can do here. I'm going to have Beth take your vitals and prepare some equipment," he said leaving the room.

"Conner, my brothers will want to wait until I'm healed again," Rebel grated out angrily.

"Calm down Rebel. We need to do whatever it takes to get you home alive. If it means waiting, then that's what we will do," he insisted.

"No! I don't mind riding slow, at a walk, but I'm not stopping," she said firmly.

The nurse entered the room and stuck a thermometer in Rebels mouth. After a moment, she said, "You have a fever and that usually means infection. The doctor is going to do the surgery here in this room so just sit tight."

"I'm going to let Darien know what's going on. I'll be right back," Conner said leaving the room.

Rebel leaned back on the tilted table and tried to relax. Conner was right. She almost died earlier this month from an infection and it would be hypocritical to be angry with the brothers for not allowing their wounds to heal then doing the same thing herself.

Conner followed the doctor back into the room and the nurse entered pushing a cart with surgical tools on it. The doctor cleaned the wound and prepared to open up the hole.

Conner took her hand as the doc injected Novocain into in her leg.

"I'm going to make a small incision so that I can see inside then I will just feel around and see if I can catch something," the doc said picking up his tool. "I would normally give you a real anesthetic for this but I don't dare without a way to monitor your heart. I'm sorry to tell you that this may hurt." He made the cut then stuck the forceps into the hole and poked around.

Rebel leaned her head back against the pain. She squeezed Conner's hand and felt the cold threat of unconsciousness close in on her.

"I got something," the doc said after a moment pulling something out of the hole. "This may very well be the culprit. I'm thinking it is bone. Maybe we won't need the surgery. I need to clean it thoroughly though, so I'm going to inject more Novocain inside the wound."

Rebel nodded and said, "We are traveling and I don't want to be laid up for very long."

"Well, from what I can see, your bleeding risk will be fairly high and if I clean it like it should be cleaned, it will be extremely painful for several days. Now you told Beth that you started penicillin yesterday?"

"Yes, but we aren't sure about the dosage and we don't have many syringes left," Conner answered.

"I can help you with that and maybe a few Vicoden but we are running short on supplies here," he said. "Beth give her one of the pain pills right now, would you? She is going to need it."

Conner glanced at Rebel nervously as the doctor prepared to stick huge swabs into the hole. She squeezed his hand reassuringly and he cursed himself for being the one needing reassurance.

"Ok Rebel, are you ready? I want you to lean back and relax. I'm going to scrub it out to make sure there isn't anything else in there. I'll be quick," the doc informed her.

She leaned back against the pillow and mentally prepared herself for the ensuing pain. Her face turned white as she tensed in agony.

"I know Rebel, just stay with me. I'm almost done with this side," the doc encouraged. Then after a moment said, "Ok, got it. Now for the other side."

After he was done cleaning the wound, he packed it with gauze and stitched the incision. "Good, you did good. Now tell me about these nasty wounds here," he said pointing to the gouges from the mountain lion.

"She was attacked by a mountain lion," Conner said simply. "I had to stitch them on the road but then she was kicked and they were reopened. So were the one's on her ribs."

The doctor looked at him seriously and said, "Show me."

Rebel weakly slid the gown so the doctor could inspect the injury.

"You did a good job. They will still heal but leave nasty scars. The holes in her shoulder look puffy," he observed.

"Yes, they were infected as well. That is why we already had the antibiotic," Conner said softly.

"Well, if we can stop the infection in your leg and you don't bleed while you ride, I think you will be just fine Rebel," the doc said helping her sit up. "But try to stay away from mountain lions and stray bullets from now on."

She laughed and said, "Thank you, I really appreciate it. One more thing though, would you take a quick peek at Conner's gunshot wound and ribs?"

The doctor turned to Conner sharply. "You were shot as well? You guys must have traveled through some rough places. Let's have a look."

Conner lifted his shirt and showed the doctor the hole in his chest. "Mine is several weeks old but it was reopened last week in a fight."

"My god! Do you realize how lucky you are to be alive? That bullet came within millimeters of your artery," the doctor said in amazement. "It is healing though and I see no sign of infection. Keep it clean and bandaged for a couple more weeks. But these broken ribs are dangerous. I can't do anything for you there. You should be down for a couple months."

Conner just nodded.

Beth handed her a bottle of pills and a handful of syringes. "Fill the syringe to here twice a day," she said pointing to the tube. "And leave that gauze in the hole as long as it will stay in there. If you aren't feeling better in two or three days, you need to find another doctor because a bone infection in this environment could be fatal."

Rebel nodded and climbed slowly off of the table.

Conner jumped up to steady her and said, "Doc, we are prepared to pay you in cash but I don't know what money is worth now days. Is there anything else we can do to repay you?"

"No, I'm afraid when our supplies run out, we will be at the mercy of God," he said sadly.

Conner opened the door to the very worried Darien and handed Rebel over to him then shook the doctors hand.

"Good luck," the doctor said.

"What happened?" Darien asked as they helped Rebel hobble out to the horses.

"The doc pulled something out of the wound and cleaned it really good. He stuffed it with gauze and showed us how much antibiotic to give her," Conner filled him in. "He said she will be in horrible pain for a couple of days."

"I will be fine, you guys," Rebel insisted. "He gave me some pain meds so there is no reason to worry."

They helped her onto Jake and mounted their horses.

"I'm sure Dylan has made camp. You can rest up tonight and we will see how you feel tomorrow," Darien said.

Chapter 11

Dylan found a secluded campsite next to a decent sized river a few miles outside of the city. "We might as well stay here until morning," he said to the others, "I'm going to assume that Rebel will need the rest."

By the time Darien, Conner and Rebel rode into camp, they had the tents set up and a fire going. The boys had taken off to try their luck harvesting a bird and Ric had prepared dinner.

It took both Darien and Conner to help Rebel off of her horse. The pain that the doctor had warned her about was crushing her now.

"I made her a spot by the fire," Dylan said very worried. "What did they find?"

Darien filled him and Warrick in on the details while Conner unsaddled the horses.

"Mom, I was so worried," Jade said sitting down beside her.

"Don't worry, Jade," Rebel soothed her with a hug. "I'm going to be just fine now. Wow, Ric. You have been busy," she smiled looking at the skillet in the fire.

Ric laughed. "I love to cook. It is my hobby and I'm having fun cooking for such a large group. I've been alone for a while." She handed Rebel her dinner. "You might as well eat while it's hot. Get yours girls, the boys can eat when they get back."

"God, I'm so pissed that we are sitting around again," Rebel said unable to contain her frustration.

Ric sat down beside her and the girls. "I know, but you will heal. We can talk the guys into moving on slowly. Just promise me that if I back you, you will stop if you need to."

Rebel smiled at her new friend and nodded.

Conner walked to the fire followed closely by the dog, "How are you doing?"

"I'm good. Ric has dinner if you are hungry," she said dodging his real inquiry.

"You'll tell me won't you Rebel? You'll tell me if you're not ok?" he pushed her.

Rebel looked into his worried eyes and said, "I'll tell you. I promise."

"Ok," he said accepting the food Ric handed him.

The brothers walked to the fire.

"So how are the ladies this afternoon?" Darien asked.

"We're good uncle Darien," Jade answered smiling. "I'm missing that bath tub though."

"Me too," Ric agreed handing food to each of the men. She added a piece of cornbread and said, "I think the cast iron skillet was worth its weight. I made the corn bread in it."

"Thank you," Warrick said smiling at the food. "I'd carry it myself to get this kind of food."

Ric smiled appreciatively.

Dylan looked at Rebel and said, "We have agreed to move out in the morning but we are going to move slow. If you need to stop, you tell us. Agreed?"

"Thanks guys, I will take it easy and stop if I need to," Rebel said.

Shane, Cayden and Danny came into the clearing packing three grouse.

"Right on boys," Warrick said smiling. "I made you a rotisserie to cook them on. I'll show you how to use it."

They sat around the fire talking and watching the boys cook their birds until dark.

Rebel hadn't moved much, afraid that the pain would show on her face. She glanced up into the darkening sky and said, "Look, it's the aurora again. You can really see it tonight."

Everyone looked up in awe of the beautiful colors slithering and swirling above them. "That means that we are still being blasted by solar storms. I wish I could see the images from the satellites and check out the CME's," Rebel said. "The sun is extremely aggravated. Do you think it's our passage through the galactic plane or do you think it's the Destroyer getting closer to us?"

"I think it is both," Dylan said. "I believe that the Mayan people gave us a true timeline and it was centered around all of this happening at the same time."

"What is happening at the same time?" Ric asked.

"The Mayan people believed that the fifth world or age, would end in catastrophe on this upcoming winter solstice," Darien explained. "On that exact date, the earth will complete its twenty six thousand year wobble and the sun's magnetic poles will flip ending its twenty-two year solar cycle. We will pass through the galactic plane and Planet X or the Destroyer is projected to pass by the earth completing its thirty six hundred year orbit. Not to mention that some scientists have predicted a geomagnetic pole shift in this time frame. We are overdue for a major earthquake on the Cascadia subduction zone and Yellowstone is overdue for an eruption. The sun's predicted once in a lifetime solar event has obviously already happened."

"That is almost overwhelming," Ric said. "How do you know all of this?"

"Well, that's the problem," Darien said. "We don't know all of it for sure. The solar cycle is fact based as well as the completion of earth's wobble. Scientist have proven that the poles have shifted before but the rest is based on theory."

"Einstein believed that a geomagnetic pole shift was possible if not inevitable," Cayden added.

"There are many predictions about this stuff from profits too. Edgar Casey predicted something about the rotational axis of the earth changing, shifting ocean basins and mountains," Dylan said. "His map shows oceans inundating all of the coasts. There will be ocean all the way to Idaho."

"That's a lot of water. Where would it come from?" Ric asked.

Rebel smiled and said, "Because of the way the earth rotates, the water is pulled to the equator. If the earths axis shifts moving the equator, the extra water that has basically pooled there will move as well."

Ric sighed dejectedly.

"There has to be a connection between the earth completing it's twenty six thousand year wobble and the passage through the galactic plane which also happens every twenty six thousand years. It's too coincidental to not be related. I'm guessing it has something to do with the gravitational pull from the black hole in the center of the galaxy," Warrick said.

"I find it amazing that the Mayan people knew about the black hole hundreds of years before we did. They believed that the fifth world would end in earthquake. The gravitational pull from the center of the galaxy would certainly do that," Shane said.

"If Planet X is out there, which I believe it is, we will most definitely experience a major geological change as its gravity tugs on earth. Some believe that it will actually pull the earth over on her side. That would be way worse than just a pole shift," Rebel added.

"Why do you believe it is out there?" Ric asked.

"Mostly because there isn't a better explanation for what is perturbing the orbits of Neptune, Uranus and Saturn. All scientists agree that something big is interfering with them. I believe that the government found it back in 1983 and covered it up. I also believe that they were keeping it off the satellite pictures that were on the Internet," Rebel said. "They announced finding a planet again last year. Remember? They said it was four times bigger than Jupiter and it was made of helium and hydrogen and it was at the edge of the ort cloud. Then they said, if its there, if its there. I never did get over that one."

"I remember that," Dylan laughed. "They knew how big it was, where it was and what it was made of then said, 'if its there'."

"Then a week later, they took down the WISE satellite which was the best satellite to detect infrared and the only way to see a brown dwarf," Rebel said. "A planet that big would certainly explain why the entire solar system is warming. It isn't just earth. The polar ice caps on Mars are melting and all of the planets have become warmer."

"My biggest fear from Planet X is that it will have traveled through the ort cloud on its way here throwing comets and meteors out of their orbits and straight into the inner solar system," Shane said. "We've already had an increased number of near earth objects fly by very close to earth in the past couple years."

"One guy online said that the I Ching supposedly ends on the same day as the Mayan calendar," Warrick said.

"What is the I Ching?" Ric asked completely into the story.

"It's the Chinese book of changes. Some say it is prophetic. It's been around for five thousand years," Rebel explained. "The Hopi people believe that we are entering into the fifth world and during the transition, the earth will go through a period of purification where trees will die and the earth will shake. The prophecy talks about the passing of the blue Kachina, then the red Kachina will arrive and right the earth's way. I believe it means it will put the earth back onto her natural rotation which just happens to be opposite of what it is now."

"I remember you telling me that The Cybil from the Roman empire, predicted that the world would last nine periods of eight hundred years and the tenth generation would be the last in 2000 AD, or something like that," Jade said.

"Sixteenth Century Mother Shipton also predicted earthquakes and changing oceans and some have related her prediction to what is happening today," Rebel added.

Cayden pulled more of the bird off of the spicket and said, "Didn't Merlin say something about a planetary catastrophe? Something like, seas shall rise, wind will blast, planets run out of their paths and run riot through the suns."

Rebel nodded, "Edgar Casey predicted that the Great Lakes would flow down the Mississippi River into the Gulf of Mexico. I have seen others say that the continent could split down the middle at the New Madrid Subduction Zone. But Nostradamus is my favorite seer. He said, 'draught and fire, everything will burn, meteors fall onto earth, time ended, stopped turning, the eagle of serpents head at center of galaxy."

"I just got shivers!" Ric said. "That is creepy."

"Are you talking about the quatrain being creepy or the fact that Rebel has it memorized?" Darien laughed.

"Funny Darien, but I'd bet money that you could recite that one as good as me," Rebel teased back. "Of course, that is someone's interpretation of his writing. The fact that on the winter solstice, the sun will rise in the center of the Milky Way and look like an eagle in its nest is fairly unnerving."

Conner sat silently listening to the exchange of horrific possibilities that could happen to the earth. Rebel had only briefly told him about some of them and it was eerie to listen to the list all at once.

"Wow!" Ric breathed. "That is all pretty ironic."

"Oh, they aren't finished," Jade laughed. "Go ahead mom, you might as well bring in the rest."

Ric looked at Rebel expectantly.

"I could quote several scriptures from the Bible but my favorite is Jeremiah 25:32 and 48:8, 'Disaster will spread from Nation to Nation. They will come like a powerful storm to all the faraway places on earth. The Destroyer will come against every town, not one town will escape. The Lord said this will happen'."

"Everyone knows the book of Revelations," Jade continued. "What was that one about the third angel?"

"The third angel sounded his trumpet and a great star blazing like a torch, fell from the sky," Rebel said.

"No wonder you are so agitated about getting home in time. I've never heard this stuff before," Ric exclaimed.

"The Book of Manuscripts in the Kolbrin Bible talks about the Destroyer also. It says something like, 'The Destroyer will appear, volcanoes, fires, water disappears and seas boil'." Rebel added. "Even Webbot has predicted that catastrophic events will peak in the year 2012."

"Are you ok Danny?" Dylan asked the completely stunned young man.

"Uh, ya," he stammered.

"Oh, I'm sorry. We didn't mean to freak you out," Jade said.

"No, I mean, are you telling me that this is what is going on right now?" he asked completely taken back by the conversation.

"We believe that at least some of these things may happen," Rebel said. "On a lighter note, here is a what if for you. Some believe that aliens biologically engineered humans. The ancient Sumerians called these beings the Annunaki. There are writings about them in Egyptian, Mayan, Incan, Aztec and Hebrew as well as many other cultures. The theory is that these alien beings used humans as slaves to mine gold for them."

"Biologically engineered? How the hell does that work?" Danny choked out.

Rebel laughed. "Well, I read someone's theory on the Internet that these beings took DNA from early human and mixed it with their own creating more intelligent human beings. Some say that these alien beings live on Nibiru and that every thirty six hundred years, the planet gets close enough to Earth for them to visit us. They say that on their previous visits to earth, they helped build the pyramids and other structures that we actually couldn't replicate today."

Danny looked at Ric then back at Rebel.

Rebel laughed again. "Danny, I don't expect you to believe everything that we said tonight. I only want you to realize that we could be facing more catastrophes in the near future."

"Well, I don't know what to believe now," he said. "Some of this sounds logical and Cayden told me that you were right about the CME taking out the power grid."

"You predicted that?" Ric asked.

"No, I just believed the predictions," Rebel corrected. "Everything that I've told you is on the Internet. Or, rather, was on the Internet. But some of it is hard to swallow and most people just won't take the time to research it."

"I'm going to have to have Darien tuck me into bed

tonight cause I am really freaked out," Ric laughed.

Darien jerked his head up and stiffened at the remark.

Everyone laughed making him actually blush.

"Well, on that note, I'm going to bed too. That is if I can actually stand up," Rebel said still smiling.

"Rebel what do you really believe will happen next?" Danny asked as Conner and Dylan helped her stand.

"I believe that we will suffer a geomagnetic pole shift. It could be caused from Planet X or the galactic plane. That means that we will be victims of many major earthquakes, tsunamis, hurricanes, tornados, and volcanic eruptions. We will most likely be impacted by large asteroids and I also believe that Yellowstone will erupt. Then I believe that the earth will be jerked to a standstill as the planet passes us," she said grimly. "Good night."

Conner helped her into her tent and under her sleeping bag. "Do you want another pain reliever?" Conner asked.

"No, I just want you," she said reaching for him.

Rebel woke up to agonizing pain in her leg as the sun was peaking through the particle filled sky. The volcanic ash and dust was mixing with clouds making the sun's rays brilliant in color.

Conner helped her dress and hobble to the fire where Warrick poured her a cup of coffee. Conner rolled a tree stump closer to the fire for her to sit on then went to find her pain medication.

"Remember that we aren't is a hurry sis. If you need some more time, please let us know," Warrick said quietly.

"Thanks Warrick. But I think I'll be ok," Rebel said.

Conner returned and handed her the tablet. "I hope these work for you Rebel. I don't want to see hurting."

Rebel looked up as Darien followed Ric out of her tent. She grinned and looked away sipping her coffee.

Warrick glanced over and grunted as they walked toward them.

Dylan climbed out of his tent and wondered toward

the coffee. "Good morning," he said searching for his cup.

Warrick picked it up from a rock by the fire then filled it and handed it to him.

"Thanks bro," Dylan mumbled. "How are you feeling Rebel? Are you sure you want to move on this morning?"

"Yes, I plan on spending the day riding under the influence of narcotics. If the pain gets too bad, I'll let you know," she answered.

Rebel noticed that Ric looked unusually happy sitting there sipping her coffee.

"Sleep well?" Rebel whispered.

Ric blushed and said, "Yes, very well."

Rebel laughed, "Good for you."

Warrick left to collect the horses and Dylan went to wake the boys. Conner left to wake the girls and Ric went to pack her stuff. Darien stayed still sipping his coffee staring into the fire.

Rebel looked at him and couldn't help teasing him. "So, good morning Darien."

"Mornin," he mumbled.

"Is everything ok?" she prodded.

"Uhuh," he mumbled distractedly, nodding his head as he watched the flames.

Rebel gave up as the boys stumbled sleepily to the coffee pot.

"What's wrong with him?" Cayden asked innocently.

Rebel grinned and shrugged.

"Let's pack the horses," Dylan hollered to the boys.

"Damn, I want some coffee first," Shane complained.

"Drink it while you ride, we will be moving slow," Dylan urged.

It didn't take long before the horses were saddled and packed. Conner helped Rebel mount Jake then turned to make sure the girls were ready.

"Is everyone good to go?" Warrick asked.

"I think so," Conner answered swinging onto his

horse.

Warrick and Dylan took the lead and Conner stayed by Rebel to keep an eye on her. Darien rode beside Ric and then the girls followed by the younger men.

They rode into the morning at a walk but at least they were moving toward home. The wound on Rebel's thigh throbbed from the pressure of the gauze packed tightly inside the hole. She felt a little better though, after two days on antibiotics.

She glanced down at Tucker who was happily trotting along beside Conner's horse. The dog hadn't left the man's side since the day he'd showed up.

"The brothers think that we will meet up with the River by nightfall," Conner said interrupting her thoughts, "They are a little concerned about the rest of that gang though. No telling which direction they would have gone last week."

"That's all we need," Rebel said. "Hopefully they are way north of here."

"You have been quiet all morning. Are you ok?" Conner asked.

"This volcano thing is freaking me out," Rebel said looking at the sun. "I'm worried about mom cause if Yellowstone goes off, they will be buried in ash." She paused for a moment, and added, "I got thinking about how many active volcano's were threatening to erupt before I left for D.C., and let me tell you, there were a lot of them."

Conner looked at her solemnly, "How many?"

"Thirty, forty at least. This pole shift is going to happen, Conner, and few if any humans will survive it," she pointed out.

"My sister in law owns a large piece of property in Montana. In one of her letters, she told me about a cave that they had found just after my brother was killed in an accident. She said that the Native Americans lived in the cave in ancient times and mentioned that it would still support life."

"You never told me that you had a brother. I'm sorry for your loss. I can't even imagine," she said sadly.

"Ya, it was some pretty rough times. He was a great guy. We were completely opposite people though. He was kind and loving and I … I wasn't. Maybe someday you will be able to meet my nephew," Conner said.

"I'd like that," she smiled. "I've read about very large ancient underground structures that supported up to thirty thousand people at a time. Can you imagine? They even had room for livestock."

"See, maybe we can survive this shit if we take a little advice from our ancestors," Conner teased.

"Have you ever heard about the Hopi Indian legend of the Ant People?" she asked.

"No, like crawl on the ground ants?" Conner laughed.

Rebel laughed with him. "No, I mean they believe that their people, the ant people, came from the earth. Everyone always thought it was a metaphoric statement, but I read online somewhere that the legend evolved from real people who lived under ground during some kind of major catastrophe, then come out of the ground when it was over, you know, like ants coming out of the earth."

"Weird, I never heard that," he pondered. "How do you know so much about the Hopi?"

"My great grandmother lived in a tiny little town just inside Utah by the Idaho border. She was really good friends with a little tribe of Native Americans that lived near there in a place called Washaki. She learned a lot about Native American culture from them and told me stories as a child. I remember visiting them there with her as a very small child. She gave Jade a necklace that she got from them and said it was very special. Jade never takes it off."

"Huh. They told her about the ants?"

"Yes, and the weird part is that some believe that alien beings came to earth and warned them of the pending doom and showed them how to survive it by going underground. Some even say that the beings still live underground today," she said grinning.

"Aliens? Do you believe that?"

"Well, that certainly isn't the only reference to extra terrestrial interaction. Every ancient culture has some kind of writing that could be interpreted as out of this world," she said seriously.

"Huh!"

"That may tie into your sister in law's cave somehow. I would love to hear about the legends that come from that area," she said.

"She is Native American, Shoshone I think. Her daddy was one of the elders. I'm going to have to get you two together," he laughed.

"If this cave of hers is what I imagine, it may be the only way to survive an eruption from Yellowstone," Rebel said looking up at the sky. "Look at those clouds."

Conner looked up. "That looks pretty bad." He turned in his saddle and looked behind them. "Wow, look back there, that looks even worse. If they collide it will produce a tornado."

Darien turned to see what Conner was talking about and said, "Holy shit! We better find some shelter." He kicked his big gilding into a gallop to catch up to Warrick and Dylan.

"This came up fast," Ric said nervously. "It wasn't like this when we woke up. I hate tornados. All these years I've lived here, I never got used to them."

Thunder clapped loudly behind them making Ric jump.

Rebel looked back at Jade and smiled reassuringly. "We are going to hole up for awhile," she said to her. "The brothers will find us some kind of shelter."

Jade nodded then glared at the sky as it started raining.

"Over here!" Darien yelled back at them. "There is a great big barn in that field. Looks empty!"

They rode through the gate and into the big doors of the structure as the rain turned to hail.

"God damn!" Warrick said slamming the doors closed, "We better take turns watching outside just in case."

"I'll take first watch," Shane volunteered.

Rebel shuttered as the hail pounded the roof of the old barn. Thunder rumbled outside and lighting flashed through the rotted boards on the walls.

"Touchdown!" Shane yelled from outside.

Dylan and Conner exchanged worried looks and walked to the door to see the beast.

"It's coming right for us!" Dylan yelled. "Get on the horses!"

Total chaos erupted in the barn as everyone tried to mount the nervous horses and grab the pack animals. The dogs started barking and Dylan's big gilding reared straight into the air.

"Hurry, god damn it!" Shane screamed throwing the doors open wide. "Run!"

Rebel slapped Jade's horse on the ass with her reins and followed the racing animal out into the pounding rain. The clouds were so dense it looked like nighttime. The wind sandblasted hail into their faces as they raced away from the raging twister.

"Keep going!" Rebel screamed at Jade through the wind. "Don't stop!"

Time slowed to a standstill as the twisting coil consumed everything in its path right on their heels. Rebel looked back and swore that they weren't even moving at all as the devouring monster gained on them.

They raced up the road, the fences giving them no way to get out of the tornados path until finally, the raging beast turned, following a gorge into the field next to them.

Jade pulled her winded horse to a stop and turned to find Rebel right behind her. "Where is everybody?" she asked in a panic.

Rebel looked around not seeing anyone. "My god, where are they?" she yelled through the rain. "Come on let's go back and find them."

They rode back to the field and were horrified to find the barn completely demolished. The horses were scattered throughout the field, milling around nervously.

Rebel could barely see through the rain but heard

Tucker barking relentlessly. "No!" she breathed. "Please no!"

Warrick was throwing boards from the crumbled structure searching. Cayden, Danny, and Lynn were riding toward them and Darien and Ric were dismounting beside Warrick, but Shane, Conner, and Dylan were nowhere to be seen.

She quickly dismounted and ran to Warrick.

"Dylan is still in there!" he yelled at her through the wind.

Rebel glanced around and spotted Shane who was badly battered sitting by Conner on the ground. Conner was holding his abdomen with both arms grimacing in agony. Rebel turned to the pile of lumber and started throwing boards. Darien, Cayden and Danny ran over and jumped into the search while the ladies checked on the wounded men.

"Here he is!" Warrick yelled and tossed another board off his brother.

"Dylan! Are you ok?" Rebel asked desperately but held her breath when she saw the piece of wood that had impaled his side under his arm.

He slowly nodded his head as Warrick and Cayden helped him stand and walk through the debris. They leaned him against the barely standing half wall and knelt down to check his wound.

"Don't pull it out yet," Rebel said as she looked around them searching for a place to set up the tents to get out of the rain. She spotted a stand of trees not far away. "I'm going to see if we can put the tents up over there."

She mounted Jake and galloped the half-mile across the field riding into the trees that grew along the bank of a small creek. She looked past the water and nearly cried out in excitement when she spied a little house beyond the trees on the other side. 'That will work even better,' she thought to herself and splashed through the creek to check it out.

The house was old and most likely unlivable but at least it was shelter. She climbed off her horse and went inside. It was furnished but she didn't see any personal belongings anywhere. There was a fireplace in the corner of the living room with a stack of wood beside it.

She raced back to Warrick and filled him in.

"Can we move them?"

"Yes, please move us," Dylan grimaced into the grumbling sky.

"We will put them on behind someone so they don't have to deal with the horse," Rebel said. "I'll go get your horses."

Once again, Jake proved himself. He was always there when she needed him, just standing there, patiently waiting for her.

She quickly mounted and rode to the huddling horses. She gathered Ace's reins and led him toward the demolished barn, the other horses following close behind.

Darien helped Conner onto Jake behind Rebel. Shane rode behind Cayden and Dylan rode behind Warrick. They trudged slowly through the rain across the creek to the little house.

Rebel helped Conner off of her horse then turned to open the door. "Cayden, there is a fireplace, would you start a fire? Here, put Dylan on the couch."

Shane hobbled in followed by Conner who was leaning heavily on Danny. Lynn and Ric entered carrying a couple of food packs.

"We will see if we can figure out something to eat," Ric said heading for the kitchen.

Danny and Cayden went outside to care for the horses and bring in the bedrolls. Rebel went to the couch and knelt down beside Dylan with the first aid kit. Warrick looked at her worriedly.

"He will be fine, Warrick," Rebel said reassuringly. "I don't think it punctured his lung or his breathing would be more labored. If it hit an artery he would be bleeding much worse. You pull the stick out and I'll put pressure on it. Ready? Go."

Warrick gently but firmly pulled the piece of wood out of his brother's side.

Dylan groaned and Rebel pushed a towel against the

flood of blood that flowed out of the wound. "That's a big hole Dylan."

"Great!" Dylan ground out.

"Jade, come here and hold this. Push hard. I need to check Shane and Conner," Rebel said going to Shane first.

"Hey little brother, what seems to be the problem," she smiled at him.

"I think my arm is broken," he said through gritted teeth.

"That's not good. Warrick, find me a splint," she said. "Darien, you are going to have to set it. How rusty is that military field training?"

"It's been awhile but I have done it before," he answered uneasily. "Are you ready Shane?"

Shane nodded apprehensively then cried out when Darien pulled the bones into place. Warrick returned and helped her splint the arm then they cleaned and bandaged the numerous cuts on his face and arms.

"K, Conner, it's your turn. What you got going on here?" Rebel asked.

"It's my god damn ribs again. Fuck! I'm sick of this shit!" he said breathing in sharp gasps.

"Shit Conner, your never gonna heal," Rebel said shaking her head. "Let me have a look just to make sure." She gently lifted his shirt and grimaced at the huge fresh bruise that covered his abdomen and side. "Jesus! This is getting serious Conner. You could be bleeding internally and your lung could collapse."

Warrick took a closer look and nodded, "That is a big bruise."

Darien nodded with concern.

"I can't do anything for you," Rebel said sadly. "You need a doctor. I have pain meds for now though."

Conner stopped her from reaching for the bottle. "Those are for you. You need them."

"I have plenty. We will find more. We'll make it our mission from now on to find pharmacies wherever we go," she laughed trying to ease his mind.

Ric and Lynn handed them food.

"Sorry, it's just soup. I warmed it in the cans over the fireplace."

"That's just fine," Warrick said smiling at her.

Rebel bandaged Dylan's wound and helped him sit up to eat.

"Fire feels good," he said trying to figure out how to eat his dinner with one hand.

"I want to find another doctor tomorrow," Rebel said. "Are there any towns ahead of us or should we go back?"

"There should be a small town about thirty miles from here," Dylan said. "But no telling if there is a doctor there."

"Ya, and that puts on a direct path toward the rest of that gang," Darien said.

"I don't want to go backward," Dylan insisted. "We should just ride on until we find a doctor."

"I agree," Conner said. "Shane, what do you think?"

"I'm fine. We will leave in the morning," Shane said firmly.

"Let's find some dry clothes and see what kind of beds are in the house," Rebel said, satisfied with the decision. Ric and the girls followed her upstairs.

It was a four bedroom house and soon everyone had found a place to sleep for the night. The wind stopped howling and the rain slowed to a drizzle.

Rebel lay awake next to Conner, unable to sleep. "What happened in that barn?" she asked him.

"Cayden and Lynn followed you and Jade out but after Darien and Ric rode out, the horses freaked and we couldn't get on them. We managed to at least get them out before the tornado sideswiped the barn, collapsing it on top of us. I was thrown into the air and landed on top of the debris after the structure collapsed," he said quietly.

"I'm worried about your breathing. A pulmonary contusion is dangerous. I want to know if you cough up blood or if you feel dizzy from lack of oxygen, ok?" Rebel said. "The pain will cause short rapid breathing so it may not be as bad as I think, but we won't know till you see a doctor."

"How is Shane? Did Darien get his arm set good?" Conner asked intentionally changing the subject.

"Yes, I think so. The danger there is a blood clot," she said worriedly. "But I'm really worried about Dylan. He is as stubborn as you and that hole is deep. I'll be surprised if it didn't hit something deep in his chest cavity. Thank god we all recently got our tetanus shots."

"You all went and got tetanus shots?" he asked suddenly amused.

"I told you that we prepared as much as possible. We knew that medications would potentially be scarce for awhile," she said defensively. "We are all EMT's too."

Conner laughed. "Well, you were right. All the precautions have paid off so far."

"Have you ever heard of Ophiuchus?" she asked intently, suddenly agitated.

Conner looked at her in surprise. "No."

"Nostradamus believed that there were thirteen signs in the zodiac. Ophiuchus is number thirteen. The unlucky sign," she said pointedly. "If we took this sign into consideration in our astrology, I wouldn't be a Sagittarius, I would have been born under Ophiuchus."

"K, I don't get it," he said confused.

"Bad Luck! I have always had bad luck. My mom always said it was a black cloud following me around but it is truly bad luck, because of Ophiuchus," she mumbled.

"You can't really believe that a zodiac sign can have that kind of power?" he said laughing again.

"Well, it sure seems that way to me!" she pouted. "How else do you explain this shit. One injury after another. We are never going to make it home."

Conner tugged her up against his wide chest and said, "I know it seems that way but we will get there. Besides, I have always had good luck so we will balance each other out."

Rebel laughed and snuggled inside his arm. "I'm

sorry. I don't mean to be so negative."

"Get some sleep and we will be on our way in the morning," he soothed.

Chapter 12

The next morning Rebel found Darien sitting on the front porch sipping coffee and Warrick pacing the front lawn waiting for Cayden and Danny to bring the horses.

She sat her cup down and looked into the sunrise. "What are you thinking?" she asked.

"I don't like that color. It's almost as if more than one volcano has erupted. Redoubt was grumbling before we left and Mount Rainier was acting up as well. I hope Yellowstone doesn't decide to join forces," he said.

"Let's just hope that if it goes it's hydrothermic not magmatic. It's possible that the magma under the caldera is somewhat solid. It is spread underneath several states so maybe some of it will be blocked and won't make it to the surface," she pondered.

"Or it will go off like it did in ancient times and blow a hole as big as the Snake River Valley," he said looking into the sunrise.

"Way to think positive," Rebel laughed as Ric walked out the door.

"What is the Snake River Valley," she asked nervously.

"The Snake River Valley is a huge ancient calderas that almost reaches across the entire state of Idaho. It is the path of the volcano as the earth's crust moved over the hot spot. Most people don't realize that the magma chamber under a volcano doesn't move but the earth's crust does. So as the crust drifts, the magma creates new openings sort of in a chain. Like the Hawaiian Islands. Yellowstone has actually erupted in what is now Idaho."

"How the hell do you know all this shit?" she asked.

"I really don't know that much. It's just how I interpret what I read and I hope that I'm telling you correctly. I'm certainly not a professional. I put this all together from researching online."

Ric nodded. "I'll bet it took a long time."

"Yes, years," she smiled then asked her brother, "How is Dylan this morning?"

"He's pretty stiff. We are going to have to go slow again. Your favorite words," he laughed with her.

"We are packed and saddled," Warrick said walking onto the porch. "We have two pack horses that can't be led. I packed 'em light cause they will just have to follow."

"Do you think that the gang is this far west? They won't go east because of the other gang and they won't go south into Lincoln city, which means that they will go west," Rebel said nervously.

"I'm worried about that too, but we don't have a choice," Darien said.

Ric and the girls filed out of the house followed by Shane. Dylan walked through the door leaning heavily on Warrick and Conner shuffled out behind them.

"Your still not breathing right," Rebel said as Darien helped him onto his horse.

He gathered up the reins and said, "Don't worry, I'll manage."

The party slowly headed toward the little city where they hoped to find yet another doctor.

The sun was trying to shine through the grayish yellow dust that still filtered through the atmosphere. The clouds had disappeared during the night and the ground was starting to dry.

"Do you see the destruction path from that tornado?" Cayden asked looking at the half-mile wide trail of debris.

Everyone nodded grimly.

Conner groaned next to Rebel bringing everyone's attention to him. His face was pale and he was breathing sharply. "Sorry," he grumbled when he noticed the attention he received. "I'm fine!"

"Ya, you look just fine," Warrick said sarcastically.

"We are almost there," Darien said. "Just hang on a few more miles.

Rebel glanced at Dylan who wasn't doing so well either. Everyone was silent as they trudged on.

Darien reined in at the outskirts of the small town

and said, "Warrick, let's check it out. You guys just hang tight for a minute."

The two rode into the city looking for the hospital or a police officer. "Over there," Darien pointed.

They dismounted in front of the police station and went into the building.

"We are looking for a doctor. Do you have one in town?" Warrick asked.

"Yes, but he is overwhelmed with patients right now," the officer said peering at them suspiciously.

Warrick glared back at him and asked, "Wounded from the tornado?"

"Well, that and…" he trailed off.

"What!" Warrick said harshly.

The poor man jumped and instinctively put his hand over his weapon.

"Easy there," Darien said stepping between the two men. "Warrick has injured family and is anxious to find medical attention for them."

The man relaxed a little and said, "Ya, I'm a little anxious too. We were recently engaged in a fight with a gang a that has moved into the high school across town."

"Are you telling me that the gang is at the school right now?" Warrick asked in a mockingly quiet voice.

"Yes, they say they are staying," the officer said looking at his boot. "We had to evacuate all the people that lived over there. I've sent word to the National Guard, hopefully they will be here tonight."

"So how did so many people get injured?" Darien asked.

"The gang opened fire into a crowd who were trying to stop them from coming into town," the officer said.

"Where is the hospital?" Warrick demanded.

"It's that way three blocks," the man pointed.

Warrick spun around and walked to the door.

"How many in the gang?" Darien asked.

"I'm guessing fifty or sixty. They are running out of ammo but they are deadly with a knife."

"Thanks for the info," Darien said following

Warrick.

They mounted their horses and rode the short distance to the hospital. Darien went inside and to the front desk where an older woman was scowling. "We need to see a doctor," he stated.

The woman looked up at the tall rugged man in front of her and her entire demeanor changed. She smiled and was suddenly fidgety. "The doctor is still in surgery, if you can call it surgery with no power. It will be at least another hour," she said nervously.

Darien flashed the woman a charming smile, trying to encourage her to help them. "We will be back. Will you please let him know we are coming?"

The woman smiled back and hurriedly sat at the desk. "I will make you an appointment. What is the injury?"

"Well, ma'am," Darien said, keeping up the charming charade, "we have a broken arm, a deep puncture wound and some broken ribs that are affecting the lung."

"Fine," she almost swooned. "I will see you in an hour."

Darien tipped his hat at her making her blush then walked out the door.

"So?" Warrick demanded as he mounted his horse.

"We can see the doctor in an hour, but I don't think we should bring everyone into town. I got a bad feeling about this place," Darien said as he pushed his horse into a run.

They rode back to the group who were waiting anxiously for their return.

"There is a doctor, but there is also fifty or sixty gang members a few blocks from the hospital," Darien said. "I want the ladies to wait here. We will take all the men with us. Rebel turn on the radio just in case."

"Fine!" Rebel said stepping off her horse.

Ric grinned and dismounted. "Should we make camp or are we riding on."

"Go ahead and make camp, Ric. We will be back to help you as soon as we can," Darien said. "Get yourselves something to eat." Then he waved the men back toward the small town.

Rebel turned on the radio and started pacing.

Darien led the seven men to the hospital. "Cayden, Danny, stash the horses then guard the door," he instructed then helped Dylan dismount.

Warrick helped Conner off of his horse and followed Shane into the hospital.

The older woman eagerly rushed up to Darien. "Follow me gentlemen," she purred, showing them to a room. "I'll tell the doctor that you are here."

Warrick laughed when the woman practically curtsied and said, "What kind of spell did you put on her?"

Darien grinned. "You know, it's the one that gets us fast tracked to the doctor."

Shane joined Warrick in another round of laughter.

A very young doctor walked in followed by a young woman about twenty-five years old. She wore jeans and a t-shirt with her hair pulled back in a ponytail.

Warrick felt Shane stiffen as she walked by and glanced at his younger brother who was trying not to look at her. He grinned and stood up and said, "I'll wait outside."

The doctor held out his hand to Darien and said, "I'm Doctor Keller, just call me Ted. We don't need to be formal these days. This is Gabrielle. We call her Gabe. So, what do we have here?"

Darien pointed at Shane and said, "My brother broke his arm, which I hope I set correctly, and Dylan here was impaled by a large stick under his arm, and Conner reinjured some broken ribs and now he can't breathe."

"Is that all?" Ted laughed. "I thought it was going to hard." He went to Shane first and inspected his arm. "As far as I can tell without an X-Ray, the break was clean and yes, set correctly." He turned to Gabe and said, "Will you prepare his arm for a cast and check those lacerations?"

As Gabe started working on Shane's arm, the doctor helped Dylan out of his shirt. "That is a nasty hole. How were you guys injured?"

"We were in a barn and the tornado brought it

down on top of us," Shane said smiling at Gabe, who returned the gesture.

Ted picked up a syringe and injected Novocain around and into the deep wound. "I need to clean this so I can see what's going on in there. I know everyone in town and don't recognize you, where are you from?"

"We are on our way back home to Idaho," Darien said.

Gabe inhaled sharply and sat up strait in her chair.

"Gabe here is from Utah," Ted said. "She was going to med school in Omaha and got stuck here visiting her grandfather when the power went out."

"Ya, this power thing is a nightmare. We got stuck out here too," Shane said.

The doctor finished cleaning Dylan's wound and looked up at him. "It's deep. It broke a rib but missed the vitals. I think it will heal just fine though if we can keep it from getting infected. I am going to put a drain tube in it. I'll need to keep an eye on it for the next week or so."

"Doc, we are hitting the road as soon as we are done here," Dylan said firmly.

The doctor eyed him for a moment then said, "It needs to be checked. You will have to find another doctor on the way then."

He turned his attention to Conner. He put his scope to his chest and listened to his lungs then carefully felt the broken ribs. "At least four of them are broken. That bruise tells me that they are broken in several places and your lungs are in danger. I wish I could get a picture of them."

The doctor stood up and paced the small room. "I can't do much for you especially if you are on the move. I'm concerned that you will puncture a lung and your heart is at risk as well. I'm amazed the lung hasn't collapsed. The only way to fix a broken rib is to lay in a bed for a couple months or so." He spun around and said, "You should be in a hospital!"

"Sorry doc," Conner said. "We are moving on. Just do what you can do."

The doctor held up his finger indicating that they should wait a moment, then left the room. He returned a couple minutes later with some kind of body wrap.

"That looks like a girdle," Shane laughed.

"It isn't a very conventional method of treatment, but it may help limit your movement. It will put you at risk for developing pneumonia so only wear it when you're moving. Take it off at night. I'm putting you on antibiotics and giving you a breathing tool. Use it," Ted said handing them to him. "Let's get the cast on Shane's arm and I'll see what I can do for pain meds."

The brothers paid the doctor and thanked him for his time. They each had a bottle of narcotics in their pocket and fresh bandages as they walked out of the hospital.

Darien helped Conner mount while Warrick held Ace still for Dylan. They were just turning their horses to leave when Gabe burst out the hospital doors.

"Wait!" she yelled desperately, "Please, take me with you!"

The men looked at each other in surprise.

"Please! I don't belong here," she begged her eyes filling with tears. "I won't be any trouble and I can get a horse."

Shane jumped off of his horse and approached her attempting to comfort her then looked at Darien.

Darien looked at Warrick who looked at Dylan. All three of them shrugged.

"I don't see any reason to say no," Darien said.

Gabe smiled and said, "Thank you so much. Give me one second." Then she disappeared back into the hospital. When she returned, she carried a large medical bag. "I had them pay me in supplies. Now I can help tend your wounds along the way."

Cayden took the bag and Shane helped her onto his horse behind him.

"I live about a half mile that way," she said pointing. "I just want to grab some cloths and get a horse."

They turned their horses toward her house but pulled up short as fifteen rough looking men crossed the street walking toward them.

Conner and the brothers all reached for their weapons leveling them onto the group.

"Don't let them in the hospital," Gabe breathed uneasily. "They will steal the supplies."

"This hospital is by appointment only," Darien said riding in front of the door, "and no large groups allowed."

"Get the fuck out of the way!" one of the men spat pointing his weapon back and Darien.

"You don't want to take us on you fuckers!" Warrick barked. "Unlike you, we are fully armed and will take you out!"

"We'll see about that!" the man ground out waving for his friends to follow him back to the school.

Dylan took a deep breath and shook his head knowing that another war had just started. He picked up the radio and said, "Rebel, bring the extra guns and ammo. Come alone!"

"Got it," Rebel answered.

Darien rode to the sheriff's office and told the officer, "Bring your weapons and anyone who can shoot. The National Guard isn't going to be here in time." He rode back to the hospital and instructed Cayden to take the horses to the back.

"We gonna do this here?" Conner asked.

Dylan shrugged, "It will be easy to treat the wounded."

Conner shook his head and grinned.

Rebel rode up with a packhorse and dismounted shaking her head, "Whose idea was this?"

Everyone pointed at Warrick.

"What?" he asked feigning innocence.

The officer strode anxiously toward them with twenty men. "We lost the last round, why do you think we will survive this one?"

"Stop being such a fucking pussy," Warrick growled. "You said they were out of ammo and we are well armed so let's get them out of your town."

Darien glanced around them trying to find a blockade so they could take cover. "Over there," he said pointing to the decorative ledge that surrounded the hospital entrance. "They won't even get close."

"Gabe, go into the hospital," Shane said. "This is gonna get bloody."

Everyone took their position against the brick wall and leveled their rifles across the flowerbeds.

"Here they come!" Warrick grinned looking through his scope. "At least fifty of them. They are walking in the middle of the road all grouped up just like the British Redcoats."

"Wait till they fire first," the officer ordered.

"No wonder you lost the first round!" Warrick growled. "Fire!"

Rebel, Conner and the brothers all fired at the same time followed by the men with the sheriff. Half the gang members fell to the ground instantly.

The officer looked around in amazement.

"Fire!" Warrick encouraged again and got the same response.

Many more men fell to the second round. The few remaining gang members turned and hightailed it back to the school.

Rebel, Conner and the brothers each took out another man before they disappeared around the corner.

"Who missed?" Warrick glowered at the men.

"Warrick," Rebel soothed. "Get off their ass. They did the best they could."

Warrick turned on the officer and yelled, "This isn't the same world it was a two months ago! You are going to have to grow some balls and act like a leader here."

The officer flushed with anger and pointed his gun at Warrick then paled when Warrick didn't even flinch. He looked past him and saw seven rifles pointed back at him.

One of the men pushed the officer's rifle down and said, "We appreciate your help here. I think we will be able to handle it now."

The doctor stepped out the door worriedly and said,

"Thank you, they would have shut us down if you hadn't been here. You can carry in the wounded."

Dylan looked at the doctor seriously and said, "There ain't no wounded."

Warrick laughed and added, "We don't work that way." Then he turned to the boys and said, "Get the horses, we're out of here."

Shane helped Gabe back onto the horse and they headed out leaving the officer to bury the dead.

"This is Gabe," Shane introduced her. "She is from Utah and is going to ride home with us."

"Hi Gabe, glad to meet you," Rebel said to her then turned to Conner. "What did the doctor say?"

"He couldn't do anything, just like you said. But he gave us all pain meds so we can ride," Conner said slurring a little.

Rebel tilted her head curiously and looked at Darien.

"The doc gave him a shot of morphine," Darien shrugged. "He will be feelin good for awhile."

"He just fired a rifle two feet from my head all doped up on morphine?" Rebel laughed. "That would have been good to know beforehand."

Darien laughed. "Ya, but he did hit his mark."

"Darien did a good job setting the break," Shane said proudly holding up his arm. "The doc just had to put a cast on it."

Rebel looked at Dylan expectantly.

"He put a drain in the hole," he shrugged. "Wanted me to stay for a week."

"But Gabe is a doctor and said she would take care of him," Shane said looking at Gabe.

"I'm not a doctor yet. I'm a medical student," Gabe corrected.

"Close enough," Darien said laughing.

"Ya, wait till you see the knife wound in Darien's shoulder and the hole in Rebel's leg," Cayden said.

Gabe looked at Rebel curiously. "How did you get a hole in your leg?"

"She was shot," Shane answered for her.

They rode into the camp that Ric and the girls had setup, surprised that they had handled it all by themselves.

"Ric, you go girl," Rebel said appreciatively.

"I made you guys something to eat," Ric said happily handing them food.

Later that evening Rebel could tell the pain medication was wearing off Conner. He was gritting his teeth against the obvious pain and a groan escaped his lips every once in a while.

Rebel sat down beside him and stretched out her leg. It was on fire after the long day on the horse and the momentary gunfight.

Gabe walked up with her bag and announced, "I have a surprise for you." She dug in her bag and pulled out a vile of morphine. "I took it off the table when I cleaned up."

"Way to go doc!" Dylan said.

"I also got more antibiotics just in case," she said with satisfaction. "Rebel, can I see your wound?"

"Sure, the gauze is starting to come out so you can help me fix it," Rebel said.

"If you are in pain, I'm sure the guys would share their medication," Gabe laughed.

Everyone gathered around the fire for coffee just as the sun dipped below the horizon. Thanks to Gabe, pain was not the main focus tonight.

Rebel woke the next morning to Cayden yelling excitedly that he hit the target with the bow. She climbed out of the tent and smiled at Conner who was propped on a log giving him pointers.

"Wow, a smile before coffee," Conner teased her.

She shook her head and walked to the fire and her coffee cup.

Shane was watching Gabe intently as she cleaned and bandaged Dylan's wound.

"Your next," she said to Rebel.

Rebel nodded and poured her cup full then sat next to Dylan. "How's it feeling?"

"Not good, sis. If it weren't for the pain meds I don't think Conner or I would be riding," he said.

"Let's keep an eye out for a place to hole up for a few more days. I doubt if we will find a place as nice as Ric's was, but I'm sure we will run into something," she said.

Dylan looked at her in surprise.

She shrugged and said, "We travel faster when we are healed. And besides, if we had to fight, we would be at a disadvantage."

"We did just fight," Warrick said as he and Darien walked up with the horses. "Let's get going before someone else decides to take us on."

"Hold up there!" Gabe said to Darien. "I want to see your wound too mister. Get in line."

"Well now, she does sound like a doctor," Darien laughed.

Gabe blushed, "Sorry, I didn't mean to be forceful. I just want to make sure none of you are critical. It's much easier to treat a wound before it gets out of control."

"By all means, Doc, treat away," Darien said still laughing.

Gabe gave Dylan his pain medication and turned to Rebel's leg. "Wow, I can't get over this hole," she said as she carefully inspected the surrounding tissue and snipped off the gauze that was working its way out. "We want to leave it in there, just cut it off as it comes out. What are these nasty lacerations from?"

"She was attacked by a mountain lion," Conner said walking up behind them. "She killed the damn thing with her bare hands."

"Almost," Rebel corrected.

Gabe visibly stiffened and her jaw dropped in amazement.

"I almost lost her to an infection a few days later," he said looking at Rebel affectionately.

Gabe closed her mouth and turned back to the wound. "This bruise didn't come from the bullet. I didn't see it last night in the dark," she mused.

"No, that came from a fight. She killed the man who kicked her though," Dylan said proudly.

Rebel laughed when Gabe's jaw dropped a second time. "That is a very short version of the story. Trust me. God! You guys make me sound like a murdering, killing monster."

"Girl," Gabe said. "I'm just glad I'm on your side! I watched your aim yesterday against that gang and it was dead on." Gabe paused looking again at the wound." I want to keep you on the antibiotics for another couple days. I'll bet that gauze will be ready to come out by then." She bandaged her leg and turned to Darien. "Let's see what you've got going on."

Darien took off his shirt and sat down by Rebel. "So doc, what's your story?" he asked while she looked at his injury.

"I wanted out of Utah so I came out here to go to school," she said.

"Is your family waiting for you back home?" Shane asked.

"Not really. My mother was never home, she traveled a lot. I don't even know where she is. My father is probably still in out there, but we don't talk much," she said sadly.

"Maybe you could just come to Idaho with us," Shane said timidly.

Gabe looked at him sincerely and said, "I think I am imposing enough."

"We would be glad to have you," Darien said nodding to Shane.

Gabe didn't reply. She was studying the wound in Darien's shoulder. "How long have you been taking penicillin? This infection is still pretty bad. I want to clean it three times a day minimum."

Darien smiled and said, "Yes ma'am." He put his shirt back on and said, "Now that the doc has us all fixed up, let's get going."

They broke camp and packed the horses.

Conner was moving slow even with the pain

medication. His face was that familiar pale color and his breathing was still erratic. He grimaced as he mounted his horse.

Rebel paced her horse next to Gabe and said, "We are going to find a place to stay for a few days. Conner doesn't look good."

"That's good news. I know men are stubborn but he is terrible. Ted, the doctor in town, was really worried about his ribs puncturing his lung. I noticed that they left that little fact out. His injury is life threatening," she said solemnly.

Rebel glanced at Conner and shook her head. "I almost lost him when he was shot. He bled so much that the doctor back there couldn't believe he was alive. He still hasn't recovered from that yet."

"I'll keep an ear on his lungs and watch him close but he shouldn't be riding," she agreed.

Later in the evening, Warrick reined in his horse and yelled back, "I see a cabin up ahead. I'm going to check it out."

He quickly returned and said excitedly, "It looks like a vacation house. No one is there. It has a well and a propane barbeque with propane," he grinned.

All their spirits lifted as they rode up to the huge cabin. "This is great!" Darien said. "Let's settle in for a few days."

They unpacked their supplies on the back deck and unsaddled the horses.

"While you guys settle in, I'm going to find a deer or something to cook on that grill," Warrick said.

"There are six bedrooms," Jade said. "Come on Lynn, they are so cool. I didn't think we would get to sleep in a bed again this soon."

Rebel and Ric took a look in the kitchen and were excited to see it was fully stocked with canned food and dry goods. They started pulling out stuff to make dinner.

"Look! Dutch ovens. I'll make us a cake and some biscuits," Ric said.

Shane, Cayden and Danny returned from staking the

horses and cheered when they heard cake.

Conner sat down on the couch sighing. He leaned back to take the pressure off of his ribs. "Oh this is much better."

"You look like shit!" Danny said to him.

"Nothin a good night in a bed won't fix," he said trying to smile.

"Ric is making cake," Shane said. "That will fix anything."

Warrick walked in and said, "Come help me with this deer. We are grilling tonight. Darien, Dylan, you are on the couch next to Conner!"

It didn't take long before dinner was ready and everyone was talking and laughing.

"I'll check the cake. It should be about done," Ric added.

"I'm going upstairs," Conner said. "That bed is calling my name."

Rebel stood to help him up the stairs and into a room at the end of the hall. She turned down the bed and helped him lay down then removed his boots. "I'm glad we stopped for a few days. You don't look good."

Conner looked her up and down and said, "Well, you are looking pretty good."

"Conner, you should rest," she said seriously.

He reached out and grabbed her pulling her on top of him then kissed her with such passion, she couldn't drag herself away.

Four days later, Rebel joined her friends and family on the back deck with a cup of coffee in her hand. "This reminds me of mom's porch back home."

"Me too," Dylan said. "I sure can't wait to get there."

"How is everyone feeling? Do we need a few more days?" she asked.

"That depends on how Conner is doing. He has the most severe injury," Darien said.

"Conner is feeling just fine," he said walking

through the door. He winked at Rebel and added, "I sure wish I could take that bed with me though."

"I wish I could take that grill and those Dutch ovens so Ric could cook like this every day," Warrick said.

Everyone laughed.

"I say we stay one more night and leave in the morning," Rebel said.

Conner looked at her somewhat surprised. "I thought you would be the one demanding we leave right now."

"I just want to make sure everyone is ok before we move on. Then we won't have to stop again," she shrugged. "Gabe, what do you think?"

"Darien's knife wound is healing nicely now that we have the infection under control. I pulled the drain out of Dylan's wound this morning and short of falling off of his horse and opening it back up, he is doing fine."

Dylan huffed, "I've never went off my horse!"

"Of course not, that would have messed up your hair and got your shirt dirty," Warrick teased.

Everyone roared with laughter.

Gabe smiled and continued, "The gauze has worked it's way out of Rebel's leg so I see no problem there and Shane is doing fine in his cast. Conner is my only concern."

It was Conner's turn to huff. "I'm ready to go. I'm feeling much better."

"Just remember, Conner, that it takes six to eight weeks to heal a broken rib and that is if you are lying down the whole time," Gabe reprimanded. "You are still at risk of one of them puncturing your lung."

Conner scowled at that. "I'm not holding up the parade! We leave in the morning!"

Darien looked at Rebel who shrugged and said, "Fine, we leave in the morning."

"I'm going to bake all day so we will have cake and bread on the road," Ric volunteered.

"I'll cook up a mess of venison to take with us too," Warrick added.

Everyone sat around enjoying the conversation well into the morning then spent the rest of the day preparing their packs to leave.

The next morning, they woke up to peach cobbler and coffee.

"Is everyone ready to head out?" Darien asked.

"Yes, the grill is out of gas," Warrick pouted.

"I wish we could watch another movie," Jade said thoughtfully.

Rebel smiled. "Isn't it amazing the things we miss when we have no power? I have missed the Internet the most. I used to brows and research for hours every day."

"I never was much for computers," Conner said, "but I do miss the television."

"I miss my x-box," Cayden said.

"Me too!" Shane agreed.

"Well, let's get the horses packed and saddled," Warrick said as he stood up. "We are almost to the river."

"I hope there is a bridge so we don't have to see you cry again," Darien said.

"Fuck you!" Warrick said flipping him the bird and stomping off the porch.

Dylan laughed and followed him toward the horses.

"I'm glad we got to restock our supplies. Whoever vacationed here was very thorough," Ric said. "I know they are heavy but I stuck a couple small Dutch ovens in the pack."

"Good Ric, it will be fine and thank you again for cooking for us," Rebel said.

"Thank you again for letting me tag along," she replied.

Rebel climbed on her horse and was relieved that her leg didn't hurt as bad today. The horses were fresh and ready to go. Jade and Lynn were chatting happily and the boys were rested and eager.

Conner mounted the gilding and grimaced in pain. He tried not to let it show but Rebel wasn't the only one who saw it.

"You might as well use the pain medication if you

need it Conner," Gabe said. "Just let me know."

He nodded and swung his horse toward the front of the group next to Warrick. "Let's go," he said.

They set the pace at a slow lope.

The sun was trying to pierce through the volcanic ash in the atmosphere producing that familiar gray yellow color that felt like doom. Rebel looked up and realized that she could still look right into the sun without hurting her eyes. She was gazing upward lost in thought when two streaks of light appeared, flashing through the heavens.

"Did you see that?" she asked Jade.

"No. What?" Jade said looking up.

"There is another one!" she pointed. "Warrick, slow up for a minute."

"I saw it. I think it was a meteor," Jade said excitedly as she slowed her horse to a walk.

"There are no scheduled meteor showers right now," Rebel said apprehensively, "but I've seen a lot of meteors lately especially since the lights went out.

"What does that mean?" Jade asked.

"It may be nothing. We have random meteors hit us all the time but if it continues, and there are a lot of them, I would start to assume that Planet X is throwing rocks out of their orbits and really causing a disturbance out in space. It could be blowing debris right at us and we could be in for some impact events," Rebel said.

"Wouldn't we see the planet by now if it was real?" Jade asked.

"Well, they say its about four times the size of Jupiter, so theoretically we will just see another star until it's as close to us as Jupiter is," Rebel explained. "Planets move fairly quickly so if its projected orbit is accurate, we should start to see it with our naked eye in a few months."

"That puts its arrival almost exactly December, 2012," Jade said. "The Mayans may have been right on the money."

"Are you guys talking about the 2012 end of the world stuff?" Gabe asked. "You think that is real?"

Everyone looked at her and said, "Yes!" in unison.

"Ok, maybe I am somewhat ignorant. Please, fill me in."

Rebel and Jade proceeded to tell her their theories about what was happening as they rode at a walk for the next few miles.

"Hey, let's stop and eat while you finish your story," Warrick yelled back.

Rebel kept talking while they dismounted and sat down to eat some lunch. "I don't mean to say that it's the end of the world but I believe it will be the end as we know it."

"Someone is coming!" Cayden said running toward them just ahead of twenty armed men that stepped through the trees.

"Don't even stand up!" one of the men said pointing a pistol at Darien. "You! Sit down!" he said to Cayden and Danny.

"What do you want?" Dylan asked angrily.

"We will be relieving you of your horses," the man informed them.

Rebel reached down and unsnapped the strap that held her weapon in the holster freeing the colt. She instinctively edged herself in front of Jade.

Dylan glared at the man unwaveringly. "You better back off right now or you won't be seeing the sun set tonight," he growled.

"Oh? You are going to fight us?" he laughed incredulously. "You're outnumbered three to one!"

Dylan didn't even blink.

The man hesitated as he tried to stare him down but looked away, his eyes going to Lynn, Jade and Gabe.

Rebel whispered into Jades ear, "If this goes down you get behind that rock! Understand?"

"Yes," she breathed nervously.

"Ok," the man laughed, "go ahead. Fight us. And once you're all dead, who is going to save the girls?" he asked tauntingly, still laughing.

"I'm your huckleberry," Warrick said in a deadly

voice as he stepped from behind a tree with his revolver leveled at him.

All twenty men turned to him in surprise and the split second distraction was all they needed. Rebel whipped out the colt and pulled the trigger at the same time Conner and her brothers fired. She shoved Jade behind the rock and took aim again bringing down a second man then a third.

The smell of gunpowder filtered through the deadly silence as Rebel looked around to make sure everyone was ok.

"I'm your huckleberry?" Darien said sarcastically bringing a roar of laughter from everyone except Lynn, Jade, Gabe and Ric, who were still sitting on the ground stunned.

"Fuck You! I had to say something that would get their attention and it worked!" Warrick defended with a sheepish grin.

Everyone laughed again.

Rebel reached down to Jade and pulled her to her feet. "Are you ok?"

She nodded silently.

Cayden helped Lynn stand and Shane came rushing to Gabe who was trembling.

"How are you doing Ric?" Darien asked walking toward his horse.

"I'm good," she said sucking in a shaking breath. "I guess I'm just going to have to get used to that."

Rebel laughed and said, "I wish that weren't so."

"You ok doc?" Warrick asked walking past her toward the heap of dead bodies.

Gabe nodded still trembling and leaned into Shane.

Darien emptied a gym bag and followed him to gather up the dead men's weapons. "I've heard you recite movies before Warrick but that's the first time I've heard Doc Holiday," he said laughing again at Warrick.

Dylan nodded and repeated sarcastically, "I'm your huckleberry."

"Shut up you fuckers!" Warrick bellowed, "Tombstone is one of my favorite movies."

Rebel laughed again and said, "Let's mount up." She wanted to get the girls away from the bloody scene.

Conner could see that Jade was still trembling so he paced his gilding next to her, trying to ease her anxiety. "Hang in there kiddo," he said softly. We will be fine, K?"

She smiled bravely and nodded, thankful that he was close.

That evening they stopped to make camp for the night. Everyone was quiet as they pitched the tents and made a fire. Warrick made coffee and Ric unpacked supplies to make dinner.

Rebel sat down next to Conner and looked into the darkening sky. Meteors were falling all over now. "I don't like this," she said.

"That planet won't hit us will it?" Conner asked looking up.

"No, its not supposed to but who knows what the government is hiding. It could sure as shit flip us on our ass though," she said softly.

"Ya, I remember the story," he breathed.

"Dinner!" Ric yelled to the boys.

Everyone gathered around the fire to eat and the conversation turned to the meteors now falling like rain above them.

"This reminds me of the depiction I saw online of the Leonid meteor shower in 1833. They actually called it a meteor storm. The story says that there were so many meteors it looked like it was raining fireballs. We will get to see the Leonids in November." Rebel paused and looked around because everyone was quiet and staring at her. "What?"

Conner smiled and said sarcastically, "Anything else we should know about this meteor shower?"

"Well, yes. The Leonid meteor shower is associated with the comet Tempel-Tuttle and we see the meteors when the earth passes through the debris trail in the direction of Leo," she pointed out then flipped him the bird.

Everyone laughed and Conner bowed mockingly.

"Rebel, I have to say that I was really impressed this

afternoon when those guys pulled their guns on us," Gabe said. "I was frozen with fear, but you, you didn't even flinch."

Rebel shrugged. "We've been preparing for shit like this for years. We thought out every scenario we could think of and men turning on each other was the first thing on the list. But still, I have to admit that I didn't think it would be this bad. I'm tired of shooting people."

"Two months ago, I would have never thought any of this could happen," Gabe said softly.

"Most people didn't. We really didn't either, but we prepared just in case," Rebel laughed.

"One thing is for sure," Ric chimed in, "I'm glad you guys walked into my life. No telling what would have happened to me if you hadn't."

"Me too," Lynn said looking at Shane and Cayden.

"Well, I say it's a good thing that Warrick is a huckleberry," Dylan said making everyone roar with laughter again.

Warrick huffed and stood up to fill his coffee cup but couldn't help grinning. "And they say television is bad for you."

Everyone laughed again.

"Stop making me laugh, god damn it! It hurts," Conner said holding his ribs.

"Speaking of hurt, I want to check wounds before we go to bed," Gabe said.

"Whatever you say doc," Darien agreed still smiling.

"Do you think it will get better as we go?" Lynn asked nervously.

"No, that's why we try so hard to avoid people. But the problem with that is that you run into the bad guys that are hiding away from authority," Rebel sighed. "I'm sure you'll feel better in the morning Lynn. Don't worry, the guys will protect you."

She nodded and followed Jade to their tent.

The next morning Conner could barely move. He

hadn't slept at all and had a horrible headache from all of the pain medication he had been taking. Gabe had given him his shot of morphine but it wasn't even taking the edge off of the pain.

Rebel woke up anxious to leave. She helped pack the horses then climbed on Jake. She looked up into the morning sky trying to shake off the gloomy feeling that had nagged at her from the time she opened her eyes this morning.

"You ok, sis?" Dylan asked as he climbed on Ace.

"Ya, I'm just feeling a little anxious today," she said.

"Hang in there. You will feel better once we get home. It should be easy riding once we cross the river," he encouraged.

She nodded and glanced at Conner who seemed very unapproachable as they started down the road.

Jade and Lynn rode close to Rebel, still a little jittery from yesterday. Darien rode behind them with Ric and Gabe stayed beside Shane. Warrick and Dylan took the lead and Cayden and Danny followed them. Conner was silent and rode by himself.

They rode at a lope without incident all day. That evening the river started to turn south.

Dylan reined in his horse and said, "We need to cross the river here, let's make camp and find a bridge in the morning."

Conner groaned as he dismounted, the pain making it impossible to even breath. He was angry that he had been injured and wasn't dealing well with life at all. He was tired of hurting and tired of everyone worrying and fussing over him.

Rebel looked over at him and noticed that his face was ashen and he looked like he was going to pass out. She rushed over to him and said, "Why didn't you say something. We would have stopped."

He just shook his head waving off her help.

She reached out again to help him over to Gabe who was unpacking her supply bag.

"Set him here," Gabe instructed as she pulled out a

syringe.

"I can set myself there!" he ground out, tired of being treated like a child. "I'm not completely fucking helpless!"

Rebel let go of him angrily. "We are just trying to help you."

"God! I'm tired of being helped. Just leave me alone for Christ sake! Both of you," he growled.

Rebel stepped away from him. "Fine! Fuck you then Conner!" She spun around to Gabe and snarled, "If those pain meds don't help his attitude, I'm going to change it with my fist!" Then she stomped out of camp.

Warrick tried not to grin as he made the fire listening to the exchange. "Conner, man, just let the ladies do their thing. You don't want to light that fire."

Conner sighed and sat down grudgingly.

"She is right to worry about you, you idiot." Gabe said stabbing the syringe into his shoulder. "You are still in mortal danger."

"Mortal danger?" he mocked.

"Oh, don't make me call her back here to fulfill that threat!" she spat. "I mean that you could still potentially die from your injuries. One wrong step, one fall from your horse and that would be it."

"Whatever!" he glowered.

"That is the problem with men! You just can't tell them anything," she said into her bag as she pulled out her scope and slapped in against his chest firmly.

Darien walked over and started helping Ric with dinner. "What's the problem Doc?" he asked innocently.

Gabe glared at Conner and smugly replied, "The patient!" Then she tossed her scope in the bag and stomped off the same way Rebel did.

Ric and Darien looked at each other then back at Conner.

Conner just leaned his head back and closed his eyes waiting for the drugs to take the edge off the pain so he could breath.

Warrick grinned and looked at Darien, "I don't think Conner's getting any tonight."

Conner's head shot back up and he glared at Warrick.

"Don't take it out on me!" Warrick laughed. "You sealed your own fate."

"Fuck!" Conner said standing up. "I'm an asshole!" He sighed and went to look for Gabe and Rebel to apologize.

He found Rebel sitting on the riverbank throwing rocks into the water and watching the meteors shoot across the sky.

"Rebel, I'm sorry. I know I'm a jerk sometimes," he said sitting down beside her.

"Hey, you don't have to apologize to me. If you don't want my help, that's fine," she said without looking at him.

"Rebel, don't be like that. I said I'm sorry."

"And I said it was fine!"

"Come on, let's go eat." He stood up and reached for her hand.

She stood without his help and walked back to camp.

The next morning they followed the interstate to an overpass near the Colorado state line.

"The earthquakes haven't damaged the bridges out here," Warrick said relieved.

Dylan grinned at him and rode across the river. Everyone followed.

"We will just ride along the freeway right into Cheyenne," Dylan said. "We should be there in a few days."

"Let's get some miles behind us then," Darien said and kicked his horse into a gallop.

Rebel watched Conner grimace as his horse matched the gildings pace. She hadn't spoken to him after they returned to camp last night and didn't offer to help him this morning. She understood the frustration of being injured though, and was trying not to be pissed off.

They rode hard stopping only to eat and get Conner his pain meds. As evening fell onto the rolling hills, the brothers slowed the pace to a walk and started looking for a place to camp for the night.

"There is a small rock bluff over there," Warrick said pointing.

They were just reining in to dismount when a streak of light flashed through the sky. There was a split second of realization before Rebel screamed, "Take cover!" But it was too late.

The meteor crashed into the ground several miles away from them. A blinding light exploded from the object just before it hit and dirt and dust billowed hundreds of yards into the air.

Total chaos erupted around them. The horses screamed and reared. The pack animals jerked loose and bolted away in a stampede.

Rebel struggled to stay astride Jake and watched as Ric and Lynn were thrown from their mounts. Gabe went off her horse and the animal almost trampled Ric. Jade was fighting her horse that reared again and spun around dumping her onto the ground.

Dirt filled their mouths and the air was thick with dust, growing so dense that she couldn't see any longer. The dogs were barking and the brothers were cussing.

Conner's gilding ran past her without Conner. She jumped off Jake and ran to the last place she'd seen him and found him on the ground unconscious just as a second meteorite slammed into the ground even closer than the first.

"Jade!" Rebel screamed. "Where are you?"

"I'm right here," Jade answered about twenty feet away. "I'm ok."

Rebel turned back to Conner who was barely breathing. She could see his white face through the thick dirt cloud. Panic started to take over her as she thought about what Gabe had said. What if he had punctured a lung?

Rebel looked around to make sure everyone else was

ok as the dust slowly settled enough to see. The brothers had regained control of their horses and Ric and Lynn were standing up brushing dirt off their clothes. Gabe and Jade ran over to Conner and looked at Rebel worriedly.

One by one, everyone gathered around the unconscious man.

"Gabe," Rebel said calmly. "Can you tell if he has punctured a lung without your bag?"

Gabe hesitated nervously. "I don't know. Oh my god! I just told him that last night." She put her hand over her mouth and tears filled her eyes.

"Gabe, just calm down. Start by listening to his heart," Rebel said trying to get her to focus. She turned to the men. "Find the horses! We need the bag!" she yelled. "And set up a tent!"

Everyone moved at once. Warrick, Dylan and Darien mounted their horses and flew after the pack animals. Cayden grabbed the sleeping bag off of Jake and Danny helped him roll it out.

Ric and Jade gently moved Conner's limbs into a more comfortable position and Lynn took off her jacket and gently put it under his head.

Gabe put her head on his chest and listened intently for several minutes. "His heartbeat is slow. Everyone be quiet so I can hear his lungs."

They held their breath as she bent down again to listen. "I can't hear any wheezing but I need my scope and I need to see his chest."

Rebel pulled the knife out of her boot and sliced his shirt open.

"No swelling yet," Gabe said mostly to herself. "Nothing visible."

Warrick rode up to them with two of the packhorses and handed the lead ropes to Cayden. "They ran for miles, it will take hours to find them."

Cayden rushed back to Gabe with her bag saying, "Thank god it was on the first horses they found."

Gabe dug for her scope and placed it on his chest. She paled and said, "His lung has collapsed." She looked up at Shane and urgently said, "Find me a syringe. Take out the plunger."

Rebel tensed and held her breath.

Gabe stuffed some gauze inside the syringe then slammed it in between his ribs. She listened to his lungs fill with air and sighed with relief.

"His breathing is extremely shallow but I think he will be ok. We need to get him out of this dust," she said.

"Set up a tent," she said to the boys. "Jade, get my water off of Jake." She turned to Conner and said, "Conner! Wake up." She wet the edge of his t-shirt and wiped his face. "Conner!"

His eyes fluttered open and he groaned in pain.

"We are going to move you into the tent," she told him waving at Cayden and Danny to help him stand.

He moaned again as the movement almost took him out a second time.

The boys helped him lay on the makeshift bed then stepped out so Rebel and Gabe could go in.

Gabe gave him a good dose of pain medication and stepped back outside.

Rebel sat down beside him and tried to calm down.

"What hurts?" Rebel asked nervously.

"Everything hurts!" he moaned through gritted teeth. "What the fuck happened?"

"Meteors. Two of them hit the ground a few miles away," she explained. "We found you unconscious on the ground again."

"My horse reared and when I reacted, pain shot through my ribs and made me fall. Then nothing," he said.

"Your lung collapsed. Gabe fixed it for now but I'm worried," she said solemnly.

"Rebel, I'm sorry about yesterday. I'm just so god damned frustrated. I need to be at my best through this journey and I've been injured the entire time." He looked away and said quietly, "I was only able to fire one shot at those men yesterday. I could barely hold the weight of my weapon. What if that would have made the difference in your safety?"

Rebel brushed his uncut hair away from his eyes and said, "Conner, I only have one rule that I live by. Its do your best. That's it, you're best. One shot was enough. Stop beating yourself up cause this isn't your fault."

He looked into her eyes and said, "Forgive me?" Then without waiting for an answer, he pulled her down for a kiss.

She instinctively leaned into the embrace and felt him wince in pain. "God Conner!" she breathed. "You aren't up for this."

"Just because I can't move doesn't mean I'm not up for it," he whispered seductively.

"You are all talk. The pain would take you out again," she laughed, relieved that he was ok.

"The pain isn't that bad. Come here. I'll prove it to you."

"Gabe said no movement," she said softly and gently pushed him back. "I'm going to check on Jade. She took a nasty tumble off of her horse. You try to sleep." Then she quickly stepped out of the tent before she changed her mind.

Everyone looked at her expectantly as she walked up to the fire. "He is fine. He'll be just fine," she told them sitting down. She looked at Jade and asked, "Is everyone else ok? Most of you went off your horses."

"I'm ok," Jade said. "I landed right on my ass!"

"Me too," Lynn said.

Rebel looked at Darien. "You guys ok? Did you find all the horses?"

"Surprisingly yes. I think overall we were lucky tonight," he replied.

Ric nodded in agreement then asked, "So what's the deal with the meteors? Will there be more?"

"There is no way of knowing. We could simply be seeing a meteor shower and there's a good possibility that it's not over," Rebel said softly. "Worst case scenario is that this meteor shower is preempting a strike from a very large rock."

"Like the one that killed the dinosaurs?" Lynn asked.

Rebel laughed, "Yes, possibly, although some believe that it wasn't an asteroid that killed the dinosaurs but a geomagnetic pole shift."

Ric inhaled sharply. "Like the pole shift you've been talking about? It could destroy all life on earth again?"

"Maybe," Rebel said. "It's possible that Planet X flew by and tipped the earth on her ass and that killed the dinosaurs. That kind of shift would have set off all the volcanoes and killed everything."

"Are we all going to die?" Danny asked nervously.

Darien broke in saying, "Danny, we believe that we can survive this thing. We aren't going to die."

"Everyone come eat," Ric said. "We will all feel better after dinner and a good nights sleep."

"I'll eat with Conner in the tent," Rebel said standing up. "Goodnight."

Chapter 13

Rebel woke up early the next morning and rode the distance to the impact crater. The rock had put a fairly large hole in the ground. It was nothing compared to the Arizona Meteor Crater but it was a crater just the same. She dismounted and slid down into the hole searching for the meteorite.

"You know, there is only a slim chance of finding that rock, it probably blew itself apart," Dylan said from above her.

She smiled up at him and said, "Ya, I know. Worth a shot though."

"I think this shit scared the hell out of Danny and Gabe," he grinned. "Ric seems to be handling it ok though."

"I found it! Or part of it," Rebel said putting on her gloves to pick up the rock. She reached up her hand and was easily lifted out of the hole by Dylan's massive arms.

They both stood looking into the crater. "What do you think this means?" Rebel asked apprehensively.

"I think we will see more of these but the big one won't be here for awhile," he said seriously. "We have time to get home."

"Well, let's get going then," she said swinging onto Jake.

They rode into camp and poured themselves some coffee. Conner was out of the tent and propped up against a log by the fire. Rebel sat beside him and asked, "How are you feeling this morning?"

"Pretty damn good, thanks to the doc," he smiled.

"You're gonna get addicted," Rebel laughed. "Good thing there isn't enough supply for the demand."

"Funny!" Conner smirked. "Are we ready to move out?"

"Yes, before something else happens. I found part of the rock," she said showing him the meteorite. "Two months ago, it would have been worth a lot of money."

"Amazing how something that small can cause so much damage," he said in awe.

"You stay here," she said standing up. "I'll saddle your horse."

Conner watched her take down the tent and pack the horses. He cursed his injury again, hating that she had to take care of him. He struggled to his feet and walked up behind her, wrapping his arms around her. "I think I love you," he said into her ear.

Rebel turned into the embrace and smiled up at him. "I think I could love a guy like you too." She handed him his reins and climbed on Jake watching him swing carefully onto his gilding.

"A guy like me, huh? And what would a guy like me be like?" he asked teasing her.

"Oh, you know, tall, built, handsome," she teased back.

"I'm not that tall," he laughed as they followed the brothers along the road.

"Well, your extra handsome so I guess that makes up for it."

Conner laughed again, "I told you that when we met."

"Ya, I remember," she said feeling her pulse react to the memory.

"Get a room," Jade teased with a grin as she rode up to them. "You two are weird."

Rebel blushed when Conner winked at her.

"Mom, aren't we almost to Wyoming?" Jade asked.

"Yes, probably a couple of days out of Cheyenne. Why?" Rebel wondered.

Jade shrugged innocently. "Just wondering. Is Danny leaving when we get there?"

"Oh, uh, I don't know. I'll ask him," Rebel said.

"No! I don't want him to know I was wondering," Jade said ducking her head.

Rebel laughed. "I will find out incognito. How about that?"

"Or, I could find out from the brothers and let you know?" Conner said.

"That would be much better. Thanks Conner," she said slowing her horse to fall back in step with Lynn.

Conner suddenly stopped his horse looking into the trees. "Hold up guys. I hear something."

Suddenly a man yelled, "Help! We need help!"

The brothers kicked their horses into a run toward the man.

Rebel watched closely as they reached him and immediately waved for them to follow. She nudged Jake into a run and raced toward her brothers.

"His wife is delivering her baby and something is wrong," Warrick yelled to her. "That house over there." He pointed to a house about a mile away.

Rebel turned to Gabe and yelled, "Follow me and bring the bag."

Gabe followed Rebel to the house and jumped off of her horse followed closely by Shane who carried the bag.

Rebel opened the door, surprised to find about thirty people gathered in the house. "Where is she?" she asked urgently.

A young woman pointed to one of the bedrooms.

Rebel opened the door quietly and said, "Hi, I'm Rebel. I'm an EMT and this is Gabe, a third year med student. We've come to offer our assistance."

"A woman stood up from the bed, completely relieved. "Thank God, I'm Gail and this is Connie. She's been in labor for fifteen hours and still no baby. I don't know what to do."

"Ok, Gail, calm down. We just need to wash up," Rebel said.

"Gabe, how are Obstetrician skills?" Rebel asked nervously as they washed their hands.

"Not much experience in this field. I'm fairly nervous," Gabe admitted.

Rebel reentered the room and knelt down beside the bed. "Alright Connie, Gabe is going to check you over and see where you're at and we will try to figure out what is going on, ok?"

The young woman nodded so Gabe went to work.

She gently felt around her belly. "He seems to be in position. Maybe he is just being stubborn."

Rebel turned to Gail and said, "I need you to time her contractions. Count them out and figure out how long in between them. Come up here and hold her hand."

Gail sat down and started counting.

Two hours later, the baby was born and everyone cheered.

Rebel turned to Gabe and said, "I'm glad you were here. I don't do babies well. I get emotionally distracted."

Gabe smiled and said, "I'm glad you were here. I needed the moral support."

Rebel left the room, leaving the baby and his mother in Gabe's capable hands. She walked outside and sat down on the porch trying to slow the adrenaline rushing through her.

Conner walked over and smiled at her. "I hear it's a boy."

She nodded trying not to show the anguish and worry that she felt for this young family as they faced their tragic future. But Conner knew instantly what she was thinking and came up to sit beside her.

"It will be fine Rebel, don't worry," he tried to sooth her.

"Conner, its not fine. We just brought a child into a world that is falling apart. How will they survive? Look around, they have no supplies and no shelter," she said choking on the emotion.

"We can warn them. It's not too late. They still have some time to get prepared. I'll have the brothers help us and we will do what we can, ok?"

She nodded her head but knew they were too close to the blast radius of the volcano.

Conner stood up realizing that there was no consoling her so he left to talk to the brothers.

An hour later, she was still sitting on the porch lost in thought. Dylan walked up next to her and sat down.

"Sis, they are going to move into Cheyenne where

they can get help. I know your upset but that is all we can do. The National Guard is there, they will be fine."

Rebel nodded without looking at him.

"We are ready to move out. Come on, I have Jake ready for you," he said softly.

She stood and followed him to the horses where everyone was waiting. She swung onto Jake and silently followed her brothers west.

That evening Rebel busied herself by helping Ric make dinner then sat down with a cup of coffee. "Darien, do you still have some whiskey?"

He looked at her sharply because it was the first words she'd spoken all afternoon. "Sure Rebel, are you ok?"

She nodded accepting the bottle then tipped it up, drinking without a cup.

Darien looked at Dylan then at Warrick. All three of them looked back at her.

"Rebel, it's been a long time since I saw you drink out of the bottle. The last time didn't end very well," Dylan said softly.

Conner looked at him curiously but kept silent.

Rebel shrugged and kept drinking.

Dylan sat down and said, "Well at least there isn't anyone out here to arrest you this time."

Warrick laughed and Darien nodded in agreement.

Conner was really curious now. What the hell were they talking about? Finally he said, "You have to tell me, it's torture not knowing."

Dylan looked at Rebel who didn't seem to notice or care if he told him. He looked around to make sure Jade wasn't around then said, "Jade came home one day from school and told her that one of her friends didn't came to school cause her step dad beat her so bad she was in the hospital. And it wasn't the first time the guy had hurt her. Rebel freaked. It took all of us to keep her from driving to his house and killing him that day. He was arrested so she was ok for a while. Then one night we all went out to the bar and guess who just happened to be there? The kid's step dad. Rebel started drinking and before we knew it, somehow got the bottle from the bartender."

Dylan paused and glanced at his sister who was still not paying attention so he continued, "Fool that he was, the guy strolled right up to Rebel and asked her to dance. I swear to god I saw the devil in her eyes when she said yes. She followed him to the dance floor and when he turned around to face her, she pounded him in the face. She beat that man damn near to death right there on the dance floor even though she was completely intoxicated. She couldn't walk but she sure could fight. We had to drag her off him. Then we had to bail her out of jail."

Conner looked at Rebel completely taken back.

"She doesn't drink like that very often but when she does look out," he warned.

Rebel tipped the bottle up again, completely lost in her own thoughts, not realizing that Conner and her brothers were watching her curiously.

Jade and Danny walked to the fire and sat down.

"Is mom ok?" Jade asked knowing that she rarely drank.

"She is going to be just fine," Darien smiled. "We will keep our eye on her. By the way, Danny wants to know if we would ride to Casper and retrieve his mother," he said getting everyone's attention. "He would like to get her and come with us to Idaho."

Jade smiled excitedly.

"Either we find a place for you guys to stay up near Elk Mountain for a few days while we ride up there and back or we all go, then cut cross country from there," he added.

"We should decide now because if we go, we will head northwest from here," Dylan said.

"What about the truck?" Warrick asked.

"I forgot about the truck. Do we want to split up to get it? Is it worth it?" Darien asked.

"I think we should definitely get the truck," Rebel said without looking at them.

"Can we find enough fuel to get it home?" Dylan asked.

"I think so. I say we stay together till we get to Cheyenne and if we can get the fuel, we will split up there," Darien said.

"I agree," Rebel said. "We should stay together as long as possible."

"Anyone else have input?" Darien asked with a grin. "Or is that the plan?"

"Sounds good to me," Warrick said. He glanced at Rebel who was mumbling to herself then looked at Jade, "Maybe you guys should hit the hay."

"Hit the hay?" Lynn asked. "What does that mean?"

Everyone laughed.

"It means we should go bed," Jade informed her as she stood up. She knew that the brothers were worried that her mother would do something crazy and they always tried to protect her from it. "Come on."

"Weird," Lynn said following her to their tent.

Rebel stood up and walked into the darkness with the bottle still in her hand.

Conner watched her disappear nervously but leaned back deciding to let her have some space.

The brothers were still talking by the fire an hour later when Rebel stumbled back into the firelight holding a six foot long rattlesnake by her knife stuck through the back of its head. She dropped it in front of Dylan's feet.

Conner's eyes widened in surprise.

"Fuck Rebel!" Dylan said launching to his feet. He pulled out his revolver aiming it at the snake as he jumped behind the rock he was sitting on. "God damn son of a bitch!"

"He almost got me," she mumbled then she spun around and threw the empty bottle into the air and whipped out her colt and shot it, showering them with glass. But when she turned back around, she tripped and fell to the ground right in front of the still writhing snake.

"Whoa, he almost got me again," she slurred with a grin.

Warrick laughed and Darien shook his head. Dylan just glared at her and holstered his weapon.

Warrick stood up and helped her to her feet then picked up the snake and removed her knife. He tossed the thing into the darkness and helped her find a seat beside Dylan who sat back down uneasily.

"God damn it Rebel, you know I hate snakes," Dylan complained.

She winked at Warrick and said, "Oh, Dylan, its dead."

"No its not and you're lucky it didn't bite you just now."

Darien shook his head again and said, "You shouldn't carry your weapon locked and cocked while your shit faced. Go get some sleep Rebel."

Conner shook his head and struggled to his feet, gritting his teeth against the pain. 'This woman is one surprise after another,' he thought to himself.

"Ah ha!" Rebel exclaimed when she saw him grimace. "You are a liar."

He looked at her wondering how the hell she remembered their conversation from the night before. "Come with me and I'll prove it right now," he said striding to the tent.

Warrick stood up and laughed as he walked past her.

"Shut up Warrick!" she spat then threw a stick and hit Conner square between his shoulders.

All three of her brothers roared with laughter.

"Why you spunky little shit!" Conner said spinning around. He strode back to her, picked her up, threw her over his shoulders then stomped back to the tent and tossed her inside. He glanced back at the brothers and said, "Good night."

The three brothers erupted with laughter again.

The sun was struggling to shine through the still dust-ridden atmosphere as Rebel poured her cup full of coffee the next morning.

"Warrick, you make the best sheepherders coffee I've ever drank," she said holding her head.

"I learned from mom," he said thoughtfully. "I think it was the only reason she liked camping."

"I bet she has a pot on all day," Rebel laughed. "I can't wait to see her again. It's amazing how much I miss her."

"Me too. She is definitely our rock ain't she?" he agreed.

"I can't wait to meet her," Conner said walking up to the fire. "She sounds like a hell of a lady."

"That she is," Dylan said following Conner to the coffee pot. "How are you this morning Rebel? Need an aspirin?"

Rebel glanced sideways at him and said, "I can't believe you guys let me drink like that again. At least I didn't wake up in jail."

"Don't blame us! We couldn't stop you then and we couldn't stop you last night," Warrick laughed.

"Ya, and no more wrangling rattlesnakes in the dark. God, you scare the shit out of me!" Dylan said with a glare.

Rebel laughed.

"Listen guys, I want to move a little faster today. I don't want to hold up the show here," Conner said firmly.

"Oh, I don't think so," Gabe said stepping up behind him.

"You heard the doc, Conner. I'm not gonna argue with her," Warrick laughed.

"God damn it Gabe. They are anxious to get home. I am fine!"

"So ask them if they want to ride ahead because you are grounded to a walk!" she said squaring off with him.

"Conner, you know she is right. We need you to heal as much as possible now so that you are strong if something happens later," Rebel said still holding her head.

He looked from Gabe to Rebel then spun around stomping off. "God damn women!" he railed.

Warrick and Dylan just grinned and drank their coffee.

The day was uneventful as they rode at a walk toward Cheyenne. Conner was scowling and impatiently whittling on a stick with his large hunting knife.

"Conner, if something spooked that horse, he'd be half a mile down the road before you gathered up the reins," Rebel reprimanded.

"At least I'd be moving faster," he growled.

"Ya, faster to the ground where I'll have to pick your unconscious ass up again!" Rebel spat back.

"Did you two get married and we missed the party?" Warrick asked grinning.

Conner scowled and Rebel shrugged.

They rode into the evening in silence.

"We are getting close," Warrick informed them. "We will be in Cheyenne tomorrow morning."

"Look," Shane said pointing. "There is a motel up there."

"Wait here, Shane and I will check it out," Warrick said riding forward.

They returned a few minutes later. "No one's around. You want to stay there tonight?" Warrick asked.

"Hell ya!" Dylan said. "I'll sleep in a bed."

They dismounted and unsaddled the horses, staking them behind the building.

Warrick built a fire and Ric joined him to make dinner.

Conner was told to sit and stay still so he was pouting in a chair on the back lawn. He was aimlessly stroking Tuckers head and staring across the rolling hills.

Rebel sat down next to him feeling his frustration. "If anyone understands, you know it is me," she said softly. "Gabe is just doing her job and I just happen to agree with her. Don't be mad."

"I'm not mad!" he said roughly.

Rebel laughed. "Whatever."

Tucker suddenly jumped to his feet whining and the puppy started howling.

Rebel looked at Conner sharply and whispered, "Earthquake."

The word had barely escaped her mouth when the

ground shuttered once underneath their feet then erupted in upheaval. Rebel launched to her feet looking around for Jade.

The building cracked and creaked and bricks tumbled from the upper level. Jade ran out the back door and stood beside Rebel.

The quake only lasted about one minute but the structure was badly damaged. Rebel turned to Conner worriedly and said, "That didn't feel close. It had to be at least a six point for us to feel it here."

"Do you think it came from Yellowstone?" Conner asked.

"At least central Wyoming," Rebel guessed. "I hope that beast isn't waking up. The magma stretches across three states. We are probably standing on it right here."

Gabe and Lynn came out the door followed by Shane, Cayden and Danny. "Is everyone ok?" Shane asked.

"We are, where are the brothers?" Rebel asked.

"Right here," Warrick said limping toward them behind Darien and Dylan.

Gabe ran over to him seeing the blood staining the hole in his jeans. "What happened?"

"He was in the storage shed and everything came down on him including a big ol' mirror," Dylan told her.

"Bring him inside. Cayden, will you grab my bag?" she asked. "Warrick, I need those jeans off."

"You get him doc," Conner teased. "It's your turn to be at her mercy."

"Fuck you Conner!" Warrick grinned as he hobbled past him.

"We'll go check the horses," Shane said.

"Ladies, let's go check the rooms and clean up," Ric said.

Conner turned to Rebel who stood watching the oddly colored sunset deep in thought. "What are you thinking?" he asked her.

She turned to him and said harshly, "We won't live long if that fucking thing erupts."

"I don't think you should get so upset over one

earthquake," he said.

"This isn't right Conner. They don't have that many earthquakes here! And if they do have one, it comes from that billowing monster in the corner of the state," she yelled pacing back and forth.

"Rebel, just calm down," he said soothingly.

"Calm down my ass! Look at that sunset. Does that look normal to you? We have seen extreme weather, experienced earthquakes, witnessed meteor impacts and know that at least one volcano has erupted. There has been nothing normal happen for the last two months!" she raged.

"Rebel, that doesn't mean that Yellowstone is going to erupt!" he said firmly still trying to calm her. "And you said yourself it could be hydrothermic not magmatic."

Rebel turned away from him trying to get a grip on her fear. "I just told myself that Conner. Just like I convinced myself that we would be safe this close to that god damned thing." She signed and slumped down in a chair, a deep frown enveloping her face.

Conner knelt down in front of her and pulled her toward him. "Hang in there, Rebel. Don't freak yourself out. We will be fine. Come on. Let's go check on Warrick."

He pulled her to her feel and took her hand in his leading her into the building.

"How's our boy?" Conner asked peeking over Gabe's shoulder at Warrick's leg.

"Took twenty stitches to put him back together," Dylan said.

"Holy shit!" Conner said. "That must have been some glass shard."

"Well," Darien said standing up. "Let's get some sleep. We will be leaving early in the morning."

Conner followed Rebel to their room and watched with concern as she slumped down on the bed. He could see that she was worried and sat down beside her. "Can't shake it?" he asked.

"It's not only us that I'm worried about. We don't know how many people are seeking refuge in our camp and we are picking up more on our way. The cave isn't big enough to save all of us," she said solemnly.

"Look, Rebel, my sister in law told me that the cave in Montana could house hundreds of people. If this volcano blows, let's just plan on moving everyone there. She would welcome all of us," he encouraged.

"We would have to get there before winter or not go until next spring. We would never make during the winter months," she pondered. "I'm sure that we have enough supplies to last till then if the ash doesn't kill us."

"It's a plan then. Now, I just happen know a way to get this shit out of your head for awhile," he said pushing her back on the bed.

Daylight broke as Warrick prepared a fire in the back yard to make coffee. One by one the small party drifted out of their rooms to gather around for breakfast.

Rebel hadn't slept well and was still edgy as she sipped her coffee. She stood up and said, "Darien, how many gas masks did we stash in the cave?"

The question silenced the entire group and everyone looked at Darien. "Four or five dozen I think," he answered getting a nod of agreement from Dylan. "Why?"

"Because I'm thinking this volcano is going to erupt," she said simply and felt the intake of breath throughout the entire group.

"Rebel, one earthquake doesn't mean it's going to erupt," he said calmly.

"I know!" she said, then grabbed control of her emotions and continued more calmly, "Sorry. I know, but there are a lot more people to protect now. We need more masks."

Darien looked at the stricken faces around him then back at Rebel. "What are you suggesting we do?"

"From here on we need to seek out certain supplies that we haven't needed out here, we need to go into the cities," she said pointedly.

"Rebel, you realize that the best place to get those kinds of masks out here is at a military base or military supply," Dylan said. "I don't see that happening."

"I know but firemen have them, hospitals may have them. We need to find them," she insisted.

"I have to say that I agree," Warrick said backing her up. "Breathing ash is the biggest threat from that thing anyway."

"We don't know how many people are in camp back home. There could be hundreds and I'll bet that no one read the letter I sent and brought their own supplies," she said shaking her head.

"Rebel, we knew that if this beast erupted, we wouldn't be able to save everyone," Darien said gently.

"We have a new option," Rebel said. "Conner has family in Montana. They have access to a cave that could house hundreds of people. I'm thinking that we may have to journey out there to survive the eruption," she said feeling a sense of hope.

Dylan and Darien exchanged glances then looked at Warrick.

"Of course, we wouldn't need to do that unless the volcano went off which I think it will," she added. "But in order to survive the initial blast, we need those masks."

"Alright, we will seek them out," Darien said.

Rebel relaxed somewhat and added, "I know that it will be dangerous and we will be utterly stealing them but I don't see another option."

"Well we will be stealing gas too, might as well go all the way," Warrick laughed. "We will start looking in Cheyenne."

"Shouldn't we have masks with us since we are riding so close to the volcano?" Lynn asked.

"Lynn, if we are within two hundred miles of that thing when it goes off, we won't be around to wear the masks," she said.

"Rebel, don't scare her," Conner reprimanded. "Lynn, we will be well away from here when it goes so don't worry."

"Sorry Lynn, I didn't mean to be harsh," Rebel

apologized.

"It's ok. I'd rather know what I'm facing," she said.

"I wouldn't," Conner grumbled.

"Let's get going. Everyone check your weapons. The city is dangerous so get extra ammunition ready and be prepared for a fast break if anything happens," Darien instructed.

The short ride into the city was stacked with tension. Everyone was on edge as they rode to the truck and dismounted.

"This truck will attract a lot of attention," Darien said. "No one has driven around for months."

"I think the ladies should stay here with the pack animals. Shane, Cayden and Danny can stay to protect them," Warrick said.

The brothers and Conner mounted their horses and prepared to ride into the city. Rebel swung onto Jake and followed. None of the men dared object.

The streets in the city were empty but they rode in the alleys to avoid being seen.

"There is the fire station," Rebel said pointing. "Let's hide the horses behind there."

They dismounted and crept to the back door.

Warrick elbowed the glass and let them into the building. "It doesn't look like anyone has been here for awhile."

"Here!" Rebel said pulling a full box of gas masks out of the closet. "We need a bag that we can tie on the horses." She found a duffle bag and stuffed the masks into it. "Get the ones out of the lockers and look for a storage in the attic or basement."

The brothers searched the firehouse thoroughly and found another box of masks that looked outdated. They stuffed them into another bag and met Rebel and Conner by the door.

"Do we want to find the hospital?" Darien asked.

"No, let's get the truck on the road," Dylan said then turned to look at the dusty fire trucks behind him. "Are those diesel or gas?"

Warrick laughed as he realized that there was probably fifty gallons of fuel in each truck. "Looks like the smaller one is gas. Let's bring the truck here and run a hose out."

"Are you sure we should risk being seen?" Darien asked. "There is most certainly a military presence and potentially fifty thousand people out there."

"I'm sure as hell not packing fifty gallons of fuel that far," Warrick said.

Darien paced the room and said, "Fine. But I think it is a risk." He stopped pacing and said, "If we can find fuel this easily, I think we should just drive to Casper."

"I agree. We could ride ahead and meet you in Rawlins. If you take the back roads it will be a straight shot back down," Dylan said.

Everyone nodded in agreement and rode back to the truck.

"You might as well head out now. We can handle getting the fuel. We will keep our horses with us just in case," Darien said.

Warrick started the truck while they loaded the horses. Darien jumped in and waited for Danny to say goodbye to Jade then they headed toward town.

Rebel and Dylan watched them drive away nervously.

"They will be fine," Dylan said feeling her agitation. "Come on, we have a long ride today. I want to get to Laramie by nightfall."

Conner mounted his gilding and looked at Rebel and Gabe. "We are increasing our pace! No arguments!"

Dylan shrugged at her and grinned then followed him into a fast gallop.

Rebel shook her head helplessly and kicked Jake into a run.

Several hours later Warrick stopped the truck behind a warehouse on the outskirts of Casper. He turned to Danny and asked, "Where is your mother's house?"

"It's just inside town on the west side," he said pointing. "I could ride over there and get her."

"We will stay with you. Let's unload the horses," Darien said.

Danny grew excited as they rode closer to his mother's house. He rode right up onto her front lawn and yelled, "Mom!" He dismounted and entered the house through the front door. "Mom!" he yelled again.

Darien tensed when he came back out with a stricken look on his face.

"She isn't here!" he said worriedly. He charged over to the neighbor's house and pounded on the door. A gruff looking man opened the door.

"Mr. York, where is my mother?" he asked him desperately.

"Danny! It's been a long time," the man said, his expression softening.

"Do you know where she is?" he pushed anxiously.

"Danny, your step dad came by last month and she left with him," he said hesitantly. "I think he took her with him back to Laramie. I haven't seen her since. I don't think she wanted to go Danny."

"Fuck!" Danny bellowed. "If he hurts her I will kill him."

The man shook Danny's hand and shut the door.

Danny stormed back to his horse and swung himself onto his back. "I should have never left her!"

"Don't worry, we'll find her," Warrick soothed turning his horse back to the truck.

"I had just finished my tour in Iraq and was discharged from the army when the power went out. I worked my way from Kentucky to Kansas City on my way home. That was when I met up with those militia guys."

Warrick and Darien listened silently.

"If this shit wouldn't have happened, I would have been here for her," he said regrettably.

"We will drive back to Laramie and find her. Now tell me about this man she is with," Darien said.

"He is a fucking prick! She married him while I was

in high school. Right after I left for college, he lost his job and started drinking. I came home that year for Christmas and she had bruises on her arms and face. I asked her about it and she said he threatened her with her life if she left. I kicked his ass and moved her out of his house that day. But I was already committed to the army and had to leave her. I sent her money though and she was doing fine."

Their conversation continued as they drove into the evening toward Laramie.

"He was convicted of assault but was released on probation. I told him that if he ever came near her, I would kill him but he always tried to call her," he said extremely upset. "She was deathly afraid of him."

"I think we should camp for the night and find her in the morning," Warrick said pulling the truck into a thicket of trees by a small river on the outskirts of Laramie. "You guys make camp, I am going to ride around the city and see if I can spot Dylan and the others."

Warrick saddled his horse and left while Darien and Danny staked their horses and built a fire.

Conner and Dylan had found a campsite on the north side of the city. They were sitting around the fire laughing with Rebel and Ric when Tucker stood up with his hackles raised, growling. Conner and Dylan jumped to their feet and palmed their handguns.

The dog suddenly stopped growling and started wagging his tail.

"It's me!" Warrick yelled into their camp. "Tell them tucker, I'm friendly."

"God, Warrick. I almost shot you," Dylan said. "What's the deal?"

"We had a problem with the kid's mom. She wasn't in Casper. Danny thinks his step dad has kidnapped her and brought her here to Laramie," he explained.

Jade appeared out of the darkness and asked, "Where is he?"

"We are camped about four miles west of here. I'll head back and let them know I found you and meet you back here in the morning." He climbed onto his horse and said, "From the way Danny talks, this guy is a real winner. We may end up in a fight." With that he rode out of camp.

The next morning, Darien, Danny and Warrick rode into camp.

Jade jumped into Danny's arms and hugged him. "I missed you," she said.

He grinned and said, "I've only been gone for one day."

"I'm sorry about your mom," she said pulling him down to sit beside her.

"I'm sure she is fine. The brothers are going to help me find her," he said appreciatively.

"Why Rebel, your coffee is just as good as mine," Warrick said laughing.

"Well, I learned from mom too," she smiled.

Darien sat down with his coffee and said, "Alright, we need to locate and extract Danny's mother from a dangerous man. We will most likely be engaged in a fight."

"Extract!" Warrick huffed.

Darien glared at him and continued, "Shane and Cayden, I think you should stay and guard the ladies. Conner, you decide for yourself if you are up to a potential fight and I don't even dare tell Rebel what to do."

Rebel laughed and stood to prepare her weapons.

"I'm in," Conner said standing with her.

"Do you have a place to start looking?" Darien asked Danny.

"He has a lot of friends down here but I remember that I was at a big ranch one time when I was young. I think it is on the east side of town about five miles from the city," he answered.

"Good, we will start there. Let's ride."

They mounted and left in a thunder of pounding hooves.

Five miles later, they reined in and walked through the gate of the large ranch and straight up to the big sprawling front porch.

The doors opened and a man walked out holding a rifle and a cup of coffee. "This is private property, strangers."

"We are looking for Miles Murphy," Danny said tilting his own rifle up a bit.

"Ain't seen him!" the man said. "Now get off my ranch."

A window on the upper floor of the house flew open and a woman screamed, "Danny!"

Danny launched from his horse and ran toward the house yelling, "Mom!"

"Fuck!" Warrick bellowed kicking his horse into a run toward the side of the house followed closely by Darien and Dylan.

The man on the porch brought the rifle up to Danny's chest as he climbed the stairs and said, "Hold on there, boy! Put down that rifle or I will put a hole in your chest."

Danny dropped the gun.

Rebel and Conner watched from the other side of the house. "We need to get inside," Rebel whispered.

Conner peeked around the corner and watched the man swing his rifle around and bash Danny in the head with the stock of the weapon. Danny slumped to the floor.

He looked past the porch and nodded at Warrick who was standing at the opposite corner of the house. The two men rushed the man on the porch. Conner grabbed the rifle as Warrick landed a huge fist in the guy's face knocking him cold.

They entered the house firing. Dylan came through the back door shooting an armed man in the leg in the kitchen. Darien and Rebel followed them into the house covering the stairs while they secured the bottom floor.

"Get in there!" Warrick said kicking three wounded men into the kitchen.

"I'll hold them here," Conner said knowing that he would be more help if he stayed out of the fight.

"I'll cover the front door," Rebel offered

preempting the order to stay put.

       The brothers climbed the stairs slowly with weapons drawn. Darien and Dylan covered Warrick as he kicked open the first door. Empty. He went to the second door and kicked it open.

       "Let her go!" Warrick growled at the man standing in the room with a knife across a woman's throat.

       Darien stepped into the doorway beside him leveling his weapon at the man.

       "Get out or I'll kill her!" the man said in a deadly voice pulling her backward.

       Warrick was unusually stricken by the terrified woman. She was beautiful with long dark hair and piercing green eyes. 'No wonder he wants her so bad,' he thought to himself. He struggled to focus on the man threatening her. "Let her go!" he warned him again.

       "Not on your life. She is mine and I will kill her before I let her go," the man screamed irrationally.

       Darien fired his weapon, putting a bullet through the center of the man's forehead.

       Warrick sprang to the woman's side catching her before the man fell on her. "Are you crazy?" he bellowed at Darien. "You could have shot her!"

       "I don't miss Warrick, you know that," Darien said calmly, stepping aside for Rebel who came bounding up the stairs. "I'll help Dylan secure the rest of the house."

       "Lauren?" Warrick said to the stunned woman. "I'm Warrick. Are you ok?"

       Lauren nodded her head slowly and tried to smile at the large man who held her.

       Rebel rushed into the room. "Lay her on the bed Warrick, she's in shock."

       Warrick paled as the woman fainted into his arms. He picked her up and gently laid her on the bed.

       "Mom!" Danny yelled bursting through the door. "Mom?"

       "She is fine Danny," Rebel said calmly. "She just fainted."

       He dropped to his knees beside the bed. "Mom.

Wake up."

Her eyes fluttered open. She sat up and grabbed Danny, hugging him tightly. "Danny, I'm so glad your home."

"Are you ok?" he asked her worriedly.

She nodded her head and looked at Warrick. "Thank you Warrick. He really would have really killed me."

Warrick just nodded without taking his eyes off of her.

"Let's get her downstairs," Rebel said not wanting her to have to look at the dead man.

Warrick and Danny helped her stand and walk down the stairs.

Danny helped her sit on the couch. "Mom, these are my friends, you've met Warrick and this is Rebel."

Rebel smiled and said, "I'm glad we found you."

Darien walked down the stairs followed by Dylan.

Warrick finally found his voice and said, "Lauren, this is my brother Dylan and this is Darien, the sharp shooter."

"Sharp shooter?" Danny asked quizzically.

"Darien shot Miles right in the forehead," Lauren explained. "Thank you Darien." She intentionally left out the fact that her head was within inches of the bullet.

"What do you want to do with them?" Conner asked walking into the room.

"This is Conner," Rebel said introducing him.

"It's nice to meet all of you," Lauren said.

"Tie 'em and lock the door!" Darien said. "Leave them to their own fate."

"I'll go to the barn and get Lauren a horse," Dylan said. "Do you ride?"

"It's been a long time, but I'm sure I can stay astride," Lauren said.

Rebel edged closer to Warrick who still stood staring at Lauren. "Hey," she whispered elbowing him in the ribs to get his attention.

He jumped then ducked his head and spun around

to follow Dylan without a word.

Rebel kept her smile to herself and turned back to Lauren. "Danny said that you would most likely want to come with us to Idaho. We have a safe camp there with supplies."

"You are willing to take us with you?" she asked appreciatively.

"Yes, you are both welcome. Do you have belongings here that you want to take with you?" Rebel asked.

"Very few," she said standing up. "I'll go get them."

"I'll help you. Danny, find something we can take those weapons in. And gather up any ammo you can find," Rebel ordered.

Darien preceded them up the stairs and covered the dead man's body with a blanket.

A few minutes later, they left the house and strapped Laurens bag onto her horse.

"That is a nice mare," Rebel said looking the horse over in appreciation.

"I'm taking them too," he said pointing to two beautiful thick stallions.

"Let's get Lauren back to camp," Darien said mounting his horse.

Danny helped his mother onto her horse and swung onto his gilding.

"Danny, I am so glad you are home," Lauren said again. "I missed you so much."

"I would have been home sooner if the power hadn't gone out," he said. "I'm sorry I wasn't here when Miles found you."

"It's fine Danny. You're here now," she smiled.

They rode the few miles back to camp and introduced Lauren to everyone there. Lauren watched Danny smile as he introduced Jade and noticed the light in her son's eyes whenever she was near.

"Your daughter is beautiful," she said to Rebel.

"Thank you. Your son is quite handsome as well," Rebel said watching the two sitting together.

Warrick sat next to them quietly fussing with his revolver.

"Would you like some coffee?" Rebel asked her. "Warrick makes a mean pot over the fire.

Warrick's head jerked up. He launched to his feet and quickly poured the beverage then blushed as he handed it to her.

"Thank you Warrick," Lauren laughed. She took a sip and said, "Damn that is a good cup of coffee."

Warrick smiled at her and sat back down.

Darien walked up to the fire and announced, "If we stay here, we are at risk of those thugs getting loose and coming after us. What do you think?"

"I say we stay," Dylan said looking at Conner who nodded.

"Me too," Warrick added.

"Fine, but we need to take turns on watch tonight," Darien said sitting down next to them. "Lauren, how many men were hanging around that house?"

"I've seen thirty five or forty different men come in and out. Some stay in the house and some in the bunkhouse but they are all friends and will be pissed that Miles is dead. Roy, the leader is a vengeful vicious prick and I have no doubt that he will come after us just for showing him up."

"Do you think we should leave tonight?" he asked her pointedly.

"Some of the guys left for a few days. I don't think he will follow us until they get back," she informed them.

"Mom, Cayden and I have put your things in our tent. We will sleep outside tonight," Danny said.

"Thanks boys," Lauren said gratefully. "I hate to kick you out of your bed."

"Not a problem," Cayden said. "We will come across another tent somewhere."

Gabe walked up and dropped her bag beside Conner. "Time to check wounds. Your first mister."

Conner groaned then leaned back and lifted his shirt.

"Oh my god!" Lauren breathed. "That is the worst bruise I have ever seen."

"And it just happens to be on the most stubborn man I have ever seen," Gabe said listening to his lungs.

Rebel laughed at Conner's scowl.

"I think you will live surprisingly," she scoffed. "Warrick, let's see the stitches."

"I'm not dropping my pants in front of everyone doc, you'll have to check me later," he said kneeling down to turn the rabbit frying on the fire.

"And that is the second most stubborn man I've ever met!" Gabe huffed. "Dylan, what about you."

Dylan pulled his shirt off and turned so she could inspect the hole in his side.

"Jesus! Are you all wounded?" Lauren asked in dismay.

"Yes, they are. Believe me mom, we are safe among these folks," Danny said proudly.

Rebel returned with her shorts on so the doc could look at her injury.

"Rebel was shot," Danny informed his mother. "But that was before I met her. She saved my life back in Nebraska. I owe her a lot."

Lauren turned to Rebel and said, "My god, I owe you a lot as well then."

Rebel just smiled.

Gabe took her time inspecting Rebel's wound. She didn't want to miss anything.

Lauren stood up to get a better look. "Rebel, how do ride with that hole in your leg?"

"It hurts, that's for sure," she admitted. "But I'm anxious to get home."

The doc stood and walked to Darien who lifted his shirt for her inspection.

"Knife wound," Lauren said softly following Gabe.

"Good Darien, this is healing nicely," Gabe said.

Lauren was clearly rattled as she held her cup out to Warrick. "Could I have some more coffee?" she asked him.

Warrick reached for the pot and poured the

steaming liquid into her cup. "I have some Jack Daniels if you need something stronger," he said softly.

"Oh, that would help a lot, do you mind?" Lauren responded putting her hand on his arm.

Warrick stiffened at the touch and slowly said, "Not at all, ma'am."

Rebel couldn't help grinning this time and turned her head so they wouldn't see.

Dylan shook his head and handed him the bottle. "It's a good thing we hid this bottle from Rebel the other night."

Rebel inhaled sharply and blushed then glared at Conner who chuckled.

"Darien, would you turn that Dutch oven?" Ric asked.

Darien reached into the fire and said, "Damn girl, that smells good. What are you cooking?"

"Peach cobbler. We needed something to offset the instant mashed potatoes," she laughed.

Lauren sat down beside Warrick who was suddenly very nervous.

"Warrick and Ric are the official camp cooks," Rebel informed her. "We definitely eat well around here."

"You cook Warrick?" she asked leaning toward him.

"Yes, ma'am. I like to eat so it kind of goes hand in hand," he said.

Lauren laughed and said, "Poor Danny, I was never a good cook. He ate better in the school lunchroom than at home."

"I hate to cook," Rebel said. "But Jade always went to her grandmothers to get good food."

"I wish you could have tried the venison Warrick grilled a few days ago," Danny said to Lauren.

Warrick stiffened again when her piercing green eyes brushed over him.

"Maybe we could do that again one day," Danny rambled on.

"I'm sorry I missed it," Lauren said still watching

him.

The comfortable conversation continued well into the night until one by one, everyone headed for bed. Cayden, Shane and Danny took first watch taking turns walking around the campsite.

Conner followed Rebel into the tent and pulled her down on top of him. "I thought I would never get you alone."

Chapter 14

"Coffee's on!" Warrick hollered waking Rebel out of a deep sleep. "Darien is chomping at the bit so let's get going."

"God, Darien, it can't be six in the morning," she reprimanded him sleepily as she accepted the cup from Warrick.

"I want some miles between us and this town," Darien said simply.

"Me too," Dylan said pouring himself coffee.

"Jade and Lynn are going to follow us in the truck. We have packed all of the extra supplies in the trailer so the horses aren't packing so much weight," Darien said.

Conner hobbled over looking for Gabe. "God, I am getting addicted!" he growled. "I can't even function without the meds."

"That's because your supposed to be in bed, remember?" Gabe said walking up with a syringe.

"Thanks doc," he smiled trying to be patient.

"Don't worry Conner, I won't let you become a junky. You will be fine once you're healed up," she said returning the smile then stabbed the syringe into his shoulder.

"Aww!" he bellowed.

"Big baby," she grinned patting his arm sarcastically.

They saddled the horses and everyone climbed on.

"We will be riding fast Lauren, if you need to stop and rest, just let me know, k?" Warrick said.

"Thank you Warrick. I think I will be fine," Lauren smiled.

"Warrick, you and Dylan take lead, I will fall behind and make sure we aren't followed," Darien said.

The sun was high in the sky before Dylan and Warrick slowed the horses to a walk. Darien caught up with them and said, "We are good so far. Let's stop and rest for a minute because I want to ride hard until dark."

They dismounted by a small creek and let the horses drink. Rebel sat down on a log and watched Conner wince as he stepped carefully toward her.

"You can't keep up this pace Conner," she said shaking her head. "You should ride in the truck."

He opened his mouth to answer but his voice was drown out by the horses that spun around and bolted in a thunder of pounding hooves. Tucker whined and the puppy started barking.

Rebel looked at Conner horrified as the ground started shaking again. Branches broke off of the trees above them and showered them with leaves.

Conner instinctively wrapped his arms around her, covering her head while the ground rolled under their feet for over a minute.

Rebel looked around for Jade as the earth grew still. Danny had wrapped himself around her the same way. Everyone seemed fine except for the fact that they were now on foot. The horses were nowhere to be seen.

"Fuck!" Warrick bellowed. "Oh, God, sorry Lauren."

Darien and Dylan roared with laughter.

"What are they laughing at?" Conner asked confused.

"Warrick never apologizes for swearing. I've heard him swear in church!" Rebel laughed.

Lauren looked around somewhat confused herself. "It's fine Warrick."

"Fuck you both!" Warrick mouthed to his brothers from behind her back and flipped them the bird stomping off to find the horses yet again.

Their laughter roared again as they followed him.

"Mom, are you ok?" Danny asked.

"Yes, I'm fine," she replied distractedly.

Rebel made sure no one was injured then left to help her brothers.

It took them an hour to gather the animals and adjust the saddles. Several of the horses were scratched up but Gabe and Rebel quickly bandaged them.

They mounted and rode fast till dusk then made camp for the night.

After they had erected the tents and cooked dinner, they sat around the fire to eat.

"That is the fifth earthquake I've felt in the last two weeks," Lauren said.

Rebel visibly stiffened and almost choked on her coffee.

"Several of them were quite big," Lauren continued.

Conner rubbed Rebel's arm soothingly knowing that this would set her off.

She stood up and started pacing then kicked a rock that was in her way and scowled when it hit her rifle that was leaning against a tree.

"Calm down Rebel," Dylan said softly. "Have another cup of coffee."

Rebel slumped back down and accepted the cup. "Thanks Dylan," she said leaning against Conner, suddenly feeling exhausted.

He wrapped his arms around her and held her close.

"Why are you so upset about the earthquakes?" Lauren asked.

"We believe that the volcano will erupt in the near future," Warrick said softly.

Rebel snuggled deeper into Conner's chest feeling completely overwhelmed.

Let's go to bed," he whispered in her ear.

She nodded so he stood and pulled her to her feet. "Goodnight," he said to everyone leading her to the tent. Once inside, he turned to her and helped her unbuckle her holster and pull off her boots tossing them into the corner.

"Do you ever think about how it would have been if we'd met under different circumstances?" he asked her.

She looked into his eyes and said seriously, "You wouldn't have even noticed me. Or worse, I wouldn't have let you close if you did."

"Oh, I don't know. I think I would have noticed and I am confident that I would have convinced you to let me in."

Rebel sighed. "I think I should warn you Conner that there is a reason I've been alone for so long. I'm really not relationship material. We really don't know each other very well."

"What are you saying? Are you regretting our relationship?" he asked looking at her apprehensively.

"No, I'm not, but you have to agree that you have a lot to learn about me. What if you hear some story that turns you off completely? I'm no angel."

"I don't care about your past Rebel. I know enough about you to know that I love you and there is nothing that could change that. "

"Nothing?" she laughed, not believing him. "I'll bet we run into something you don't like sooner or later." Then she shook her head. "Let's not talk about it. I'm just feeling a little weird tonight."

Conner tugged her down onto the sleeping bag and kissed away her anxiety.

It felt like Rebel had barely fallen asleep when Warrick stormed into camp yelling, "Get up! They're here!"

She launched to her feet and pulled her jeans on. She grabbed her rifle and scrambled out of her tent pulling her t-shirt over her head. Conner was moving a little slower as he followed her outside.

"How close?" she asked as she ducked back in and grabbed her holster and strapped it around her waist.

"They are camped about five miles away. They didn't see me so we have the advantage but they are preparing to attack," Warrick explained.

Rebel pulled her boots on and stuffed her knife inside them. She opened her pack and pulled out extra clips of ammo.

"I'm so sorry," Lauren said trembling. "I didn't think they would follow us this far."

Warrick walked up and smiled down at her. "Don't worry Lauren, we won't let anything happen to you."

Cayden and Shane lined up all the extra weapons

against a log and checked their handguns.

"How many Warrick?" Darien asked.

"Thirty at least," Warrick said softly.

Dylan stopped buttoning his shirt and stared at him. "Fuck! Are they mounted?"

"Yes," he said shoving his revolver into the holster.

"Should we wait for them or go after them?" Rebel asked.

"I want them away from the ladies," Darien said. "Not that you're not a lady Rebel," he smiled.

"I know what you mean," Rebel smiled back.

"I don't want to get too far away from camp though, in case they circle around," he continued.

Conner looked at Rebel nervously and said, "I think you should stay here with them."

She glanced at him dismissively then turned back to her brother without comment.

"There is plenty of cover. We could move a half mile out and wait but that will only work if they come straight at us," Dylan said.

"I bet they will," Warrick added.

"K, let's do it," Darien agreed. "Shane, Cayden and Danny, you are there in the trees just out of camp. Don't let them near the ladies if they get past us. Just make sure you see what you're shooting."

"Ya, don't shoot me!" Warrick said walking away.

They followed him into the thick brush where each of them found a spot to ambush the men coming toward them.

Conner looked over at Rebel apprehensively. He was nervous that she would get hurt. He shrugged off the feeling and pulled out his bow and placed it next to the arrows he had leaned on a tree in front of him. He pulled his rifle into his shoulder and sucked in his breath in anticipation of the pain.

Rebel rested her rifle across a tree limb at shoulder height. She looked through the scope and scoured the terrain in front of her.

"Make sure that it's them before you fire," Dylan reminded them.

"It's them!" Warrick said looking through his binoculars. "He's wearing the broken nose I gave him." He set the glass down and picked up his rifle.

"They are heavily armed," Darien added. "Looks like they are wanting a war."

"And we are going to give 'em one," Warrick smiled wickedly.

"They are in range. Rush the second shot cause they will scatter after the first one," Darien warned. "Fire!"

Rebel squeezed off her first round and took aim on a second man while he was disorientated. She watched him topple off of his horse before looking for a third target. She hesitated as their horses reared, she didn't want to unnecessarily kill one of the animals.

Total chaos erupted in front of her as men were shot or thrown from their startled horses. She watched through the scope as they tried to take cover. She pulled off another shot dropping a third guy before he took cover behind a tree.

Conner fired again and she heard him groan in pain. She glanced at him and could see the color leave his face. She turned back to her task and searched for another shot but found no one in the open.

Warrick and Darien advanced a few yards down hill and barely ducked behind some trees before bullets started flying back at them.

Rebel ducked her head down. The men stopped firing and silence echoed through the trees around them.

"They're gonna flank us!" Conner and Darien yelled at the exact same time, jumping up to reposition themselves.

Rebel caught the movement of a tree branch out of the corner of her eye. She focused in and saw a man's shoulder. She aimed and fired. The man screamed.

"He was close!" she yelled to the others setting down the rifle and reaching for the colt. She heard a twig snap behind her and spun around into the chest of a very large man.

He looked down at her rifle and laughed as he reached out and grabbed her around the throat.

She stared calmly into his eyes as she slowly raised the pistol and squeezed the trigger. His expressions change from satisfaction to confusion then to shock as he fell on top of her, taking them both to the ground.

Rebel struggled to get the huge man off of her. She pushed the nearly three hundred pounds of dead weight with no success. Suddenly the body was thrown from her like it was a feather. Dylan and Darien both reached for her at the same time.

"Thanks," she said once again on her feet.

Then a shot rang out from where the boys were positioned. All three of them bolted toward camp.

Conner seen them run and was about to follow when he saw three men sneaking toward them from behind. They hadn't seen him so he picked up his bow and knocked an arrow. He gritted his teeth and drew back, releasing the arrow into the closest man to him. The man slumped silently into the dense foliage. He drew back again hitting the second man.

Warrick watched the second shot with a new appreciation. He knew the third man was out of range by the time Conner drew back the third time so he pointed his rifle and fired.

Conner stepped from his hiding spot and slapped Warrick's hand in a high five. He picked up his rifle, barely able to grasp it. "You go ahead, I'll cover your back," he said.

Warrick nodded and took off at a run toward camp. He ran into a small clearing and watched in horror as a man leveled his handgun at his sister. "Rebel!" he yelled jumping the five feet that separated him from the man and landed right on top of him sending his weapon flying into the dirt. He pounded his fist into his face then a bloody hand-to-hand battle erupted.

The two men pummeled each other with their fists each doing damage and spilling blood.

Conner walked slowly into the clearing, surprised by the fight.

"Stay with him!" Rebel yelled then turned to join the gun battle that was going on closer to camp. She snuck through the brush and realized that the men were getting way to close to her friends. She decided to drop down beside Shane and Cayden so she could watch for the men heading in their direction.

She found a boulder and knelt down behind it then looked through her scope and saw Danny and her youngest two brothers. She looked the other way and saw several men sneaking through the trees toward them.

Rebel put one of the men in her crosshairs and squeezed the trigger. The man crumbled to the ground. She waited patiently for a second target. Suddenly a woman's scream pierced the morning silence, ringing through Rebel's soul. 'Jade'!

She bolted through the trees and into their camp just as Lynn fired her pistol at a man who was advancing on her and Lauren. The shot clipped him in the arm totally pissing him off. He roared in anger and lunged at her.

Rebel's shot didn't miss. The bullet blasted a hole in the man's chest and he folded right in front of the poor girl who dropped the weapon and started crying hysterically.

Rebel glanced around. "Where is Jade?" she yelled.

"She went with Cayden," Ric said then screamed, "Look out!"

Rebel spun around just as a huge fist slammed her square in the mouth. She stumbled backward, her colt flying out of her grasp. She regained her balance as the man came at her reaching for his pistol. She spun around with a kick that knocked the weapon from his hand.

He glared at her and raised his fists then yelled, "That was my brother you bitch. I'm gonna kill you!"

"Bring it you fucker!" she spit through the blood running out of her split lip then ducked as he stepped in and swung at her. She slammed her fist into his teeth as hard as she could swing.

He staggered backward, surprised that this small

woman had injured him. She took advantage of the hesitation and launched forward jumping high into the air. She came down with all of her body weight landing a superman punch into his nose. Her stomach rolled as she felt his nose shatter under her fist. She fell to the ground with him and quickly rolled back to her feet.

He grabbed his nose with one hand and growled in anger as he lunged at her, swinging his long arm at her face.

She ducked but caught his fist in the shoulder. She stepped under him and pummeled her fist into his stomach, almost dropping from the pain that exploded in her hand. She ignored it and quickly spun around and bashed him in the face with her elbow.

She grabbed her colt as he fell backward and shot him before he stabilized himself. The man slumped to the ground, dead.

Rebel turned around to find Jade standing behind her and watched her eyes as they followed the man to the ground and stayed fixed on the blood draining from his back.

Rebel grabbed her and held her tight. "Oh, Jade, I'm sorry."

Jade started trembling and said, "Is everyone trying to kill us?"

"No babe, we just aren't running across the good people." She turned to Ric. "I want you guys to take cover over there under that overhang. Take her and try to calm her down. I will cover you."

Ric nodded, visibly shaken from the events.

"Are you ok?" Rebel asked Gabe as she picked up her rifle and handgun.

Gabe just nodded and followed Ric. The five women huddled in the small alcove absolutely terrified.

Rebel wiped the blood from her mouth. "Fuck! That's all I needed." She climbed to the top of the dirt bank and squatted down behind a fallen tree scanning for anyone she didn't recognize.

Several shots rang out in the trees in front of her

then the valley grew silent. Rebel held her breath wondering what was happening. After several minutes, Conner, Danny and her brothers walked into camp.

Rebel jumped down off of her perch and walked over to them.

"What the fuck happened to you?" Conner yelled seeing the blood dripping off her chin.

"She saved us!" Lynn cried running to Cayden and burying her face in his chest.

Ric wrapped her arm around Darien and said pointing, "That man came out of nowhere and tried to kill us. Rebel shot him, then that guy came in pissed that she killed his brother. She fought him and I'm glad to say, kicked his ass."

"If it weren't for her, that man would have shot us," Lauren said stepping closer to Warrick who wrapped his arm protectively around her waist.

Gabe was completely silent holding on to Shane tightly.

Danny wiped the tears off Jade's face.

Conner looked at the five women then back at Rebel. "Do you always have to show us up? Here we are out there thinking that we are the ones kicking ass and come back to find out you saved everybody!"

"Well, you wanted me to stay in camp," Rebel laughed.

"Because I thought you would be safe," Conner glowered, finding no humor in the situation.

Rebel turned serious and asked, "Have we already found something you don't like?"

Conner scowled at her. "I'm trying to protect you."

"Ya, well don't!" she scowled back.

The brothers laughed and walked closer to check out her face.

"It's not my face that hurts," she said holding up her obviously broken hand.

"Jesus Christ Rebel! I should have been here," Conner said, growing more agitated.

"Conner, I told you not to say shit like that!" she

fumed. "You were doing your part. I don't need to be babysat like a child."

Warrick laughed and patted Conner on the shoulder. "You really need to learn how to talk to her, brother. Don't worry, it only took us thirty years."

"Shut up Warrick!" Rebel spat then winced at the sharp pain in her lip.

Gabe stepped forward finally getting control of her emotions and said, "Come here Rebel. Let's get you fixed up. Shane, baby, could you get my bag?"

Warrick raised his eyebrows at his brother and sarcastically mouthed, 'baby' to him as he walked past and received a fist in the shoulder and a middle finger for his effort.

Dylan laughed and rolled a log over so Rebel could sit down on it.

Conner paced behind them as Gabe braced and wrapped her hand.

"My god, Conner, sit down before you drive me crazy. I know damn well that your ribs hurt way worse than a couple of broken knuckles," she reprimanded.

"Fuck ya, I'll be they do too especially after firing his rifle so many times and I watched him pull two and a half shot from the bow," Warrick said.

"Two and a half shots?" Dylan laughed. "How does that work?"

"The first two found their mark but the third guy was out of range before the arrow flew. But he had 'er drawn back though and that's half of it," Warrick said seriously.

Everybody laughed.

"I want to pack up camp," Darien announced. "We have no way of knowing if there are more of them out there hiding. I want us inside some kind of house or building. Something we can defend ourselves from."

"I need to stitch your lip Rebel. It is split all the way through," Gabe said.

That silenced the camp as everyone came closer to look at her face.

"Rebel, I want you to stop fighting. It scares the shit out of me," Conner said.

"Conner!" she growled.

"Hold still!" Gabe said firmly.

The brothers laughed again and walked away to pack the horses.

Rebel had been right about Conner's ribs. He was in so much pain that he could barely climb onto his horse. He glanced at Rebel and scowled. The answer was yes. They had found something he didn't like.

Darien rode forward at a walk as he searched the countryside for some kind of shelter.

Dylan rode beside him and said, "Isn't there a little town a few miles up ahead that has hot springs? I could sure use a hot bath."

"Good thinking. There are motels there and the population is small," Darien agreed.

Several hours later, the small posse rode to the edge of the very small quiet town.

Conner was instantly on edge. "I got a bad feeling about this town."

"Warrick, Dylan, let's ride in and check it out. Turn on the radio and wait here, Rebel," Darien said kicking his horse into a gallop.

The brothers rode into town staying off the main street. As they drew closer to the public hot pool they heard yelling and glass breaking. Darien motioned for them to dismount and they crept forward on foot.

"What the fuck?" Dylan said watching the obnoxious party going on in the pool. Eight men were sitting in the water obviously drunk and boisterous.

One of the men waved to someone behind the dressing room and all three of the brothers inhaled sharply when a woman was hurtled into the shallow pool. A man jumped in behind her and grabbed her roughly.

"Don't look like she's enjoying the party," Dylan whispered.

"Fuck no she ain't!" Warrick growled. "And neither is she!" he said pointing to another terrified young woman in the corner surrounded by intoxicated men.

"How many men do you see?" Darien asked.

Warrick scanned the space then looked up into the motel that stood next to the pool. "I'm seeing nine in the pool and possibly a couple more in the motel."

"Fuck! Here we go again," Dylan said grabbing his rifle off of his horse.

Just as they stepped toward the pool to intervene, they heard a man demand, "Release the girls you sons 'a bitches!"

Darien looked toward the voice that belonged to an older man wearing a sheriff's badge and watched him turn red with anger when the only reply was laughter.

"Or what?" they demanded.

The poor sheriff carried only a shotgun and hung his head in helpless frustration.

Darien nodded to his brothers and stepped up behind the agitated man.

The sheriff looked up in surprise as Darien yelled back, "Or we will shoot you where you stand. Put your hands in the air now or we fire!"

All nine men froze and looked strait at them in surprise. One of the men looked at his weapon on the side of the pool.

"Go ahead," Warrick said." Make my day!"

All of the men lunged for their weapons at the same time.

Warrick grinned and fired. Darien and Dylan fired with him and they didn't stop until there were nine bodies on the ground.

The girl's screamed in terror then raced to the sheriff.

"Well, did it really make your day Clint Eastwood?" Dylan laughed.

"It did when he died from a Sudden Impact," he laughed.

Rebel and Conner heard the shots and quickly mounted and raced into town followed closely by the boys.

They slid to a halt in front of her brothers looking around confused.

"What the hell?" Rebel bellowed. "You scared the shit out of me."

The sheriff hadn't said a word yet, just stood there stunned by their actions trying to calm the hysterical young women.

Darien looked at him calmly and said, "Sheriff, we didn't mean to step on toes here but we could see that you were outgunned and seriously outnumbered. We couldn't stand by and watch them hurt these young ladies."

The sheriff found his voice and said, "No, no, we are deeply in your debt. Where the hell did you come from anyway?"

"We were just passin through hoping for a hot soak," Dylan laughed.

Rebel looked at the dead men in the pool and the crying girls and guessed what had happened. "Don't you have back up here? Why were they taken, and who the hell were those men?"

The sheriff looked at Darien and hung his head, "Those assholes have taken over the town. We just stay indoors and pray when they are here."

"I can't believe that you don't have enough men here to stop them," Dylan said in amazement.

The sheriff sighed and said, "They killed everyone who crossed them including my deputy. Most of our weapons have been confiscated and the others are out of ammo. Those of us that couldn't leave have basically been held hostage here with no way to defend ourselves."

"Did you send word to the National Guard? I'm sure they are in Cheyenne," Dylan asked.

"We sent word and have heard nothing! That was two weeks ago. They don't have time for us! And I am just one man!" he ground out. "One helpless old man!"

"How many people are still in town?" Darien asked again.

The sheriff looked at him hopefully, "Are you willing to help us? I mean, you already did but would you help again?"

Warrick looked at the battered young women and growled, "We will kill them all if they are hurting the ladies!"

Rebel watched as the sheriff almost leapt with joy.

"We gather for dinner every night at the old church down the road." He looked straight at Darien. "Come eat with us and I'll introduce you to my little town then you can help me save it."

Darien took a deep breath and looked at Dylan then back at the desperate man. "Alright, we will meet you for dinner. We have about twelve people with us."

"Good, good," the man said with a spark brightening his eyes in anticipation. "Bring them."

"Ok then, see you at the church," Dylan said walking toward his horse.

Darien followed him then led the group back out of town.

"This town is like a fucking Hitchcock movie," Dylan mumbled as they rode back to where they left the women.

"They need our help Dylan. This town is in trouble here. They take the girls, damn it!" Darien said determinedly as he dismounted beside Ric.

"Well your intuition was right on again Conner. I really wish you would quit doing that," Rebel laughed.

"What is it? What's going on?" Ric asked.

"The people in that town are being held hostage by a group of murdering rapists!" Rebel said.

Warrick bristled at the reminder and looked at Rebel, "How many men did the sheriff say were coming?"

"He didn't say. We will go eat dinner with them and find out. Danny and the boys found a pasture with a barn up the road. Let's leave the horses and our stuff there," Rebel said.

Dylan raised an eyebrow at her questioningly.

She smiled and said, "I was thinking we could rest for a day. We might as well save the world while we're here."

They quickly stashed their supplies and tack and

walked to the church. The Sheriff met them at the door excitedly. "Come in, I want you to meet the towns people."

Rebel, Conner and the brothers looked around the room at the hundred and fifty expectant faces looking back at them.

"My god Darien, there ain't a man in this room that can fight!" Dylan breathed.

A gentle looking older woman came out of the kitchen saying, "For goodness sake, come sit down. I'm Joan by the way and you've met my husband, Fred, the sheriff. Dinner is almost ready."

The room erupted with conversation, everyone talking at once. The sheriff held up his hand and said, "Ok, ok, quiet please. Sit down and we will talk while we eat." He turned to Darien and pointed to a table.

Dinner was served buffet style under Joan's strict supervision. Rebel ate quietly beside Jade and Conner and tried to ignore the curious looks they were getting.

"So, sheriff, "Darien said, finally breaking the silence, "tell me exactly what the hell is going on here."

"Most of those men were from the Rawlins State Penitentiary. They are criminals and should have been left to starve in their cells. They don't bother us in here, in the church, but at night, when they start drinking, they always go looking for trouble," he said quietly.

"You never told us how many there were," Dylan pointed out.

"There are at least sixty of them," he said looking down, "minus the ones you took out tonight. They were left to hold down the fort while the others went for supplies. They have completely depleted our supplies here."

Joan broke into the conversation with tears in her eyes. "They took all of the guns except Fred's shotgun. Most of the people left because they were so afraid. But some of us had nowhere to go. The worst thing is that they keep taking the girls. We can't stop them."

"How did they get control? I don't get it," Darien asked.

"One by one before anyone knew what was going

on, they went to each house and either killed the man or scared him into leaving. My deputy and I tried to stop them but they shot him," Fred said squeezing Joan's hand.

"So where do they sleep?" Warrick asked. "And when will they be back?"

"I expect them back tomorrow. They will want liquor and women!" he spat.

"They took over Cassidy's hotel by the pool. She didn't get out of there for a week. Poor thing hasn't said a word since," Joan said giving in to her sobs.

Dylan stiffened and slammed his fist on the table. He looked at the startled people around him and said, "Can I have a word with you guys outside?"

Darien, Warrick, Conner and Rebel followed him outside to the front lawn.

"We have to stop them. We need a plan," Dylan said disgustedly.

"I say we wait till they get in the pool and open fire while their weapons are out of reach. Then burn the hotel to flush out the rest," Conner said.

"Just like Billy the kid," Warrick nodded with a grin.

"We are going to have to start the fire first so they can't hit us from the upper floor," Darien pointed out.

"What about the people?" Rebel asked. "We don't want them taken as hostages."

"We will have them stay in the church behind some kind of cover and arm them with the extra weapons. I'll bet some of those people can shoot," Dylan said.

Everyone nodded in agreement.

"I just want to point out that this is premeditated murder. This isn't self defense," Shane said. "Not that I care, but we should at least think about it for a second."

"One," Warrick counted. "Happy?"

"They are committing major crimes and there is no law to help. We will do this tomorrow just before dinner. We don't want to disturb the routine around here and create suspicion," Darien said without a second thought.

"Let's find out where they are getting their alcohol

and make sure it is stocked. They might not fight as well if they are drunk" Rebel said walking back inside.

"That theory didn't work for you," Dylan teased as she walked away.

All the brothers laughed when she flipped him the bird.

The sheriff was impatiently pacing as they walked back in. He eagerly patted Darien's shoulder and said, "Well?"

Darien looked down at the man and whispered, "Sheriff, look around this room and make sure you can trust every person in it. Take your time because all of our lives depend on it."

The sheriff paled as he looked at each person in the room. He looked back at Darien and nodded.

Darien stepped forward and said to the anxious group, "I want everyone to listen to me carefully. Do not react loudly. No yelling, no clapping. Understand?" He waited as everyone nodded. "We are going to try to help you. We have developed a plan that may work if you are willing to help us."

Everyone in the room inhaled hopefully.

"We will carry out our objective tomorrow. It is vital that no one talks about this. Not one word and wipe the hope off of your faces. You need to go about your day as if it were yesterday," Darien instructed. "We will meet for dinner tomorrow night exactly like you do every day. Do you understand?"

"Fuck Darien, they aren't military recruits," Warrick mumbled.

Darien ignored Warrick and said, "Thanks for dinner, we will see you tomorrow night."

Rebel waved for their little group to follow and led them out. They stayed in the shadows and silently walked back to the barn.

"What are the chances that no one blabs about this?" Rebel asked.

"I say pretty slim," Warrick growled.

"I think you underestimate them," Darien said.

"They are desperate and I think they will pull this off."

"No fire tonight. Let's just roll out the bags on the floor of the barn," Dylan said.

"I'll take the boys and inventory the extra weapons and ammo," Warrick said.

"I'll help the ladies prepare theirs," Rebel said.

Later that night, Conner could sense that Rebel was still a little pissed off at him. He hated it when they weren't getting along. He decided to try and change the mood so he took her hand and said, "Let's go for a walk. I have a surprise."

She followed him to a small creek and looked at him curiously when he stopped.

"The water is warm," he said leaning down to put his fingers in it. "Let's go skinny dipping."

She paused for a moment then grinned and quickly stripped and jumped in.

He laughed and followed her.

"Shh, we have to be quiet," she smiled as he swam up to her and wrapped her in his arms with a kiss.

Rebel was anxious when she woke up the next morning. She walked to the unpacked bag holding the coffee pot and kicked it.

"I know what you mean," Warrick said laughing. "If only we could drive into town and find a Starbucks."

"That's when you know you're addicted!" she scowled.

"For sure!" Warrick agreed.

"I think I can help you with this dilemma," Ric said smugly. She bent down and pulled out a can of sterno. "Warrick if you can figure out some kind of stand to put the pot on, I believe this will heat your coffee."

Rebel squealed and hugged Ric.

"What the hell is sterno?" Warrick asked looking at them as if they'd lost their minds.

Rebel laughed but Ric managed to keep a straight face and said, "It's basically heat in a can. Just light it here."

"K, I'll take it from here then," Warrick said. "Thanks Ric, I think you saved us."

Conner moaned as he tried to get up off the floor. "God, somebody please just shoot me now."

Dylan laughed and helped him up. "Can you at least take out some of those thugs first?"

Conner laughed with him. "Speaking of that, I think I better stick to hand guns tonight if you will trade me one for my rifle."

"Whatever you need. Take your pick," Dylan said.

Warrick handed Dylan a cup of coffee while Conner inspected the extra weapons.

"Let's head to the church and get working on the barricade," Darien said. "Fred told me that the ladies sometimes work on quilts during the day so some movement won't attract any attention and I want to see if we can get a count when they ride in."

"I'll put the weapons in bags and pack them on one horse," Warrick said. "We will be able to go in and out of the back door without being noticed."

"I'm afraid," Jade said. "This isn't just protecting us from a threat. This is intentionally going into battle where you are outnumbered five to one."

"I know Jade," Rebel said soothingly. "But we are well armed and skilled."

"And injured," Jade pushed on growing agitated. "How are you going to shoot with a broken hand?"

Rebel hugged her and said, "We will be fine."

"Come on guys, let's get this day over with," Warrick said gently.

Rebel walked beside Jade to the church and opened the back door for her to enter. The brothers packed the bags of weapons inside and laid them out on a table in one of the small rooms.

"We don't have ammo for half of them, just what's in the chamber," Dylan said looking over the guns.

"I'm not planning on them having to use them at all," Darien said. "Danny, Cayden and Shane, you guys are their front line. You will be positioned there, there and there," he pointed out the window. "Don't let them past you."

The boys nodded quietly.

"Did the sheriff restock the liquor store?" Warrick asked.

"Yes, and I'm hoping they stop there first so we can get a look at them," Darien said.

Later that evening, Joan started cooking dinner as planned. People started showing up and the room buzzed in anticipation of the evening.

Darien told the sheriff to meet everyone at the door and send back the men and boys that could shoot.

Dylan and Warrick handed out the weapons and ammunition.

The sheriff walked into the room and said, "That's everybody. Was there enough to go around?"

Dylan nodded and handed him Conner's rifle. "That one needs to be returned."

The sheriff nodded and turned to leave as a beautiful woman walked in. "Hello Cassidy," he greeted her nervously.

The woman ignored the sheriff and stared expectantly at Dylan. Her haunting hazel eyes wrapped around his heart as she looked through him into his soul.

"Give her a gun Dylan," Rebel said.

Dylan couldn't seem to move. He was lost in pools of blue green and never wanted to be found.

"Dylan!" Rebel said again.

He jumped back into reality and quickly offered her the pistol in his hand.

Cassidy unwaveringly held his gaze as she accepted the weapon then turned and exited the room.

"Did you feel that?" Warrick asked. "I think the temperature went up twenty degrees in this room."

"Fuck you, Warrick!" Dylan said still looking at the door.

"This is a church boys, do you think you could hold off on the swearing for a minute," Rebel reprimanded.

Warrick huffed and stomped to the door. "Let's do this!"

Rebel picked up her rifle and followed him out of the room.

The main doors burst open and a very hysterical woman ran in screaming, "They took the twins! The twins! They are only sixteen years old!" The woman dropped to the ground at the sheriff's feet crying.

"Fucking psychos!" Warrick yelled stomping out the front doors.

"Sounds like they are here," Conner said following him.

"Well, it ain't murder now!" Shane growled.

Rebel looked anxiously at Darien and Dylan then followed them with a new determination.

"I'll set the fire then cover the front door," Conner said. "Rebel you've got the back door. Please be careful."

"We've got the boys in the pool," Warrick said. "Make sure you don't hit the girls."

Rebel crept around to the back of the hotel while the brothers positioned themselves for the slaughter. She made herself comfortable behind a dumpster in the alley and laid the extra clips beside her. 'Four rounds in each clip one in the chamber,' she thought as she put the crosshairs on the door. 'This is the day the pump will prove itself'.

Smoke wafted out the open window on the bottom floor and she only counted to two before all hell broke loose. The brothers started firing and the men in the pool started screaming.

Two of the men ran from the pool toward the back of the hotel. Rebel dropped one before he reached the side of the building and the other before he recovered from the shock of the first shot.

The back door of the hotel flew open and three men burst outside stumbling over each other. Rebel emptied the clip and grabbed the backup stuffing it into the rifle as a fourth man exited the burning building. She squeezed off the shot and watched through the glass as stunned horror filtered across his face.

'Three more shots,' she reminded herself then heard Conner empty his revolver. She held her breath as silence settled over the little town.

"Don't shoot! We are coming out!" she heard one of the men yell down from the second floor. She waited impatiently unable to see what was going on then jumped when she heard four shots ring out at the same time.

"You ain't worth feedin!" Warrick yelled to the dead men.

Conner peeked around the corner of the building, waving to let her know it was him. He motioned toward the back door and they entered the burning building.

"They didn't have the girls with them. They may still be in the building," he said clearly upset.

They met up with the brothers and carefully cleared the first floor then climbed the stairs. The smoke was thick and the flames were climbing the walls.

"We don't have time to be cautious!" Rebel yelled and kicked one of the doors open. "Just find the girls!"

Warrick stuck his head out of a window and yelled, "Shane! Cayden! Cover the hotel doors."

He stepped back into the hall and started kicking the doors open.

"Here they are!" Conner yelled from down the smoke filled hallway.

"They are tied! Those bastards were going to leave them here to burn!" Rebel exclaimed. "I'll get them out. You guys check the other rooms."

Rebel untied the hysterical girls and said firmly, "Follow me and stay by my side." She led them through the flames that now consumed the hall then down the stairs and out the front door. "This is Shane, he will take you to your mother. Stay beside him!"

Shane stopped her when she turned to go back into the hotel. "Rebel, you take them to the church, I will help the guys. I insist!" he added firmly.

Rebel nodded and said, "Come on girls."

They ran along the sidewalk and across the street to

the churchyard. The doors flew open and the girls' mother ran out and wrapped her arms around them. "Thank you Rebel. Thank you so much."

"Get back inside," Rebel said and ran back to the hotel.

The building was completely engulfed in flames now. "Conner!" she yelled into the door.

"We are coming out!" he yelled back.

He, Shane and Warrick came out the door and doubled over coughing. Dylan and Darien followed half carrying another woman between them.

"Jesus!" Rebel yelled.

"There were four more men up there," Darien said still gasping for air. "But we checked every room. There was no one else in the building."

"She is injured. We need to get her to Gabe," Rebel said leading the way back to the church.

The church erupted in cheers as they walked through the doors.

"Gabe! I need you here!" Rebel yelled helping the injured woman into one of the classrooms.

Gabe ran into the room and started checking her over.

The Sheriff strode over to Darien and grabbed his hand. "We are in your debt! Thank you."

Conner crumbled into a chair and leaned back trying to ease the pain in his ribs. The brothers sat down around him exhausted.

"Dinner!" Joan yelled to the room. "You boys don't move. We will bring yours to you."

"That would be great," Warrick said without lifting his head from the table.

Rebel joined them and everyone ate in silence.

Dylan suddenly jumped to his feet and Rebel looked behind her to see what he was looking at.

Cassidy walked up to their table and laid the handgun down. "Thank you," she said looking into his eyes.

"Would you like to sit down?" he asked her pulling out a chair.

She sat down across from Rebel. "I really wanted to kill them myself," she said softly.

"I know," Rebel said gently. "They're gone now, you're safe."

Cassidy put her hands over her face and started crying.

Dylan panicked not knowing what to do and looked at Rebel for help.

She motioned for him to put his arms around her.

He followed the advice and smiled when Cassidy sunk into his embrace.

Warrick rolled his eyes and stood to get more coffee.

"Oh no you don't. We are going to wait on you hand and foot," Joan said taking the cup from his hands.

He sat back down with a blank look on his face. "Did she just appear out of nowhere when I stood up?" he whispered.

"I told you, Alfred Hitchcock," Dylan laughed.

Rebel laughed with them then stood to check on Gabe and the injured woman.

Conner followed her and asked, "Is she going to be ok?"

"She was raped and beaten probably daily for some time. Physically, she will heal but emotionally, I don't know." Gabe looked around the church solemnly and said, "You guys did a good thing here today."

"Rebel," Darien called. "The sheriff says that there is another motel just up the road that we can stay in."

"That's great. I'm ready for bed," she said. "We can get our stuff tomorrow."

Rebel led the way out the door waving to the people in the church.

"That building is going to burn for days," Conner said regretfully as they walked past the motel. "I'm sure glad we got everybody out."

"First thing in the morning we will bury the bodies and help clean up," Darien said. "I'd do it tonight but I don't think it is safe out here yet."

"There it is!" Cayden said excitedly pointing to the motel up the road.

Rebel opened the first door for Jade and Lynn then went into the next room and sprawled on the bed. "I'm tired," she said into the pillow.

Conner leaned his rifle against the wall and shut the door. He pulled off his boots and lay down beside her. "How tired are you?"

She rolled over and said with a grin, "Not that tired."

Chapter 15

Rebel woke the next morning to laughter and loud conversation. Conner wasn't in the room so she rolled to her feet and opened the door looking down the street. Men were loading bodies onto a wagon and women were throwing buckets of water onto the blood soaked sidewalks.

Conner rode up to the door with her bags and said, "Good morning."

"Morning," she said accepting the bag. "They are up early."

He looked back up the road and smiled, "Darien told them that we came this way to soak in the pool so they decided to give us that in return for clearing the trash out of their town."

Rebel smiled. "It's good to know that there are still good people out there."

"I'll find you some coffee," he said turning his horse back up the road.

Rebel took her time getting dressed. She wasn't in the mood for company this morning let alone a town full of zealous people.

Conner came back packing the coffee and said, "They have decided to have a celebration tonight and we are the guests of honor."

Rebel rolled her eyes. "Conner, I don't want to go to a party. I want to sit on my ass and rest till tomorrow then head out."

"Sorry. I'm not the boss and the minute Fred said they were gonna roast a pig, the brothers were in," he said grinning.

"Great," she moaned.

"Here, one of the ladies sent this for you," he said holding up a bathing suit with a grin. "I can't wait to see you in it."

Rebel raised her eyebrow at him and jerked it out of his hand.

He laughed and said, "The pool is cleaned up and ready and Jade is waiting for you. Come sit with us, k?"

Rebel nodded and strode to the bathroom to put the suit on under her cloths. When she returned, he took her hand and they walked to the pool.

"Mom! The water is great, come on in," Jade called out then splashed Lynn in the face.

Ric, Gabe and Lauren were sitting on the stairs waist deep in the soothing hot water surrounded by her brothers.

"Come on Rebel, the water is legendary for its healing powers," Conner urged, pulling off his shirt.

She smiled and stripped to her bathing suit and jumped in.

They soaked, swam, splashed and talked all morning.

The sheriff walked up to them and said, "The women are real excited about the party tonight and are getting all duded up over at the hair salon. They asked me to invited you ladies to join them when you're done here."

"Thank you," Rebel said seeing the excitement on Jade's face. "I'm sure the girls will enjoy it."

"They've been cooking all morning. Should be one hell of a feast," he laughed as he walked away.

"Let's go Lynn, I want to do my hair. They are eating at four and it will never dry in time," Jade said.

The girls climbed out of the pool and rushed back to the motel.

"Are you coming Rebel?" Ric asked.

Rebel shrugged not really interested.

"Come on, it will be fun. We haven't put makeup on for weeks," she urged. "It will make you feel better."

"Fine," Rebel gave in. "I'll meet you there." She watched as the three women followed the girls excitedly. "Fuck! I'm not up for this," she said climbing out of the water.

"Go have some fun Rebel. It won't hurt to enjoy something for once," Conner said resting his chin on his arms over the side of the pool. He bit his lip to silence the groan of pleasure that threatened to escape his lips as he watched her bent over to pick up her jeans.

She glanced at him as she pulled them up, instinctively knowing what he was thinking. "Conner, you are such a boy," she smiled at him then walked away.

The salon was buzzing with chatter when Rebel walked through the door.

"Come in," one of the ladies said. "We have makeup and old style rollers. Can I style your hair for you?"

Ric could see that Rebel was feeling a little overwhelmed so she jumped in and said, "Why don't we find her a dress first."

"A dress? Find me a dress?" Rebel exclaimed.

"Adrian owns the clothing store next door and she has offered us dresses. Come on, let's go find something," Ric said.

Rebel followed her into the store and browsed through the racks of cloths. She stopped when she noticed Cassidy sitting behind the counter and walked over to her and said, "Hi Cassidy, how are you today?"

The woman tried to smile and shrugged.

Rebel sat down next to her and said, "They are trying to find me a dress. A dress! I haven't worn a dress since I was twelve years old," she laughed. "Probably the last time I went to church."

Cassidy actually did smile at that.

"What are you wearing tonight?" Rebel asked her.

She paused then shook her head and said quietly, "I don't think I'll go."

"Oh come on. I'll tell you what. I'll wear a dress if you do," Rebel said looking directly into her eyes expectantly. "We will go and feel uncomfortable together, k?"

Cassidy smiled again and said, "Ok."

Rebel put her hand over hers encouragingly and softly said, "I know you've been through hell Cassidy. I can't even imagine. Just keep fighting. Don't let it ruin your life."

Cassidy looked at her with tears in her eyes. "I just can't even face the day sometimes. These people look at me with pity and scorn. I want to just climb in a hole and die."

"I know and I'm asking you to keep trying. Don't give up. I'll do anything I can to help you," Rebel said wrapping her in her arms. "Come on, we have a party to go to."

Cassidy stood up with her and wiped her tears. "I'm not wearing pink or flowers."

Rebel laughed and said, "Me either!"

Later that afternoon, Conner and the brothers were sitting around a table on the front lawn of the church drinking beer. The pork was being sliced and the Dutch ovens were being pulled out of the fires. Fresh fruit cobblers were set out and the door to the liquor store was open wide.

Jade, Gabe and Lynn walked out of the salon and crossed the street. Danny, Cayden and Shane stood up, stunned by the sight of the three beautiful women walking toward them.

Warrick grinned and bowed, "Ladies."

Jade smiled at him then blushed as Danny almost tripped over a chair because he couldn't take his eyes off of her.

Cayden held out his hand and led Lynn to the table.

Shane hadn't moved, just stood staring at Gabe. And she just looked right back at him. "You are beautiful," he said finally.

"Thank you," she smiled. "You shine up pretty good yourself."

He laughed as he walked up to her and took her hand. "Can I offer you a chair?"

She nodded and let him lead her to the table.

Conner and the brothers watched the six of them laughing and chatting together as they waited for dinner.

"Seeing them together gives a man hope for the future," Darien pondered then looked at the others wondering why they were silent. He followed their gaze and sucked in his breath. "My god!"

Lauren and Ric were walking across the street toward them.

Warrick and Darien jumped to their feet trying not

to look like teenagers at a high school dance.

Darien strode to Ric and picked her up twirling her around. He bent down and kissed her then said, "Absolutely gorgeous."

Lauren walked up to Warrick who was fidgeting nervously. "Hello," she smiled.

"Hello Lauren. You look very nice tonight," he said. "I saved you a chair by me. Hope that's alright."

"That is wonderful," she purred. "Thank you."

Warrick followed her to her chair and grabbed his chest imitating a heart attack as he passed Dylan.

Dylan laughed then looked up when Conner nudged him to get his attention.

Rebel and Cassidy walked out of the salon together chatting happily as they crossed the street.

"Is Rebel wearing a dress?" Warrick asked completely taken back.

"She sure as fuck is!" Conner breathed barely able to keep his heart in his chest. "My god, how did I get so lucky?"

"We will never know!" Darien teased.

"Jesus, I thought she was beautiful before but… look at her. I've never seen her with makeup on and only in jeans," he mumbled to no one in particular.

"She isn't always a gun slingin, bronc riding, brawling, tom boy, Conner. She is a woman sometimes too," Jade said laughing.

"Obviously so," Conner said nodding in agreement as the two women stopped in front of him and Dylan. They launched to their feet.

"I convinced Cassidy to wear a dress too so that I wouldn't feel so out of place," Rebel said. "Please excuse my bare feet though, I wasn't about to wear heels."

"You both look fantastic," Dylan said without taking his eyes off Cassidy.

Cass ducked her head and Rebel could feel the tension building inside her from two feet away.

"Please," he continued, "sit here by me."

Rebel watched the fear and mistrust melt into hope

on her face as she smiled.

"I'll sit next to you," Rebel said giving her some much needed moral support.

Cassidy inhaled deeply and sat down.

Dylan looked at Rebel again nervously. She motioned for him to sit down and smiled when he pulled his chair closer to her timid friend.

Rebel turned to Conner and said, "Hello handsome."

Conner let his eyes trail slowly over her wickedly beautiful body that perfectly filled out the tiny slip of a dress she was wearing. Her breasts rested just out of sight but tantalizingly close to the seam, and he had to rip his eyes away from them. The tiny straps did nothing to hide the perfectly shaped muscles of her shoulders and long arms. Her stomach was so flat and shapely that he almost couldn't resist putting his hands around it. The hem barely hid the bandage that covered the bullet wound in her muscular thigh and when he glanced down at her sexy, tanned bare feet he had to force himself to breath. He sucked in his breath and whispered, "Hello my little spit fire."

Rebel had to clench her jaw and her fists to keep the rush of pounding blood from breaking through the walls of her veins while Conner practically raped her with his eyes. She caught her breath and slowly sat down beside Cassidy with a grin.

"I'm glad you're getting your eyes full because it's probably the last time you will ever see me in a dress."

"How disappointing," he teased. "I always knew there was more to you than muscle shirts and holsters."

Dinner was served and the party was on. Everyone ate, drank and laughed deep into the night.

Conner could barely contain himself as he impatiently waited to get Rebel back to their room. He could not get over how she looked dressed up with makeup on.

Finally, she leaned over and whispered, "Have I tortured you enough? Are you ready to take me to your bed?

He launched to his feet and picked her up, carrying her away as she laughed, waving goodbye to her friends and family.

Conner opened his eyes the next morning to loud angry voices. His head was pounding from drinking all night and he had barely slept at all. He peeked out the window to see Rebel and Darien in the middle of a heated conversation. He pulled on his jeans and stepped out the door barefoot.

"What's going on guys?" he asked glaring at the sun that pounded on his head.

Darien took a deep breath. "I'm trying to convince her that we should stay at least a couple more days then she should take the truck and drive the ladies home," Darien said looking away.

Warrick walked up and stuffed a cup of coffee in her hand. "Everyone is in agreement, Rebel," he said quietly.

"It's not up to everyone!" she ground out. "Shane can take the women. The rest of us need to stick together! And we need to get on the road today, tomorrow at the latest. We are just wasting time here after that."

Dylan, Darien and Warrick all looked at Conner hoping he would step in and back them up.

Conner hesitated for a moment. He'd been in this exact position before and it hadn't turned out well for him. He looked back at them then sighed and said, "Rebel, I agree with them. The women have been through enough. Take them home."

Rebel's eyes flashed as she turned on him. "I expected you to side with them." She turned and walked away from them heading out of town into the forest. She needed to clear her head and think.

"Fuck! You guys just led me to the slaughter," he said to the brothers as he watched her disappear into the trees. "She will never get over this one."

"Yes she will, cause she knows we're right," Darien said. "It just takes all of us to make her stop and think about it."

Rebel hadn't walked a hundred yards into the forest when she found herself right in the middle of someone's campsite. She froze realizing her error. She had been so preoccupied with Conner and her brothers that she hadn't been paying attention to her surroundings.

"Well, look what just walked into our house, boys," a deep hard voice said.

Ten men circled around her.

"Conner!" she screamed as loud as she could before a large fist slammed into her face. She vaguely heard the man tell his friends to hide her before they all disappeared in darkness.

Conner, Darien, Dylan and Warrick all heard the scream and bolted into the forest that she had disappeared into only minutes before. Tucker ran in front of them as if he understood that she was in danger.

They sprinted into the campsite and slid to a stop in front of eight rifles.

"Where is she?" Conner demanded barely able to contain beast that was fully awake and a heartbeat away from erupting out of him.

A man with a deep scar across his cheek laughed and said, "Don't worry about it. Your dead anyway. We will take good care of her."

Conner lost control of the animal inside him and exploded on the man.

At the same time, Tucker came flying through the air landing on the man next to him, snarling viciously as if to say, 'this one is mine'.

The other men jumped in surprise giving the brothers the split second distraction they needed to launch their assault. They moved in shoving the rifles away from them and swinging fists.

Conner pounded the guy in the face knocking him cold and reached for his handgun. He cursed when he realized that he'd left it sitting next to his boots at the hotel. He turned to the closest man to him and ripped the rifle out of his hands bashing him over the head with it then ducked as another rifle swung around to him. He swung his fist the full length of the barrel and found the man's face, knocking him cold.

The man Tucker had hold of screamed in terror as the dog latched onto his throat with a deadly growl.

Conner turned just as first man recovered from the gun beating and charged him, hitting him at a dead run with his arms wrapped around him. They crashed to the ground.

His lungs deflated as he impacted the dirt and he couldn't breathe. The man crawled on top of him and started pounding him in the face with both fists.

Conner took several hard blows before he could suck in enough air to push through the flying fists and shove the guy off of him. He rolled over and climbed to his feet then growled as the man advanced again throwing his fist. Conner blocked the swing and pounded his fist into the man's face, breaking his jaw. The man shrieked in pain and fury then in a full-blown panic, swung his fist aimlessly at Conner catching him in the ribs with a lucky body shot.

Conner dropped to his knees, the pain from his ribs threatening to render him unconscious. He fought off the blackness and heaved himself at the man, taking him back to the ground. Conner held him down and beat him in the face with his fists over and over until Warrick pulled him off.

"Come on. I think you got him. We have to find Rebel," he said.

Conner stood up and spit blood on the ground beside his bare feet and stood over the body wheezing.

"Jesus Christ, Conner!" Warrick yelled. "You're barefoot. And it sounds like you fucked up your lungs. Fuck!"

Conner looked down at his feet and shrugged. He looked at his dog and said, "Tucker, go find her. Go get 'er boy." He shrugged off the anxious looks from the brothers, and followed the dog down the mountain."

Tucker raced through the trees looking for Rebel, followed by four worried men running behind him.

Rebel became conscious being dragged through the forest by two men. It took a second for her to remember the events that led up to this moment. She could taste the blood gushing from her nose and the deep cut on her cheek stung viciously. She glanced up at the two men holding her and knew she was dead. The men were armed with rifles and both of them were very large. She pictured the men back at camp and knew that they would stop Conner and her brothers from finding her.

One of the men, a Hispanic looking guy, stopped and asked, "Where are we going?"

"How the fuck should I know?" the second man answered rubbing the tattoo on his baldhead.

"I say we take her to the motel and ask Ruben," the Hispanic guy said.

"No way! We aren't supposed to be back to town till in the morning. He would be pissed if he knew we were here already," the bald guy said.

Rebel looked around her and saw a branch lying next to her leg. She inhaled deeply and made her move. She jerked her arms free from the unsuspecting men and picked up the two-foot long weapon, swinging it as hard as she could across the bald guys face, knocking his rifle out of his hands as he fell backward.

The Hispanic man stared at her in surprise for a moment then lunged at her. She stepped into his attack and slammed her left fist into his stomach, doubling him over. She grabbed the top of his head and wrapped her fingers in his hair and shoved his head down hard as she could at the same time bringing her knee up into his face. The connection sounded like a pumpkin being smashed to the ground.

The man stumbled back and fell on his ass holding his shattered face with both hands, blood pouring between his fingers.

The bald man scrambled to his feet and faced her with a scowl as he wiped blood from his mouth. "You're dead now!" he said in a chilling voice.

Rebel clenched her fist, feeling the pain in the broken knuckles and knew this fight was gonna hurt. She stared unwavering into the man's cold eyes and waited for him to move.

He brought up his fists and swung with a quick

punch, hitting her in the side of the head as she ducked. She stepped in and slammed her fist into his jaw, staggering him back a step. She nearly dropped to the ground from the pain in her hand.

He recovered faster than she did and lunged at her, tackling her to the ground. She head butted him in the nose and he howled as his blood spilled onto her chest. He heaved her to her feet and backhanded her so hard she damn near lost consciousness again. He growled with hatred and kicked her, landing his boot in her thigh.

Darkness closed in but she fought to stay conscious as she rolled to her feet and staggered up trying to see through the blackness in her head and the blood draining down her face.

The man smiled through the blood dripping down his own mouth and came at her again. She gathered every ounce of strength she could and spun around with a head kick that caught him right in his temple. He sprawled to the ground.

She kicked him in the abdomen then hobbled quickly out of his reach.

He rolled to his feet with murder in his eyes.

Conner and the brothers topped the ridge and saw the horrifying bloody fight down in the valley.

"Rebel!" Conner yelled when he saw the size of the man she was fighting and the blood running down her face. He raced down the mountain, afraid he wouldn't get there in time. He watched her sway and prayed she could fend him off for just another minute but almost stumbled in fear as he watched a second man stand up and circle around behind her.

Rebel knew she was going to lose this fight when the Hispanic man stood up behind her. The bald guy grinned unmercifully, knowing that the two of them could take her down quickly.

Suddenly, Tucker ran past her and launched himself onto the Hispanic man, taking him to the ground. The man shrieked in fear, flailing his arms wildly as the dog went for his throat.

Rebel anticipated the distraction and actually smiled when the bald guy glanced at the dog attacking his friend. She stepped forward and pummeled him with a left hook that shattered his teeth then followed the swing with her elbow, smashing it into his broken nose.

The man staggered back, stunned by the power hidden inside the woman in front of him. He was moving much slower as he lunged for her again.

Rebel held her ground, patiently waiting for him to get close enough then shoved her body upward, head butting him right in the chin. His head snapped backward and blood showered the ground around them as he fell to his knee. He growled as he slowly climbed to his feet, looking at her in amazement.

She faced him once more, fighting the darkness still trying to overtake her and looked him dead in the eye. She was so weak she could hardly stand and tested every muscle in her body trying to stay on her feet. Suddenly a shot rang out and they both turned to see Warrick standing there with his pistol in his hand. She swayed in relief and felt her knees go out from under her as the big man dropped to the ground.

Conner raced past him and wrapped his big arms around her as she slipped into darkness, unconscious.

"Rebel! Rebel," he said into her hair. "Oh my god."

Warrick pulled the dog off of the half dead man on the ground and stood over him. "What are we going to do with this mess?"

Conner laid Rebel on the ground strode to Warrick taking the pistol out of his hand. He pointed it at the man's head and fired without the slightest hint of emotion. He handed the weapon back and strode back to Rebel, gently picking her up. "We need to get her back to Gabe."

Warrick stared after him and Dylan looked at Darien who shrugged.

"Give her to me Conner," Darien said taking his sister into his big arms.

Conner could hardly breath as they hiked up the

mountain and stopped at the top of the ridge. He started coughing and leaned over spitting blood on the ground.

"His lung is collapsing again!" Dylan said leaning over his friend.

"I'm ok, we need to get Rebel back to town," he wheezed and stumbled forward determinedly.

The brothers glanced at each other worriedly and followed.

They must have been quite a sight when they walked into town, each of them covered in blood and bruises. Everyone came rushing toward them.

"Mom!" Jade screamed running from the pool. "Mom, are you ok? What happened?"

Rebel moaned, opening her eyes then wiggled out of her brother's grasp.

"Get my bag!" Gabe yelled, racing toward them.

Warrick helped Conner onto the bed in their room and Dylan motioned for Rebel to sit in the chair.

Jade helped her and knelt down to check her wounds.

Gabe ran in wrapped in a towel and said, "What happened, god damn it! Conner, you were supposed to be resting."

"We met up with some men just out of town," Warrick said. "They asked for a fight, so we gave them one."

Dylan smirked and Darien actually smiled.

"Who were they?" Shane asked as Gabe shook her head and pulled her scope out of the bag, putting it to Conner's chest.

"They were headed for the motel," Rebel said getting everyone's attention. "They must have been on some kind of mission and returned early but were too afraid to tell their boss so they were camping out there until morning. They had no idea that their friends were dead."

"Jesus! He has punctured his lung!" Gabe said fearfully. "I don't have any way to fix this. I don't have the equipment."

"There has to be a hospital here somewhere. A

clinic or something. Shane, go get the sheriff. Hurry!" Darien said.

Shane bolted out the door and returned minutes later with Fred.

"We don't have a hospital but we have a fairly well equipped clinic up the street," Fred said very concerned.

Gabe looked at Darien fearfully. "Carry him to the clinic carefully, but hurry or I'm going to lose him." She turned to the sheriff and said, "Fred, are there any doctors or nurses here?"

"The doctor left, but Brittany is a nurse. I'll go get her and meet you in the clinic," he said rushing out the door.

Rebel took Conner's hand and held it as the brothers packed him to the clinic.

Brittany ran into the clinic and threw open one of the doors. "In here!"

The brothers lay Conner on a table and watched the chaos helplessly.

Gabe rushed past them and started opening drawers searching for instruments. "What is your education level and experience?" she asked the girl.

"I'm an LPN," Brittany answered. "I've worked in this clinic for two years."

"Good, I need to put a tube in his chest. Can you help me find what I need?" Gabe said taking control of the room. "Rebel I need you to wait outside."

"Not a chance," Rebel said weakly looking into Conner's eyes. He squeezed her hand encouragingly and winked.

"Fine but you sit at his head and don't touch him. You haven't scrubbed up," Gabe said firmly.

The brothers filed out of the room and sat down in the lobby.

"I hope they can fix Conner quickly cause Rebel needs stitches all over her face and her leg was bleeding badly again," Dylan said.

"Did you see that fight? I'm fucking impressed," Warrick said. "She just might have finished him off."

"And don't forget she has a broken hand and a

bullet hole in her leg," Dylan said frowning.

"Remember how dedicated she was when she was learning to fight? She spent hours practicing, sparing with anyone who would accept the challenge," Darien added.

"I don't think she missed a day in the gym for the last five years," Dylan laughed.

"Well, it paid off. She just held her own in a fight with two armed men twice her size," Darien said.

"She could have been killed," Dylan pointed out. "We need to make sure that never happens again."

Darien and Warrick solemnly nodded in agreement.

"I'm making her take the truck and go home. Conner won't be able to ride now. Maybe this will convince her," Darien said hopefully.

"Fucking Conner. He beat that guy to death with his fist," Warrick smiled. "And did you see the look on his face when he blew that guy's head off?"

Dylan nodded. "I'd say rage was an understatement."

Thirty minutes later, Rebel followed Gabe out of the room. "He is going to be ok," she informed them.

"Thank God!" Warrick said standing up to pace the room.

Gabe turned to Rebel. "It's your turn, follow me," she said leading her into the room across the hall.

Ric and Jade stood up and followed the two women into the exam room.

Gabe pointed to the table and peered at the deep cuts on Rebel's face as soon as she was seated. "Rebel, this has to stop. You can't be fighting like this."

"What do you want me to do, Gabe? Do you think I enjoy getting my ass kicked all the time?" Rebel spat.

"Mom, she is right. You are going to get hurt really bad one of these times," Jade agreed fearfully.

"Look you two, when the threat is over, I will retire. But until then, I will do whatever it takes to protect you. Got it?" Rebel said firmly. "And this one was self defense so get off my ass!"

"You have several deep gashes on your face and another one over your eye. There is an even bigger one on the top of your head that is probably covering a severe concussion. You've ripped the stitches out of your lip and your entire face will be black and blue within an hour. And that's just your head. I haven't even seen your ribs or your leg yet!" Gabe exploded.

"Well, should I wait until later to show you my hands?" she ground out.

"God damn it! You've broken more bones in the right one and probably some in the left!" Gabe exclaimed.

"Just fix me up coach and send me back in," Rebel said mockingly.

"Rebel, even I have to object to this," Ric said. "You can't tell me you don't like to fight cause I know better. But you are going to be killed one day."

"I haven't once gone looking for a fight! But I'm sure as hell going to finish the ones that find me!" Rebel yelled. "Now everyone get out! Gabe, you hurry up with the stitches or I'm leaving without them!"

Jade and Ric sulked out into the lobby. The brothers stood when they saw the look on their faces.

"What did she do?" Dylan asked.

"She kicked us out of the room," Jade murmured.

"We told her that she should stop fighting and she flipped out," Ric said.

"She only fights when she has too," Warrick defended. "She won't just stop because we tell her too."

"She has at least one concussion and both of her hands are broken. She can barely walk on that leg and she looked like she fought the heavy weight champion! You three are going to have to do something!" Ric said firmly, pointing her finger at them.

"She did just fight a heavy weight!" Warrick said proudly. "In fact she fought two of them at the same time."

"Not funny!" Ric said.

"We are going to send her home in the truck," Darien said softly. "The trick will be getting her to agree with us."

"I can help you with that," Jade jumped in smiling deviously. "If I get in the truck you know she will go with me. She would never let me drive away alone."

"Good idea Jade!" Dylan said standing up. "Don't say anything today, we will break the news to her tomorrow."

"Gabe will have to go with Conner," Ric pointed out. "And Lynn should go to."

"It's a good plan. We will prepare everything she needs and find enough fuel to get them there," Darien said excitedly.

All the brothers stood when the door opened and Gabe followed Rebel out of the room saying, "Now please go lay down and rest Rebel."

Rebel looked at her and said, "I'll be staying here with Conner." Then she hobbled into the small operating room without another word.

"Doc, how long before Conner can ride in the truck?" Dylan asked.

Gabe looked at the three brothers. "At least three days if everything goes well. Why?"

"We are going to make Rebel take the truck and go home. You will have to go with them," Darien said as Shane and Cayden followed Danny through the doors.

"She will have to go where?" Shane asked.

"We are sending Rebel and Conner home in the truck and he will still need medical attention," Darien said gently. "Jade and Lynn will go as well."

"At least they will be safe at home," Cayden said looking at Shane who nodded.

"Go find a hospital bed that will roll into Conner's room. Rebel will want to sleep there tonight," Darien said to his younger brothers.

Rebel lay awake all night listening to Conner's chest gurgling. Her entire body ached from the beating she'd received and her head was pounding from the concussion.

She eased out of her makeshift bed at the first sign

of sunlight and groaned in pain. Conner was still sleeping so she stepped outside onto the sidewalk. She slid down onto a bench and watched Warrick build a fire on the church lawn up the street.

Darien walked up and sat down beside her. "How's your battle wounds?" he asked.

"Hurts," she said simply.

"I know everyone is on your ass about fighting, we are all worried about you, but I just wanted to say that your skills are impressive. You really are a warrior, Rebel."

"Feels more like I'm a punching bag," she said softly. "If only I weighed two hundred pounds and had big fists."

"When are you going to stop trying to be something your not? Just be yourself Rebel, and let us be the muscle," he gently prodded.

"I know your right Darien. I just regret being the one who has to be taken care of," she sighed.

"You have certainly pulled your own weight out here. All of your hard work has paid off. You should have no regrets at all. But now it is time to step back off the front line. Ok?" he urged.

She slowly nodded her head as Warrick walked up with coffee.

"How's our warrior princess?" he asked.

"I feel like I got my ass kicked," she said grudgingly.

"Oh hell no. You beat the shit out of those guys!" Warrick exclaimed. "I think you could have finished him."

Rebel shook her head. "He would have killed me if you wouldn't have showed up when you did."

"That's what we are here for, sis. You did great," Dylan said seriously.

"Thanks," she shrugged.

"How is Conner?" he asked.

"His lungs gurgled all night but Gabe said he is going to be fine," Rebel said glancing at the clinic.

Dylan sat down on the curb and sipped his coffee distractedly. Warrick leaned against a light pole and crossed his arms over his chest and Darien looked down at his boots.

Rebel looked at her brothers curiously and said, "What is going on. I feel some kind of intervention approaching."

"Jade has offered to take the girls home in the truck," Darien said flatly.

Rebels eyes narrowed as she waited for him to continue.

"Conner, Gabe and Lynn are going with her and they are hoping you will go too," Dylan added.

"You sneaky bastards!" Rebel exclaimed. "I can't believe you would use her against me."

Warrick grinned and said, "We don't have all that much to work with so we are going to use whatever ammunition we can find."

"Look, sis, you are injured and Conner can't ride at all now. Just get him home." Darien said then added, "And this is your chance to get Jade out of danger."

Rebel slouched back in her seat and folded her arms across her chest.

The brothers stayed smugly silent, knowing that they had won.

They spent the next couple of days preparing the truck for the drive home. Rebel hadn't said much, spending most of her time sitting at Conner's side. He was recovering nicely, finally able to breathe freely again.

"I think today is the day," Gabe said after listening to his lungs. "I hear no air escaping into his chest. We can leave in the morning."

Rebel helped pack their bags and watched the brothers load the horses into the trailer.

"We can only fit four head so if something happens to the truck, Jade and Lynn will be riding double," Darien said.

"Nothing will happen to the truck. There is plenty of fuel and the engine is sound," Warrick pointed out.

Jade, Lynn and Gabe said goodbye to the boys and climbed in behind Conner. Tucker and Lucky found a spot in the back and laid down.

"We put extra weapons and ammo in the tack compartment just in case," Darien said as Rebel climbed behind the wheel. "Love you sis."

"Be careful. Love you too," she said turning the key. She waved as they pulled onto the road and drove away.

The brothers breathed a sigh of relief still not believing that they talked her into leaving.

"Let's get going too," Darien said turning to saddle his horse.

An hour later, everyone sat on their horses waiting for Dylan.

"Where the fuck is he?" Warrick said impatiently.

"There he is," Darien said as Dylan walked around the corner holding Cassidy's hand and carrying a bag.

"Cass wants to join us," he announced taking the reins to one of the extra horses and helping her onto the animal.

"Good to have you," Ric smiled.

Cass smiled back and said, "I promise I won't slow you down, I am an accomplished rider."

"Let's move fast then," Darien said leading them into a fast run.

That evening Rebel turned the truck onto the lane of their property deep in the mountains of Idaho.

"I can't wait to see grandma!" Jade said excitedly.

"Look at the small city she has created here," Rebel exclaimed.

"There she is!" Jade yelled as they pulled up to the cabin. She launched out of the truck and wrapped her grandmother in her arms.

Tears rolled down Kira's cheeks as she hugged her granddaughter. "Jade!" she said. "I'm so glad your home."

"Mom, this is Conner," Rebel said introducing him.

Conner shook her hand and said, "I just couldn't wait to meet you Kira. They all talked about you the entire way."

Kira smiled, "All lies I hope."

Conner smiled.

"This is Lynn and Gabe," Rebel said.

"So nice to meet you."

"Uncle Neil!" Rebel yelled as he walked up to the porch and hugged her tightly.

"My god girl, who the hell have you been fighting?" he asked holding her away from him to look her over.

Rebel shook her head and said, "Our worst nightmare. Just like we thought. All of the scum crawled out of their holes."

"Your room is ready," Kira said. "Let's get you settled in."

"Mom, there must be a sixty people here. Look at what you've done," Rebel said admiring the organized little camp.

Kira smiled and led the way into the house.

"Conner is grounded to the house for a month," Gabe said. "I will need help holding him down."

Uncle Neil laughed and said, "Don't worry, we've had practice doing that." He glanced at Kira who smirked at him.

"Why, what happened?" Rebel asked following him into the house.

"Your mother was injured in a stampede, broke a couple ribs. And she is more stubborn that you are," he said pointing at Rebel fondly.

Conner started to laugh but stopped himself when his ribs shot him with a blast of pain.

"Jade, you and Lynn can sleep up in the loft," Kira said. "Evie and Neil have the third room."

"I'll take care of the horses and unload the truck," Neil said ducking his head as Rebel turned to look at him curiously.

Tucker whined and leapt up on the bed with Conner making them laugh as he lay down beside him and put his head on his chest.

"I guess I'm on the couch," Rebel shrugged with a smile then looked around and said, "Dad hasn't showed up yet?"

"No. But I didn't think you were expecting him for awhile," Kira said.

"Ya, he was pretty set up at his house but I was hoping he would be here by now," she said worriedly.

"He'll come Rebel. Don't worry," Kira soothed.

Chapter 16

The entire next week was spent laying around healing and catching up with tales about their journey.

Gabe completely took over the small clinic and Conner grew stronger each day. The bruises on Rebel's face faded to a yellow color and the stitches were removed from her cuts. Her left hand was much better but Gabe had put a cast on her right one.

The days passed slowly and Rebel grew more restless with each passing hour. The ground shook almost daily from small earthquakes and the ash in the sky thickened so that the afternoon looked like dusk.

The morning of the eighth day home, Rebel walked onto the porch and announced to her mother and Conner, "I'm going to find them."

Conner stood to object and Kira held her breath worriedly.

"I talked to uncle Neil and we are leaving this morning," she said firmly.

"Fuck!" Conner spat. "Sorry Kira."

"Rebel, please don't. I just got you home," Kira pleaded.

"Mom, they have women with them. I have a bad feeling that they are in danger. I'll only be gone two days," Rebel said.

"That's only if you can find fuel!" Conner said trying to hide his anger.

"Conner, I'm not arguing with you. We are going!" she said stomping toward the clinic.

"Gabe, I need you to prepare me a first aid kit. I'm going to find the brothers."

Gabe looked at her friend for a moment then nodded in agreement.

Rebel returned with the supply kit and sat it next to her bag beside the truck. Her uncle led the horses to the trailer without looking at Kira.

Kira and Conner watched from the porch as they

climbed into the truck and headed down the lane.

Conner slumped down in his chair and said, "Kira, no offense, but that is the most stubborn woman I have ever met."

Kira nodded in agreement wiping the tears from her eyes.

After seven days at a fast pace through Wyoming, the brothers reined in to camp for the night on the outskirts of Jackson Hole.

"Almost home," Warrick said. "I'm figuring two hundred miles or so from here."

"Thank god!" Lauren said climbing off her horse. "My ass hurts."

"We'll follow the highway through Teton pass and into Idaho tomorrow," Dylan said.

"I always wanted to visit Jackson Hole, I just never made it out here," Ric said.

"Its a fun little town but its become very commercialized over the last twenty years," Cass said. "But you can find some kick back fun out at the Bar J Ranch."

Lauren laughed in agreement. "Those guys are fun."

The boys built a fire and stood the tents while the ladies started dinner. They had just finished eating and were chatting happily when a major earthquake rippled through the ground underneath them. The horses jerked free and stampeded away again and trees quivered above them.

Lauren screamed as a tree cracked next to them and fell in slow motion into the middle of their camp. Everyone was able to jump clear except Ric who was kneeling next to the fire. The branches sparked and erupted in flames so quickly that everyone was singed by the heat blast.

Darien dove across the shuttering ground into the flames and grabbed Ric firmly in his grasp then heaved himself backward toward Warrick and Dylan who dragged the two of them out of the fire.

He bent over the badly injured woman screaming her name, as the earth grew quiet. He looked fearfully at his brothers shaking his head in disbelief. "Why?" he asked choking on the word.

Lauren and Cass rushed to his side trying to assess her wounds.

"Warrick, find the supplies that Gabe left us," Lauren said worriedly.

"We need to move her Darien, the entire forest is going to burn," Dylan yelled.

Everyone jumped into motion as the burning tree ignited others around it. Warrick grabbed his rifle and the medical kit. Darien gathered Ric into his arms and Dylan followed with as many weapons as he could carry.

"There is a clearing just over there by the creek," Shane said pointing.

Darien lay Ric down on the bank of the creek in the clearing and started looking for her injuries. Danny and the two younger brothers ran back to camp to gather more supplies before they burned. Warrick and Dylan went searching for the horses.

Ric opened her eyes and tried to speak.

"Shh. Don't try to talk Ric," Lauren said. She looked up at Darien's pale face and said quietly, "Send someone to town to find a doctor."

Darien didn't move, just looked back at her as he realized that she was telling him it was bad. He inhaled deeply, trying to focus and stood up looking for his brothers.

Warrick and Darien rode into the clearing with the horses and handed them to the younger boys. "Tie them good. The fire is coming."

Darien strode up to them. "Ride into town and bring her a doctor," he said in a deadly quiet voice. "Use any means available."

Warrick looked at Dylan completely understanding the tone. He looked back at Darien and nodded then they turned their horses and raced into town.

Lauren and Cass made a bed for Ric inside one of the tents and waited for Darien to return so he could carry her inside. He gathered her into his arms and placed her gently on the sleeping bag then sat down beside her.

"Darien, I think she has broken her shoulder and collar bone," Lauren said softly. "But worst than that, she has a huge bruise down the length of her back and I'm worried that she is bleeding internally."

He stroked Ric's face gently without responding.

Shane, Cayden and Danny stood beside the water watching the fire grow into a blaze that ripped through the forest unrestrained. The flames lit up the night.

"That will never stop out here," Cayden said. "It will burn uncontrolled across three states unless it rains.

"We will be lucky to get out of here for days," Shane agreed.

Warrick and Dylan rode through the darkness at a full gallop and into the small empty town right to the hospital doors. They dismounted and walked into the dimly lit building.

"How can I help you?" a woman said from behind the counter.

"We have a badly injured woman in our camp. She needs a doctor," Dylan said.

The woman stood up and walked toward him saying, "There is only one doctor on staff and injured people are arriving every minute with injuries from the earthquake. You will have to bring her here."

"We can't move her," Dylan argued. "And there is a raging fire heading this way."

"Sheriff!" the woman bellowed. "They say there is a fire burning."

The sheriff walked over and said, "Where is the fire?"

Both brothers pointed east.

"We need a doctor to come with us," Warrick said again, urgently.

"What's going on?" a very fit, trim man in his early fifties asked walking toward them.

"A tree fell on our friend and she is badly injured," Dylan said dejectedly. "Are you a doctor?"

"Retired army doctor," he said. "I just help out here when I can.

"Would you be willing to ride with us in the dark on horseback, surrounded by a raging fire, and risk your life to save a beautiful young woman?" Dylan asked sarcastically.

The man looked around the room for a moment then smiled, "Absolutely. Show me the way."

Dylan looked at the man incredulously.

"A true hero," Warrick said slapping him on the back.

"Put him on Ace and get him out there then send the boys back for me," Dylan said.

Warrick and the doctor raced through the dark, smoke filled forest to the clearing.

"In there!" Cayden said taking the horses as they dismounted.

The doctor entered the tent and opened his bag saying, "Everyone step outside please."

"Come on Darien, it's only for a moment," Lauren encouraged.

Darien stood and exited the tent with the ladies.

Warrick had built a fire on the creek bank and offered him coffee. "She'll be fine man," he said standing next to him.

"Tell me about the doctor," he said anxiously.

"His name is Theron, retired army doctor. He volunteered without hesitation. He's from the Midwest. Said he was going to meet some friends here for a vacation but then the power went out and they never showed up. He's just been hanging out ever since," Warrick said.

Darien listened distractedly then asked, "Where is Shane?"

"He rode back to town to get Dylan."

Darien turned eagerly to the doctor as he climbed out of the tent. "Doc, please tell me she will be ok," he pleaded.

"She has several broken bones and is bleeding internally. I can't treat her here. I need to get her to the hospital," Theron said in a typical doctor voice.

Darien sagged with grief so Warrick took lead and

asked, "How do we move her doc?"

"We will have to make a stretcher and pull it behind one of the horses. I can stabilize her for the ride and I have pain meds to make the journey as comfortable as possible," he said. "But we need to hurry, I want to leave at first light."

"We will have the stretcher ready," Warrick said nodding to Cayden.

The sun had barely peaked over the blazing mountain when Darien lifted Ric onto the stretcher and followed by her side as Warrick led the animal toward town.

Dylan followed leaving the young men in charge of camp.

Rebel knew that something was wrong when they drove to the top of the summit on Teton pass. Flames lit the evening sky, illuminating the entire valley.

"My god!" Neil exclaimed. "I bet last nights earthquake caused this."

She nodded in agreement and drove anxiously down the side of the mountain. They pulled into the outskirts of Jackson Hole and parked the truck in a parking lot safe from the fire.

"Feed the horses in the trailer tonight, just in case," she told her uncle. "Let's check the hospital first."

Rebel and Neil strode through the doors of the hospital and Rebel launched into Warrick arms when he stood from his seat, completely surprised.

"Uncle Neil," he said shaking his hand. "You let her talk you into this?"

"She would have gone without me so I figured I should tag along just in case," he laughed.

"Who is hurt?" Rebel demanded. "Why are you here?"

Warrick ducked his head and said regretfully, "It's Ric. A tree fell on her. She's hurt pretty bad. The doc said he stopped the bleeding but I can tell he is worried."

"Can I see her?" Rebel asked worriedly.

"Darien is in there with her, I'll show you her room," he said striding down the hall.

Rebel opened the door and slid quietly into the room. Darien stood in surprise and wrapped his arms around her.

"Darien, I'm so sorry. I had a feeling that something was wrong and decided to come find you."

"Rebel, I should be angry but I am so relieved. I didn't know how we were going to get her home," he said sitting back down.

"How is she?" Rebel asked walking to her bed.

"She has broken bones and was bleeding inside. But the Doc did surgery and says she will be fine now. She just needs to regain her strength."

Ric opened her eyes. "Rebel, you drove all the way back here just for me?" she teased her friend with a smile. "You look much better than the last time I saw you."

"Well, I hate to break it to you but you look a lot worse," Rebel teased back.

Ric laughed and squeezed her hand. "Theron says I'm gonna live, though I don't feel like it."

"As soon as you're up to it, we will drive you back in the truck, k?" she said. "I'll let you rest now."

Rebel turned to leave just as the doctor walked in.

"Rebel, this is Theron, Ric's doctor," Darien introduced him.

"Nice to meet you doc," she said shaking his hand. "How long does she need to stay in the hospital?"

Theron laughed and said, "Straight to the point, huh? Well, the incision should heal in a week or so but her shoulder is shattered. That will take a bit longer."

"Doc, how long till I can walk around," Ric asked trying to find out when it would be safe to ride in the truck.

"I'd say you could probably get out of bed in a couple days," he answered. "But you won't want to move much."

Rebel winked at her and left the room.

Warrick and Neil stood as she entered the Lobby.

"We leave in two days. Warrick, I'll need more fuel for the truck. Let's go check on everyone else."

Warrick told Darien their plan and followed Rebel to the vehicle. They drove through the blackened trees to the small clearing that housed their campsite.

"Rebel's here with uncle Neil!" Cayden yelled as they pulled in.

Rebel hugged her brother and said, "Will you take care of the horses?"

He nodded and headed to the trailer. Dylan and Shane hugged her and shook Neil's hand.

"Good to see you uncle," Shane said.

Lauren stepped out of the tent and rushed to her. "Rebel, what are you doing here?"

"I thought you'd be sick of riding by now so I decided to come get you," she laughed.

"Thank god," Cass said walking up to them.

"Cass! I didn't know you were here. I'm so glad to see you," Rebel said.

"How's Ric?" she asked with concern.

"She is doing great. We will take her home in two days," Rebel said. She turned to her brothers, "Tomorrow I want you to load the tack compartment with any extra supplies. I will be taking Ric, Cass, and Lauren back with me. Uncle Neil is staying to help you with the horses."

The boys nodded as they followed her to the fire.

"I really missed you guys. I can't wait until everyone is home safe," she said.

Dylan handed her a cup of coffee and said, "How is mom? Everything good back home?"

"Yes, she did great. There are a lot of people there, some I don't recognize but she had the camp running smooth," Rebel smiled. "She misses all of you."

They talked for several hours then Rebel stood up and said, "I'm going to sleep in the truck. See you in the morning."

Two days later, Rebel drove the truck into town.

Neil and Warrick went to work siphoning fuel out of the stalled cars and Rebel walked to the hospital to check on Ric.

"Are you ready?" she asked her.

"Yes, but Theron isn't happy about me leaving. We explained to him that I would be under the supervision of another doctor by nightfall, but he still wasn't satisfied," Ric said.

"No, I'm not satisfied," Theron said, walking into the room. "I'm disappointed that my patient is putting me out to pasture and replacing me with a younger, prettier version."

Rebel smiled, "Well doc, I see only one way for you to reclaim your status."

He looked at her inquisitively, "And just how is that?"

"You could ride with us and stay with her until she has healed," Rebel said simply.

The doctor was overcome with curiosity, "Just what exactly are you proposing?"

"I am inviting you to come with us, unless of course, you are committed to this town," she said slyly.

He huffed and fidgeted with his scope.

Darien walked through the door and straight to Ric. He kissed her and said, "I'm going to miss you. Are you ready to go?"

She nodded then looked back at Theron. "Well? What did you decide?"

Darien looked at him curiously, "Decide what?"

"I invited him to ride home with us," Rebel said looking at him expectantly. "What do you think, doc?"

"Well, I ..." he looked at them for a moment. "I guess I could handle some new scenery."

Ric smiled and said, "Go pack your stuff, we'll leave as soon as you get back."

An hour later, the five of them loaded into the truck. Rebel hugged her uncle and brothers and climbed behind the wheel.

"We will be home by tonight," she said as she pulling the truck onto the road.

Conner sat on the porch beside Kira and Evie watching the lane as he had done for the last three days. Tucker lay at his feet snoozing. "She should have been here by now," he said standing to pace the small space.

"Conner, you just said that and hour ago," Kira reminded him.

"Sorry," he mumbled sitting back down.

"Evie, don't we have some whiskey stashed in the house somewhere?" Kira asked her friend.

"Yes!" she grinned. "I'll go get it."

She returned with the bottle and poured the liquid into their empty coffee cups.

"That should make you feel better," Kira said to Conner who hurriedly threw back the drink.

He reached out for another shot and sat back to sip on it.

Suddenly, Tucker jumped to his feet and ran down the lane barking.

Conner stood excitedly, "It's them!"

The truck pulled around the bend and Conner launched off of the porch then cursed the pain he'd just inflicted upon himself.

Rebel jumped out of the truck and raced into his open arms. After a moment, she broke away and introduced Cass and Lauren to Kira and Evie. "This is Ric," she said as she helped her friend from the truck.

Theron opened the door and stepped out just as Gabe ran up.

"Everybody, this is Theron, Ric's doctor," she said.

He tipped his head in greeting and glanced over the faces of his new friends. His eyes stopped on Kira and stayed on her.

"This is my mom, Kira," Rebel said noticing that she was staring back at him just as intently. She smiled. "Let's get Ric to Darien's room, I'm sure she is exhausted from the ride."

Theron tipped his head again to Kira and helped Rebel take Ric to the bunkhouse.

They got her settled on the bed and Rebel left her in

Gabe's capable hands so she could join Conner on the porch.

"I was right Conner. They wouldn't have been home for weeks if I hadn't gone after them," Rebel said.

Conner smiled and kissed her then turned to the doc. "So Theron, how did you let this little vixen con you into coming all the way out here?"

Rebel mocked a shocked face at him.

Theron laughed and accepted the whiskey from Kira. "Thank you," he said, his eyes drifting over her face.

She smiled and sat down to hear his story.

"I didn't really have any ties back in Jackson. I was just stuck there after the power went out so when she invited me, I accepted the offer. I am always up for a new adventure." He smiled and glanced at Kira again.

Kira inhaled deeply and reached for the bottle to pour herself another drink.

Rebel laughed and said, "See, I didn't kidnap him or anything."

Gabe walked onto the porch and sat down on the steps by Rebel. "Ric is sleeping," she said then turned to Theron. "She is lucky you were there. As her friend, I want to thank you. So what is your specialty?"

"Oh, I'm just an old retired army doctor. Nothing special here," he grinned.

Kira poured another drink.

"Well, I'm glad you're here. I was only in my third year of medical school and these guys overestimate my skills," she said.

"Whatever!" Rebel exclaimed. "You saved both mine and Conner's lives. You can't overestimate that."

Theron laughed, "That's true. Good for you."

"Are you going to stay? Will you teach me more?" she asked eagerly.

He glanced around and said, "I don't have anything drawing me away, so I guess I can stay awhile."

Rebel laughed this time when Kira swallowed her drink.

"Rebel, I don't mean to pry, but I noticed that you and Conner are pretty banged up," he said expectantly.

"They got into a fight," Gabe explained laughing. "And believe me, it wasn't the first one."

Theron looked at Rebel curiously, "With each other?"

"No," Gabe laughed then turned serious. "It was actually ten against five from the way I hear it. Rebel took two of them out herself."

This made him draw back in surprise. "You fought two men?"

Rebel shrugged and said, "Ya, but Tucker helped me out."

Conner stiffened remembering the terror he'd felt as he watched her fight the huge man. "She has been banned from fighting now though," he said trying to relieve his agitation. "The brothers have grounded her."

Everyone laughed knowing that they had no control over her what so ever.

Theron looked around confused.

Gabe leaned in and said, "She is a tough little bitch and if someone threatened us right now, she would kick their ass."

Everyone roared with laughter again. Everyone accept Conner who leaned back in his chair and swallowed more whiskey.

"And that ain't nothing compared to what her brothers would do," Gabe continued. "I've seen shit that you wouldn't believe."

"All right Gabe, don't scare the man," Rebel laughed.

"The bottom line is that you are safer here than anywhere else thanks to these guys," she said leaning back on the railing.

"Only if the mountain don't blow," Rebel said looking into the distance.

"The mountain?" Theron said confused again.

The rest of the evening was spent talking about the end of the world as they knew it.

The brothers, along with Danny and Nick, rode at a lope across the Teton pass and into Idaho. Their supplies were packed on five horses and the other twenty head just followed along, their hooves shaking the ground as they thundered up the road.

Late that afternoon, Warrick heard gunfire and waved at everyone to slow up. "Did you hear where that came from?" he asked.

"The ricochet echoed through the trees so I couldn't tell, but it sounded close," Darien said.

They walked around a corner and right into a shockingly bloody scene. Two young boys were kneeling down crying beside a man who was bleeding fiercely from a bullet wound to the chest.

All seven of them drew their weapons.

"What happened here?" Darien asked.

The boys jerked up fearfully with tears rolling down their faces.

Shane dismounted and walked closer. "It's ok, we won't hurt you. Who shot this man?"

One of the boys who looked about eleven years old pointed and said, "Three guys. They took our sister and our horses."

Warrick growled and took off in the direction he pointed, followed by everyone but Shane and Cayden who stayed to protect the boys.

Cayden dismounted and ran over to the bleeding man with the medical bag.

Shane pulled out a washcloth and pushed it hard into the bleeding wound. He looked at Cayden telling him with his eyes that his wound was bad.

Cayden turned to the small boys and opened his arms saying, "Come here." They ran to him and sobbed into his shoulder.

Warrick could see the riders ahead of him through the trees. He pulled out his rifle and using the open sights, still at a full gallop, shot one of them in the back of the head.

He heard a girl screamed as the man tumbled off of his horse.

The other two looked behind them in surprise and kicked their horses faster.

"The girl is in front of the man on the right," he yelled at Darien who was riding up beside him.

Darien pulled up his rifle and fired, dropping the man on the left off of his horse.

The third man threw the girl from his racing horse trying to distract them and kicked the animal again.

Nick and Danny stopped beside the girl and the three brothers raced forward with determination.

Danny jumped off of his horse. "Are you ok?"

The stunned, hysterical girl nodded sobbing uncontrollably.

He smiled soothingly and said, "We found your brothers. Let us take you back to them, ok?"

She nodded again, still unable to stop sobbing.

He helped her stand and gently boosted her onto his horse and led the animal through the trees toward the road then helped her dismount next to the wounded man.

The girl raced to her dad's side still crying.

The man grabbed her hand and tried to smile.

"Dad!" the girl wailed.

Shane and Neil feverishly tried to stop the blood from flowing out of his wound.

"This is a god damned shame!" Nick said.

The three kids were still kneeling over the man crying when the brothers rode up to them.

"What the hell are we supposed to do now?" Warrick asked.

"We can build another stretcher like the one we used for Ric." Darien said. He walked over to the kids and said, "Where do you live?"

The girl looked up at him and said softly, "A couple miles that way."

They rigged the stretcher and slowly moved the injured man home.

"There it is," the girl said excitedly as their mother

ran out the door.

"Oh my god! What happened?" she asked running to the man.

"Some guys tried to take me," the young girl said. "These men saved me."

The woman looked at them and breathed, "Thank you so much. How can I ever repay you?"

"No need ma'am," Darien said. "We are just glad we could help."

"Please, come in and rest. I have dinner ready. Come eat."

Everyone dismounted and helped her move the injured man into the house then gathered around the fire that burned just out the back door.

Darien helped the woman stabilize the injured man then stepped out to join them.

Warrick stuffed the coffee pot onto the fire and looked at his brother. "We might as well unsaddle the horses and camp here tonight."

They all nodded in agreement.

Four days later, they rode up the lane to their cabin, home at last.

Rebel ran down the porch steps followed closely by Kira. Soon the entire camp was beside them.

The camp erupted in happy conversation, everyone relieved to finally be home and together again. A large meal was planned to celebrate the end of their journey and everyone jumped into the preparations excitedly.

Several hours later, the Dutch ovens were pulled out of the fire and the meat was ready on the grill. The large group sat down to eat and a happy atmosphere hovered over the camp.

The next morning everyone gathered on Kira's front porch with their coffee, talking and laughing, thankful to be together again.

"I thought dad would be here by now," Dylan said.

"Me too," Rebel agreed.

Warrick set his cup down and said, "I think we should go get him."

Darien nodded.

"We could take the truck. We may not find enough fuel to get it back here but it would get us there quick," Dylan said.

"I'll go with you," Rebel said.

Conner stiffened. He felt much better after a couple weeks in bed but wasn't sure if he was up to another cross-country ride.

"I'm sure we can handle it Rebel," Warrick said.

"Ya, well what if you can't. The crazy rednecks out here are sure to be mounted and well armed," she said. "And I'm worried that there aren't enough supplies in the small towns. They might be aggressive."

Conner shifted in his seat becoming more agitated.

Rebel glanced sideways at him and said, "What?"

"I don't want you to go," he said simply. "It could be dangerous and I don't think you need to put yourself in harms way,"

"Well it's not up to you," she scowled.

He glared at her and said, "Rebel, there is no reason for you to go."

"I'll go simply because I want to. I don't need a reason."

He stood up and angrily walked into the cabin.

"Rebel, he is just worried about you. You are a half crazy redneck yourself," Dylan said.

"Maybe so, but I am one that don't need to be told what to do!"

"I think we should leave in the morning," Warrick said. "Something could be wrong down there."

"I'll be ready," Rebel said and walked into the cabin to ready her gear. She stepped past Conner into her room. "We are leaving in the morning if you want to go."

Conner followed her to the bedroom and leaned against the door jam. "Rebel, please understand that I just worry about you."

She glanced at him but continued with her task.

He silently watched her ready her bag and weapons then shook his head and said, "Why do you do this? Why do you insist on testing fate?"

"What would you have me do Conner, hide from life in a closet? You know I won't live like that."

"I would think for Jade's sake that you would at least attempt to stay out of danger as much as possible."

"Don't you dare bring her into this!" she said angrily stepping toward him. She threw her bag at his feet by the door and looked deep into his eyes. "I guess we have found the one thing that will test our relationship Conner. You have a decision to make here. Either accept me for who I am or not at all." She turned and stomped outside.

He leaned his head back and sighed.

"She's always been like this," Kira said softly, walking up to him. "I share your concern but I've found that it doesn't do any good to argue with her."

He looked at her sadly and said, "I don't know how you handle it. She is so stubborn. I don't know what I would do if anything happened to her."

Kira smiled. "Conner, all you can do is stand by her side and do your best to protect her. That's all the brothers have been able to do all these years. But don't try to hold her back cause that's when she pulls away."

He nodded and turned to pack his own bag.

The next morning, Rebel tossed her bag into the tack compartment of the trailer then loaded Jake. She glanced at the cabin wondering if Conner had decided to go.

Darien loaded his gilding and waited for Dylan to load Ace.

"It will be a tight ride with five horses," Warrick said leading his gilding along with Conner's.

"They'll be fine," Darien said. "It's only a few hours."

Rebel climbed into the back seat and smiled when Tucker jumped in and found a spot in the back.

Conner climbed in behind him and looked out the

window without saying anything.

"Let's go," Darien said. "We should be at dad's house by dinner."

Rebel waved at Jade and Kira as the truck started down the lane.

Later that day they neared a small town just outside of the Craters of the Moon National Park.

"Look at that," Dylan said pointing to an old warehouse on the outskirts of the town. "It looks like dad's team."

"It is them. There's his wagon," Warrick said. "And that's his sheep camp."

"It looks like they are camping here. I see a fire pit out front," Dylan said. "Something must have happened. It looks like they have been here for a few days."

"I don't like being this close to the INEL. I think they store spent nuclear rods there," Rebel said. "We need to find him and get out of here."

Darien pulled the truck behind the building and they all climbed out.

"I'll go check it out," Warrick said. "You guys unload the horses in case we need to go look for him."

Rebel led Jake out of the trailer and was preparing to saddle him when she suddenly heard someone yelling just down the road. She swung onto the horse bareback and started toward the sound.

"Rebel, just wait for us," Conner said fearfully.

Rebel ignored him and rode down the block keeping on the sidewalk close to the buildings. She came to the end of the road and looked around the corner.

Her dad and forty or so people were cornered in a large parking lot in front of a store trying to defend a stack of supplies from a group of thirty well armed men.

Rebel pulled out her handgun and cursed herself for not grabbing her rifle. She eased Jake out into the open and rode toward the back of the group of men. She knew that Conner and her brothers would be right behind her and decided to try to distract the men so they could surround them. The timing would have to be right or she would be vulnerable out in the open.

She rode within pistol range and asked, "What seems to be the problem here?"

The men shot surprised looks back at her. She glanced at her dad who smiled, knowing that she wasn't here alone.

"None of your business!" one of the men yelled at her. He wore a ragged cowboy hat and t-shirt and had piercings all over his face."

"None of my business? You are trying to steal supplies from women and children and you don't think I would consider that my business?" she asked calmly.

"Ride on lady before you get hurt," the man said with a sneer.

Rebel smiled at him sarcastically. "I have a better idea. You guys ride on, then I won't have to kill you."

The men all laughed.

"You think you can kill all of us?" the man asked with a grin.

She knew that she had their complete attention now. Hopefully the brothers would see what she was doing and move into position to cover her.

"You know, I have traveled all across this country over the last few months and I have run into nothing but bad people," Rebel said shaking her head in disgust. "I'm truly disappointed in the human race. Instead of people helping each other, they attack each other, steal from each other and kill each other."

The guy grinned spitefully and waved his arm at his friends. "I'm helping them, trying to feed them. Now move out before I change my mind."

"You're not getting it. I'm not going anywhere. But you are. I have you outgunned here. Take my word for it and don't make me prove it," Rebel said. She knew that Conner and her brothers would be in position by now.

The man turned to his friends and laughed. He leveled his weapon on her and said, "Lady, are you crazy? I think your bluffing. Go ahead, prove it to me."

Rebel could see that her dad was trying to send the women and several kids around the side of the building to safety. She noticed seven of her cousins in the group and knew that they were all good shots. They all raised their weapons while the men were focused on her and prepared to back her up. She needed to get them a few more minutes.

Conner and the brothers watched nervously as Rebel held the men's attention while they got into position to cover their friends and family.

Rebel slid off of Jake and pushed him out of the way. He made a big target and she didn't want him to be injured. She leveled her weapon on the men as she strode toward them.

All of them turned on her now with their guns drawn. She walked up so close to the man in the hat that his gun was almost touching her chest before she stopped and glared into his eyes.

He stepped back in surprise and glanced uneasily at his friends. "You are crazy. Now get back on the horse and get out of here or I'm going to shoot you."

"What we've got here is a failure to communicate," she said in a deadly voice keeping his gaze locked with hers. "You've got to ask yourself one question. Do you feel lucky?"

The man paled. He was obviously confused because her words and tone of voice didn't match. She was being sarcastic as she quoted Clint Eastwood and Strother Martin but her tone and body language told him that she was deadly serious.

Warrick grinned and whispered, "I'm not the only one who quotes movies. She has a pretty good list herself. That's the movie 'Cool Hand Luke' and of course 'Dirty Harry'."

"What is your story lady," the man said to Rebel trying to ease his own stress.

Rebel didn't move or change the glare on her face. "I've come here to chew bubble gum and kick ass, and I'm all out of bubble gum."

The man looked nervously at his friend again, still

unable to figure her out.

Dylan almost laughed out loud. "That's from the movie 'They Live."

Conner glared at the brothers not at all comfortable with their lack of concern in this situation. "I don't think she should be quoting movies while there is a 9mm dialed in on her chest."

One of the men behind the pierced man laughed. "She's just fucking with you Larry. Shoot her."

Rebel raised her eyebrow still holding the man's gaze and quoted Geena Davis, "Be afraid, be very afraid. Out here, due process is a bullet." She had to focus so that she wouldn't smile as the man recognized the John Wayne quote.

The man sucked in his breath and adjusted his hat nervously.

Warrick and Dylan both covered their mouths so they wouldn't laugh out loud.

"That's 'The Fly' and 'The Green Berets'. Come on Conner, you have to admit it's funny," Warrick said. "She is trying to figure out if they are murdering bastards or just desperate."

"I don't give a shit either way. They are pointing a weapon at her and I'm gonna kill them just for that," Conner said with a scowl.

Rebel knew that she was pushing her luck but couldn't resist. She smiled at the pierced man and said, "I am just fucking with you. Now just ride away and we will forget this whole thing."

"We ain't riding nowhere you crazy bitch!" the other man yelled and stepped toward her, pulling the hammer back on his revolver.

"I see dead people," Rebel said softly and winked at the man in front of her. He turned white as a sheet then jumped as over a dozen rifles exploded into the group of men. Over half of them fell and the remaining few just stood there stunned.

She smiled at the now trembling man. His eyes were

wide with surprise and fear as he looked back at her.

"Have you ever danced with the devil in the pale moon light?" she asked still grinning.

He choked and dropped his weapon. All of the other men followed his lead, dropping theirs and slowly raising their hands into the air.

"Is that enough proof for ya?" she asked sarcastically. "Now walk away."

They all turned and stormed off.

"Haley Joel Osment in 'The sixth sense'," Warrick laughed raising his hand to give Dylan a high five.

"Jack Nicholson, 'Batman'," Dylan said with a grin slapping his brothers hand.

Conner just glared at them then looked at Darien who was silent but wore a grin.

Rebel ran to her dad and hugged him tight. "Dad, I was worried about you."

"Rebel, I wish you wouldn't stare down pistols like that. I was worried about you," he said hugging her tight.

Conner and the brothers walked up.

"Dad, this is Conner," Rebel introduced them. "Conner, my dad, Marshall."

"Nice to meet you," Marshall said as they shook hands then turned to the brothers. "Boys!"

They all shook hands with him then greeted their cousins.

Conner pulled Rebel aside and said, "Rebel, that was dangerous and stupid. You toyed with them while staring down the barrel of a gun. Thirty guns! Don't do that again!"

"I see you still haven't made your decision," she glared at him. "It's going to be a long ride home." She turned away from him and walked back to her dad.

"So what happened here?" she asked ignoring Conner.

"We stopped to rest because one of the kids wasn't feeling well. We decided to get a few supplies from the store but these guys showed up and tried to take them. It wasn't like they couldn't go in and get their own," Marshall said with a scowl.

Rebel nodded then turned toward Darien and said, "We could put the women and kids in the truck and get them to the cabin. Can we find fuel?"

Darien nodded. "I think so. We could clean out the trailer and put blankets down so they are comfortable. They would be home in a matter of hours."

"That would be good," Marshall said. "I think these guys may come back with friends."

Rebel looked at him and said, "There are more of them?"

"Yes, I heard them talking amongst themselves. They are from somewhere in Nevada and some are from California. People are moving up here to the mountains to get water. They were bragging that their group was a mixture of gang members, ex cons, and renegades."

"God damn it!" Rebel said. "I've had enough of the scum in the human population. Where the hell are all the good people?"

"Rebel," Marshall said soothingly, "the good people aren't traveling. They are probably holed up somewhere safe. These guys are marauders that don't have anywhere to go. No homes, no family. It's only natural that they group together."

"Come on, let's ready the truck and get some of these people safe," Darien said. "If those guys come back, we will be ready."

"We might as well fill the extra trailer space with supplies from that store. No one else is around to use the stuff," Dylan said.

Several hours later, the trailer was cleaned up and loaded and the truck was filled with gas. All of the women and children and a number of the men climbed in for the journey to the cabin.

Rebel waved goodbye, relieved that they would be safe very soon.

"Let's ride. We have about four days ahead of us," Dylan said after they hitched the teams to the wagons.

Rebel glanced at Conner as she climbed on her

horse. He hadn't said a word to her all afternoon. He glanced back at her then turned to his horse. She shrugged, deciding to give him some space to work out his inner conflict. She nudged Jake into a lope beside the four horse team of Clydesdales pulling the supply wagon and the two thick quarter horses pulling the sheep camp.

Conner took lead with Warrick and Darien, and Dylan fell behind with the cousins.

They rode hard into the night trying to put some space between them and the band of renegades that would most likely follow from the small town behind them.

Hours later, they stopped to make camp for the night. Rebel stood her tent and unrolled her sleeping bag. She didn't look at Conner who was sitting by the fire, just climbed into bed.

The next morning Rebel woke up early, instantly aware that Conner was asleep in his sleeping bag next to her. She watched him breath for a moment then stood up to get dressed.

"I don't want to fight with you," he said after a moment, startling her.

"I'm not fighting," she said as she strapped on her holster.

"I don't want to argue either."

"Good, then don't." She glanced at him then sighed. "Let's just forget it and move on," she said. "Come on, I need some coffee."

Her family was all gathered around the fire when they walked up. The cousins were harnessing the teams and Warrick was cooking breakfast.

"Mornin," Dylan said. "You were right, Conner. They are following us."

Rebel looked at Conner surprised. "You knew they were following?"

"Just had a feeling, that's all," he said.

"The team is taking the fast pace well, so maybe if we keep it up today, they will give up," Darien said.

"Ya, and if they don't, we will give them another movie marathon," Warrick said with a grin.

Everyone laughed except Conner and Marshall.

"I had a few more but I figured that I was pushing my luck," Rebel laughed.

"We wouldn't have been able to keep from laughing out loud much longer," Dylan said. "The look of confusion on the guys' face was classic."

"I thought he was going to pass out when you said the Batman quote," Warrick laughed.

"Come on, let's get going," Conner said once again very aggravated. He knew now that she would do what she wanted no matter what he said. Obviously the brothers had already gone down this road and knew better than to try to control her.

Rebel saddled Jake and climbed on while Marshall took up the leads to the team.

"Dad, the team looks great," she said.

"Todd, there in the lead, was injured in a pulling contest last year. Do you remember? He still wasn't completely healed until now. That's why I waited to join you guys on the mountain. But I think he is good to go now," he said.

Rebel nodded. "They work very well together. It's been awhile since I've seen them."

Darien rode up and said, "We are ready. Dad you take the lead with Warrick and Conner. Dylan and I will cover from behind with the cousins."

Marshall slapped the leather lightly across the wide haunches of the massive animals and they stepped out together in perfect unison. He urged them gently once more and they transitioned smoothly into a lope.

Rebel paced Jake beside the wagon and the group moved at a good pace up the road.

Several hours later, Dylan rode past them and said something to Warrick then waved them to a stop.

"The men following us just closed the distance to about half a mile. I think we should look for a place to defend ourselves before they catch us in a bad spot," Dylan said.

"Mackay is up the road a bit. If those men believe that there are police there, they could make a move on us here before we get closer," Darien said.

"We will be there before dark so they may wait until tomorrow night," Rebel said. "I'm not sure they will attack in daylight."

"I think it's possible that they will," Conner said. "We don't know how many there are which gives them the advantage. If they are confident in their numbers, they may not hesitate to make their move in daylight."

"I say we keep moving. Dylan and I will take a radio and several of the guys and fall back to keep our eyes on them. We will alert you if they make a move so you can secure the wagons," Darien said. "Everyone else, ready your weapons."

Dylan nodded and followed him back down the road.

Conner and Warrick took lead and Rebel stayed beside the wagon as they continued on again at a lope.

Rebel rode nervously waiting for the radio to warn them of incoming danger. She glanced up at Conner who was keeping an eye out ahead of them. She knew he was anxious and figured that he was more worried about her than anything else.

She was frustrated that he was trying to change her. He should know by now that she didn't like being controlled. On the other hand, she was trying to be patient with him. She knew he was just worried about her and his concern was based on the fact that he loved her. He glanced back at her and she shook her head wondering how the hell he could always sense when she was watching him.

Conner could feel Rebel's eyes on him and glanced back at her. He still couldn't figure out how he had allowed her to crawl into his heart and dig in like a tick. God, she was so reckless and stubborn, constantly putting herself in danger. How was he ever going to deal with her risky behavior?

Suddenly, the radio came to life, startling them both out of their thoughts.

"They just changed course," Darien said. "I think they are going to flank the town. Probably want to stay out of sight. We are coming up."

Warrick waved them to a walk as they waited for the others to catch up.

Darien galloped up next to them and said, "They moved off of the road. I'm guessing that they are going to ride up onto the mountain and go around the city. We counted roughly forty of them and several of them were women."

Rebel raised her eyebrow curiously. "Women?"

Dylan laughed, "Ya, rough looking women."

"If they are still wanting to mess with us, it will be after we pass the city," Darien said. "Let's make camp on the outskirts of the town. We will ride through in the morning."

"There is a good spot just up the road about a mile," Warrick said. "I remember it from working out here a few years ago."

They continued talking while they moved at a walk to the campsite.

"There is a small creek upstream that dumps hot water into this small river," Warrick informed them.

Rebel laughed and said, "You guys go for a swim while I cook dinner." She unsaddled Jake and helped Marshall remove the harnesses from his teams. Then they started a fire and broke out some supplies to make dinner.

"It's been a long time since we went camping together Rebel," Marshall said. "I'm really glad you guys came down to get me."

"I'm glad too dad. I've missed you," she said.

"So tell me about your venture across the U.S. Dylan called me after he dropped you at the airport and told me about the solar flare and warned me about the power outage. But when he said you went to Washington alone, I was worried."

"It was a long dangerous ride. Conner and I were both shot and I think everyone of us was injured at some point. But we got the kids and made it home. I guess that's what counts," she said. "The brothers just got back a few days ago. Conner is still suffering from some severely broken ribs."

Marshall glanced at Conner who was setting up the tent. "So tell me that story."

"We met in West Virginia and traveled together from there. His family is in Montana. He wants to go check on them as soon as he can."

"He seems like a good man," Marshall said.

Rebel nodded and said, "He is. If only he would stop telling me what to do. But other than that, I'm thinkin he's a keeper." She stood up to pour coffee into their cups.

Marshall laughed. "Good for you. I want to see you happy."

One by one, the men finished cleaning up and gathered around the fire to eat dinner.

Rebel waited until they all returned then went to her tent to get her bag so she could bath in the warm creek. She walked upstream looking for a secluded spot to undress.

Conner watched her leave and experienced a deja vu when he glanced over at their tent and seen her rifle leaning against it. He was almost able to stop himself from following her. Almost.

Rebel slid into the warm shallow water and quickly washed then leaned back against the smooth rocks and looked up into the darkening sky. Suddenly, she felt someone watching her and glanced around to find Conner standing on the bank.

"If I'm not mistaken, this is the second time you have spied on me bathing in the river," she said with a grin.

"Please don't punch me in the face this time," he smiled. "It's not my fault. My legs just walked me here on their own."

"Well, are you coming in? The water is perfect," she invited.

He quickly undressed and waded into the water and sat down on a rock beside her.

"Are you still mad at me?" she asked.

"I'm not mad. I'm worried. Are you still mad at

me?"

"Are you going to quit telling me what to do? Or more specifically, what not to do?" she asked.

"I won't be able to stop doing that Rebel. You are so unafraid. I feel I have to be afraid for you," he said softly.

"I'm sorry Conner. I don't mean to scare you. But god damn it, I won't just stand by and do nothing when someone needs help. Besides, I'm not used to someone worrying about me. Until now I was only accountable to myself. Jade was grown and moved out. Mom was busy with uncle Neal and Evie. The brothers were usually working out of town. So you have to understand, I'm needing an adjustment phase."

"I do understand," Conner said with a sigh. "I'm still trying to adjust to giving a shit about someone other than myself. It's been a long time for me too." He sighed in frustration. "I want to protect you but I can't when you run off and put yourself in danger."

"I don't need you to protect me. I know you want to but it's not your job."

"It is if I love you."

"No Conner, not even then. You knew how I was before you fell in love with me. You can't change the rules after you start the game," she said.

Conner shook his head trying to hide his distress. "God you are a stubborn woman."

"Ya, but if I weren't, you'd be so bored," she laughed.

He looked at her and couldn't help pulling her toward him. He quieted her objection with a passionate kiss.

Chapter 17

The next morning, everyone drank their coffee while they packed up camp and saddled the horses. The air was filled with tension. The road they were traveling on went right through the middle of the town and on the other side, a large group of dangerous men were most likely waiting for them.

Conner and the brothers all took lead so that they could keep an eye out in front of them and the cousins took position close behind and around the wagons.

Rebel rode next to her dad as they started through the small town. The buildings were empty and the streets were quiet. Someone had pushed all of the cars off the road and parked them in the parking lots in between the abandoned stores. It was eerily normal looking as they rode through.

"How long before you expect company?" Rebel asked Conner.

"As soon as there is no risk of police and I don't see any police here," he said looking around.

Marshall pulled his rifle from beneath the seat and leaned it up next to him.

Rebel dug in her bag for extra clips for her rifle and handguns and put them in her pocket.

Conner pulled back to ride beside her and Dylan fell back to ride on the other side of the wagon.

"I think we should continue at a walk so the horses will be fresh if we need to move fast," Darien said.

Everyone nodded in agreement.

"Maybe they went over the mountain to Ketchum," Rebel said hopefully.

"We could hope, but I doubt it," Dylan said. "No, we will run into them before we get to Challis."

"What the hell is that?" Warrick asked looking through his binoculars. He pointed up the road. "Behind that stalled truck."

"It's them," Conner said looking up the side of the mountain. "They are trying to ambush us."

Marshall pulled the team to a stop and glanced around for a place to secure the wagons.

"Over there dad, put the wagons against that rock faced ridge. It's hard to shoot straight down so we can defend you easily," Darien said.

"I think we should go get them," Rebel said. "We need to take them out or they will follow us all the way home."

"I agree," Warrick said. "Guerilla warfare."

Conner nodded and looked anxiously at Rebel. "You stay here and help Marshall guard the wagons."

"Conner, stop telling me what to do!" she growled.

"I'm with him on this one," Darien said.

"Me too," Dylan agreed.

Warrick crossed his arms over his chest obviously backing the others.

"Fuck you guys!" Rebel yelled at them then dismounted. She stomped off railing in a rage, "Sons a bitches! Always gangin up on me!"

Marshall smiled and moved the wagon into position.

Rebel stayed silent until everyone except three of her cousins and her dad left for the fight then angrily scanned the area with her glasses. The road was clear behind them with the mountain on one side and an open meadow on the other. The road curved just beyond the stalled truck a half-mile ahead of her.

She looked up on the ridge satisfied that no one would be able to get to them from there. There was a risk that some of the men could get around Conner and her brothers and attack the wagons from the road behind or in front of them.

"We will only get a moment's notice if someone comes around the corner," she mumbled to her dad.

"It's within rifle range so we will only need a moment," he said.

Rebel nodded trying to relax a little. "Eight against forty. That's not very good odds."

"If anyone could pull it off, it will be them. It won't

be the first time your brothers were outnumbered five to one," he laughed.

Rebel smiled. "They were always fighting weren't they?"

"Yes they were. I've heard about your fights too."

"Who's the blabber mouth? I didn't want you to know cause I knew you would worry," she said.

"They are proud of you and can't help bragging," Marshall laughed. "I'm proud of you too even though I don't like it when you fight. Your mother blames me for your roughneck ways. Once when you were very young, maybe four or five, I put you on one of the horses and just let you go. She objected. I told her that you had to learn to do it by yourself. She was pretty mad and yelled, "Are you going to teach you how to spit too?"

Rebel laughed. "What did you say?"

"I told her that you would probably learn that from your brothers," he smiled.

"I hope I didn't disappoint her. It just wasn't in my nature to be a girly girl," she said softly.

"You never disappointed her. She was always proud of your basketball skills and your riding skills. Even your fighting skills the way I hear it. I always said you don't have to wear boots to be a cowboy and you don't have to wear a dress to be a woman," he said.

"She wanted a little ballet dancer and got a prize fighter instead. But I did give her Jade. She is definitely a little princess."

Marshall nodded with a smile.

"Shit!" Rebel exclaimed grabbing her rifle. "Someone is coming."

A group of men were coming around the bend in the road. They stopped beside the truck and took cover to aim their rifles.

"Get back!" Marshall yelled. "They are going to fire at us."

Rebel ducked as a bullet flew past their heads and waved for everyone to get behind the wagon.

"If they injure one of my horses, I'll kill them

myself," Marshall said with a scowl.

"I don't want to fire this close to the team either so I'm going to circle around and flank them so I can get a shot," Rebel said then left before her dad could object.

She went behind the wagon and scaled the rock face of the mountainside then crept along the ridge until she was above the truck and the men were directly below her. She looked through her scope trying to find a shot but the men on the other side of the truck. One of them moved and was about to fire when she suddenly seen an arrow pass cleanly through his chest.

The startled group jumped when one of their companions dropped to the ground dead beside them. Then a second man fell. They scrambled around to her side of the vehicle.

Rebel took aim and was just about to pull the trigger when she heard a twig break right behind her. She spun around and was surprised to be face to face with one of the women holding a handgun.

"Don't point that gun at my friends," the woman said.

Rebel calmly looked her up and down. The girl was in her late twenties and had tattoos and piercings all over her face and arms. Her hair was very short and she wore a tank with camo pants and boots. Then she noticed that the woman had all the signs of a crack addict.

"Don't point that Glock at me," Rebel said calmly. "Where did you get it by the way? The officers out here don't pack 'em. FBI or U.S. Marshal?"

The woman smiled a cold heartless smile and said, "Good guess. He was a Marshal. Chased us from L.A. I've put it to better use than he did though."

Rebel's eyes narrowed in anger. "I see. I'll tell you what. Why don't you gather up your friends and go back to where you came from. We don't need your type around here."

"Oh ya? And what type is that?" she sneered.

"Murdering, drug dealing, psychos," Rebel

glowered. "I'd imagine that it's hard to cook your shit now that the power is out."

"Shut the fuck up!" the woman yelled raising the weapon threateningly.

Rebel spun around with a kick and knocked the weapon out of her hands then followed with a right fist to her face, knocking her cold. She picked up the girls weapon and turned around to find herself standing in front of three men and another woman.

"You people are sneaky," Rebel said raising the Glock at them, surprised at herself for not hearing them walk up.

"You just knocked out Sky," one of the men said then looked at the other woman. The woman was about the same age as Rebel and was clearly pissed off at her.

The men moved to surround Rebel so she pushed the safety off of the weapon.

One of the men started laughing and said, "That gun ain't loaded. I wouldn't give that doped up bitch a loaded gun."

"Shut the fuck up Mitch. Don't talk about her that way," the woman said then glared at Rebel and pulled out a knife. "Maybe you want to try to knock me out too."

"Sure, why not," Rebel said sarcastically. "Now back up boys and let us ladies have some fun here."

All three of the men looked at each other in surprise and stepped back.

Rebel stuffed the weapon in her waistband and faced the woman. "Maybe you should tell me your name so I can put it on your marker when I kill you," she said spitefully.

"Amber, but you won't be killing me today," the woman said then lunged at her, swiping the knife.

Rebel dodged the weapon and slammed her fist into her nose while she was off balance.

Amber flew backward and landed hard on her back. Her lungs deflated and she couldn't breathe. Blood drained out of both nostrils drenching her shirt.

Rebel shook her head in disappointment. That was

why she never liked to fight women. There was just no satisfaction. Even an unskilled man at least gave her some kind of response. Now that her adrenaline was pumping she was really in the mood to kick some ass. She dropped her fists and looked hopefully at the three men. "Anyone else want to go?"

"My name is Ryan but I won't fall so easily," one of the men said. He was in his early thirties and didn't look like he was a drug addict. His eyes were sharp and though his hair was uncut, he was somewhat clean.

"Thank god Ryan. I thought I was in for a boring day," Rebel said. She circled around him waiting for him to move. "So why are you hangin out with these guys? You don't seem to be like them."

"Like them?" he asked moving in with a swing.

She easily dodged his fist and swung back landing her fist into his chin. He stumbled backward surprised but quickly recovered.

"You know," she said, "strung out on crack. No self-respect. Typical tweaker."

Ryan smiled at her then swung again, his fist making contact with her cheek. Rebel responded with a blow to his eye that opened a one inch long cut that instantly poured blood down his face. He hesitated, once again surprised. She punished him with a fist in the nose.

Once again he found himself off balance. He scowled at her and growled, "I'm not a tweaker." He tried hard to hide the frustration of being hurt by her. "I met up with them in California. I just followed cause it was safer to travel in large numbers."

Rebel swung again and pummeled him in the chin. He wobbled, this time barely able to keep on his feet.

"Yet you don't mind watching them kill people," she said coldly.

Ryan shook his head clear and said, "I don't kill people." Then he swung at her again.

Rebel once again ducked his fist and pounded hers into his jaw. He instantly crumpled to his knees. "You are still an accessory!" she yelled and planted her fist in his temple, knocking him out.

She stood over him and shook her head in confusion. This man should have been a much better fighter. She looked at the other two men in frustration and said, "Maybe you should both fight me at the same time."

"Good idea," one of them sneered. "I'm Mitch, this is Cole."

Cole nodded in agreement and they both stepped in.

Rebel couldn't help smiling as she quickly stepped in and planted a right hook in Mitch's face then spun around with a kick to Cole's head. She battered Mitch again in the face before he could recover from the first hit.

Cole regained his balance and smashed his fist into her jaw.

She responded with a rocket to his face that sent him sprawling then turned to Mitch and hammered her elbow into his eye. He dropped to the ground.

"Come on! Get up! Both of you," she yelled now very annoyed. She looked around her as Amber stood up and lunged at her with the knife again. Rebel grabbed her arm and twisted it behinds her back, forcing her to drop the knife then shoved her out of the way.

Cole came at her with a vengeance and hit her in the shoulder as she ducked. She swung around and kicked him in the side of his head again, this time knocking him out.

Mitch hesitated for a moment as he watched his friend hit the ground. He looked at her with his eyes wide, unable to cover his surprise.

Rebel didn't wait. She quickly stepped in and drove her fist into his nose then stepped back as his eyes rolled back in his head. She spun around and bashed her fist into Amber's jaw as she ran at her once more, silencing her scream of rage.

She looked around her at the five people lying on the ground and shook her head again. Five against one and she was barely bleeding. She shrugged and gathered up their weapons then kicked them awake.

"Clasp your hands behind your head and move that

way," she said pointing her colt toward the wagon.

Slowly they made their way down the mountain and walked toward the wagon where Conner and her brothers were waiting impatiently for her to return.

"What the fuck, Rebel?" Conner said looking at the cuts and blood on her captives. "Five of them?"

"What the hell are we going to do with them?" she asked ignoring Conner's worried frown.

"We will have to take them with us to the next town and see if the police can put them in their jail," Marshall said trying to hide his grin.

Conner seen it though and scowled.

"Ten or fifteen of them got away. Ran like spooked deer," Warrick said. "But they are out there. We won't make it to Cheyenne tonight now so it's possible that we will run into them again very soon."

"I'll go gather some of their horses while you guys bind their hands," Conner said.

Rebel whistled for Jake and put away her weapons then helped her dad check the harnesses on his teams.

Conner returned with the horses and he and the cousins helped their captives climb on. They each took the reins to one of the horses then the group moved out at a lope.

They rode into the evening then reined to a walk to search for a place to camp for the night.

"Over there. That will be easy to defend," Dylan said.

Rebel dismounted and unsaddled Jake then built a fire to make dinner.

The brothers tied the captives to the back of the wagon and helped Marshall unharnessed the team.

"I need to pee!" Amber yelled. "You can't keep me tied up like this."

"I'll take her," Conner said as he walked over to untie her.

"You can take me anytime," Amber purred seductively as she looked him up and down. Then she rubbed her entire body against him he pulled her to her feet.

Rage exploded through Rebel. She stomped over and grabbed the woman away from him. "I'll take her," she said glaring at Conner.

"I need to pee too," Sky whined.

Conner reached down to untie the younger woman. "I'll help you take them Rebel, just calm down."

"This is me calm!" Rebel gritted through clenched teeth. She pulled out her knife and put it against Amber's throat. "Don't you dare fuck with me. I'm gonna break your face the next chance I get."

Amber's eyes widened in fear.

"Real calm," Conner grinned.

She jerked the woman behind a tree and said, "Hurry up! I've wasted enough time with you."

Conner turned his back on the women and glanced at Rebel. Her reaction to Amber's tactics had surprised him. He'd never seen her so pissed off and couldn't help grinning.

"You think that's funny?" Rebel said so only he could hear her. "Be careful or I'll let her keep you."

He laughed and said, "Come on Rebel. Give me some credit."

"I'm gonna give you something all right," she threatened then turned to take the women back to the wagon.

"Rebel, I have their food here," Warrick said.

She took the plates and practically threw them at the captives. "This is bullshit. I think we should just tie them to a tree and leave them."

Ryan scowled at Amber as Rebel turned away from them. "Stupid bitch. I told you not to piss her off."

Sky looked at Conner and smiled, "I wouldn't mind a round with him myself. He is scrumptious."

Rebel overheard her and stopped dead in her tracks. She stood there for a moment trying to calm her rage but couldn't. She turned around and slammed her fist into Sky's face knocking her out a second time. Then she turned to Amber and said, "The only reason your alive right now is because I don't want to give my dad the wrong impression of me. But don't think for a second that I won't shoot you. You might want to warn that little crack head too when she wakes up."

"Is there a problem Rebel?" Dylan asked walking up to them.

"No problem yet," she said glaring at Amber. "I'll take first watch."

She picked up her rifle and stepped out of camp to listen for any movement from the group of men that would probably try to rescue their friends tonight. She was agitated with herself for over reacting to what that woman had done to Conner. Jealously wasn't something she'd had to face for a long time. The more she thought about it the more aggravated she became. She couldn't get it out of her head as she walked through the trees on the side of the road.

Suddenly, she heard a horse whiney in the darkness. God, she hadn't been paying attention for several minutes. How far had she walked? She looked around her and realized that she was a long way from the campsite. She ducked behind a tree and pulled out her colt trying to see through the darkness then noticed almost twenty men standing just of the road thirty yards in front of her.

"I heard something," one of them said as he stepped toward her.

"Your full of shit Larry. I didn't hear anything."

"Shut up Jeff! Someone is out there," he said.

Rebel instantly recognized the man they called Larry. He is the one that she had antagonized with the movie quotes. Jeff was the one that threatened to shoot her just before her brothers fired their rifles.

They walked up to within twenty feet of her position and stood there listening. Rebel felt completely trapped for a moment, unable to move. She peered through the branches at them and waited, hoping they would walk away.

But luck just wasn't on her side. Larry was determined to find something and stepped closer. He was now within a few feet of her and wasn't going to give up.

"Come on Larry. We have to see if they have Amber. I'm going to kill those sons a bitches if they took her," Jeff said.

"Fine. But I know someone is out there," Larry said as they turned back to their horses.

Rebel let out her breath and watched the men ride past her toward the wagons. "Shit," she breathed. "How am I going to warn the brothers?" She followed them until they were far enough away from the brothers to give them enough time to prepare and close enough for them to come to her rescue quickly, then she aimed her colt and fired.

Total chaos erupted as the man she shot fell from his horse. She heard everyone in her camp move just as the group of men in front of her turned on her. She quickly stepped behind a tree and fired again. She needed to give Conner and her brothers time to get to her.

Suddenly someone grabbed her from behind and jerked her into some thick brush deep in the trees. She flung her head back and slammed it into the man's chin, forcing him to lose his grip on her.

"God damn it!" he howled covering the deep gash on his lip.

"Look, it's the movie freak," Jeff said.

Larry let go of his chin and glared at her. "I knew it was you. Got us outgunned this time?" he asked sarcastically then jumped as gunfire exploded through the trees.

"Yes, I do. They will be here any second," Rebel smirked.

"It won't be soon enough," Jeff said and swung his fist trying to knock her out. His face paled and his breath rushed out of him when she blocked the punch and slammed her fist into his abdomen.

She didn't stop with one hit. She pounded him over and over in the same place until several of his ribs were broken and he dropped to his knees in agony. She turned to Larry and said, "Don't mess with the bull young man, you'll get the horns."

Larry swung at her and clipped her jaw with his fist. She returned the strike and split his top lip then spun around with an elbow to his nose.

He stumbled back in surprise then came at her again.

She hit him again and said, "Just in case you didn't recognize that one, it's from the movie 'The Breakfast Club'. The actor was Paul Gleason. I have many more. Do you want to continue our little game?"

"Fuck you," he said trying to catch his breath through the blood flowing down his chin.

"You talking to me?" she said as she circled him and waited for him to move. "Are you talking to me? Come on, guess the movie."

He growled and swung his fist again.

"Wrong answer," she said as she planted her fist in his eye. "That was Robert De Niro in 'Taxi Driver'."

Larry covered his face with both hands and yelled, "Stop hitting me! You are crazy."

"Insanity runs in my family. It practically gallops," Rebel said. "If you guess that movie, I won't hit you again."

"I don't know," Larry wailed.

"It was Cary Grant, you idiot. Everyone knows that one. The movie is 'Arsenic and Old Lace'," she laughed then pummeled him again without mercy.

Jeff tried to stand up so she turned and planted her boot into his broken ribs then turned back to Larry and smiled. "Ok, I got one you will know," she said then pulled out her colt. "Say hello to my little friend."

Larry stood up straight and glanced at his friend writhing in pain on the ground. He looked back at her and said grudgingly, "Godfather."

"Part two. Who was the actor?" she asked putting her gun to his head.

He wiped the blood from his chin and said, "Al Pacino."

"Very good. It's kind of fun ain't it? Now take the shoelaces out of your shoes."

Larry bent over for a moment then handed her the laces.

"Turn around," she said and tied his hands. Then she tied Jeff who groaned at the movement. "Conner, I'm over here!" she yelled through the trees.

Her brothers crashed through the brush moments later followed closely by Conner who looked at her in exasperation.

"Don't say it Conner," she said still pissed off. "Don't you say a fucking thing." She turned and followed her brothers and the captives back to the wagons.

Dylan tied the men with the others and turned to Rebel. "I'm guessing that they caught you because you had to give away your position to warn us that they were coming."

"Yes, but it was my fault. I wasn't focused and practically walked right up to them. I have really got to get my head clear," she said.

"Dylan," one of the cousins yelled, "your dad took a hit."

Rebel panicked when she glanced over and seen her cousins circled around her dad. She raced to them and asked, "Dad, are you ok?

"He was shot in the leg and hurt his ribs when he went down," her cousin said.

Rebel knelt down beside him. "Damn it dad."

Marshall squeezed her hand and said, "I think I'll live Rebel."

Rebel and Darien cleaned and bandaged his wound then propped him up by the fire.

"We got the bleeding stopped and the bullet went through so if we can keep it from getting infected, he will recover," she said softly. "Did we get all of them this time?"

Darien nodded solemnly. "They are the only survivors," he said glancing at the people tied to the wagon.

Rebel filled her coffee cup and sat down beside Marshall.

Conner walked up to her and said, "Let me clean you up Rebel, you're still bleeding."

"Thanks Conner," she said and leaned back while he washed and bandaged her face.

"None of these people can fight," she said thoughtfully. "Take away their guns and large numbers and none of them would survive."

"Hey!" Larry yelled from behind the wagon. "Something is wrong with Sky."

Rebel stood up and walked over to the girl. She scowled and said, "Symptom of withdrawal. Was she using crack or something else?"

"None of your business," Jeff yelled.

"Good, I don't want to help the little bitch anyway," Rebel said and turned to leave.

"Wait," Larry pleaded. "Let her have her shit. Its just crack."

"I will not let her have her shit," Rebel said. "She will be fine if its just crack. She will puke and shake and maybe ache a little but it won't kill her. Let me know if she has a seizure."

"You are a cold heartless bitch!" Jeff yelled at her.

"And you are murdering, thieving, drug dealing scum. Your friends shot my dad and I hope you all rot in hell," she said angrily then glanced at Ryan who was quiet. Something told her that he wasn't really tied to this group. Her instincts were screaming that there was something up with him. She turned and walked back to the fire.

"That guy Ryan isn't one of them. Something is different about him but I can't put my finger on it," she said to Conner and the brothers. "He is quiet but hears everything and he watches every movement."

"Sounds like a professional. Maybe he has police training," Conner said.

"He volunteered to fight me but fell way too easily. Maybe you should get him alone tomorrow and talk to him. See if you can figure it out," she said. Then she thought about the Glock and what Sky had said about where she got it. "Would you be able to tell if he was a U.S. Marshal without his badge?"

"Not if he's a good liar."

"We need to let Sky loose and follow her to her bag.

She told me she got the Glock from a Marshal. Maybe she took his badge too."

Conner nodded. "Tomorrow I'll talk to him and see if it's a possibility. If it is then I'll leave Sky's rope loose when she has to use the bathroom. Hopefully she won't release the others."

"She won't. She will go straight for her drugs. The bad news is that we just killed almost sixty men. That won't look good if he is what we think."

"My bet is that he would have done the same thing if he could have," Conner said then stood up. "Come on, let's go to bed."

The next morning, Rebel left Conner sleeping and went to find coffee.

Dylan filled her cup and said, "We will be in Challis by this afternoon."

"Good, I'll be glad to get rid of those guys. I woke up feeling like all the good people are gone and we are surrounded by nothing but people like them," she grumbled.

"Don't worry about it Rebel," Warrick said. "Let's just get home and away from them."

Rebel looked around wondering why Conner wasn't up yet. She stood up and walked to the tent.

"Conner, are you ok?" she asked as she pushed the flap open. He was just pulling his shirt over his head and she noticed that the bruise still covering his broken ribs was growing larger.

"God Conner, you should have stayed home," she said.

"You should have stayed home too," he replied without looking at her.

"And you say I'm stubborn," she said and stomped back to the fire.

Conner smiled and followed her. He filled his cup and sat down beside her. "I'm going to take Ryan for a walk. You guys feed the rest of them while we are gone."

Rebel nodded and dished up their plates while he untied the man and led him into the trees.

Several minutes later, he returned and retied him to

the wagon. He nodded to Rebel and untied Sky to take her to the bathroom. Rebel untied Amber and followed them.

After they were done, Rebel tied Amber and Conner sort of tied Sky. Then they busied themselves helping the brothers harness the teams and take down the tents.

They were almost packed up when Rebel looked up and noticed Sky slinking over to the pile of saddles and tack that they had piled up from the horses they had gathered up the night before.

Conner eased closer so he could see which bag she was digging in then walked over and grabbed her arm. He retied her and picked up the bag.

Rebel looked over his shoulder as he sifted through the stuff inside. He pulled out a badge.

"You were right. Ryan is a U.S. Marshal. These guys killed his partner," he said showing them the picture on the badge. "He told me his partner's name and ID number. He infiltrated their group so he could eventually bring them in."

"I knew it. I could sense that he didn't want to hurt me when we were fighting. He was just keeping in character. Go untie him, there is no reason for him to keep up it up now that they are all dead."

"I'll go get him," Dylan agreed.

Ryan followed him back to the fire and said, "Sorry for the deception. I wasn't sure how this was all going to play out yesterday." He looked at Rebel and laughed. "I about shit when you called it so accurately on the Glock. Sorry I hit you, but damn girl, I was worried that you would hurt me. You fight very well."

Rebel smiled. "Don't be sorry about that. I could tell you were holding back. That's how I figured it all out. I'm just glad we can turn them over to someone. I'm sick of them."

"Ya, I'll take it from here but I don't know what I'm going to do with them either," he said.

"We will ride with you to the next town and look for the local police," Rebel said handing him his partner's weapon and badge. "Come on, let's move out."

Later that afternoon, they rode into the little town.

"There's the sheriff's office. I'll go inside and see if anyone is there," Darien said.

He came out a moment later followed by an officer.

"This is Ryan, U.S. Marshal," Darien said. "He will need to use your facilities here."

The officer shook hands with Ryan. "Nice to meet you. I'll help with whatever you need."

"Ryan," Rebel said, "I feel that I need to warn you that we are all in danger from a potential pole shift that I believe could happen any time now. You need to find shelter. A cave would be best because I also believe that Yellowstone will erupt. "

Ryan looked at her with a strange expression. "Pole shift?"

Rebel explained to him what a pole shift was and how to prepare for it. "You may be able to save the people in this town," she said then shook his hand and said goodbye.

Their group moved out at a lope and Rebel was relieved to finally be back on the road toward home.

Two days later, they once again rode up the lane to the cabin.

Kira walked out the door of the cabin and said, "Glad you made it Marshall, everyone was worried about you."

"Thanks for inviting me," he said sincerely.

She smiled and said, "You can put your camp there between the cabin and the barn. But first, maybe you should meet Theron. He is a doctor and can fix up your injuries."

Rebel helped him to the small clinic and introduced him to Theron and Gabe. "I'll meet you at dinner," she said.

An hour later, over a hundred people gathered together to eat. Rebel walked up to where her dad was sitting and asked, "Are you sure you should be out and about?"

"I'll be just fine Rebel. Sit here beside me."

She sat down and everyone enjoyed another dinner full of stories about their journey to the mountain cabin.

The days grew hotter as summer came to the little cabin hideaway turned small city. The garden was growing and the pasture was thick with grass for the livestock. The sky cleared up and earthquakes become scarce. Everything was calm.

Rebel woke up early one exceptionally warm morning and took her coffee to the porch to watch the sunrise. She had grown uneasy in the past weeks wondering if they were experiencing a calm before the storm. She looked into the prelit sky and froze, terror ripping at her gut as she caught a glimpse of a huge star illuminating the horizon, drowning out the other stars with its bright light. A mere moment later the sun broke over the mountain, dowsing the light of the massive object.

She sat trembling, unable to move as realization flooded her. Planet X. The Destroyer. Whichever it was, it was now closer to earth than Jupiter.

"Rebel?" Conner asked urgently as he walked out the door seeing the fear on her face and trembling hands. "Rebel, what is it? What's wrong?"

Rebel looked at him with wide eyes and said softly, "I saw it. The planet is here."

Conner was taken back by her reaction. He had rarely seen her afraid and concern pulled his brows into a scowl. "What do you mean? How do you know?"

She pointed a still quaking hand into the air and breathed, "I saw it just before the sun came up. A massive star, bigger than Jupiter."

Warrick walked up the stairs and instantly knew something was wrong. "What!"

"She said that she saw the planet," Conner said looking into the morning sky.

Warrick followed his gaze. "Are you sure?"

Rebel nodded still unable to control the fear racing through her. They had been right. All those so-called conspiracy theorists on the Internet had been right.

Darien and Dylan strolled toward the cabin and

stopped short at the sight of their sister.

"Rebel?" Dylan said worriedly then looked at Warrick.

"She said she saw the planet," Conner repeated.

The two brothers looked at each other then slowly climbed the stairs.

"It's there," Rebel pointed. "In the direction of Orion. I caught a glimpse of it just before the sun came up."

Tension filled the air as reality settled upon them. It was said that the giant mass would cross the solar system going around the sun and between Jupiter and Mars bringing it very close to earth. The gravitational pull would no doubt cause the pole shift that they had been talking about for years.

Darien sat down heavily. "We knew this was going to happen. We shouldn't be so surprised."

Dylan and Warrick sat down next to him and nodded.

Conner paced back and forth nervously. "I'm sorry but I didn't think this would really happen. Not that I didn't believe you but really, what are the chances?"

"I have to say that it took me by surprise too. It was just there, blindingly obvious," Rebel said finally able to speak.

Kira strolled out the door somewhat surprised that everyone was up so early. "Morning," she said quietly.

Ric walked up the stairs a moment later.

"Rebel seen the planet," Dylan said.

"What?" Kira exclaimed incredulously. "When?"

"Just before the sun came up," Rebel repeated.

"My god! It's real then," Kira breathed uneasily.

Rebel nodded and everyone was once again consumed by a heavy silence.

Ric looked at her nervously then looked at Darien. "What does that mean."

"It means that everything we were afraid of is really going to happen," Darien said.

Rebel stood up and started pacing. "I'm going to stay up all night and get a good look at it before the sun comes up in the morning."

"Me too," Warrick said getting excited. "We can sit around the fire and all get a look."

Rebel sat back down and tried to pull herself together. "We need to open the cave and make sure it's ready."

The brothers nodded.

That evening, Warrick built a fire and made coffee. Rebel was surprised at the large group that gathered around to join the all nighter in hopes of seeing the dreaded planet. The conversation naturally turned to the anticipated events that would accompany the damn thing when it swung close to earth.

Jade turned to Rebel and asked, "So, why haven't we seen it until now?"

"Well, I'm certainly not an expert in astronomy but I do know that in the Northern Hemisphere, Orion is visible in the winter months. It dips beneath the horizon for a couple months in the spring. Right now we can only see it in the predawn sky. I don't know why I didn't think about it that way before, and it was just by chance that I got up early this morning and caught a glimpse of it."

A mixture of dread and excitement surrounded them as darkness settled in. Conner glanced at Rebel feeling her agitation and took her hand encouragingly. "What will happen now, if it's really coming? You said that it could flip the earth over or cause the pole shift."

Rebel squeezed his hand and said softly, "First, we have to distinguish between the pole shift theory and the earth being pulled over. The pole shift will cause the crust of earth to shift with the poles when they move. That is something we can actually survive now that we are home and in the safety of the cave but if this planet tips us on our ass, that is an entirely different thing."

Conner looked at her expectantly.

She paused, not wanting to freak them out then said softly, "Some believe that the planet will come at us with its north pole facing earth. If that is the case, just like any magnet, it will push the earth's magnetic north away and attract the South Pole with such force that the entire planet will topple over and that isn't something we would survive."

"Are you sure that it will do that to us?" Jade asked nervously.

"No Jade, no one knows for certain what will happen. The projected path may be different or maybe it will come in straight at us and not mess with the poles. Maybe we will just slow down instead of stopping. If that is the case, we could simply experience a few more earthquakes and get a once in a lifetime view of a huge planet then go on with our lives."

"I hope that is what happens," she mumbled.

Rebel scanned the horizon for several hours then suddenly stood up pointing, "There it is!"

The planet peeked over the horizon overwhelming the stars around it with its immense size. Everyone around the fire launched to their feet, completely taken back by the sight.

"My god, the reality of it is undeniable now," Jade said.

Rebel watched the object until the sun's light overtook the night sky, fading the stars into the background. She inhaled deeply and sat back down deep in thought.

"How long till it gets here?" Conner asked quietly.

Rebel shrugged and said, "The Mayan's tried to tell us. Their calendar marks the date of arrival on this coming winter solstice, December 21, 2012. I'm betting that the date is as exact as the rest of their calendar."

"What do you think will happen first then?"

"Earthquake, bigger than has ever been experienced by humans before. Everything will be thrown to the ground, the buildings the mountains and us. Oceans will consume continents just like Atlantis and new land masses will rise."

Conner glanced around at the frightened people beside him. "Rebel, what are our chances of survival? You planned on living through this, is it possible?"

Rebel smiled through her fear and said encouragingly, "If we live through the initial movement of the crust, and our mountain stays intact, and we aren't flooded by ocean, we could survive."

Jade stood up and said firmly, "We are going to be in the ten percent of humans that live!"

Everyone cheered as if she were encouraging them to win a game.

Rebel looked toward Wyoming and the big volcano. She had intentionally left out the fact that an eruption from the massive monster was now eminent and would most likely kill everyone.

Conner followed her gaze and read her mind. He kept quiet though realizing that she didn't want to destroy all hope for the others. "Rebel, I would really like to see your cave."

Darien stood up excitedly, "I'll give you a tour. There are still places in there that we haven't explored and I think now is a great time to do it." He led them to the opening and slid the cover, revealing the mouth of the cave. He lit a lantern and entered the massive chamber.

"Wow, this is much larger that I would have guessed," Conner said.

"It took us years to find just the right piece of property. Rebel searched relentlessly until she found this one," Darien said proudly.

Conner looked around in appreciation. The ceiling was twenty feet tall and the walls ran almost sixty yards deep into the mountain. Several smaller openings stretched in different directions opening into fairly decent sized rooms.

Rebel stepped beside him and said, "I wanted something big enough to protect a hundred people or so. This cave will only temporarily house that many. Only about fifty people could survive for a long time in here. But it will keep us safe for a short time."

"That may be just long enough Rebel," he smiled then looked at the rows of water and food that lined the walls.

"Come on," Darien said. "There are a number of small openings in the back that I want to check out."

Conner stepped forward curiously but stopped when Rebel didn't follow. "Aren't you coming?"

"No, claustrophobic remember?" she laughed then turned back to the door.

"Oh ya, I forgot," Conner smiled and followed the brothers to investigate the cave.

Rebel poured herself a cup of coffee and sat down on the porch by Kira. "At least we know now. No more guessing," she said sadly.

"We are ready Rebel," Kira encouraged. "We have a good chance."

Rebel nodded and let her mother's words sooth her.

Chapter 18

Summer turned to fall and everyone watched the planet get closer and closer each day. Rebel decided to turn her fear into energy and finish getting prepared for whatever it was that was coming with it.

Conner and the brothers built a smoker and cooked pounds of jerky and smoked salmon.

The garden was ready to harvest and potatoes, squash, apples, carrots and pumpkins were stored in the coolest part of the cave. The beans and corn were set out to dry.

Rebel looked around, satisfied that they would be able to ride out the winter with their supplies. "I say we have Thanksgiving early to celebrate the success of our first harvest up here," she said.

Everyone excitedly agreed.

The next day, the large meal was prepared.

Ric laughed with Kira and Lauren as they prepared fresh peach cobblers in the Dutch ovens. Jade and Lynn picked blackberries and strawberries and Gabe helped Cassidy cut lettuce, spinach, chard and tomatoes to make a salad.

Conner and Darien shelled and cooked corn on the cob while Dylan and Warrick grilled the meat. Shane and Cayden helped Marshall peel potatoes and onions and Danny and Theron sliced watermelon and cantaloupe.

"This is just like a huge family reunion," Rebel laughed as everyone brought their camp chairs together to eat.

She sat down next to Conner, Kira and Jade, across from her dad and brothers. She raised her cup and said, "To the year 2013 and to all of us being here to see it."

Everyone cheered and happily enjoyed the good food and good company.

The next morning, Rebel sat down on the porch with Conner, her mother and her brothers to watch Planet X just before the sun came up. It was now almost half the size of the moon and growing each day.

Dylan looked across the valley in front of them and noticed the trees shaking on the mountain ridge across the river. He stood up and pointed, "What the fuck is that?"

Rebel jumped to her feet, "It's an earthquake, a shockwave."

They watched in horror as the massive ripple rolled down the mountain, across the meadow and straight at them.

"It's going to hit us like sound hits the sound barrier. Jade!" Rebel screamed. "Get out of the loft!"

Time stood still as the ground beneath them lurched sideways then lifted, heaving the porch into the air. The cabin behind them creaked just as Jade appeared in the doorway.

Rebel grabbed her hand and ran down the stairs followed closely by the others. Once down on the ground, she turned to watch the distinct ground wave as it continued east.

"I've never seen anything like that before!" Warrick yelled.

"It was like a ocean wave across the ground, like a tsunami," Dylan said.

Rebel never took her eye off of it as it continued across the landscape. "Wave energy. It's heading for the volcano."

Suddenly the ground shifted with such a sudden violent motion that it slammed everyone to the ground as if a carpet had been ripped from beneath their feet.

Before Rebel could recover her breath, the earth jolted several feet again and trembled underneath her. She looked up into the sky and clearly saw the sun move lower in the horizon that it had just risen from.

The cabin groaned and trees across the entire mountainside snapped and crashed over. The corral splintered and the barn collapsed. The cover over the barbeque fell and the woodpile crumbled.

Rebel sucked in her breath barely able to breath through an invisible pressure surrounding her, pushing on her chest. She slowly sat up, the quaking ground keeping her from standing. Her head felt like she was in a vacuum and her ears started ringing. She looked at Jade worriedly and then to Kira. "How long is it going to shake?" she whispered.

Many minutes later the ground grew still and the pressure released their lungs.

Rebel rushed to Jade, "Are you ok?"

Jade nodded and helped Kira to her feet.

Conner pulled Rebel into his arms and held her trembling body until she calmed. He let her go and looked at the devastation around them.

Ric and the other ladies walked over from the bunkhouse and people all over the camp came out of their tents. Marshall climbed out of his sheep camp and Theron opened the door of the clinic. Neil and Evie walked out of the cabin.

"The cabin held together, barely," Dylan said.

"The barn and corals are leveled," Warrick added softly.

"Is it over?" Kira asked nervously.

Everyone looked at Rebel expectantly.

"Guys, I wish I knew but no one ever said exactly what would happen. It's all theory."

They didn't take their eyes off of her.

"All right," she said as she started pacing. "That felt like a magnetic jolt, I'll bet the magnetic field of Planet X collided with ours and sent a shockwave across the earth. We experienced a magnetic jolt back in 2010 on the winter solstice. Remember? There was full moon that night and a week later thousands of birds and fish died. It moved the earth on her axis."

Darien nodded. "They never did officially accept that fact. But since then, the number of earthquakes have increased by a hundred percent."

She glanced toward the volcano. "The mountain didn't go off though, thank god. A pole shift would take a minimum of two days and possibly months. Someone check a compass."

Darien pulled his compass out of his pocket. "It's off by twenty four degrees."

"K. That has happened before in the last year or so. Wait a minute and see if it flips back," she said.

"So that's it? It's over?" Ric asked.

Rebel gazed at her agitated friend. "I doubt it Ric, the planet is still coming closer." She looked at the nervous people in the camp. "Look, we are just going to have to take one day at a time. That planet is going to be close to us for at least six more months and it could take several years for our solar system to cross through the galactic plane. But at least we made it through round one."

"Let's get shit cleaned up," Warrick said. "If Rebel knew more so would we."

Dylan turned toward the cabin, "I can't believe it stayed up. That quake had to have been a ten."

"Nice design Dylan," Rebel said appreciating his construction skills.

Everyone nodded in agreement.

"I'm going to ride out and check the livestock," Neil said.

"I'll go with you," Darien added.

They spent the day cleaning up the camp and trying to come to grips with what had happened earlier this morning.

Later that evening, Rebel sat alone on the porch waiting for dinner. She looked up into the sun curiously wondering why it was still so high in the sky at six o'clock in the evening.

"Darien," she hollered and waved her brother over. "Look at this. We need some way to chart it."

Darien stepped onto the porch and looked into the sky as she pointed to the sun.

Kira emerged from the cabin and followed their gaze. "Aden, bring out the calendars."

Aden rushed up the steps with an arm full of papers and placed them on the table.

"Here is our calendar of earthquakes and these are

the temperatures. We also documented meteors because there were so many there for awhile," Kira said proudly.

"Wow, mom, this is great," Rebel nodded appreciatively. "Look, this calendar has sun rise and set times and moon cycles. Is your watch still working, Darien?"

"Yes, I always knew this old thing was worth keeping so I put it in a faraday cage," he laughed. He looked at his watch and said, "Right now it's six thirty five p.m."

"According to this calendar, the sun should set at eight twenty six," Rebel pointed out.

"Well that don't look right," grumbled Kira.

"No, it doesn't," she agreed. "That means that the earth's rotation has slowed."

"You said that the pole shift could cause the earth to stop and start rotating backwards," Conner said.

"Yes, I did," Rebel said quietly looking back up at the sun. "We need to document the exact times and compare them to this calendar. I wish I were good in math. Then I could tell you the exact reduction in speed."

"Dinner!" Ric yelled.

"Come on, we will figure this out over some supper," Darien said standing up.

Rebel followed him to the tables and took her plate looking at it distractedly. "I'm not very hungry," she said.

"Me either," Conner agreed.

"I think I'm going to save this for later and go work on my charts," Rebel said.

"Rebel, don't let it consume you, k?" he said as she stood up.

Jade laughed and said, "Consume her? You haven't seen anything yet. We've seen her do this before. She just might forget all about you Conner."

Conner laughed and said, "That bad huh?"

"Jade, I didn't forget you guys. I was just preoccupied," Rebel said defensively then looked at her daughter quizzically. "Did you feel forgotten?"

Jade laughed again. "Let's just say that it would have been a good time to be a teenager. I could have gotten away with anything."

"You were a teenager," Rebel mused.

Jade shrugged with a grin, making Conner laugh again.

Rebel spent the next several days trying to describe the size of Planet X and writing down the sunrise and sunset times. She documented the earthquakes that rumbled through the camp every few hours. The earth had definitely slowed, causing the sun to stay in the sky longer each day.

"So what are you seeing Rebel? Anything that helps us figure this out?" Conner asked.

"No, I'm just not educated enough. The only thing that I know is the day is now almost two hours longer than it was a few days ago."

"We are still slowing down."

She nodded, "At least the earthquakes are small, but I bet that won't last."

"It's going to get cold," Conner said sitting down beside her. "I'm worried about the kids sleeping in the tents."

Rebel looked up at him in surprise. "Do you think we should move them to the cave?"

"We are only a few months away from the winter solstice. I think we all should sleep in there just in case. The cabin may not survive another quake like that last monster."

"You're right. I'll talk to the brothers at dinner," she said gazing at the tents scattered about the camp.

Conner stood up and wrapped his arms around her.

She leaned into his embrace and tried not to think about the future.

The moment was shattered when Neil raced into camp and slid his horse to a stop in front of the porch, showering them with dirt.

"There is a large group of people being chased up the main road! They found cover but will fall to the attack if we don't hurry," he yelled. "The brothers are bringing in the horses."

Rebel ran into her room and strapped on her holster

and picked up her rifle. She slid past Conner who was grabbing extra ammunition and ran out the door.

She race outside and whistled for Jake who came right to her. She snapped a lead rope onto his halter and swung onto his back without a saddle, kicking him into a run behind her uncle and five other men already heading down the lane.

"God damn it!" Conner roared as he threw his saddle onto his big gilding. "She's going to get herself killed one of these days."

All five of the brothers nodded and watched her leave as they hurried to saddle their horses.

Rebel, Neil and the others rounded the corner at the top of the mountain just in time to see thirty or so men advance on the large group of people with their weapons aimed. Several men stepped out to defend their women and children and were instantly shot for their bravery.

Rebel couldn't control her rage as she pulled her rifle to her shoulder and fired without stopping. One of the men in the front line fell to the ground and the others looked up at her in surprise as she fired again.

"Get the supplies!" one of them yelled, and they quickly turned their attention back to their task. One of them grabbed a small boy to use as a shield as the men advanced on the group trying to take their supplies. Another brave man tried to keep one of the men from a young girl and was shot at close range.

Rebel didn't slow her racing horse as she closed in on their position below her. She kicked the big gilding, urging him over a cliff ten feet above the group of men. The horse launched over the cliff and landed right in the middle of them, trampling several and killing one. Rebel dropped the rifle and pulled out the colt, emptying the clip in a spray around her. Eight men dropped instantly. She launched off the horse and pulled out the .22 firing fifteen rounds at close range, wounding many more.

Neil and the others dismounted and took cover behind some trees and started shooting trying to give her cover.

She pulled a clip from her pocked and shoved into the weapon and quickly fired again, emptying the clip a second time.

The men ran from the woman who had just jumped her horse off the mountain and landed in the middle of them. They took cover inside the trees. Then several of them ran toward the group of innocent frightened people causing several of the women to shrieked in terror.

Rebel grabbed her rifle and took cover behind a tree while she reloaded all of her weapons. She glanced up and watched several of the men grab hostages. She fired, killing one of the men before he could reach a terrified young girl.

The others bolted forward, each of them grabbing a woman to hide behind, and pointed their weapons at their heads.

"Stop shooting or we will kill them!" a tall dark haired man yelled.

"Let them go or I will kill you," Rebel yelled back.

Suddenly she caught a glimpse of an arrow passing through the neck of one of the men. The woman he was holding screamed as he slumped to the ground.

Rebel was a good shot but didn't dare try a close shot like that.

But Darien did, he put a bullet in the forehead of another man who was holding a woman.

"Let her go!" Rebel yelled to the last man standing.

The man looked for his companions and soon realized that they were all down. He let the woman go and held up his hands.

Not good enough. Warrick shot him in the chest.

Dylan shot a man trying to sneak around to the side of them.

The few remaining men took off running into the trees knowing that they were outgunned.

Rebel walked to the group of people and was instantly surrounded, praised as their hero.

"Follow me," she said. "Let's get out of here."

Conner, Neil, and the brothers covered them from

behind as they made their way to the safety of their camp.

Once there, one of the men reached out his hand to her and said, "I'm Father Mcaffey. That was some kind of rescue. Thank you for your help."

Rebel shook his hand and said, "Why are you moving this late in the year?"

"They burned the church that we were staying in leaving us with nowhere to go and we needed water," he said sadly. "Every water source from here to the Snake River is controlled by someone. People are dying because they won't share it."

Neil walked over and reached out his hand, "I'm Neil, sorry for your loss today."

"It would have been much worse if you hadn't showed up," the father said solemnly.

"What did they want from you?" Neil asked.

"Revenge!"

"Revenge for what?" Rebel asked curiously.

"We turned some of their group over to the National Guard for stealing our food storage and burning our church," the father said hanging his head dejectedly. "They used to be a hundred strong."

"Darien, will you tell Ric we are having friends over for dinner?" Rebel said trying to lighten the mood. "And see if dad brought those big ole army tents that he used to set up for the reunions."

"Follow me Father, let's get your people set up for the night," Darien said.

Rebel turned to the cabin and walked up the stairs.

Conner stomped over to her clearly pissed off. "I am going to ask you nicely one time to never pull something like that again," he gritted out trying to control his anger.

She stepped back down the steps until she was looking him square in the eye and said in a deadly quiet voice, "You will not ask me that, nicely or not. I am what I am and you will not change that."

Conner looked at her in amazement and opened his mouth to respond when suddenly the ground erupted beneath his feet. He slammed to the ground, the impact knocking the air out of his lungs.

The porch heaved and flipped Rebel down the stairs sending her sprawling head first into the railing. She felt the blood run instantly down her face but fought through the fog wondering where Jade and Kira were.

She crawled back up the stairs and across the broken planks of the porch to the cabin door. "Jade! Mom!" she yelled trying to stand.

"In here!" Jade yelled back. "Grandma is hurt."

The ground continued to rumble but Rebel stood and wobbled to Jade. A sudden jolt toppled her once again to the floor next to her mother and daughter. The cabin creaked, loosening the construction and spilling debris on top of them.

"Jade, crawl to the door and get out. I will stay with grandma," Rebel urged.

Rebel watched her crawl out the door as she pulled Kira toward the thick log table and slid it over them just as the ground rolled in another shock wave bringing the entire structure down on top of them.

Conner was rushing toward the cabin door just as Jade climbed out. He grabbed her and launched them both off the porch as the cabin collapsed.

"Rebel!" he yelled in horror, scrambling back up the now leveled porch.

The ground rumbled aggressively for many minutes as Conner dug through the wreckage trying to clear a path to the door. He desperately glanced around for help but knew it wouldn't come. The bunkhouse had collapsed as well and the brothers were searching for their friends underneath piles of debris.

Jade climbed to her feet and looked at the crumpled house in front of her and couldn't help but think back to last spring. She looked around, overwhelmed by the deja vu. This whole nightmare had started with the same exact event that had just taken place. She shook her head clear it then rushed to help Conner find her mother and grandmother.

Tears ran freely down her cheeks as she called out to

them remembering the fate of the people in D.C. She looked at Conner trying to gain some reassurance.

Conner could feel Jade's pleading eyes on him and he stopped for a moment to comfort her. "Jade, we will get to them in time, I promise."

She nodded and turned back to the cabin picking up another board.

Several others from the camp soon joined them and together they burrowed their way through to what was once the cabin door.

Conner turned back to Jade. "Where did you see them last?"

"In the kitchen, they were on the floor in the kitchen about twenty feet from the door."

"She would have gone under the table," Conner said anxiously then yelled, "Rebel!"

Rebel faintly heard her name through the fog of darkness that had consumed her moments ago. She fought to clear her head and looked down at Kira. "Mom, are you ok?" she pleaded. "Mom?"

Despair overwhelmed her when there was no response.

"Conner!" she cried from their little cave under the remains of the once beautiful cabin. She tried to move but pain washed over her and she became distinctly aware that the table had tipped over on them, confining both of her arms and crushing her chest.

"Conner!" she shrieked suddenly engulfed by hysteria from her dreaded claustrophobia. She screamed again and closed her eyes tightly, fighting the unreasonable madness that devoured her.

Conner heard her shriek in terror and grabbed the table, heaving it off of her. He took both of her hands in his and said soothingly, "Rebel, it's ok. I got you."

Rebel opened her eyes and looked deep into his and allowed them dispel the paralyzing terror that had ravaged her.

"Grandma!" Jade cried seeing the blood on Kira's

head.

Kira stirred and moaned trying to sit up.

Dylan and Warrick rushed over to help her stand then half carried her onto the clearing in front of the porch.

Conner reached down and plucked Rebel from the debris on the floor and followed the brothers. He set Rebel down in a chair next to Kira and turned to look at the carnage that surrounded them.

Not one tent was left standing. The bunkhouse lay in ruins and children were crying. Half the population of the camp were injured, many of them fatally.

Conner glanced at the bunkhouse and sucked in his breath as he watched Darien and Shane pack out Theron's still form.

Kira gasped in horror and slowly stood up.

"He's alive," Darien yelled. "Gabe, we need you here."

Kira sank back into her chair in relief.

"He was the only one inside," Warrick said. "Thank god the others were cooking out here."

Gabe rushed over to Theron and bent down to check his wounds. Panic eroded her self-confidence and she looked up at Rebel. "I can't do this without him. There are too many wounded."

Rebel could see her apprehension and stood up to help her. She turned to her brother and said, "Dylan, open the cave and find some sort of beds or cots for the injured. Warrick, we need the supplies out of the clinic. Darien, Conner, your with me and Gabe."

She turned to her younger brothers, "Cayden, Shane, bring the injured to the cave, the most serious first then set up the big tents and help everyone get settled. And send in Marv and Jerry."

Everyone moved at once following Rebel's lead.

Gabe followed the boys packing Theron into the cave and knelt down beside him. "Theron," she said worriedly. "Theron, can you hear me?"

He moaned in pain but opened his eyes.

"Where are you hurt?" she asked.

"My arm and my leg on the left side. They are broken, I can't move them."

Gabe turned to Darien, "Check the breaks and prepare a brace while I check the others." She turned around overtaken by the number of injured people that now lined the cave floor.

"Take it one at a time Gabe," Rebel said encouragingly. "We will help you."

Hours later, they had stabilized everyone in the cave and helped the others regroup for the night.

Rebel looked sadly at the row of dead people covered in sheets at the edge of the camp as she sat down next to Father McCaffee. "We won't save everyone. It's my biggest regret."

He sighed sadly and nodded, "Mine as well."

"The cave is too small for everyone. How do you choose who gets in?"

The kind man turned to Rebel and said gently, "Protect the innocent and defenseless. You've already shown me that you are selfless so my advice is that you follow your instincts."

Rebel nodded her thanks and stood up. She turned to Conner and her brothers with dread in her heart from the sacrifice she was about to vocalize. She looked at them sadly and said, "I want the women and children to sleep in the cave from here on out. The men will bunk in the tents." Then she turned and walked away.

They watched her leave knowing that she had made a very hard but logical decision, then turned to find the tents.

Rebel helped Jade and Kira prepare their beds inside the cave then set up her tent just outside the cave door.

Conner stepped up to her and took her badly bruised arms into his hands. He kissed the bruises then said, "Rebel, I want you to sleep in the cave with the others."

Rebel looked up at him struggling to push back the anger that threatened to surface again. "Conner, that sounds a lot like your earlier request. I accepted you for who you are and I expect the same in return. I know you are worried about me but don't try to change me."

"God damn it Rebel, that's not what I'm trying to do," he said softly. "I just need you safe."

"Conner, I won't ask someone to do something that I won't do myself. If I order you and my brothers to sleep outside then I will sleep outside as well."

He nodded, understanding her logic.

Rebel relaxed a little, her anger melting away. She leaned up and kissed him then smiled, "Besides, I'd risk my life to sleep with you one more time."

He couldn't help smiling. "Come on then, let's go to bed."

They had just barely fallen asleep when the aftershock hit. Rebel grabbed her jeans and climbed out of the tent. She looked into the starlit sky at the planet that was now almost as big as the moon and knew instinctively that this earthquake was the big one.

She stayed on the ground to avoid being thrown down. Conner crawled out next to her and took her hand anticipating the ominous outcome. They watch helplessly as the big military tent that housed the men folded onto itself, settling on top of them. Tucker whined beside them.

The ground jerked sideways then surged upward severing their hand connection and flipping them backwards away from each other. Rebel rolled to a sitting position but jumped aside when rocks rolled down the mountain above the cave landing just in front of her. She looked up and gasped as a major portion of mountain soil was torn loose and hurtled downward, slamming to the ground in front the cave opening, completely enclosing it.

The few surrounding trees that were still standing toppled over in a loud crash as the surface lurched repeatedly back and forth.

They endured the thrashing of being tossed around for well over five minutes as the earth heaved and pitched underneath them. Finally the ground grew still and she shot to her feet to check on the men.

Darien was the first one out followed closely by Warrick and Dylan. She waited impatiently until she saw

Cayden and Shane help Marshall out of the small opening in the canvas.

Her uncle climbed out and said, "We have more injuries, help me get the tent off of them."

Rebel pointed silently to the opening of the cave and all of the men inhaled sharply in unison.

"Dig the shovels out of the barn, we'll dig them out," Darien yelled.

Rebel helped her uncle get the injured people out of the tent and looked anxiously at Conner as he shoveled dirt.

"We'll get to them, don't worry," he said encouragingly.

Rebel looked up at the planet again and growled, "You fucker!" She shook her head angrily, "God I wish I could fight that fucking…."

Conner looked up at her when her words faded off. She was staring into the sunrise with her mouth wide open. He followed her gaze and stepped toward her in surprise. A huge blazing ball of light was streaking from the atmosphere toward the earth's crust.

"My god," he breathed. "Is that…?"

"Asteroid," she raked out.

Everyone around her stopped working and stood silently watching the deadly rock as it closed in on its target.

"We need to get into the cave. Now!" Rebel yelled.

"Are we in the path of the shock wave?" Shane asked nervously.

"A ten mile wide rock will send a blast wave three hundred miles. That one looks pretty big," she said. "And if it comes apart, the pieces could impact hundreds of miles away."

"You know what Rebel? Sometimes I wish you didn't know all of this shit. I'd almost rather die ignorant," Conner scoffed.

Rebel ignored the remark. "It could cause another earthquake. That won't be good if it hits close to the volcano," she added her eyes following the asteroids path. "My god! It's going to practically slam right into it."

Darien looked over just as the rock plowed into the ground somewhere in Wyoming.

"Hurry!" Rebel yelled again. "The volcano will really be pissed off now."

Cayden started shoveling faster.

"I'm through!" Warrick yelled.

Conner looked at Rebel who was looking in the direction of the impact and counting to herself. "What are you doing?" he asked confused.

"The shock wave will be here in about thirty seconds if it's going to reach us," she said without looking at him. "The Tetons might be big enough to block it, so maybe..."

Her voice trailed off as the ground started quaking once again.

"Get them into the cave! Hurry, everyone climb through the hole," she urged.

Rebel helped her brothers with the injured men then climbed through the small hole into the cave. "Darien, there are a lot of people in here, how much oxygen can get through the back entrance?"

"If it doesn't get buried, it will be enough for a day or so," he said softly.

She slowly nodded her head trying not to show her anxiety of being locked underground. "K, maybe we should take turns outside digging. Four of us at a time. That way, we will have time to get back inside if something happens."

"We'll take the first round," he agreed with a grin. He knew how bad his sister hated being in the cave. "And Rebel, don't worry. We will be fine in here." He picked up his shovel and waved to his brothers then followed them back out.

Rebel turned to the large number of frightened people huddled around the cavern. "Ric, let's get everyone something to eat. There are boxes of prepared foods in the back corner."

She helped Ric and Jade pass out the food eyeing the cave walls that shuttered every few minutes. When everyone had something to eat she poured some water in a bowl for the dogs then walked to the hole that her brothers were working on and looked out. "I feel much better now that the opening is bigger," she said.

"I think it's big enough for now, let's get back inside," Warrick said.

Darien scanned the mountain across from them and yelled, "Get in! It's another ground wave!"

Rebel looked out and watched the earth roll like the ocean as the wave traveled toward them.

Warrick grabbed her and shoved her inside then turned back to Dylan, "Don't forget the shovels, we might have to dig our way back out."

The entire mountain heaved and Rebel felt the ground move sideways. The next jolt cracked the thick rock wall and everyone shrieked in terror. Another slide piled dirt in front of the cave entrance once again trapping them inside.

Minutes ticked by, the quaking never letting up. Rebel thought her body was going to shake apart.

"How long is it going to last?" Jade cried covering her ears in panic and sinking back into Danny's chest.

Rebel looked at Conner and for the first time questioned whether they would actually make it out alive.

Conner looked into her eyes seeing her strength fading. "No Rebel, don't give up. We've come so far."

She looked at the weeping people around her and tears filled her eyes. "I don't think we'll make it, Conner."

He dropped to his knees in front of her and wrapped her in his big arms. "I love you," he whispered in her ear. "We have to make it because I want more time with you. I haven't got enough yet."

He held her tight for many minutes until finally, the earth grew quiet. He lifted his head and looked into her eyes. "Please don't give up."

She nodded slowly and squeezed him one more time before they climbed to their feet and picked up the shovels.

Several hours later, everyone in the cave climbed outside into the dusty daylight. The landscape was completely leveled. The mountain across the river was a hundred feet shorter and the displaced dirt had filled in the valley. Not one tree was standing and dust billowed around them like low-lying fog, allowing them to see only yards away.

Several of the horses trotted past them shaking their heads as if they were proud to have survived.

Rebel looked toward the volcano but couldn't see anything past the haze. "I can't see it. We have no way of knowing what the volcano is doing," Rebel moaned nervously.

"Rebel! Come look at this!" Warrick yelled from the top of the ravished mountain ridge pointing to the west.

Rebel and Conner hiked up to the top and stared, completely astonished at the sight below them.

"Is that the ocean?" she choked out in disbelief.

Conner nodded, unable to speak.

Kira climbed up beside them and exclaimed, "Oh my god! Is that…?"

Conner nodded again.

Darien pulled out his compass and said, "It was a pole shift. Look, north is now that way." He pointed to what used to be west.

One by one, the entire camp hiked to the top of the ridge and stood in awe at the sight of the majestic Pacific Ocean lapping at a mountainside in the middle of Idaho.

Rebel looked around at her family then grabbed Jade's hand on one side and Conner's on the other then turned back to the unbelievable view. "It has really happened. We have experienced a geological pole shift."

She looked back at the volcano and added, "And it's only a matter of time before we witness the massive eruption of a super volcano."

"Will we make it?" Jade asked. "Will we really survive?"

"I still don't know Jade, but like Conner said, we have made it this far."

Rebel turned to the group of people around her and said, "Come on, we have work to do. This isn't over. We are still in danger. Gabe, we need to check on the injured. Uncle Neil, see about the livestock. Jade, you and Ric dig out something to eat. Darien, we need to uncover the spring and make sure it is still flowing. Father McCaffee, say a prayer, we are going to need all the help we can get."

Everyone nodded and glanced back at the new ocean for a moment then turned to reorganize and prepare for the next round.

Rebel searched through the dusky sky looking for a cloud of ash over the volcano. The dust was finally settling some, but still blocked her view. She tried to put it out of her mind as she worked on the injured people in the cave.

Ric yelled for everyone to come eat and the group sat around the battered camp together in silence.

One of the women from the church stood up and said, "Rebel, I want to thank you for helping us. You risked your life to save us then opened your doors to us and shared your supplies. If it weren't for you, we would not have survived the past few days and I pray that God looks after you and yours in the same way."

Everyone cheered and looked at Rebel expectantly, obviously needing some kind of response.

She stood up and said, "Thank you. We have always believed that we should take care of each other. Sadly, I haven't seen that very often during this catastrophe." She paused and looked around for a moment then continued, "I'm going to need your prayers because I can't count the number of men that I have killed in the past few months and even though I did it to protect innocent people, I don't know if God will forgive that. I do know, however, that together, we will survive and life will continue on earth."

Everyone cheered again.

Father McCaffey stood and the camp went silent. "We owe these people our lives and prayers. Thank you from me as well. Rebel, I do believe that God will forgive those who are as kind and giving as you people are. I pray that he will protect us through the coming months and help us survive."

Rebel nodded her thanks to him and stood to leave. She glanced to the east and froze in terror.

Everyone stood and followed her gaze to a massive billowing ball of ash and steam erupting into the sky over the corner of Wyoming.

Rebel crumbled back into her chair and said, "Father, I hope your prayers are answered because our chances of survival just plummeted to almost zero."

Conner looked at Rebel then back to the volcano. He took her hand and squeezed it encouragingly. "Rebel, lets get to the cave in Montana."

She looked into his eyes, fear enveloping her as she nodded in agreement. She turned to her brothers and said, "Dig out the masks and prepare for a cross country journey. Its several hundred miles from here and there will be no roads. We will be lucky to make it. Neil, what about the horses?"

"We lost several head but surprisingly, the rest of them survived."

Rebel stood and looked into the crowd. "My family and I will be moving on to Montana. It will be a rough ride. You are welcome to go with us. If you decide to stay, you are welcome to use this camp. The cave will protect you and the spring is still flowing." She heard the gasps and whispers among the people at the sudden decision as she walked to the cave.

Conner followed her inside and watched her gaze at the injured people that lined the floor.

"Most of them will have to stay because they won't survive the trip. It is going to be long and cold."

He nodded and glanced at Theron and Marshal sitting together chatting like old friends. He smiled and said, "I guess those two will be on the front seat of the wagon."

"It will take days to prepare for this. We will have to load the supplies and gather our gear. I need to know who is going and who is staying."

"I'll have Kira schedule a meeting over dinner and we will get it figured out. The brothers are preparing fresh beef from the downed animals they recovered this morning.

We have plenty of horses and saddles. Everyone can ride so we can put the supplies on the wagons," Conner pondered.

"Here we go again," Rebel smiled.

Conner laughed and bent down to kiss her. "We will be fine, Rebel."

Later that evening over a big dinner, Rebel once again stood to address the large crowd of people. "As I said this morning, some of us are preparing to move. I need to know by tonight, who will be going with us. Come talk to me before you leave so that we can make our plan. Also, later tonight, Father McCaffee will lead us in a funeral for our fallen friends."

Once again, Father McCaffee stood after Rebel sat down. "We appreciate the offer, but everyone in my group will be staying. We are grateful that you are allowing us to stay here under the protection of your cave and offer our help to anyone else who would like to stay here."

Rebel sighed sadly praying that they would be able to survive here.

Aden sat down beside Kira and opened her notebook ready to document the names of people who were committing to the journey to Montana. She started with Rebel, Kira and Jade and continued with the brothers, Marshall and Uncle Neil. She added Conner, Danny, Ric, Lynn, Lauren and Cass, then continued with Gabe and Theron. She glanced at Rebel and timidly wrote her name on the list.

Rebel patted her knee then smiled as her seven cousins added their names to the list. Several of them were married and some had older children. Most of the young families with small children decided to stay.

Dylan sat down beside her and said, "We have fifty-six saddle horses plus dad's two teams and roughly eighty head of cattle left. There are forty-three saddles and plenty of tack. It took us hours to dig it out of the barn."

"Good, there are roughly forty or fifty people on the list so that leaves several pack animals. I want to leave the calves, anything that won't handle to trail. I don't think we should try to take more than fifty head. Do you think we should take the mares and foals?" she asked.

"They are old enough to handle it. I'm sure they will be fine," he encouraged. "Dad's wagon is in good shape and the team should handle the weight of the supplies if there is some kind of road or trail." He paused and looked at her seriously "I don't think there will though, Rebel. We will be lucky to get the supplies through."

"Dad and Theron can't ride. Neither can Evie. If we lose the wagon, we will lose more than the supplies. And if the ash starts to fall, we will lose all of the large animals. We may all end up on foot."

"Maybe that is all the big bastard is going to do. It looks like just a portion of it went off."

"It was just steam probably from the lake when the water was displaced but I really think that it's just showing off. It is going to try to kill us yet," she said sadly. "I just hope it waits till we get to Montana."

Conner silently listened to the conversation, realizing that this trip was going to be rough. The cattle and the wagons would slow them down and time was not on their side if they wanted to make it there before winter. He glanced at Rebel and read the concern on her face. She looked over at him and he smiled encouragingly.

Rebel stood up and said, "Everyone on this list, meet me for coffee in the morning so we can start our preparations." She turned and walked to the cave to help Gabe change bandages.

Early the next morning, before the sun came up, Rebel stood looking over the newly placed ocean that lapped at the mountainside below her. She looked into the clearing sky at the massive planet that was responsible for the chaos and death that surrounded her. There were still some time before the winter solstice and she knew that the devastation wasn't over yet. A geomagnetic pole shift like the one they had just witnessed was completely different than the threat of the planet slowing to a stop or being dragged onto her side. She couldn't help the anxiety that washed over her and wondered again if they would actually survive to ring in the New Year.

Conner walked up next to her and was once again awestruck at the sight of the Pacific Ocean. "It's not over yet, is it?"

Rebel shook her head no and sighed. "How many people died between here and what used to be the West coast? The east coast will have suffered the same fate. At least I don't puke anymore every time I think of the suffering. God, I wish I had Internet so I could see what the hell was going on."

"I was thinking yesterday that I probably wouldn't have survived this if I hadn't met you," he said softly. "I can't believe how lucky I am."

Rebel turned to him and smiled. "You would have made it Conner, but I'm glad we made it together. Now if we can just hold out for a little longer."

He wrapped her in his arms and kissed her with all of the love he possessed in his heart and she returned it passionately.

He took her hand and said, "Everyone has gathered for your meeting. Let's get this trip planned and start the preparations."

As they walked back to camp, she said, "It's just my luck that I finally have beach front property and I'm going to move."

Conner laughed.

Everyone looked up as she walked to the fire. Warrick handed her a cup of coffee then turned to help Theron hobble to his chair.

"As you know," she started hesitantly, "this is a bad time to journey cross country in the mountains of Idaho and Montana. We will be facing very cold temperatures and rough terrain. The going will be very slow because of the cattle and wagons. Some of us are injured and we will have several young people with us. But, I have faith in the fact that if we are properly prepared, we will be successful. We will all be riding so we can save the wagons for our supplies.

Aden has a list of things that I want you to have with you on your horse."

She started pacing in front of the fire as she continued. "Dad and Theron will man the supply wagon. Dad has cleaned out the sheep camp so we can turn it into a cook wagon. Mom and Evie will drive it. Ric will be in charge of packing the supplies that go in there. Everyone should have a warm bedroll and a tent. Pack your own mess kit and coffee cup. You will need winter clothes, hats, boots and especially gloves. Leave anything you're horse can't carry and hopefully one day we will come back to retrieve our personal belongings."

She paused again, sipping on her coffee. "Warrick will make sure that everyone is armed. If we happen to run into survivors, they will be desperate and we may need to protect ourselves and our supplies so prepare your minds for confrontation. Darien will hand out the masks and you need to take care of them. They just might save your lives. We will leave the rest of them for the people who stay here."

Rebel looked around at the drawn faces of the people in front of her and knew that they were apprehensive. "On a lighter note, just think of this as a long hunting trip or camping trip. A cattle drive vacation like the one in the movie 'City Slickers' except in the cold," she smiled.

Everyone laughed.

"We need to sort the supplies and make sure that the people who are staying have what they need as well. Any questions?" she asked.

"When do we want to leave?" Dylan asked.

"The sooner the better. I'm thinking three days. We should be ready by then. Let's go to work!" she said clapping her hands together.

Jade turned to Conner with a grin and said, "That's what she always said during our basketball games when she was our coach. After a time out she would clap her hands like that then slap us on the ass. I sure miss those days. I wish you could have seen her back then. She didn't like to lose."

"Her determination to win may be the reason we are

all still alive," he smiled back at her. "Are you ready for another long ride?"

"Ya, I guess. I love to ride horses, but this is pushing it. I'm worried about mom though. She hates the cold worse than anything. She always wanted to move out of Idaho because of the weather. And she hates Montana."

"Why does she hate Montana?"

"We took a trip out there once and it snowed the entire time. And it was May. We were almost run off the road by a truck. The snow bank was huge and we almost plowed right into it. She calls it a snow ridden, god forsaken state," she laughed. "But she loves the mountains and trees and always says it's a shame that the beauty up there is wasted in the cold."

Conner laughed and looked at Rebel. "She is something."

Jade nodded then stood up and said, "I hope everyone has warm coats and boots."

Chapter 19

The next several days were spent sorting and loading supplies onto the wagon and packing their gear for the long ride. The men prepared the horses, replacing shoes and sorting tack.

Dylan helped Father McCaffee prepare to rebuild some structures with the lumber from the unusable cabin. Marshall helped Darien ready the harnesses for the teams and the women packed the cook camp. Warrick sorted through the weapons and ammunition. Gabe packed their medical supplies and showed Jerry, the LPN, how to treat some of her patients who were staying.

On the third day, everything was ready. Rebel walked to the fire as the sun came up and smiled at Warrick and Dylan who were already drinking coffee while they cooked breakfast.

"Are we ready?" she asked as she accepted a cup from her brother.

"Ready as we will ever be," Dylan smiled. "Neil has the cattle rounded up and the horses are waiting down by the river."

Conner walked up to them and said, "Here we go again."

Rebel nodded, "At least we don't have to travel across the entire U.S. this time."

After breakfast Darien stood up. "I'll go bring up the horses," he said waving at Shane and Cayden to help him.

Rebel saddled Jake and rubbed his neck fondly for a moment before she strapped her gear behind the saddle. She buckled her holster and checked her weapons before sliding them home then turned to help the guys finish loading the packhorses.

Marshall climbed onto the wagon next to Theron and took up the reins to the team of giant Clydesdales and slapped them across their rumps. He took the lead followed by the cook wagon where Kira held the reins sitting next to Evie.

Neil and the brothers circled around the herd of cattle and pushed them into a slow walk behind the wagons.

Rebel looked back and waved at Father McCaffee then fell in step beside Jade and Ric. Silently they rode into morning.

Several hours later, Darien and Dylan ran past them to check the road ahead and make sure that it was clear. The landscape around them had changed drastically. Mountains had been split or leveled and riverbeds were displaced spilling water into the valleys. But so far, the road was passable.

The plan was to follow the highway north along the river to lost trail pass then cut across to the Interstate and follow it up through Helena. The pavement, if it was still there, would make it easier to get the wagons and cattle through.

Rebel looked around, still amazed at the destruction from the massive earth shift. Trees were leveled and structures were crumbled. Nothing had escaped the power of the quake.

"Look at that," she said pointing to the flooding river below them. "The dam was demolished. We are going to have problems crossing the some rivers along the way."

Jade nodded nervously and glanced back at Danny who was helping with the cattle. "Can the cattle swim if they have to?"

"Yes, but its dangerous. I would be more worried about getting the wagons through. God, I never thought that we would be following the Lewis and Clark trail across the continental divide pushing a herd of cattle traveling in a wagon train."

Jade laughed. "I never really thought about it that way either. We are just like the pioneers."

Later that evening, they stopped to make camp for the night beside the flooding river. Rebel and Conner helped Theron and Marshall off of their perch on the wagon and laughed when Kira hobbled toward them.

"God, my butt hurts," she smiled. "Jade, grab my

camp chair, would ya?"

Jade returned with their chairs and helped Ric build a fire.

Rebel pulled out the Dutch ovens and started dinner. "I'll help with dinner, then I'll take a turn watching the herd so the brothers can rest before their shift."

"I'll ride with you," Conner said, knowing that she wasn't comfortable in the dark.

"Thanks, will you saddle one of the extra horses for me?"

He nodded and turned to set up the tent before they left.

The brothers rode into camp and dismounted, eagerly seeking their dinner.

"God damned slow sons 'o bitches," Dylan complained. "It will take us months to get there at this speed."

"Dylan, its not even three hundred miles. At twelve miles a day, we should be there in a month," Rebel laughed.

"I'm used to loading them into trailers and moving them at seventy five miles an hour," he laughed back.

"Conner and I will take first watch so you guys can rest up. How are they traveling?"

"We have a few stragglers but they are moving out alright. Let 'em spread out pretty good to bed down. We left them about three hundred yards back just in case something spooks them. We don't want them stampeding into camp," he said.

Conner rode up with the fresh horses and asked, "Are you ready?"

She nodded and followed him to the small herd of cattle. They rode in silence around the herd for several hours until Cayden and Shane rode up to relieve them.

"Get some sleep, Rebel," Shane smiled. "Goodnight.

Several days later, they stopped to camp just across the Montana state line at the top of lost trail pass.

"We will turn here and cut across to Butte. There

are several rivers in our path and most likely, no bridges," Dylan said anxiously.

Warrick choked on his coffee and looked at Dylan sharply. "We can't expect to swim the wagons across the rivers. Let alone the kids on horseback."

"We may not have a choice, Warrick," Dylan argued.

"Let's just take one day at a time here, guys," Rebel broke in. "We will figure it out when we get there."

Ric handed them their dinner and said, "I'm going to need you to harvest a deer or something for tomorrow if you could. I don't think we should open the storage just yet."

Conner accepted his plate and said, "I'll go have a look around first thing in the morning. It should be interesting to see how the wild game dealt with this whole crust of the earth moving thing."

"Back to venison already," Shane complained.

Rebel woke up alone the next morning and walked sleepily to the fire. "I'm sure glad you guys get up and build the fire in the mornings. I hate the cold."

"Ya, we know. And you hate mornings," Dylan teased handing her a cup of coffee.

"But really, I feel a little spoiled not having to make my own coffee very often."

"We don't mind sis, we rarely make dinner anymore. Everyone has a place and we all seem to be working well together," Darien said.

"How are the horses holding up to the extra hours?"

"We are using the pack horses for the night shift but we sure could use a few more," Warrick answered.

Conner rode into camp and dropped a deer off of his horse.

"That's a nice buck," Dylan said standing up. "I'll help you skin him."

Ric walked to the fire and said, "Thanks, Conner. That should feed us for a couple days. I'll prepare a place for you to hang the hindquarters in the camp. I'll use the front shoulders first."

He nodded to her and went to work on the animal.

Neil and Danny rode in from their shift watching the herd and switched to fresh horses.

"Better eat, we will be ready to leave in about thirty minutes," Rebel said.

After two days of slow riding, they stopped to look at the very small town of Wisdom just across the Big Hole River. Like Dylan had predicted, the bridges had crumbled.

"The river is flooding but it doesn't seem to be very deep," Dylan pointed out. "We should be able to cross it without Warrick getting his gun wet."

"Fuck you Dylan," Warrick laughed.

Rebel smiled and looked at Jade. "Just stay on the horse. Trust him, he will get you across."

Jade nodded bravely and looked anxiously at Kira. "Will grandma be ok?"

"We will all be just fine. Just stay by me."

Darien and Conner started across the frigid river to guide the team pulling the wagon. The huge animals followed without incident and Kira pushed her team in behind them. The water came up above the horses' shoulders but they trudged through.

Once everyone was on the other side, Rebel turned to help gather the cattle coming across. "That went much more smoothly than I thought it would," she said as the brothers reached her. "We may not be as lucky the next time."

"Let's make camp just outside of the town. Then we will ride in and see if there are survivors there," Darien said.

They set up camp then Conner, Rebel and the brothers mounted for the short ride to the badly damaged little town.

"My god, everything is leveled," Dylan said as they rode past the tumbled structures. "It must be like this everywhere."

"I'm sure it is global," Rebel agreed.

Conner pulled his horse to a stop and said, "There is someone here. I can feel it."

Rebel and her brothers pulled out their weapons and looked around.

"There. By that log structure. Part of it is still standing," Conner pointed.

"Hello," Rebel yelled as they rode closer.

Warrick rode around behind the building and suddenly came racing back. "There are remnants of a big fire and a lot of foot prints. Fuck! We shouldn't have set up camp this close to the town."

"They would have seen our fires anyway," Rebel soothed then rode closer to the structure and dismounted.

Tucker followed her, barking excitedly.

"Rebel, don't get that close. You don't know who's in there," Conner reprimanded.

She ignored him and followed the dog through the small opening. A small, terrified young boy was sitting in the corner of the room looking at her with wide eyes.

"It's ok," she said softly. "I won't hurt you, neither will Tucker. Are you here alone? My name is Rebel. Are you hungry?"

This got his attention and he quickly nodded yes.

"If you want to come with me, I will get you something to eat," she encouraged. "Come on."

He moved uneasily toward her.

"It's ok, we are just traveling through town and stopped to see if anyone was here. Follow me." She climbed back outside the hole and waited.

He timidly poked his head out catching Conner and her brothers off guard.

Warrick started laughing and said, "Well if that ain't something. How the hell did he survive this shit?"

"Do you want to ride my horse with me?" Rebel asked him and his face lit up.

"There he is, the big buckskin. His name is Jake," she continued trying to ease his anxiety.

The little dude walked up to the big gilding and

reached out to pet his nose.

"We need to move out in case whoever is staying back there comes back," Warrick urged.

Rebel picked the boy up and put him in her saddle then swung on behind him. "This little guy is hungry. We need to get him back to camp and feed him."

They rode into camp and dismounted. Rebel lifted the boy down and said, "Come over to the fire. They are cooking dinner there."

To everyone's surprise, the kid took right to Warrick. He followed him around everywhere he went and sat down by him while he ate his food.

"Warrick, see if you can get him to talk," Rebel said.

Her brother looked at the boy and said, "What is your name?"

The kid looked up at him still chewing a mouth full of food and said, "Ty."

"Are you alone out here?"

Ty shook his head no then said, "They kicked me."

Warrick and Conner both stiffened.

"Who kicked you? Was it a man?" Warrick asked.

Ty nodded again. "They hate me."

"They? How many of them?" he urged.

Ty shrugged.

"Do you live in the town?"

Ty nodded yes.

"Where is your mom?"

"She's sleeping."

Rebel inhaled sharply and stood up to pace around the fire.

Darien stood up and said, "I want you to stay in pairs by the herd and two of us will guard the camp as well. Keep your weapons ready."

"I'll take first watch. I doubt if I could sleep anyway," Rebel said picking up her rifle.

Conner followed her to the outside of the camp and sat down next to her against a tree. "We need to find out who those men are."

She nodded in agreement and added, "I think we should try to find the kid's house and see if we can get him some clothes," Rebel added. "He isn't wearing any shoes."

Tucker perked his ears up and Conner jerked his head up. He put his finger to his lips. "I hear them."

Rebel raised her rifle and listened. "There they are. Riding along the river."

They watched the fifteen men ride into the little town then Rebel stood to inform the brothers.

"There are fifteen of them," Rebel informed Darien. "They rode to the structure where we found Ty."

"Watch them close, I'm sure they know we are here. I want to break camp early and get the wagons and the herd on the move. Keep me informed," he said.

Rebel and Conner took turns sleeping and watching the men until daybreak. Darien had the camp up and ready to roll when they walked to the fire.

"Grab a cup of coffee Rebel, we are moving out," Warrick said, eyeing the little boy following him around.

"The kid needs cloths. I want to go into the town," she informed them. "Those guys may not be as bad as we think."

"Once we get everyone moving, we will take you in," he said drawing a nervous glance from Conner.

Rebel turned on him daring him to say anything.

He looked back at her clearly concerned and said, "Please Rebel, just do this once for me. I know I'm being selfish but damn it, I have a bad feeling. I don't want you to go."

Rebel could see that he was trying to compromise by asking instead of telling her what to do so she to let him have his way this time. "Fine, Conner, but you two need to make sure you get everything that kid needs for the trip. Dig through the debris at a store if you have to but get him set up." She turned and mounted Jake then pushed him into a run to catch up with the wagon.

Conner looked at Warrick, completely surprised that she had complied. Warrick was just as surprised and grinned as he lifted the kid up onto his horse.

Together, along with Dylan and Darien, they rode into the town.

"Where is your house?" Warrick asked Ty who pointed up the road.

Warrick dismounted in front of the collapsed structure and told the kid to stay on the horse. Darien, Dylan and Conner stood guard with their rifles ready while he dug through the debris, trying to find the kids' winter clothes.

"I found his room, and his coat and boots," Warrick hollered as he stuffed a backpack full of clothes from what used to be his closet. He yanked several blankets from the buried bed and rolled them up then walked through the debris. He jumped when he saw the kid's parents buried under the boards.

"Company comin," Conner said quietly nodding down the road. He and the brothers waited as the fifteen mounted men rode toward them.

Tucker growled and sat down next to Conner's horse.

"What the fuck are you doing?" one of the men asked as they stopped about twenty feet away.

"We are finding the kid some clothes, what the fuck are you doing?" Warrick growled back to him.

Conner noticed that Ty turned pale and was about ready to jump off the horse to get away from them. "Ty, stay on the horse. We won't let them hurt you," he said to stop his retreat.

"Why do you think we would hurt the thievin little bastard?" the man asked.

Conner leaned forward in his saddle and looked him in the eye, "Just a guess, I guess."

Tension filled the air as the two men stared at each other.

The man glanced at Conner's rifle and knew from the cold look in his eye that he would kill him so he waved to his friends to follow him and they turned back down the road.

Warrick swung onto his horse behind Ty and said,

"Let's move out."

They turned their horses the other way and thundered out of town.

"I was scared," Ty said after they slowed to a walk.

"Don't you worry, little man, you can go with us and we will look out for you, ok?" he asked then smiled when he nodded his head excitedly.

Warrick rode up to the cook wagon and threw Ty's pack and blankets inside then handed him over to Rebel. "I think we got everything he needs. Those men scared the shit out of him though. I'm going to ride behind the herd and keep watch. I think they will follow us."

Rebel nodded and rode up to Marshall and Theron. She asked Ty if he wanted to ride in the wagon and he quickly nodded yes so she passed him over and laughed as he perched himself on the seat between them. Then she turned to help guard them.

They pushed on for about twelve miles before stopping to make camp for the night. Rebel could tell that the guys were a little nervous about those men following them because they pushed the herd up beside their camp instead of leaving it behind them.

Everyone but Warrick and Dylan rode into camp.

Darien strolled over to Ric and planted a kiss on her lips. "We need to feed the guys so we can rotate out. Can I help you with dinner?"

"No, we have it covered. You should sit and take a break yourself," she smiled.

He poured a cup of coffee and sat down by the fire watching her bustle around.

"I'm taking first watch, Rebel," Conner said as he switched to a fresh horse. "Want to ride with me?"

She nodded and pulled her saddle off of Jake. He glanced at her curiously, sensing her tension, so she smiled and said, "I'm just a little anxious tonight. I'm feeling a little vulnerable because we can't run from danger and we can't hide either. We are just out here."

"I know. We all feel the same way. Go get

something to eat and I'll saddle your horse," he said turning her toward the fire.

She quickly ate and checked her weapons then followed Conner toward the herd of cattle.

The night was cold and heavy with thick threatening clouds that hung low in the valley. Darkness enveloped them. The cattle were agitated, milling around instead of bedding down.

Rebel couldn't shake the anxiety and it was making her horse nervous. He pranced around, pulling on the bit and tossing his head. She glanced at Conner and noticed that he and Tucker were looking into the darkness very intently. She rode up next to him and whispered, "What is it?"

"They are out there watching us," he said softly. "They may be contemplating stealing our supplies and livestock. Maybe you should go get the brothers."

"I'm not leaving you out here alone. They will come to relieve us soon."

"If we have to fire our weapons, it will stampede the cattle. This is a dangerous situation," he said worriedly.

"Here comes our relief," she pointed.

Dylan and Warrick rode up to them and instantly knew something was wrong.

"Those men are out there watching us," Rebel informed them.

"Ride back and put the camp on alert, Rebel. Bring Darien back with you," Dylan said.

Rebel turned her horse and galloped back to camp. Darien was still sitting by the fire and she quickly informed him of the new situation.

"Wake up the men and let them know so they can guard the camp," he said. "I'll ride out to the herd. You may want to help them here."

Rebel woke up the men then mounted her horse to ride the perimeter of the camp. As she rode to the far side, she thought she caught a glimpse of movement about thirty yards from the supply wagon. She pulled out the colt and circled around moving toward the trees.

Suddenly, someone lassoed her with a rope, yanking

her off her horse. She gripped the colt tightly determined not to drop it as she was dragged behind a horse for several hundred yards.

Rebel waited for him to stop and as soon as the tension was out of the rope she raised the colt and fired.

"God damn it!" another man yelled through the darkness. "You just shot Willie. Fuck!"

She swung her weapon toward the voice but couldn't see anything. She crouched down realizing that they may not be able to see her either. Then she heard it, the faint whimper of a gagged woman.

"Shit!" she breathed as she slid out of the lasso and crawled toward a tree.

Conner was on edge as he scanned the darkness in front of him. Suddenly Tucker bolted toward the camp. He quickly followed, trusting the dog's instincts. Just outside of camp he heard a gunshot so he slid his horse to a stop and jumped off to follow dog on foot.

He froze and experienced an eerie Déjà vu when he heard a man say, "Where the fuck is she?"

He reached for his knife and silently crept toward the voice trying to catch any kind of movement.

Rebel silently crept to where she thought she heard the woman whimper and damn near tripped over her in the darkness. She crawled up close and peered into Aden's fearful eyes. She gave her a reassuring smile and quickly pulled out her knife and cut the ropes that bound her hands and mouth. She motioned for her to be silent and follow her.

Aden nodded and they moved forward, slinking through the darkness toward cover.

Suddenly a man wrapped his arm around Aden's neck from behind and growled, "Where do you think you are going?"

Rebel spun around and said, "Let her go!"

Conner froze again when he heard Rebel say, "Take me instead." He watched the man shove Aden away from him and reach for Rebel.

She smiled coldly into his eyes as she allowed him

grab her hair and jerk her head back then she turned and exploded with a punishing fist to his ribs. She followed quickly with a left uppercut in the chin that rattled his jaw and snapped his head back then unleashed another bomb back to his ribs.

Conner couldn't help feeling admiration when the man lost his grip on her and doubled over in pain. He walked up behind him and grabbed him by his hair pulling his head back. He put his knife to his throat and said, "Ladies, you are wanted back at the fire."

Rebel nodded and grabbed Aden's hand, leading her back to camp. She knew that Conner didn't want witnesses for what he had in mind.

She helped Aden sit down and said, "Shane, gather up the others somewhere you can protect them." Then she turned back to help Conner.

Conner let go of the man he was holding and watched him fall to the ground dead then turned to look for the others. He noticed Tucker stalking three men in the darkness still searching for Rebel. If he had his bow, this would have been easy. He was still nervous about firing his weapon and setting off the herd so he stalked toward them waiting for one of them to step away from the others.

It happened sooner than he had hoped for and he quickly stepped in behind him and sliced his blade across the man's throat then drug the body back into the darkness.

Once again, Rebel found herself watching Conner execute their attackers. She was just outside his line of sight and watched as he took out a second man. The third man suddenly realized that he was alone and panicked. He bolted straight toward Rebel.

She stepped out from behind the tree just as he raced past and slammed her fist into his face, knocking him cold.

Conner walked toward her shaking his head. "You just couldn't help yourself, could ya?"

She grinned and said, "No."

Conner reached down and yanked the man to his feet and shook him awake. They took him back to camp and tied him securely to the back of the wagon.

"Rebel, stay here and guard the camp and no more fighting. You boys come with me, the brothers may need our help," Conner ordered as he mounted his horse.

Rebel's eyes narrowed and a deep anger started boiling inside her as she watched them leave. How dare he order her to sit and stay? Let alone stop fighting. She glanced over at Aden who was clearly rattled. "Are you ok? God, did he hit you? I didn't see the bruise in the dark."

She nodded and said, "I thought I heard something so I stepped out of my tent and bam, fist in the face. Out cold. I don't know why you like to fight Rebel. It sure hurts. But I am really glad you can. Thank You."

Rebel smiled and turned to Ric. "Will you build up the fire? I'll just be right out here." She wanted light in the camp but wanted her eyes accustomed to the dark so she walked to her gilding and retrieved her rifle then paced in a circle around the camp. There were still ten men out there and she was very agitated.

Her anger with Conner grew with every step she took. She thought that they were over this whole thing. Why did he continue to think he could tell her what to do! Just as she completed her circle back to the other side of the fire, she saw someone slinking across the open ground a hundred yards from the camp. She crept forward and met the man in the darkness.

When he saw her, he stopped. "You're that crazy bitch who rode the horse off the cliff and killed half my men."

Realization hit her hard and she struggled to keep her focus in the midst of her surprise. These are the men that attacked Father McCaffee and his people.

"And you're the fucking prick I let get away, you murdering son of a bitch!" she angrily spat.

His face turned cold as he lifted his handgun to her chest.

She nodded smugly when he realized that hers was already poised at his.

They stared at each other for several seconds, both realizing that they would kill each other if either fired.

Rebel thought about what Conner had said and smiled obstinately. "Let's settle this old school," she said lifting an eyebrow in anticipation. "You up for a little hand to hand?"

He grinned at the challenge in her eyes and eagerly nodded in agreement. They both holstered their weapons and faced each other for the fight. Silently they stepped in a circle around each other patiently waiting for an opening.

Rebel grew bored and stepped in with a quick jab to his chin. He grinned again and returned the blow. They pummeled each other for many minutes. She could taste her blood and see his. They continued back and forth, neither of them overpowering the other.

'Finally,' Rebel thought, 'someone worth fighting.' She could sense that he was starting to wear down so she put a little more power behind her strikes.

His grin disappeared as she kept the pace, hitting him over and over in the face. He struggled to keep his guard arm up but every time it slipped, she pounded him. Angry and exhausted, he started to get sloppy and she was able to duck or block most of his punches. And still she kept hitting him.

After a few more minutes, he couldn't take anymore and lunged at her in desperation. She instantly slammed him to the ground then kicked him in the face. He screamed as her boot smashed his nose.

She hadn't heard Conner and the brothers ride up and was just about the pounce on him and beat him to a pulp when she heard Conner yell, "God damn it, Rebel!"

She stepped back and snarled, "What?"

He shook his head at her, astounded at the amount of blood that covered her face and hands then jumped when Dylan fired his weapon and looked down to see that the man had pulled his gun to shoot Rebel.

"Thanks, Dylan," she mumbled as she picked up her rifle and stomped back to camp, glaring at Conner as she strode passed him.

She walked to the fire and slumped angrily into a chair, crossing her arms over her chest in frustration.

Gabe stood up and silently went for the medical bag.

Conner stalked into the firelight and said, "I don't want you fighting anymore!"

"Too fucking bad," she growled.

"I mean it Rebel! I can't take it anymore."

"Don't take it then, Conner," she said in a deadly voice standing up to face him. "And while your not taking it, you can get your shit out of my tent!"

"You would choose fighting over me?" he asked incredulously.

"I will choose being able to choose over you," she stated angrily. "I'm glad you finally made your decision."

He scowled at her angrily then spun around and strode to his horse and galloped into the darkness.

Gabe sat the bag down and said softly, "Rebel, let me clean you up."

Rebel slumped back into her chair so Gabe could work on her face.

"I'm with Conner, I don't like it when you fight," Jade said quietly. "Grandma and grandpa hate it too."

"I know you guys don't like it but her fighting skills saved my life tonight," Aden pointed out still trying to calm down.

"Saved me back in Wyoming," Lynn added.

"Me too," Lauren said softly.

Jade looked at them and sat down, hanging her head. "Saved me in Iowa."

Rebel closed her eyes and didn't respond.

"Come on everyone, let's try to get some sleep. We have eliminated the threat and secured the camp," Darien said.

"We have eliminated the threat!" Warrick teased his brother. "What he means is that we killed those fuckers so they can't hurt you now."

"You forgot one," a voice said from behind the

wagon.

Rebel sat up in her chair.

Darien and Warrick looked at each other in surprise.

Dylan glanced at his sister and asked sarcastically, "Rebel, did you save that one to fight later?"

Everyone laughed when Rebel flipped him the bird.

"We'll just let him go when we leave," Darien said softly so the man couldn't hear him. "Who are these guys anyway?"

"They are what was left over from the mongrels that attacked Father McCaffee's people. They are murdering bastards!" Rebel said, her anger clear in her voice. "But the extra fifteen horses will help."

"I think I should stitch that gash on you eyebrow, Rebel, or it will leave a nasty scar," Gabe said.

"Fine," Rebel answered leaning back in her chair and closing her eyes again.

After Gabe was done, she said goodnight and climbed into her tent.

It wasn't dawn yet the next morning when Rebel woke up. She built a fire to make coffee, still angry about the events from the night before. She hadn't slept well and her patience ran out well before the coffee was ready. She kicked a rock with a scowl and glared at the pot.

"Good morning Rebel, kill anyone today?" Warrick teased her as he strolled to the fire.

"The day ain't over yet," she laughed. They had just talked about the movie 'City Slickers' before they left. She loved how Jack Palance played the tough cowboy guy.

She looked at her brother and said, "Why is it that I like to fight so much? Do you like to fight? You fight all the time. Is it because you like to or do you only fight when you have to?"

Warrick sat down and said seriously, "I must admit that I really enjoy a good fight." Then he grinned and said, "There ain't nothin quite like it."

Rebel nodded her head and started pacing.

"I only fight when I have to," Dylan said with a

wink and sat down with a huge grin.

"That's because it messes up your hair and wrinkles your shirt," Warrick laughed.

"Fuck you," he smiled.

"I realize that I am a woman and fighting isn't exactly a womanly thing but who gives a shit what the norm is. I know I don't."

"Do you enjoy fighting women as much?" Darien asked joining their conversation.

"No. I tried that and it's too easy," she replied.

"So it's the challenge that you like most."

"I guess. I haven't fought for awhile and I kind of missed it," she shrugged then started pacing again. "But, I don't go out looking for fights. They just seem to find me all the time. Last night, we both had our weapons drawn. We both realized that we would kill each other if we fired, so we compromised and both put our guns away. Isn't that a fight finding me?" she ranted. "I didn't go seek it out. It just happened."

The brothers looked at each other and nodded in agreement.

Warrick stood up and poured coffee into her cup then made the rounds with the pot.

She sipped the hot liquid barely able to hold still. "Ok, I admit that I'm a little abnormal. I watch football instead of chic flicks. I drive a truck instead of a cute little car. I prefer whiskey to wine. I fight instead of cry. I wear jeans instead of dresses. What is so wrong with that? Does that mean I am less of a woman?"

"Nothing is wrong with that, Rebel," Conner said stepping up to the fire and pouring coffee into his cup. "It's the reason I fell in love with you. And I can assure you that you are all woman."

Rebel eyed him suspiciously.

He slumped down in his chair and looked at her seriously. "I'm sorry. I know that it's not my place to tell you what to do. I let my fear for you override logic but you're right, who the hell am I to tell you what you can and can't do." He shook his head dejectedly.

She was surprised by his complete change of heart and said, "Why does it scare you so bad? I think I have proven that I can hold my own, so why are you so afraid for me?"

"Rebel, when I came up over that ridge and saw you fighting that huge man back in Wyoming, my heart just stopped. I still can't get it out of my head. He would have killed you and I would have had to watch it."

He stood up and paced the fire. "He almost did kill you, god damn it. Jesus, what if we hadn't been there."

"That's not fair Conner! You picked the one fight that I didn't choose to use as an example. I always measure the opponent and know well before we go to blows whether or not I will win. I knew I'd lose that fight before it started but you know as well as I do that I didn't have a choice in that one."

He shook his head solemnly and said, "I won't stop you again. You can fight whoever you want."

"Good, cause I think you and I need to go a round," she challenged, still angry.

He inhaled sharply in surprise and mumbled, "I didn't mean me. Why do you want to fight me?"

"Because it's the best way to learn. I've watched you fight and want to experience it firsthand. I made them fight me," she said pointing at her brothers.

They all nodded.

"Fine," he said. "Maybe someday we will find a gym and go a round then."

"I got a hundred bucks on Rebel!" Dylan said.

"I'll raise you a hundred," Warrick added.

Conner pretended that he was insulted and flipped them off.

The brothers laughed and stood up to saddle their horses.

Conner glanced at Rebel still unsure if she would accept his apology.

She looked back at him still not ready to forgive him. Suddenly she caught a glimpse of a flashing light and launched to her feet just as a meteorite slammed into the ground only a few miles away. "The cattle will stampede! Get to the horses!"

Conner jumped up and ran to his horse as Rebel whistled for Jake.

She panicked when she heard the cattle coming and looked up to see them heading straight for camp. "Mom! Get everyone on the wagon!" she yelled then swung onto Jake this time without a saddle or a lead rope. She pointed him toward the herd with her legs, thankful that he responded.

Conner was coming up around the front of the herd but she knew that one horse wouldn't make a difference so she fell in line behind him desperate to turn them away from camp.

The lead steer turned with them just in time for the body of the stampede to pass by without running over the tents.

Dirt and dust filled the air around them as she rode back to camp to saddle her horse so she could help round up the fifty head of livestock that were now scattered across a hundred acres.

Several hours later, they all gathered around the fire to eat.

"This little venture hasn't started out very well," Rebel grumbled as she sat down with her food. "I hope it isn't going to be like this the entire way."

"We might as well stay here tonight. None of us have gotten much sleep. Conner didn't sleep at all," Warrick said.

Rebel nodded and scowled as it suddenly started to rain.

Several days later, they crossed the continental divide and stopped to look down on the city of Butte. Every building in the city was flattened and it looked like a giant pile of lumber and debris had been dumped into the valley.

It had been raining constantly for days and the slow,

wet, cold ride had made everyone grumpy. Rebel was worried because she couldn't keep her eye on the volcano or look out for meteors with the heavy cloud cover.

"Let's camp up here, just off the Interstate," she called out. "I don't want to risk taking the herd down into the city because that pit was still toxic the last I read and it has spilled out of its banks," she said.

Everyone dismounted and stood their tents then gathered around the fire to eat.

"I'm sick of this rain!" Rebel complained. "I'm going to bed. Call me when it's my turn to ride the herd."

Everyone followed her lead and soon the camp grew quiet.

The next morning Rebel woke up to sunlight, alone in her tent. She quickly dressed and stepped outside. She walked to the fire where Darien and Dylan were drinking coffee." Why didn't you wake me up for my shift?"

"Conner wanted to let you sleep in. He mentioned that you haven't slept well lately. Are you ok?" Dylan asked.

"I'm fine," she said as she filled her cup and sat down beside him. "The god damned cloud cover gives me claustrophobia. I'm glad it has cleared off."

Ric handed her breakfast and said, "The brothers want to get moving, better eat."

"Thanks Ric," she said with a smile. "How are you holding up?"

"I'm good. I had to dig to find the hot chocolate cause Ty thinks he has to have coffee like Warrick," she laughed.

"It's so strange that he attached himself to Warrick of all people," Rebel laughed. "Where is he anyway?"

"He is on his own horse now, following Warrick around the herd."

"What? He is only four or five years old."

"I've seen pictures of you riding when you were two, Rebel. You shouldn't be surprised," Dylan said.

"That's true," she nodded.

"Well, let's get going. The ladies are all packed up and ready," Darien said.

The wagons rolled out and the brothers pushed the herd into a walk behind them. The cattle were getting used to following the wagons and were much easier to deal with lately.

They all looked sadly at the fallen structures as they picked their way down the interstate through the city.

"It is such a shame. This city has a really cool history and there used to be some fantastic historical buildings here. Makes you wonder if we shouldn't rebuild our structures out of stone like the ancients," Kira said.

"I'm going to go have a look around," Darien said. "It's possible that there are survivors here."

Rebel sighed and said, "God, I hope they are decent people if there are. I'm sick of only running into the bad ones."

"Will you stay with the wagon and help Uncle Neil and the boys protect the ladies just in case?" Darien asked her.

She nodded and watched the brothers ride back into the city.

That evening, the brothers hadn't caught up to them by the time they stopped to make camp. Rebel stood in the middle of the road looking back toward the city nervously.

"They will be fine, Rebel," Conner said walking up behind her. "Come on, let's get something to eat."

She followed him back to camp and sat down next to him by the fire. "What if they found people who need help?"

He looked at her sadly. "Rebel, I know I don't have to remind you, but we won't be able to save everyone. We simply can't stop. It would put all of us in danger."

She nodded and said, "I know, but if there are survivors and they don't find adequate shelter, they won't survive."

He smiled encouragingly, "The brothers will warn them. Try not to think about it."

Several hours later, the brothers rode into camp. Warrick dropped several bags on the ground and said, "I found the kid some better winter gear and I found you something Rebel."

She smiled in surprise and said, "What is it?"

He dismounted and handed her two pair of boxing gloves and headgear.

"It's the only way I will let you fight Conner. I doubt if we will run into a standing gym anywhere out here," he laughed. "I found a sporting goods store and dug through the debris."

"That's what took us so long," Dylan laughed.

"Thank you Warrick," she said. "So you didn't find any survivors?"

"No, if they are out there, they have more than likely found shelter in one of the mines," Darien said.

Rebel nodded and sadly looked back at the city silently praying for the thirty five thousand souls that once lived there.

Chapter 20

Two days later, their journey was halted once again when Dylan rode back to the wagon and said, "The road is demolished up ahead. The ground shifted so hard that the both lanes have dropped thirty feet. You guys wait here while we scout for a new path for the wagons."

"I'll go with you," Conner said as he waved Darien up from his post beside the herd.

An hour went by before they returned with smiles on their faces.

"What could possibly have happened to make you all so happy," Rebel asked.

"We found a fairly easy path for the wagons but better than that, we found some hot springs," Darien said. "It's just up the road a couple of miles. We will camp there tonight and get a bath."

Rebel helped them get the wagons through the rugged path then followed them to the once beautiful resort. Just like everything else they'd seen along the way, it was completely leveled.

"Over here," Warrick hollered. "This must have been the outside pool. The concrete is cracked, but the hot water is still flowing and it's pooling about three feet deep. Help me clear the debris."

Rebel helped the women set up their tents and Ric start dinner while the guys cleaned the pool.

"I didn't bring a swim suit," Jade complained.

"Just go in your unders," Kira laughed. "No one cares."

"After dinner, I'll take a shift on watch so the guys can soak," Rebel offered. "They have been behind the cattle the entire time."

Conner handed her dinner and said, "I'll go with you."

It was well after dark by the time Cayden, Shane and Danny rode out to relieve them. They rode back to camp and unsaddled the horses.

"Everyone has gone to bed. Let's go find the pool," Conner said with a grin. "I can't wait to feel hot water again."

She looked at him still angry and not ready to forgive him but followed him to the hot springs. She silently watched him undress. Her body responded with an unbridled jolt of lust at the sight of his tantalizing bare chest and masculine form. She shrugged off her anger and undressed then followed him into the water.

"God, its hotter that I thought it would be," she said.

"Not nearly as hot as you are," he said as he pulled her into his arms.

The next morning, Rebel was awakened by a violent earthquake. She quickly climbed out of her sleeping bag and pulled on her jeans. Conner was right behind her as she stumbled to the main fire where everyone was gathering.

"I knew the last few weeks of silence were just the calm before another storm!" she pouted. "Come on, the cattle will scatter."

They spent most of the day gathering the herd and rounding up the horses then quickly talked themselves into staying one more night. Everyone took turns in the pool then settled around the fire for dinner.

"So, Rebel, I've been wanting to ask your opinion about what we could expect in the next few months. The pole shift was bad but not really what I expected," Ric asked.

Rebel glanced around at the anxious faces of her family and friends. She hesitated for a moment then said, "I don't think its over yet. The continent may have moved a little when the poles shifted but I think the quakes were just all of the plates readjusting, sliding under each other. It was more than likely caused by the earth's reduction in speed. The planet hasn't reached its closest point yet and may very well still flip the earth on her ass."

Everyone sat in silence, contemplating the severity of the situation they were facing.

Rebel stood up and looked into the sky. "I hate

being the bearer of bad news. I hate looking into your eyes and telling you that we may not survive. I have tried to convince myself that we will live through this but you know, I don't know if we will. The volcano is going to erupt, probably all of them and I for one don't want to live to see an ice age."

She started pacing and continued ranting, "This has happened before and scientists believe that when it did, the human population was reduced to five thousand. Five thousand!"

Darien stood up and pulled out a bottle of whiskey and slumped back in his chair.

Rebel had to change the subject. She reached out her cup for Darien to fill it and said, "They think that the equator may end up in Alaska. It used to be there and it may very well settle there again."

"Well if it does we will be in the warmest part of the world. If we survive, you will have warm beachfront property in Idaho," Dylan said trying to lighten the mood.

She smiled at him and tried to accept the encouragement but couldn't shake the ominous feeling that rushed through her. She glanced around again and realized that they were all counting on her to supply the hope that they needed to continue on. She sat down and said, "Maybe Dylan is right and all those wishes of a warm beach will actually come true and we will live long enough to enjoy it."

"I'm sorry we look to you for the information, Rebel. We don't mean to put you on the spot. "Darien said softly. "But you're the only one who can give us an educated guess."

"I know, Darien. I just hope I'm wrong and this whole thing is done. Maybe we will just shake a little while the plates settle and go on with our lives."

He smiled and handed her the bottle of whiskey. "If not, you might as well die happy."

Everyone but Conner laughed with him. He had felt Rebel's agitation growing over the last few weeks and knew that she was on the verge of erupting just like the volcano.

He knew that she was still angry with him and there was intense tension between them. He watched her swig the whiskey from the bottle and couldn't help wondering what tonight would bring. She didn't drink often but when she did, she was very unpredictable.

She handed him the bottle and he shrugged, deciding to join her and get smashed.

"How much whiskey do you guys have anyway?" he asked suddenly curious.

Darien laughed and said, "When Rebel told Warrick to stock up on supplies, he bought cases of coffee and more cases of whiskey."

Warrick grinned and said, "I just packed the essentials."

Everyone roared with laughter.

Eventually everyone started drifting off to bed. Rebel and Conner were still passing the bottle around with the brothers and Ric and Gabe were chatting on the other side of the fire.

Rebel couldn't drink away the anxiety that gripped her soul so she stood up and started pacing in front of the fire. She turned to Conner and said, "Tell me more about this cave. You said it had running water and plenty of room."

Conner nodded and said, "Did I tell you that it's haunted?" He didn't believe in ghosts and if he had been sober, wouldn't have brought it up.

"Haunted? By what? What could possibly be haunting a cave?" she asked with a grin.

"Native American Ancestors. They protect it. Supposedly, it's a portal to another dimension," he smiled. "Lissa told me that she saw some kind of apparition in there. It warned her to prepare for disaster and promised to protect those who are worthy."

"Huh, what if we aren't worthy?"

"I don't know, she didn't say."

"So what's it like in Wilson? Did you spend much time out there?"

"Yes, I spent almost a year up there helping them

repair the lodge after a terrible fire and have been back several times."

"So you have friends there?" she asked suddenly curious about his past.

He nodded then grew nervously silent.

Rebel looked at him and her stomach lurched as she realized why he was suddenly looking away from her. "You have girl friends there?"

The brothers glanced at each other apprehensively. Rebel was not normally a jealous person but she was fully drunk and they knew that she harbored harsh emotions after everything she went through with Jade's dad.

Conner knew that a big can of whoop ass had just been opened and stammered a little when he said, "That was a long time ago, Rebel."

Rebel knew that she was drunk and irrational when jealousy exploded through her out of control. She took a deep breath and tried to force the image of him with another woman out of her head but it wouldn't fade. She grabbed the bottle and tried to drown it but still it infiltrated her mind.

Conner glanced nervously at the brothers who shrugged helplessly back at him. He looked back at Rebel and watched her grow more agitated with each ticking second.

She stood up and staggered toward the pool trying to regain some control of the unreasonable anger that flooded through her. She knew that he had a past. Why was it so hard to deal with all of a sudden? Probably because she was still angry with him and feeling a little insecure about their relationship. The images that her imagination created played over and over in her delirium until she was almost out of her mind.

"Fuck!" Conner said when she was out of hearing distance. "I stepped right into that one, didn't I?"

"She knows she's wrong to be jealous. I can tell she is trying to control it. She went through hell that year Jade's dad left and we knew she never got over it. But you're the first guy she's cared about since then so I have no idea how she will react. We can't help you brother," Dylan said.

Conner stood up and paced by the fire clearly upset. He turned to them and said, "God, I'm already on thin ice. What do I do?"

Warrick grinned and said, "Might be a good time to box. I know that is one thing that will make her feel better and maybe if we are here, she won't beat you half to death."

Conner smiled and said, "Thanks a lot."

"Come on, let's get away from camp so mom don't get upset. Jade is right, she hates it when Rebel fights," Dylan said.

Warrick grabbed the gloves and followed them to the cleared area by the pool. Ric and Gabe walked behind them apprehensively and found a seat to watch.

Warrick walked up to Rebel and traded her the bottle for the gloves without a word.

She glanced down at them and smiled a vicious, mindless smile.

Dylan saw it and turned to Conner, "Dude, she is going to kick your ass." Then he sat down by Ric and Gabe with a wide grin on his face.

Darien silently laced Conner's gloves knowing full well that he wouldn't hurt his sister and couldn't help feeling sorry for the man. He slapped him on the back and sat down by his brother.

Warrick secured her headgear and smiled, "Go get him."

Conner waited for her to turn around and said, "Rebel, I'm sorry. I know your upset but what can I possibly do?"

"Nothing, Conner. Nothin you can do. Its fine," she slurred then smashed her fist into his face.

He staggered back and wiped the blood from his lip, once again amazed at her strength. "God damn, you are going to kick my ass aren't you?"

She smiled wickedly again and slammed a powerful blow into his ribs.

He doubled over in pain and caught an uppercut in the jaw.

"Conner, man, you'd better fight back or Gabe here will be up all night trying to fix you," Warrick laughed.

Conner looked at them and sighed. "God, this is ridiculous. I can't fight …"

She cut off his words with a hammer to his mouth then spun around and kicked him in the side of the head.

"Fuck!" he yelled finally getting pissed off. He glared at her. She was serious about this. He didn't want to hurt her but standing here getting the shit beat out of him was not the best option.

She moved in again but he blocked her swing this time and swung back. She ducked his fist and slammed hers into his nose and smiled when she saw a fire light in his eyes. "You know, I have something of a beast inside me too. Let's let them out to play."

"You don't want the beast Rebel. Let's just have some fun here and be done," he said firmly and got the full force of her fist in his face again in answer.

Warrick laughed and gave Dylan a high five.

Conner struggled with his anger, sincerely afraid that he would hurt her if he unleashed. He was drunk and wasn't sure if he would be able to turn it off.

"Go ahead and fight, Conner. We won't let you hurt her," Darien assured him.

Conner relaxed a little. They would certainly be able to stop him if he lost it. He looked back at Rebel and decided that this would be a good opportunity to teach her a lesson. He raised his fists and circled around her.

She knew exactly what he was thinking when his demeanor suddenly changed. 'Lesson my ass, you fucker,' she thought as she gathered her focus and let the adrenaline flow through her. She waited for him to move, preferring to respond rather than attack.

He moved in with a swing but she ducked under it and swung her leg under him, knocking both of his out from under him. He crumpled to the ground and groaned as her boot slammed into his stomach. He lunged at her but she easily danced out of reach then stepped back in and pummeled him in the side of his head before he could get to his feet. He felt the beast move and focused on her face, trying to keep it at bay.

"I can do this all night Conner. Either you fight me or bleed."

'Teach her a lesson,' he thought again as he stood up and stepped in with a swing that impacted her head.

She intentionally let him hit her so that he would realize she wasn't going to break and could tell that he was still holding back when the blow didn't knock her on her ass. She fired a bomb that split his eye open and followed it with an elbow to his chin.

The beast was coming alive now that he was bleeding and he knew that he was going to loose control. And still she came at him, battering him over and over until his anger completely overrode his fear of hurting her. She stepped in with one more jab to his face and that was the last straw.

Rebel smiled as his eyes darkened, instantly sensing that he was finally ready to fight her. She allowed the picture of his beautiful body lying with another woman to wash through her mind, knowing full well that it would drive her to punish him. And it did.

If he thought she was strong before, he was shocked now. They clashed in battle, each of them landing pulverizing blows. She never tired as she responded to his every move and countered every swing. They brutalized each other as the minutes ticked by.

Suddenly, she unleashed with a powerhouse that damn near dropped him. He was so stunned by her power that he hesitated and she landed a second one that put him on his knees. Then she stepped up with a knee to his face and knocked him out cold.

Dylan stood up and said, "Ok Rebel, that's enough."

She stepped back angrily and yelled, "The headgear gave me an advantage. It's not fair!"

"I didn't make you wear it for you. I did it for him. I've seen him kill men with his fists and he would never have forgiven himself if he'd hurt you," Warrick said pointedly.

"I killed a man with my fist too!" she said with growing anger.

"I know Rebel," Warrick said softly, "but just trust me on this one."

Conner opened his eyes and groaned in pain.

"Good fight Conner. You were very noble," Darien teased.

"Noble my ass! I wasn't just letting her kick the shit out of me," he said still stunned that she had knocked him out. "Jesus Christ Rebel! How do you fight like that?"

Darien helped him to his feet and laughed. "We all wondered the same thing, believe me."

"Did she beat all of you?" he asked trying to gather his wits.

"Pretty much," Warrick smiled.

"They weren't fair fights!" Rebel yelled still unable to control her emotions. "You put me in padding so you can't hurt me and I know that you all hold back."

"Protected or not Rebel, you won this round," Conner stated still not believing it himself.

"Whatever!" she said throwing her gloves at his feet and stomping away. "It's not a fight if I don't bleed."

Darien grinned and Warrick just shook his head.

"Never satisfied!" Dylan said.

Gabe and Ric stood up, both very impressed by her skill.

"I don't mind as much when she's in head gear," Ric said.

"Goddamn, Conner, you are going to need several stitches," Gabe laughed.

"Oh, you think that's funny, huh?" he grinned. "Maybe you could stitch my pride back together too."

The brothers all laughed and followed their sister back to the fire.

Rebel picked up the bottle and slouched down in her chair ignoring Conner while Gabe stitched his face. She was still full of anger and even though it was unreasonable, it felt real.

She drank until she passed out.

The next morning, she woke up late. Everyone was eating breakfast when she walked to the fire desperate for a cup of coffee.

"Good morning, Rocky," Dylan said with a grin as he poured coffee into her cup.

"Morning," she growled glancing at Conner who was watching her silently. His face was black and blue, his lips were pulverized and he had stitches closing several cuts on his face.

She looked away and sat down feeling everyone watching her. "What?" she asked in exasperation.

"Nothin," Darien laughed.

"God, I'm hung over. Why did you guys let me drink so much?"

"We were afraid to take it away from you. We didnt want to look like Conner if you got pissed off," Warrick laughed.

"Fuck you guys," she said but couldn't help the grin that tugged on her lips.

"Come on, let's move out," Darien said. "We have a long day ahead."

Rebel rode silently for many miles thinking about how she had reacted to the thought of Conner's past. The jealousy had again taken her completely by surprise. Maybe she had over reacted because there was a possibility that she may have to endure being trapped in the same space with one of his 'friends'. Whatever the reason, it was completely irrelevant. She knew that he loved her and her irrational behavior last night was not cool. She owed him an apology. But at least she wasn't thinking about the end of the world.

Conner had intentionally kept his distance from Rebel ever since he had packed her to her tent last night after she passed out. He knew that she would have to deal with her jealousy in her own way. Still, he felt bad that it had come out like that. He glanced over at her and was once again amazed that she had knocked him out. Ya, he had been drunk, but she had been as well. He would have to deal with that in his own way.

Darien waved at them to stop for the night. "We should be near Helena by tomorrow night," he said as they dismounted.

Rebel unsaddled Jake and went to help Ric with dinner. She still didn't feel like talking to anyone so kept busy inside the cook camp.

Jade climbed inside and leaned against the counter. "What's wrong, mom?"

Rebel looked up at her and said, "I got drunk and over reacted to something Conner said. Then I made him fight me and now I'm not sure how to deal with it all."

"Just talk to him, he seems pretty understanding," she urged.

"Yes, he is. That's part of it I guess. I'm fairly surprised that he is dealing with me and my crap," she sighed. "Did you know that your mother is a little weird?"

Jade laughed and said teasingly, "Yes, I did know that. But really mom, you always told me to just be myself. You can't change for someone. Maybe you should take some of your own advice. I have a feeling he likes you just the way you are."

Rebel stopped and looked at her. "How did you get to be so smart?"

"Grandma," she laughed then gave her a hug. "Come on, come sit by the fire."

Dylan handed her coffee as she sat down and Ric followed with a plate of food. Conner handed Jade a plate and sat down beside them.

"So tell me Rebel, really, what is your secret. How is it you fight so well?" he asked seriously.

Rebel was quiet for a moment. She knew that this was Conner's way of asking her to put it all in the past. To forgive and forget. She stared into the fire, still not ready to look him in the eye and said, "There is no secret really. I'm stronger than most women and that always surprises my opponent. I'm much quicker than most men so it throws them off and if I can get them to bleed, they get pissed off and sloppy. Men can't handle being cut by a woman."

Conner nodded, silently waiting for her to continue.

"I use all of that to my advantage and it gives me an edge but because I'm not as strong as most men, I had to learn how to hit as hard as them. Most untrained men normally throw a punch using just the strength of his arm. I have to hit with the full strength of my entire body weight behind my arm. Follow through, like following through when you serve a volleyball or swing a baseball bat."

He nodded again.

"There are disadvantages though. I have to reset and prepare for each swing so I'm unable to repeat the blow very fast. And it takes a lot more effort to hit that way so I have to stay in extremely good shape and keep my muscles strong. If not then I can't hit with enough force to compete with a man. I am really good at sensing movement, which gives me a split second lead. But my biggest advantage is stamina. I can always outlast them. I've never fought anyone that could wear me out. I haven't been to a gym since all this shit came down though, and I can tell that I'm losing muscle strength."

"God, I'm glad I waited this long to fight you then," he smiled.

"We seriously thought about taking her underground and making some real money betting on her in the ring but mom wouldn't let us," Dylan laughed.

Kira raised her eyebrow at him and huffed.

"Mom, I'm sorry. I know you hate it when I fight," Rebel said. "I know you all do but god damn it, its my only bad habit. And up until recently, it was the only thing that would put this planet X shit out of my head."

Rebel glanced at Conner who actually blushed. "Its just who I am and I expect all of you to accept it. And just for the record, I know that it wasn't really fair of me to ask all of you to fight me. And with the exception of last night, I didn't do it so that I could prove myself or beat you. The whole point was to learn from you."

"You seriously wanted to hurt me, didn't you," Conner laughed.

Rebel finally looked into his eyes and couldn't help the grin when she said, "Yes."

Conner held her gaze for a moment, silently telling her that he loved her and that everything would be ok then leaned back and asked, "So what did you learn from them?"

"Well, Dylan prefers to fight using marshal arts. If you can keep him on his feet, he gets frustrated. He gives off little signals when he moves to take you to the ground, so I learned to watch for them and counter them. Warrick is just the opposite. He prefers to box so you can get under his skin if you take him down several times, then he becomes uncomfortable and gets upset. Darien is like a bull. He blows out of the chute in a ball of fury and goes right after you. If you can keep out of his way for a few minutes, he gets impatient. I basically use their emotions against them."

"It's amazing. I had no idea. And just for the record, I think you fight very well. I'm impressed," he said sincerely.

"You have to be impressed," Warrick teased. "She beat your ass."

Conner shook his head and smiled. "Yes she did. But how? How did you beat me, Rebel?"

"You beat yourself, Conner. You weren't fighting to win. You were just trying to teach me a lesson and when you failed, you lost the fight."

He looked at her surprised and asked, "How could you possibly have known what my intention was?"

Jade laughed this time and said, "Psychologist remember? Her specialty is body language. She knows what you're thinking by the way you move or look and always knows when you speak. I could never lie to her, she could always see right through it."

"That must have been terrible growing up," Conner laughed.

"It will be terrible for you too," she teased.

He smiled and said, "It already is."

They continued talking well into the evening then climbed into their tents.

The sun was just peeking over the mountain the next morning when Rebel stuck the pot of coffee on the fire.

She had come to terms with her irrational anger and was feeling much better now that she felt Conner would accept her for who she was. She looked over and watched him and Warrick work on a tire on the wagon.

"Did you see that planet this morning? It's getting close. I'm worried about these quakes, four or five a day is bad news," she said.

"I know," Conner said without looking up. "The cattle are constantly agitated. It makes moving pretty slow but I think we are on schedule. It will more than likely snow on us before we make it to Wilson though."

"Ya, we are pushing it with the weather. Montana is known for putting down feet of snow in the early winter. I hope it holds up for a couple more weeks."

Darien and Dylan rode in from their watch and tethered their horses then sat down to wait for the coffee.

"The roads are getting pretty bad. It seems like the mountains were damaged more than the valleys," Darien said. "I hope we don't have to go cross country."

"Rebel did you see the meteor shower last night? It looked like it was raining fire, I bet many of them hit the ground," Dylan said.

"It would be pretty ironic if we were hit by a large asteroid the same time the volcano went off," Darien added.

"It is very likely that the planet is being orbited by many large asteroids. The earth's gravity could pull them right into us," Rebel said pouring coffee into their cups. "It would also make sense that the impact tremor from an asteroid hitting us would set off the volcano. So it just might possibly happen that way."

Warrick walked over to the fire with Ty right on his heels. Ric handed Warrick his coffee cup and Ty his hot chocolate.

Rebel grinned when the little boy sat down and imitated Warrick sipping his coffee.

An hour later, the wagons rolled out followed closely by the herd of cattle. Conner paced his gilding next to Jake and Rebel noticed that he was unusually quiet.

"What's wrong? You seem on edge," she said.

"It's just one of those feelings. I think we are being followed. We are going to wait until we top that ridge then ride back and check it out."

"I'll go with you."

He looked at her protectively then choosing his words carefully said, "Your mom and Evie are sitting ducks up there, so are Marshall and Theron. We might want to have someone stick close to protect them."

Rebel smiled knowing full well what he was trying to ask her by not asking. She glanced at her mother then back at him and said, "Ya, I guess your right. They are pretty vulnerable."

He looked into her eyes and knew that she knew exactly what he was saying. "Thank you, Rebel."

She smiled again then turned to Jade and said, "Ride close to the wagon for the rest of the day, k?"

Jade nodded and trotted up next to her grandma so she could visit with her.

Rebel looked back at Conner and said, "Riding with these cattle and this amount supplies is like flashing gold under the nose of a thief. If there are desperate people out there, they will do anything to get their hands on them."

Conner nodded, unable to conceal his concern. "Make sure your weapons are ready."

They continued the slow trek up the mountain in silence. As soon as they topped the summit and started down the other side, Conner, Dylan and Darien rode back the way they had just came from to check out their new threat.

Warrick waved them to a stop near the bottom of a valley in front of a rock cliff.

"Set up the tents right next to the rock and pull the wagons in front of the tents." He turned to Shane and Cayden and said, "Push the herd down into that clearing by the creek. If something spooks them, they are less likely to run uphill."

Rebel knew he was nervous because he had intentionally sought a campsite that was easily protected. She watched him put Kira and Jade's tents in the middle and theirs on the outside. Then he unsaddled the horses and put all of the tack in front of the wagon as a shield.

Something was going on and Conner hadn't mentioned it. He had intentionally left something out and Rebel was determined to find out what it was. She unsaddled Jake and led him down to the creek to drink. She unsnapped his lead rope and watched him wander off to graze then strode back to the fire that Warrick had built on the pavement by the cook camp.

"Warrick, what is going on? You picked this spot for a reason. Does Conner know more than he told me?" she asked.

He looked around to make sure no one was within hearing distance and said, "There are a lot of them. He thinks they have been following us for several days and if they are going to make their move, it will most likely be now, before we get to Helena."

"God, why didn't he tell me?"

"Because he wanted to make sure first. That's what they are doing now. It may not be anything to worry about."

Rebel started pacing and mumbled, "He has been right before, every damn time in fact. What do you think?"

"I think we should circle the wagons and prepare our weapons but I don't think we should cause a panic just yet. Let's wait and see what they say when they get back."

Rebel nodded then left to set up her tent. She set out her stuff and as she was digging through her bag, she ran across her bulletproof vest and set it beside her rifle. Then she filled her coat pockets with extra clips and ammunition for her weapons. She tucked her jeans into her boots so that she could have easy access to her knife and slid her handguns into the holster.

Jade looked at her mother curiously as she approached the fire and knew that she was preparing for confrontation. She didn't say anything though recognizing that there was probably a reason why she hadn't said anything.

Rebel tried not to think about the impending attack

as she helped Ric and Warrick prepare their meal. She sat down beside Jade with her food and smiled encouragingly at her. "Keep your hand gun close and sleep in your clothes tonight, just in case."

Jade nodded and whispered, "What's going on?"

"I'll let you know as soon as I find out, k? They are checking it out right now. Don't worry, it may be nothing."

Jade nodded and silently ate her dinner.

Warrick, Shane and Cayden stood up to watch the herd so that the others could come in and eat.

"Rebel, turn on your radio and keep me updated," Warrick said as he left.

Conner, Darien and Dylan looked anxiously at the huge camp below them that must have housed almost a hundred men.

"Well, you were right," Dylan said. "Fuck! Where could they have come from?"

"It makes sense that any survivors would seek each other out and group together. Its possible that there are women and children with them," Darien added.

"Maybe they are just traveling to hunt and seek shelter," Dylan said hopefully.

But Conner's gut told him differently. He scanned the camp looking for signs that they were friendly. "I am going to get closer and see if I can hear anything. We need to know what their intentions are."

"We will try to cover you, but man, this is dangerous," Dylan breathed.

"I'll be silent. Just hang back so they don't see you," he said. "If anything happens, you leave me. I won't have you injured protecting me because that would be a death sentence to the others." He kicked his horse into a gallop toward the camp.

As he approached, he slowed to a walk and rode as close as he dared then dismounted and continued on foot. The camp was loud and boisterous telling him that it was mostly men. He crept toward one of the fires so he could hear what they were saying.

"Beef steak and women! It don't get better than that nowadays," one of the men said.

Conner clenched his fist angrily. The cattle and supplies weren't the only thing they were after. He focused on staying silent, hoping that they would give him some indication of when they planned to attack. He glanced around looking for weapons and saw that every man had a gun.

"Get some sleep!" a very rugged looking man said as he walked up to the fire. "We will strike just before dawn while they are asleep."

"Fuck!" Conner said under his breath as he turned back to his horse. He rode back to the brothers and said, "They are planning to hit us just before dawn. God, this is a strategic nightmare."

Darien nodded grimly as they started back toward their camp. "We need to get the women and children away from the wagons and cattle. Should we put them on horses so they can run if they have to or on foot so they can hide?"

"God, man, I don't know," Conner said nervously. "I'm going to go with mounted. Then if they get through this, they can continue on."

"I agree," Dylan said. "I'll have Warrick meet us so we can make a plan.

Rebel set up her chair beside the wagon just outside the light of the fire. She looked down at Tucker who hadn't left her side all night. "You feeling it too?" she asked him.

After awhile, she got up to pace around the camp. As she passed her tent, she stepped inside and put on the vest then swung her rifle over her shoulder. She continued tracing her path and ended up on the road staring blankly back up the summit.

The night was completely silent and the darkness that enveloped her was thick and heavy with tension. She couldn't help worrying that Conner and her brothers may have run into trouble. Suddenly, the radio crackled and Dylan's voice came across.

"Warrick, meet us at the top of the ridge."

Rebel turned and whistled for Jake then led him back to camp to retrieve her saddle. She knew that Shane and Cayden would stay with the cattle so she quietly rode a wide circle around camp while she waited impatiently for the guys to return. Finally, Tucker turned his attention up the road and wagged his tail.

She was pacing by the fire waiting for them to dismount and when she saw the alarm on their faces, her heart caught in her throat.

"Rebel, I want you to get the women and kids on horses. All of them, even Evie. Take them away from the camp and the road," Darien said.

"Evie's never been on a horse and neither dad or Theron can ride with their injuries. Why? What the hell is going on?"

"Rebel, there are roughly eighty men on their way to steal the supplies and cattle. And that isn't all they are after," Conner said then paused to let the implication of that sink in before he continued. "We have less than twenty men in this camp and may not be able to stop them. You will have to protect the women. You will have to take them to the cave if we fail here tonight."

Rebel's knees grew weak and she started trembling. He was telling her that they weren't going to survive this fight. She looked at her brother's solemn faces and realized that they planned on fighting to the death to save them but it wouldn't be enough.

"No. There has to be another way. We can run. We can all run," she said almost hysterical now.

"You just pointed out that some of them can't ride. They won't be able to keep up. Besides, we have to at least try to save the supplies or none of us will survive anyway. There is a small chance that they are short on ammo and we will pull this off," Darien soothed her.

"Well then I'm fighting with you. Mom can take the women."

"Rebel, come on, you know we are right. If we fall,

they will need you. You are their last defense."

She looked at her brother trying to regain control of her emotions. He was right and she knew it but she also knew that she would never be able to hide while they were being slaughtered. She spun around and stomped off to wake up the camp.

Conner watched her walk away praying that she would stay with the women but knew in his heart that she wouldn't. He hesitated for a second then ran after her and grabbed her into his arms. He bent down and kissed her then looked her in the eyes.

"Rebel, I love you. God, I can't believe how much I love you. I want to spend the rest of my life with you. Will you marry me?"

She looked up at him completely taken back by the urgency in his voice. She had never expected this from him. Especially now as they faced what could possibly be the end. She reached up and brushed his hair off his brow and said, "I love you too, Conner. Yes, I will marry you."

He sighed with relief and smiled as he took her hands in his. He looked down at them and was suddenly overtaken by how small they were. She was tough as nails but so small. He was determined to protect her.

She looked at him curiously.

He kissed her again and said, "Rebel, please, stay safe." Then he sadly turned to help saddle all of the horses.

An hour later, Rebel led the group of women and children through the fallen trees away from their camp. She glanced nervously at Evie who was barely staying astride. They had picked out the most gentle of the horses for her to ride but she was very upset.

Theron and Marshall decided to cover the men with their rifles. They took the three teenage boys with them and hobbled to their hiding place up on the ridge overlooking the camp.

Conner, Danny, the brothers and the cousins mounted their horses and rode back up the mountain to prepare the front line of their defense. They were hoping to reduce the number of assailants in a surprise attack then separate and hit them again from each side as they approached.

They dismounted and crouched behind a natural barrier beside the road. They didn't have to wait long. They heard the army of men approaching before they could see them. Darien signaled for them to ready their weapons and then fire as the men came into view.

Rebel jumped when the roar of gunfire sounded through the darkness. She glanced toward the summit but continued onward, still not satisfied that the women were far enough away. Suddenly, she came upon a huge opening in the mountain. It wasn't a cave but a massive overhang that had somehow withstood the earthquake. Upon closer inspection she realized that it was solid rock and waved at everyone to dismount.

"Tie the horses and hide in there," she said helping Evie down. "If you have a weapon, take position at the outer edge. Hopefully you won't have to use them but if this goes wrong, don't hesitate to kill those sons 'a bitches because they won't hesitate to kill you."

She looked at Jade and Kira and said, "I'm going to ride back down and stand guard. I'll call you on the radio and warn you if they are coming. You should be safe here."

Slowly she rode back down the mountain toward camp until she found a small ridge that offered her a good view of the valley. She peered into the darkness listening to the battle that raged up on the summit. Then silence. She knew that the men would reposition for a second attack and struggled with the decision to go help them. She looked back to where Jade and Kira were hiding and decided to wait a little longer.

The surprise attack had gone better than Darien had hoped for. All of his cousins were excellent shots so together they had significantly cut the number of men in front of them. He signaled for everyone to move to their next position and mounted his horse.

They split up and took position in the cover of brush on each side of the road where they would wait for the men to advance.

Conner reloaded his rifle and knelt down beside Warrick. "They may split up and send some of their men to flank us along the creek."

Warrick nodded and said, "Hopefully dad and Theron will be able to see them from above and send out a warning shot."

"Here they come," Cayden said looking toward the pavement. "I'll follow your lead."

Conner waited until the group of men was in between them then fired. Rifles exploded all around him sending more of their attackers to the ground.

The leader of the group kicked his horse into a run and raced past them followed closely by the rest of his army.

Conner and Warrick launched onto their horses in pursuit, firing into the body of men.

Theron and Marshall opened fire from their post on the ridge surprising the lead man into turning down into the valley. They rode right into the herd of cattle scattering them.

Rebel rode closer now confident that they were on the other side of the Interstate and well away from the women. She heard Conner and her brothers riding toward the camp to prepare a defense from there and decided to help them this time. She watched them dismount and slap their horses out of the way then take cover.

She scanned the valley, thankful for the small amount of predawn light that was now starting to dispel the darkness. From her position up on the hillside, she could see that the army of men were regrouping and realized that they were going to surround the camp and attack. She started downward but knew that she was too far away to make it in time.

The attack came in a rush and she watched in horror as fifty or so men circled around her family and friends with guns blazing. Her breath left her as three of her cousins fell to the ground. Shane took a bullet and Uncle Neil crumpled in a heap. Terror then rage filled her soul.

They were all going to be slaughtered right in front

of her eyes. She kicked Jake faster hoping that he could see well enough now to jump the logs in front of him without her guidance. She brought her rifle to her shoulder and started firing.

She traded the rifle for the colt as she neared a group of ten men in front of her. They turned in surprise as the big gilding plowed through them like a bowling ball, knocking them to the ground. She turned him around and emptied the clip, taking out eight of them then traded it for the .22 and put several rounds into the other two men who were trying to find cover.

Conner looked up and watched Rebel's big gilding level ten men in a full out run. His stomach tightened in fear knowing that she would be right in the middle of this fight now. His attention was quickly jerked back to the fight as bullets ripped past his head.

Rebel ducked Jake behind a tree and stuffed a fresh clip into each of her handguns then kicked him toward several men preparing to fire at her men. She raced past them shooting on the run.

Theron and Marshall had hobbled down the hill to help and took position behind a tree firing at a small group of men that were trying to sneak around the camp.

Rebel pulled Jake to a stop and scanned the brush for a target. She noticed that several men were creeping toward Marshall and Theron so she started toward them.

Conner glanced up at her and followed her gaze. The rugged leader and two other men were almost in range to fire on her dad and he held his breath as she rode at a walk up behind the unsuspecting men and fired. Two of the men dropped instantly but the leader spun around and shot her.

Conner launched to his feet and raced toward her as she crumpled off her horse. Then the leader turned on him and fired, hitting him in the thigh. He dropped to the ground then scrambled to his feet and hobbled as fast as he could toward her. But before he could get there, the guy picked Rebel up and threw her across Jake then mounted behind her. He waved at his men to follow and raced up the road with the remainder of his army right behind him.

Silence fell over the battlefield and Conner just stood in the middle of the road unable to believe what had just happened. He picked up her colt and stared after her in shock. The brothers rushed up behind him silently sharing his agony and Marshall hung his head in sadness.

Darien turned to Cayden and Danny and said," Take the women some food and bring Gabe and Ric back with you."

Conner suddenly jerked his head up looking at them hopefully then limped to Rebel's tent. He dug threw her bag and emerged excitedly.

"She was wearing the vest. I'm going after her! She won't survive long with them."

Darien stopped him from mounting the horse and said, "Hold up a minute. You need to stop the blood from pouring out of your leg or you won't make it a mile. We'll get you fixed up and go with you."

He looked down at his leg and nodded in agreement knowing that he was right.

By the time Gabe got to camp, Dylan had Shane propped up in front of the fire and had somewhat stopped the bleeding from the gunshot wound that had ripped through his ribs just under his arm. But Uncle Neil was injured badly and couldn't be moved. Theron was feverishly trying to slow his bleeding.

Gabe rushed to his side and went to work trying to help him stop the bleeding and assess his injuries. Finally, they had him somewhat stabilized so they turned to Shane.

"God," she said sadly. "You are so lucky Shane." She left him with Theron and walked over to Conner.

"Gabe, I'm going after Rebel so just do your best to keep me from bleeding out."

She looked up at him and nodded, knowing that there would be no arguing with him on this one.

The brothers were mounted and waiting when he hobbled to his horse and swung on.

Darien turned to Cayden and said, "See what you

can do about gathering the herd but the women and injured are the top priority. Keep your weapons ready in case some of them come back. Dad and Theron will help you guard camp."

Cayden nodded and sat down protectively next to Shane and watched them ride away.

Chapter 21

Rebel once again became conscious being dragged between two men who propped her up against a tree stump then walked away. She kept her eyes closed and listened to what was obviously men preparing fires in a camp.

Her shoulder was on fire from the impact of the bullet striking her vest. Thank god it was her left side so she still had full use of her shooting arm.

She opened her eyes slightly and looked around at her kidnappers. There were roughly thirty of them and she could tell that they were very angry. They had just lost over half of their company and she could hear them talking about revenge.

They would probably take most of their anger out on her and she knew that she was in danger. She thought about Conner and her brothers and fear ripped through her at the thought that they would come after her and probably be killed trying to save her.

The rugged leader walked up to her and kicked her in the leg. "Wake up!" he yelled.

She glared up at him angrily.

He reached down and yanked her to her feet. "Where are the other women?" he growled.

"As if I would tell you," she ground out.

He backhanded her across the face and she landed hard on her ass.

"Don't worry. We will find them after we finish off the men."

Rebel climbed to her feet in front of him with her fists clenched. He sneered at her and she couldn't help herself, she slammed her fist right into his nose, knocking the sneer of his lips and sending him staggering back several steps.

The men around them erupted in movement, murmuring in astonishment.

"You little bitch!" he snarled unable to hide his surprise then smiled at his men who were waiting for his response. "Don't worry. I like it rough. We are going to get along just fine."

Rebel's gut wrenched at the thought and stepped in again with every ounce of her body weight behind her fist and smashed it into his jaw, knocking him cold.

All of the men surrounded her and she felt her confidence crumble in the face of so many opponents. She was certain that she wouldn't survive the day.

Two of the men grabbed her and drug her to a tree and tied her hands around it. "This will do just fine," one of them said into her ear with a menacing smile. "The boss will want to finish this."

It took a moment after the men stepped back to their boss for Rebel to come to grips with the wave of claustrophobia that always overtook her when her hands were tied. She closed her eyes tight and focused on breathing until she was able to think rationally. She lifted up her boot and dug out her knife. She sliced through the rope just as the bloody, rugged leader walked up behind her.

"So, you think your pretty tough huh? Well, let's just see about that."

She spun around swinging the blade at this throat but his reflexes were better than she expected for such a large man and the knife sliced a gaping hole across the top of his shoulder.

He looked down at his wound angrily and lunged at her. She stepped sideways and hammered her fist down into the side of his head, the impact combined with his momentum sending him sprawling in the dirt. She slammed her boot into his gut then stepped back to recover.

The men circled around them again as the rugged leader slowly climbed to his feet. He looked at his men again somewhat embarrassed then quickly replaced the emotion with a grin and said, "I think she wants to fight." He looked her up and down and said, "I will consider it foreplay."

The men all cheered their encouragement.

Rebel knew that even if she beat the big man, she would still have to face thirty more. She watched him turn to her and quickly decided that she didn't care. She tightened her grip on the knife and swung her fist again, this time breaking his nose before he could even raise his arm to block her.

One of the other men moved in to intercept, but the big man said, "No! She is mine! I will break her. Then I'm going to kill her." He wiped the blood from his face and raised his fists.

Conner and the brothers carefully picked their way toward the men who had kidnapped Rebel, staying completely out of sight. They dismounted and hid the horses well out of hearing distance and quickly moved toward their camp.

"God damn it. Here we go again," Conner said when he looked through the circle of men and saw Rebel pounding the big rugged man.

"Jesus, there are thirty of them. We need to take them out before they all turn on her," Dylan said.

"If it was dark, I could go in and take them out one at a time," Conner mumbled then added, "I can do it in daylight, it will just take more time." He pulled out his bow then turned to the brothers and said, "I will go down and take out as many as I can from behind without being seen while she has their attention. You guys get in position to cover us with the rifles."

The brothers looked at each other for a moment then nodded in agreement.

"Don't fire unless you absolutely have to. Give me some time so I can reduce their numbers," he said then turned toward the camp.

They watched him with apprehension as he ghosted in and out of the trees just outside the camp.

With masterful precision, Conner killed several men with arrows then crouched down as a man walked his way. He stood up behind him and in one motion put his hand over his mouth and his knife across his throat. He drug the body back into the brush and moved to his next target.

Rebel scowled at the big man as he circled her. "You

pathetic pig. I've already won this fight," she said to antagonize him.

"This fight hasn't even started yet," he said back.

"Thirty against one. That tells me you have no confidence in your ability."

"They won't touch you. Will you?" he asked his men without taking his eyes off of her.

They all said no.

"Good," she said and moved in quickly with a bomb that bashed in his already broken nose. She followed with a spinning elbow that opened a gash above his eye sending more blood down his face. She danced away with a smile and said, "Don't make this too easy or I'll get bored."

The man was absolutely astonished and struggled with himself, trying to decide if he should have his men kill her right now.

She read his mind and said, "You fucking chicken shit! Need your friends to protect you from a woman?"

He growled and lunged at her, now so angry that he was fighting blind.

She spun around and pounded her boot into his temple knocking him flat again. Then before he could stand up, she plowed him in the side of the head with her fist.

Conner watched the circle of men move in toward her and had to fight himself to stay back in the shadows.

Dylan put his finger on the trigger of his rifle, holding his breath.

"Is she fucking toying with him or what?" Warrick asked apprehensively.

Rebel felt the anxious group ease forward as their boss went down again. She stepped back and said, "Ok, ok. I'll let him get up."

They eased back and curiously watched her allow their boss some space.

Conner continued to pick off the stragglers as the main group of men focused on the fight.

Rebel waited patiently as the big man climbed again to his feet. "Are you ready this time?" she said to him. "Do you need a drink or maybe a hug from your mommy?"

He growled and pulled his gun on her. "Fuck no! All I need is this."

Rebel noticed Conner out of the corner of her eye and knew that the brothers were out there with their weapons aimed. She wanted to keep the men's attention on her and off Conner so she said, "Don't you do it, Billy." She looked at the men and said, "You're all little Billy bastards." Then she laughed at herself thinking of her brother. 'Young Guns II' was another of his favorite movies.

The man in front of her paused and tilted his head curiously at her statement.

"Don't you watch movies?" she asked then stepped back trying to keep their attention on her. "I'm truly disappointed. I can't believe that you can't finish this fight. I thought you would be a worthy opponent. Don't you want to at least bruise my face before you shoot me?"

She looked at the group of men watching her very closely. "You will follow a leader that can't even make me bleed? He outweighs me by over a hundred pounds!" She knew that the men were disappointed and it would be easy to turn them against each other.

The big guy looked around, instinctively knowing that his men were looking down on him.

"Come on, give it one more shot. I'll go easy on you this time," she encouraged, trying to find an advantage.

The men all nodded their encouragement.

The big man looked around realizing that he was loosing their respect and holstered his gun. He raised his fists angrily, knowing that he had no choice if he wanted to save face.

Rebel smiled and thought about the movie again. "You just killed yourself," she said then she stepped in and sliced her blade cleanly across his throat so fast that his men didn't even realize what had happened.

The big man looked at her in horror as he tried to hold back the flood of blood that spilled down his chest. She put her hand on his gun and it slid easily out of his holster as he sank to the ground. She turned on his men and almost smiled as they looked back at her in surprise.

"Here we go!" Dylan said watching her swing the weapon on the men.

The brothers opened fire the second Rebel pulled the trigger.

Conner fired from behind them and the men all dropped before the big man was dead.

Rebel looked around and breathed a sigh of relief. She looked at Conner who stepped up beside her and wrapped her in his arms.

"I almost died when he shot you. Thank god you put on the vest."

She nodded and whispered, "I'm sorry, I know how bad that image hurts."

He held her for a moment then stepped back and handed her the colt. "Good fight. I don't think he even touched you did he?"

"No, but that's usually how it is with bullies. He didn't want to fight but had to just to save face. What a bastard."

The brothers rode into the camp and dismounted giving their sister a hug.

"This could have been bad Rebel," Dylan said. "Maybe there is a God."

Rebel looked around at the massacre and said sadly, "If there is, I'm going straight to hell."

"Take Conner back to camp before he bleeds to death. Send Cayden to get the women. We are going to gather up their horses," Warrick said.

Rebel nodded and climbed on her horse then followed Conner toward the pavement. She had intentionally put her injured family out of her mind until now but had to ask. "Conner, I seen our guys fall." She hesitated, unable get the entire question out.

"Shane took a bad one but he will survive. Uncle Neil is critical and I'm sorry to say that two of your cousins and three of their friends didn't make it," he said softly. "But admittedly, that's better than I expected."

Rebel nodded as tears filled her eyes and they rode the rest of the way in silence. She dismounted by the fire and instantly went to her uncle's side. He smiled up at her weakly and squeezed her hand.

She turned to Cayden and said, "Its safe now, go get them. Keep a close eye on Evie. After dinner we will all attend the funeral."

Two days later, Gabe finally gave in to uncle Neil who insisted that they move on. They made a spot for him inside the cook camp and Shane climbed onto the bench between Marshall and Theron. Conner insisted on riding and actually growled at Gabe when she objected.

Slowly they trekked onward until the once beautiful city of Helena emerged in front of them.

Darien rode up next to wagon and said, "I want to camp on the outskirts tonight and ride through the city tomorrow."

It started snowing as they were eating dinner and didn't stop all night.

Rebel climbed out of her tent the next morning with a scowl. "Winter is here I guess."

Jade grinned at Conner and said, "I told you."

"Told him what?" she asked as she poured her coffee.

"That you hate the snow and cold," Jade said.

"Yes I do. When this shit is over, I don't care where the beach ends up, I will be there."

"Let's move out," Darien yelled. "We are going to ride ahead and watch for people. Rebel, I will need you back at the herd."

She nodded and stood to saddle Jake.

That afternoon, they were past the city. The brothers went back to check it out.

Conner was riding on the right side of the cattle and Danny was on the left.

Cayden rode up to him from the back and said, "Rebel disappeared. She was back there a few minutes ago but now she's gone.

Conner looked behind them wondering where she would have gone. "Thanks Cayden, I'll go see if I can find her."

Rebel was distracted as she rode behind the slow moving herd, thinking of all of the death that she had been responsible for. She shuttered with regret and wondered how many people had actually survived the pole shift. Suddenly, Jake started dancing underneath her and pulling on the bit. He suddenly jumped sideways as a huge grizzly bear stepped out of the brush beside her trying to catch one of foals. She recovered her balance and grabbed her rifle, pulling it to her shoulder.

The bear stood up on his haunches and roared, spooking Jake again just as she pulled off the shot. The bullet slammed the bear in the shoulder as he lunged at her horse, swiping her off of him with a powerful blow.

Conner rode to the back of the herd and stopped, looking into the brush, listening. A rifle shot rang out in front of him so he kicked his gilding and raced through the thick downfall toward the sound.

Rebel knew that she couldn't take down the eight hundred pound, pissed off monster in front of her. She pulled out her handgun and fired at him but another swing impacted her shoulder, sending the weapon flying out of her reach.

She climbed to her feet with her knife in her hand, trying to keep out the reach of his massive front paws but he was injured, pissed off and very fast. There was no way of outrunning him and she knew that it would be almost impossible to kill him with a blade.

Conner rode into a clearing and paled when he saw Rebel a half mile away, facing off with a huge grizzly. Jake was bleeding and Rebel's shoulder was ripped open telling him that the beast had knocked her off her horse.

The bear had several deep gashes across his face from her knife and he could see a bullet hole in his shoulder but the animal wasn't going down.

He pulled up his rifle and took aim but hesitated as

she moved in toward it with another swipe of her knife. "Move out of the way, God damn it!" he yelled but knew she wouldn't hear him.

The bear stood up on his hind legs, towering over her with a heart-stopping roar. She quickly slid between his paws and stabbed her knife into his chest then jumped back out of his reach. He roared again and swung his big paw at her again, knocking her flat.

She tried to scramble to her feet but he came down right on top of her and grabbed her shoulder in his huge mouth and wrapped his 7" claws around her torso. She almost panicked when she felt his long teeth sink deep into her flesh but forced herself to focus and plunged her knife into his neck over and over.

The animal growled and was about to rip her shoulder apart when she faintly heard a gunshot then felt the weight of the animal sink onto her almost smothering her. She struggled to get out from under the beast, instantly threatened by a wave of claustiphobia. Suddenly two big arms wrapped around her and pull her out.

"Rebel! My god. Are you ok?" Conner said worriedly looking her over.

She nodded and looked down at the huge grizzly bear. "He was trying to get one of the foals."

"Will you ever stop scaring me to death?" he said hangin his head. "You are going to make me lose my mind."

She smiled up at him and said, "Conner, I warned you that I wasn't relationship material."

He just shook his head and hugged her tightly. "Go back to camp and have Gabe check your wounds. I'll find your weapons."

Rebel rode into camp and everyone jumped to their feet.

"My god Rebel!" Kira yelled helping her to a chair. "Gabe, bring the bag! What happened?"

"Grizzly. He just came out of nowhere and knocked me off the horse," she explained. "Conner shot him."

"Ya, but not before she damn near killed him with the knife," Conner said walking up. "I'm always late saving you."

Rebel laughed and said, "You were just in time Conner."

Gabe knelt down and once again started stitching her wounds.

Later that evening Rebel sat up by the fire until the brothers returned. They were pissed to find out that she was attacked and they weren't there to help.

"I'm fine you guys. You can't be by my side every minute," she said impatiently. "Damn it, it could have been anyone."

Dylan sighed and changed the subject. "We didn't see anyone in the city."

"There has to be survivors somewhere, doesn't there? Is everyone dead?" she asked sadly.

"I'm sure that they have found shelter Rebel. People survived. It's a big world."

She nodded and stood to go to her tent. "Good night."

Two days later, they reached wolf creek and turned off the freeway onto the highway going north. It was now snowing every day and the earthquakes that rattled the ground beneath them were growing in number.

"We are almost there," Conner said as he poured coffee into Rebel's cup. "Just a few more days or so. Rebel, I think I should ride ahead to Wilson and prepare a place for the livestock. I should give them a heads up and let them know we are coming."

Rebel looked at him over her cup, trying to hide the sudden jolt in her stomach. "Are you sure that's necessary. It may be dangerous for you to ride alone."

"I was going to ask if you think I should take some of the others with me? Only those who can ride fast and Jade if you would entrust her to me."

She stared deep in his eyes and said, "Of course I would."

He smiled. "Theron said he would drive the cook

camp with Evie if Kira would like to go. I hear she is quite a horsewoman."

"Yes, she is."

"Rebel, I would ask you to go but I already know the answer."

She looked away and nodded the answer to the question hidden in the statement. She wouldn't leave her brothers with fifty head of cattle and over a hundred head of horses to deal with let alone Shane and Uncle Neil.

He sighed and said, "I'll let everyone know at dinner."

Rebel stood up and silently went to help Ric prepare their food. Everyone gathered around the fire and she sat down beside Jade to eat.

Conner sat down and said to everyone, "I have decided to ride ahead to Wilson. I will take some of you with me but only if you can commit to riding fast."

Jade looked at Rebel curiously.

"You and grandma might as well go, Jade," she said. "You will be off the trail in two days and safe in the cave."

Kira looked at Evie apprehensively.

"Oh Kira, go with Jade. Theron said he would drive the team and keep me company. I'm not riding another damn horse if I have to dig my own grave," Evie threatened. "Besides, I won't leave Neil."

Everyone began talking excitedly.

"I'm staying," Gabe said. "I won't leave Uncle Neil either and Shane needs me as well."

"I'm staying too," Ric said. "But I think one of the boys should go with you to help protect them. You are injured Conner."

Lynn and Jade looked at Danny and Cayden hopefully.

Conner laughed and said, "I'll take Cayden and Danny if you can do without them."

"I'll take one of their shifts behind the cattle," Rebel offered.

"I will to if you show me how," Ric said laughing.

Darien looked at her with a smile and said, "We will

do just fine. Take them with you. Now boys, if anything happens, get him his bow quick then hide with the girls."

Everyone roared with laughter again.

Conner rolled his eyes with a grin and said, "We will leave in the morning. Like Rebel said, you should be inside the cave in two days if we ride hard so get a good night's sleep."

After they had cleaned up dinner, Ric and Rebel helped Kira and Jade prepare their cooking gear and food supplies to be loaded onto two pack horses. Gabe made them a nice first aid kit and Warrick made sure they were armed and had extra ammo.

Rebel sat down by the fire, satisfied that they had everything they needed for their journey. She looked at Conner and said, "What if you are attacked or something."

"We will be fine Rebel. I'll take good care of them."

"I know but I'll still worry."

"Come on, let's go spend some time together before I leave," he said and stood up leading her to their tent.

The next morning she hugged Jade and Kira and watched as half their group rode ahead then turned her horse to help get the cattle on the move.

Ric followed her and said, "I've never worked cattle before. I'm fairly nervous. Those two bulls look pretty mean."

Rebel laughed and said, "They really aren't as mean as they look. These guys are pretty trail worthy now. The first few days were terrible. Mostly we just keep the stragglers moving and make sure that if they are spooked, they don't break to the sides."

Ric nodded.

"You're riding one of the better horses so trust him and give him his head. He is very cow savvy and will do most of the work for you," she added. "I'm really glad you stayed Ric."

She smiled and said, "Me too."

It started snowing and the large flakes started piling up fast as they trudged up the road.

Two days later, Conner led the group through the little town of Wilson and up the mountain along a winding road. They were riding around a sharp curve in the road when he suddenly felt a strange sensation that made the hair on the back of his neck stand up. He glanced around and noticed that the wind was swirling just off the road ahead of them. He turned his head to watch as they passed by.

He shrugged it off as weird and continued on to Lissa's lodge. He looked at the once beautiful cabin, sadly remembering the amount of work his brother and sister in law had put into it. It looked like they had reconstructed a huge room off of one of the wings that had smoke coming out of a hole in the roof.

"Hello," he hollered assuming that they were inside the room.

Gage ran out and yelled, "Uncle Conner, it's so good to see you."

"I hope you don't mind that I brought you some company," he smiled as he dismounted and shook hands with his nephew. "This is Kira and Jade. Ladies, my nephew, Gage."

He smiled at them then looked at his uncle. "Are you kidding? You know how mom is. The more the merrier."

Lissa came up to them and hugged her brother in law affectionately. "Conner, how have you been? I've thought of you every day and hoped you were ok," she said then stepped back to look at him. "My god, I forgot how much you look like your brother."

"Why thank you ma'am," he said and hugged her again.

"Come on, get everyone inside. Gage, help them with the horses and gear."

"Lissa, I have more people coming. They are bringing fifty head of cattle and many horses. I don't mean to barge in on you but we think that the volcano is going to erupt soon and I remembered your letter about the cave. I didn't know where else to go," he said softly.

"I would have been angry if you hadn't come. They are all welcome. So come, introduce me to your friends then tell me more about the volcano," she said taking his arm.

He smiled and turned to Kira waving at her to follow.

Lissa led them into the large room where the huge fire was burning and thirty or so people were sitting around it.

"Please sit and have some coffee. It looks like you better get off that leg," she said glancing down at the blood on his thigh. She turned to the large group of people. "This is Rob's brother, Conner, if you don't know him already."

Conner smiled and shook hands with Dallas, the sheriff and his nephew's friends then said, "Rebel is on her way but this is her mother Kira and her daughter Jade." He continued with the introductions and turned back to Lissa who was grinning.

"What?"

"I just can't wait to meet the woman who would tolerate you, Conner," she laughed.

Jade laughed too and said, "Its an even match I think cause I didn't think my mom would meet anyone that would tolerate her either."

Everyone laughed feeling completely at home and sat around the fire talking well into the night.

The next day, Conner and the boys helped Gage and his friends repair the fence around the resort for the incoming livestock.

Kira and Lissa spent the day sharing stories about their families and talking about Rebel and Conner. That evening, though, the conversation turned to what Rebel thought was going to happen in the coming months.

"That's why we brought all of our supplies and the livestock. It's possible that we may have to spend a lot of time in this cave," Conner said.

"So you think that the volcano will go off and we will enter a volcanic winter that could last several years possibly followed by an ice age?" she said worriedly. "And you think that we can survive that in this cave?"

"Yes, we do. But the worst part is the possibility that the earth could be tipped over. It will be much worse than what has already happened. She isn't sure that it will happen, but if it does, it will be catastrophic."

"Well then, I am grateful that you are here to help us," she said. "When can we expect all of this to happen?"

"Any day. I can't believe it hasn't happened already."

Lissa glanced at Kira then looked back at Conner. "As soon as your people get here, we will go into the cave."

He nodded and sipped on his coffee silently watching the fire.

The next morning, he walked outside and stood looking down the lane that led to Wilson. He missed sleeping next to Rebel, missed watching her drink her coffee by the fire. He missed everything about her.

Lissa smiled as she walked up behind him. "You really fell for her didn't you?"

He nodded and said, "I've never loved like this before. I never really understood it. I mean sure, I've loved, but never on this level."

Lissa nodded. "I'm glad you got to experience it Conner. It's a wonderful thing."

"I'm sorry, Lissa," he said sadly. "I am truly sorry that you have to live without the love of your life. Now that I really know what it means, my heart aches for you."

She smiled up at him and said, "Don't hurt for me Conner. We loved a lifetime's worth before he died. I'll see him again."

He nodded and said, "I'm going to get her. Will you let Kira and Jade know?"

"Yes, be careful," she said and smiled again as he raced to the corral to get his horse.

Rebel cursed the cold as she climbed into her sleeping bag alone again. She thought about Conner and was amazed at how much she missed him. Never in her wildest dreams would she have believed that she could fall so deeply in love with someone. She drifted off to sleep dreaming that he was beside her.

The brothers were still sitting by the fire when Tucker suddenly ran into camp excitedly. Darien stood up curiously and smiled when Conner walked up behind him.

"Good to see you. Everyone settled in at Wilson?" Dylan asked.

"Yes, Lissa welcomed us openly and we have readied the pasture for the livestock," he said. "I thought I'd come back and help you bring in the herd."

"Sure ya did," Warrick laughed. "I'm thinking that you came back for some other reason."

Conner almost blushed when he said, "I'm going to go find that reason."

The brothers laughed as he walked to Rebel's tent.

He quickly undressed and climbed under the sleeping bag taking her into his arms.

She woke up completely surprised and wrapped her arms around him. "I missed you."

"I missed you too."

The next morning, they strolled happily to the fire and sat down sipping on their coffee.

Ric smiled and said, "Nice to see you, Conner."

Gabe laughed and waved as she walked by to check on Uncle Neil.

"So, you couldn't wait one more day to see her?" Dylan teased.

"That's when you know you're addicted," Warrick laughed using Rebel's own words. "

"Funny, Warrick," she smiled but her smile suddenly faded as another massive cloud of steam rose above the horizon. She slowly stood up and started trembling as the plume wafted into the air high above the mountain.

Conner followed her gaze to the billowing cloud that drifted high into the atmosphere.

She shook her head and said, "We may not make it in time. You should have stayed at the cave."

"No, I belong right here with you."

"We need to hurry."

The camp erupted in activity as they prepared to leave.

"Don't worry Rebel," Conner encouraged. "We'll make it."

They mounted and rode back to the cattle urgently pushing them onto the road.

"Thank god you took mom and Jade to Wilson," Rebel said as they rode behind the herd. "At least they will be safe."

That evening, Conner waved everyone to a stop and said, "Let's camp here for the night. Wilson is right over there."

Rebel looked around and from their vantage point could see the volcano was still erupting steam and ash. "Let's get something to eat and move out early in the morning."

Snow started falling in the middle of the night and piled up, growing deeper with each hour. Rebel was out of bed before the sun and was pacing the fire when Conner climbed out of the tent.

"I can't watch the volcano with this cloud cover," she said impatiently.

Conner pulled her down on his lap and kissed her. "I love you and if I died tomorrow, I will have died the happiest that I have ever been."

"You love me even though I'm always cranky? And even after I beat you up? And even though all I think about is the end of the world?" she teased.

"Yes, all those reasons and many more."

She smiled and said, "I love you too Conner, now get me some coffee."

He laughed and tossed her onto her own chair then stood up to fill her coffee cup. He sat back down beside her and held up her lion claw necklace that now held the bear's claws in between them.

She smiled and took it from him admiring his work. "I love it. Thank you."

"It's a warriors trophy," he smiled then shook his

head. "My little spit fire."

She wrapped her arms around him and kissed him.

Soon they were back on the road, riding through many inches of snow.

That afternoon, Conner once again led his party through the little town of Wilson and up the winding road to the Lodge. Suddenly he felt the same sensation that he felt the last time he had ridden around this curve. He looked apprehensively at the side of the road and inhaled sharply when the wind started swirling again.

"What's wrong?" Rebel asked.

"Nothing. Nothing's wrong," he said turning in his saddle to watch the phenomenon.

She followed his gaze but couldn't tell what he was looking at. When he turned back to her his face was pale.

"You look like you seen a ghost, Conner. What was it?"

He looked at her sharply then shrugged. "I don't know. I thought I heard something."

Rebel knew that he wasn't telling her the truth. Something was bothering him but she let it go for now.

They rode up the lane and into the clearing in front of the ruins of the once beautiful lodge. Conner waved Theron and Marshall toward the newly rebuilt room.

Cayden and Danny ran out the door and waved the livestock toward the gate of the pasture and Gage rushed over to help Shane off the wagon.

Conner smiled fondly at his sister in law when she stepped up next to him expectantly. "Lissa, this is Rebel."

Rebel laughed when she passed up her hand and wrapped her in a welcoming hug instead.

"It's so nice to meet you. I just couldn't wait."

"Nice to meet you too," Rebel said then turned to introduce the rest of their group.

Conner and Darien helped Uncle Neil inside onto a cot that Lissa had prepared for him. Gabe fussed over his injuries for several minutes then sat down beside Rebel and Lissa by the fire.

"Rebel, I think we should remove the stitches on your face so that we won't have to worry about it later. Conner's too," Gabe said.

"Good idea, Gabe."

Lissa watched as Gabe carefully removed the sutures and asked, "Rebel, do you mind if I ask how you were injured."

Rebel hesitated not wanting to make a bad impression. "The cuts on my face are from a fight." She shot a glance at Conner who smiled back at her. "Fighting is one of my hobbies. Mom hates it."

"You like to fight? And…, what about Conner?"

Rebel laughed at the hidden question. "Conner and I went a couple of rounds and I am responsible for his stitches. I was in headgear though so he isn't responsible for mine. They came from a different fight."

Lissa looked at her surprised then flashed a glance at Conner.

He just shrugged with a grin.

"Well, I guess everyone has a passion," she smiled.

Gabe looked at Lisa seriously and said, "She might say it's just for fun, but her fighting skills have saved all of our lives. I am deeply in her debt. We all are. I didn't like it at first, but I got used to it. She is really good."

Conner strolled over and laughed. "She's so good that she knocked me out."

Lissa couldn't hide her dismay. "You knocked him out?"

Rebel looked up at him and smiled. "I was in padding so he couldn't hurt me. It really wasn't a fair fight."

Lissa looked back and forth between them for a moment then laughed. "I'm sorry Conner, but she must be good if she can knock you out. Even if she was in padding."

He nodded and said, "I'm telling you. She whipped my ass."

Everyone laughed as Conner sat down for Gabe to remove his stitches and change the bandage on his thigh.

"Conner, how did you get shot?"

"Some men tried to steal the livestock and supplies.

We ended up in a gun battle. Rebel killed the guy who shot me though," he said smiling at her.

Rebel inhaled sharply and said, "Lissa, I hope you don't think I'm some kind of monster. It sounds pretty bad in that context."

"It's not the same world out there, I know that. We have to do what we have to do," she said with an understanding smile. "So what about the injury on your shoulder?" she asked, watching Gabe change the bandage.

"She fought and killed a grizzly bear," Conner said.

"My god, Rebel."

Rebel shrugged and said, "Conner helped me. Lissa, I'm feeling like kind of an animal here. I'm really not a fighting, killing monster."

"I don't think that," she laughed. She could tell that Rebel was uncomfortable so she changed the subject. "Tomorrow, I will show you our cave. We can pack your supplies down and get it prepared for our long stay," Lissa said.

"I'm looking forward to it. Conner told me a little bit about it but I can't wait to see it for myself," Rebel said.

"And I would love to hear the rest of your theories about this Planet X and what it will do to Earth," Lissa replied.

They talked late into the evening then everyone decided to continue their conversation over coffee in the morning.

Conner signaled her to follow him outside where he had set up their tent. "We can sleep inside if you want but I thought some privacy would be nice."

She smiled and followed him into the tent.

The next morning, the sky was clear except for the huge ash cloud hovering over the corner of Wyoming. Rebel stood staring at it, watching for any new sign that the entire caldera was going to explode.

Conner stepped up and handed her a cup of coffee. "No change?"

"No, but I think it will happen soon. Somehow, I can just feel it."

"Come on, Lissa is excited to show us the cave."

Rebel followed Conner inside the large room and smiled when Lissa rushed to her excitedly.

"Rebel, I want you to meet some friends of mine. "This is my dear friend Millie and this is Larry."

Rebel smiled, "Nice to meet you."

Lissa led her to a very frail looking older Native American man that was sitting on a blanket in front of the fire.

"This is Larry's grandfather, Lone Eagle. He is a Kalispell Shaman."

Rebel held out her hand to him and said, "Nice to meet you Lone Eagle, I am…"

"You are The One," he exclaimed climbing to his feet. He took her hand in his and stared deep into her eyes then looked at Lissa and said excitedly, "Where did you find The One?"

Lissa was taken back for a moment as he looked back at Rebel and started mumbling in his native tongue. He raised her hand along with his into the air and closed his eyes. "Nko'o simmu'em esel spukani."

"One woman, two suns. Grandpa, I don't understand. No one speaks Salish anymore. Say it in English," Larry urged.

"The woman of the two suns. She is The One," he said looking back at Rebel lowering his arms. "The female warrior that comes with the two suns."

Rebel inhaled sharply as she realized what he was saying.

"It's not a planet," she whispered. "It's a sun, a brown dwarf. The Destroyer!"

He nodded eagerly then suddenly swayed. She quickly reached out her other hand to stabilize him. A strange sensation fell over her as she helped him sit down on his blanket. She felt as though she were floating, looking down on the room from above. She quickly let go of his hands and stared at him, clearly shaken.

"Grandpa, tell me about The One," Larry said breaking the spell.

"I'm tired. We will talk later," he said still looking at Rebel.

She regained her composure and said, "It was very nice to meet you Mr. Lone Eagle. We will talk again."

He nodded closing his eyes, then started humming a haunting chant.

Lissa looked at Larry who shrugged.

"Come on, Rebel. I'll take you to the cavern," Lissa said tugging her away from the old man. "He called you a warrior. Does that seem odd considering you told me last night you like to fight?"

Rebel nodded and said, "It does seem strange."

"Come on, let's go look at the cave. The passageway is very dark and long. We have the lanterns ready and have packed a lunch."

Conner met them at the cave entrance and said. "I'm really excited to see your cave, Lissa."

She smiled and handed him a lantern then followed Larry inside.

The passageway was small at first but grew bigger as they followed it deep into the mountain. After awhile, it opened into a large cavern.

"This is the smaller of the two caverns," Lissa said, then waved them on and turned into one of the two tunnels that split off from the large space.

They trekked on for thirty or so minutes when suddenly they stepped into a massive opening. It was so big that the lanterns light didn't reach the walls on either side of them. The sound of rushing water rose up from the bottom of a deep crevice beside them.

Lissa smiled and said, "This is our cave."

Rebel was taken back by the size of the huge space. She followed Conner looking at the small rooms carved into the walls and the rock stairs that led up to each level. "My god," she breathed. "Its like a city. It's massive. Bigger than I could have imagined."

"Lone Eagle says that this is sacred ground," Lissa said. "He said that our people used this cave to hide from the white men but our ancient ancestors used it to hide from another danger. He told us to prepare for the time when this danger would come again."

"What danger exactly?" Rebel asked. "Did he specify?"

Lissa nodded and continued, "He said that the sky would rain danger. That it would rain death. No one could change what the sky would do."

Rebel listened intently at her words almost holding her breath.

"He told us that the star and the moon and the sun would come together in a line, then the land would shake and the waters would boil. It would rain fire when the stars fought in the sky."

Rebel's mouth opened in surprise and she could barely breath.

"Come here, I'll show you." She led her to one of the carving on the wall. "Here, see the star that looks like a monster with its mouth open? And I think that is earth right in its path."

Rebel was amazed by the whole thing. How ironic that she ended up in an ancient cave that tells the same story on its walls that she had been researching for years. She looked at Conner who was obviously thinking the same thing.

"This is incredible. There is definitely enough room for all of us," he said.

"We have spent years acquiring supplies and preparing the cave for the danger that Lone Eagle warned us was coming. But, I still haven't shown you the best part." She waved at them to follow her. "We didn't find it for several months but it was well worth the wait."

She stepped onto a narrow trail between the edge of the crevice and a rock wall. Eventually the trail widened and Rebel could feel moisture in the air.

"I hear a waterfall," Conner said.

"It's just ahead. Watch your step here," Lissa said as

she descended downward.

The trail opened into another large space in front of them. The humidity was so high that it almost felt as if it were raining. As they stepped further inside, they could see light coming from unseen source above them.

Rebel looked up in amazement and noticed that vegetation was growing in the crevices of the rocks. "Where is the light coming from?" she breathed.

"We don't know. We've searched for the source and can't find it. Come here, look. We planted tomatoes and squash and watermelon just to see what they would do," she said pointing to the plants. "They grew bigger than I have ever seen."

"Lissa, I can't tell you how amazed I am over this whole thing. I don't know what to say," Rebel said. "When Conner told me about this cave, I had no idea that it would be this impressive. This will save our lives if the volcano erupts. It gives me hope that we may actually survive. Thank you so much for welcoming us into your oasis."

Lissa started back down the trail toward the others and said, "Rebel, from what I heard from Lone Eagle, you may be our savior as well. I'm starting to believe that we were destined to be here in this mountain and you were destined to come here."

Conner looked at Rebel and realized that it had been pure chance that they met each other in West Virginia. The timing had to have been perfect or they would have missed each other completely. He looked at Lissa and wondered about the chance of this all being predestined.

They slowly made their way back to the main cavern and sat down with the others to eat lunch.

"Obviously, because of the time it takes to get down here, we haven't completely moved in yet. But we can certainly bring everyone down to pick out a spot and stash some of their stuff," Lissa smiled. "It will take some time to get your supplies down, so we should start right away."

"I wish we had a way to freeze some wild game because the ash from the volcano will kill the large animals,"

Rebel said thoughtfully.

Lissa suddenly stood up. "We do! I forgot to show you. There is a section of the cave that is ice all year round."

Rebel stood up too and started pacing. "If we have water and can grow vegetables and store meat year round, we will be able to live for several years down here if we have to. I can't believe it. It feels like I'm in a dream and don't want to wake up."

Lissa hugged her tightly. "Together Rebel, we will save our friends and family. Let's get to work."

Rebel nodded and followed the group back to the surface. Once outside, she went straight to the wagon and started sorting their supplies. Lissa joined her and together, they spent the next several days directing the huge task of organizing and moving everything to the cave.

The next day, Rebel stood watching the corner of Wyoming while she drank her coffee. Conner and the brothers joined her and sensed the newfound hope that she was feeling.

"We have all of the supplies secured and have set up a nice kitchen area with the cooking utensils. We put the boys in charge of packing firewood down. What else do we need Rebel?" Darien asked.

"The only thing left is to start harvesting game. I'm going to say the more the better. Take Larry and anyone else who wants to hunt and fill that ice cave full of meat. I think that is all we can do for now," Rebel said. "We will leave the cattle until the last minute."

Larry came toward them obviously flustered and said, "Excuse me, but grandpa is saying that he dreamed that some of our people are in danger and we have to go get them. He is asking for you Rebel. I'm sorry."

"Oh, Larry, don't be. Let's go see what's going on," Rebel smiled.

They all entered the structure and the entire crowd turned to them.

Lone Eagle walked to her and took her hand, "You have brought with you the only way to save them. The horses. Take the horses and bring the people here. All of the horses. There are many and they are trapped."

Rebel looked at Larry then back to the old man. "Where are they trapped? How long is the journey?"

"Three days. Larry will show you the way."

She nodded and turned to Larry, "Give me a minute to prepare then we will leave." She turned to her brothers who nodded telling her that they would go as well.

"We will go get the horses," Dylan said. He really liked the old man and had sat by him around the fire listening to his stories every night. He was eager to see if his dream came true.

Lissa helped her secure her bedroll and supplies and said, "Rebel, I don't understand why he wants you to go. This is all very strange."

"I don't understand either Lissa, but I'm willing to go on a little faith here. Especially after everything that has happened so far. Besides, if there are survivors out there, they deserve our help," Rebel said.

"Thanks Rebel. Be careful."

It took some time to prepare the hundred or so head of horses but soon they were ready to go. Conner, the brothers, Larry and Dallas mounted and looked at Rebel.

She looked back at Lone Eagle.

"The mountain is waiting for them," he said.

Rebel nodded hoping that he meant that the volcano wouldn't erupt until they got back. She kicked Jake into a run and led the men down the backside of the Elk Horn Lodge.

Three days later Rebel woke up with an ominous feeling. She paced by the fire drinking coffee and glaring up into the clear cold sky.

Conner joined her and unconsciously started pacing beside her.

"What's up with you two this morning?" Dylan asked.

"Weird feeling," they both said in unison.

Dylan raised his eyebrows curiously then turned to

the others. "I don't take that lightly. Check your weapons and be prepared for anything."

"Grandpa told me to go over that ridge and look to the north," Larry said.

Rebel nodded and looked toward the mountain just as a meteor flew through the sky above them. She waited to see if it impacted and winced at the flash of light. A huge billowing dust cloud surged into the atmosphere.

"Did you see how far away that hit? I couldn't tell," she asked.

"No, let's get going before something else happens," Conner said.

They mounted the horses and quickly rode up the side of the mountain. When they reached the summit, Larry pointed.

"There, there is the cave," he said.

"Look at that," Dylan said getting everyone's attention.

Rebel looked across the valley and saw a huge fire coming at them from the next mountain range. "We need to hurry and get them out of there," she said.

Jake suddenly reared and tried to bold back down the hill.

"What the hell Jake?" Rebel yelled then was almost swallowed into a huge crevice that ripped open on the trail in front of them. The ground shifted sideways and quivered for a second then erupted in a massive convulsion, shuddering then rolling until it finally just heaved upward.

"Jesus Christ! What kind of earthquake is this?" Conner yelled.

Several minutes later, the ground lay still beneath their horses and everyone looked at each other shocked. Conner looked at Rebel, whose face was suddenly pale. He followed her gaze and his jaw dropped when he realized what she was seeing.

The cave had been completely camouflaged beneath a landslide that covered the entire entrance.

"They are trapped," Conner mumbled.

"Conner, they weren't trapped until we got here,"

Rebel said softly. "How did he know?"

Dylan tilted his head sideways contemplating the implication of the strange event.

"That fire is coming. We need to get them out!" Darien said moving downhill.

They followed him into the valley and started moving rocks and debris from the cave entrance. One by one they helped almost fifty people out of the cave and onto the horses.

"Hurry," Darien urged. "It's growing and coming right for us."

Conner tossed a little boy up on the horse behind his mother and helped a teenage girl mount then climbed onto his gilding. "K, hang on, we need to move fast."

The brothers led the way back up the mountain carefully avoiding the new cracks in the earth. They rode as fast as they dared across the summit and away from the firestorm that was right on their ass.

Darien and Dylan set the pace and didn't stop. They rode at a gallop into the afternoon.

Rebel glanced up at them and knew they were risking the horses but felt they had no choice. Finally she yelled, "We have to rest the animals!"

Dylan reined to a stop and yelled, "Switch to fresh horses. Quickly."

Darien looked back at the fire and said, "It's pacing us Rebel. I've never seen a fire travel so fast. Either we risk the horses or risk ourselves."

"It's because all of the timber is laying on the ground and dry. The wind is pushing it, fueling it. There is nothing to stop it," Warrick said.

She looked back at the frightened people and said, "Some of them can't keep the pace. What are we going to do?"

"They are going to have to. We have to keep moving," Darien said pushing his horse into a gallop.

Rebel dropped behind encouraging everyone to hurry. She looked behind them and recognized that her brothers were right. The fire traveled uphill way faster than the horses and just as fast going down. She was worried. It was a three-day ride to get home and Warrick had said that nothing would stop the fire. They needed a miracle.

Lissa was keeping a close eye on Lone Eagle as he sat cross-legged on his blanket in front of the fire. His eyes were closed and he was mumbling under his breath and rocking back and forth. Suddenly he stood up and started chanting loudly.

Kira looked nervously at Lissa. "What is he doing?"

Lissa shrugged then inhaled sharply as the old man started moving in distinct steps around the fire.

"He's performing a rain dance. I haven't seen it for a long time. Something is very strange about all of this," she said nervously.

They watched as the old man became louder and his movements grew into a full out dance. Several of the men around the fire stood up and joined him.

Everyone around them grew silent as they chanted and danced. The fire flashed and grew bigger and a gust of wind blasted past them causing the flames to dance eerily as if imitating the men.

Lissa held her breath realizing that there was something bigger going on than she had imagined.

Rebel could feel Jake weakening underneath her as they pushed the animals to their limits trying to stay just out of reach of the massive firestorm that seemed to be gaining on them. She looked back praying for the miracle that would be their only savior. Then she noticed huge thunderheads that seemed to just appear over the mountain in front of them. "It's going to rain. Look." she yelled pointing to the cloudburst.

The sky erupted with color as lighting pierced through the clouds and thunder clapped so hard that the horses jumped. Rain pelted them with such force that she had to duck her head to keep it from stinging her face.

Dylan pulled the horses to a walk and looked

around in confusion. "Where the hell did this come from?"

"I don't know, but it will slow the fire. Thank God! It may give us a chance to rest the animals," Darien said.

Dylan looked at Rebel and said, "Does this seem weird to you?"

She nodded her head and said, "The timing is very strange. This just appeared out of nowhere."

The large party galloped through the pounding rain until they reached a clearing beside a small lake at the bottom of a valley.

Darien looked back at the fire and said, "I think we should be able to rest for a couple hours. Let's get the people something to eat."

Rebel unsaddled Jake and let him go. She decided to ride one of the extra horses from now on. She wasn't willing to ride him into the ground if things took a turn for the worst. She pulled her coat up around her neck and turned to help cook dinner for the large number of people.

After they had eaten, Darien stood up and said, "I know your tired but we have to move on."

Everyone stood up and climbed back onto their horses and followed him into a gallop. They rode well into the night under the pounding rain that continued without pause.

Finally, the brothers chose a large clearing to stop and allow the people to sleep.

Rebel lay awake next to Conner and watched the fire glow just over the ridge. She had given her tent to a group of younger children and chose to sleep out in the open by the fire. Her mind drifted to the rain that just happened to arrive in their most desperate hour. She couldn't shake the feeling that it was just too coincidental.

Conner watched the emotions play across her face and instinctively knew what she was thinking. "Maybe we are just lucky," he said.

"That is some kind of luck. I've never been lucky so I'm having a hard time believing that."

"Try to put it out of your head Rebel. You need to

sleep."

She nodded and snuggled close to him trying to calm her mind.

The sun wasn't up the next morning when the brothers stoked the fire and put on the coffee.

"We need to move out," Dylan said. "The rain has slowed the fire but it is still coming."

"At least now we don't have to push the horses quite so hard. They wouldn't have made it much further," she said thoughtfully as she poured coffee into her cup. "Jake was failing fast."

Soon they had everyone on the horses and were making good time. The rain lightened and Rebel could sense that they were finally pulling ahead of the monster that chased them.

They pushed on with very little rest until they finally reached their destination and rode up the lane to the Elkhorn Lodge.

Rebel helped the people dismount and watched the reunion as everyone came out of the structure excitedly. Lone Eagle stepped to the door and nodded at her as if to say 'Thank You'.

She nodded back and was overtaken by a strange feeling. Somehow, he had helped them and she was determined to find out how.

Jade and Kira rushed to her and hugged her tightly.

"I was worried Rebel," Kira said. "Something is weird here. I had the strangest feeling while you were gone."

"Lone Eagle did a rain dance," Jade said. "It was really cool. All the men helped him.

Rebel's eyes shot toward the old man who still stood smiling in the doorway. "A rain dance?" she mumbled.

Dylan looked at her and grinned. "A rain dance. I should have known." He shook his head and turned to take care of the horses that had just saved all of their lives.

Lissa walked up to them and said, "Rebel, I don't know how to thank you and your family. They said that they wouldn't have survived if you hadn't been there."

Rebel looked into her eyes and said, "Lissa, those

people weren't trapped until we got there. An earthquake caused a landslide and buried them right in front of us. That old man had to have premonitioned that. He seen it before it happened."

"He is a Shaman, Rebel," Lissa smiled.

"But I don't believe in that stuff. I don't understand the things he has said about me."

"I don't understand it all either," she admitted. "But I can testify that I have seen some unexplainable things and there is something to all of this."

"He said that I brought the only thing that would save them. The horses. If we hadn't been mounted, the fire would have killed us. This is all very weird," she said softly.

"I'm just glad your home mom," Jade said. "Lets go get you something to eat."

Rebel nodded and followed them into the large room where many people came up to her and thanked her for saving them.

Conner, Dallas, Larry and the brothers entered the room and everyone erupted in applause. They handed them plates of food and cleared a spot by the fire for them to sit. Rebel smiled, relieved that everything had turned out.

She turned to see a tall man emerge from the group they had just saved. He held out his hand to her.

"Thank you from all of our people. I am their leader, John Timminboo.

Rebel shook his hand and smiled, "I'm glad we were able to help you."

Lone Eagle came up beside him and said, "This is the fire keeper. She is The One."

John stared at Rebel for a moment then smiled. "Grandfather saw you coming in his dream. It is good to meet you. We share ancestors."

Rebel tilted her head at Lone Eagle curiously. What the hell did he mean, fire keeper? Related?

Lone Eagle just smiled back and said, "Get your food. You will need your strength." Then both men went to sit by the fire.

Chapter 22

The next morning, snow began to fall again and it didn't stop until the ground was buried under several feet. Rebel was leaning on the fence looking into the pasture at the livestock and wrestling with the fact that they wouldn't be able to save them after the eruption. She watched Jake as he pawed at the snow and was overcome with sadness.

"There is a place for them," a soft voice said from behind her.

Rebel swung around surprised by the old man and asked, "Where?"

He smiled at her and said, "I will show you. Take me in the wagon."

She hesitated for a moment unable to believe what he was telling her. Then she nodded and waved at Conner and Dylan. "Will you harness dad's team and help Lone Eagle onto the cook wagon. He is going to show us something."

"Of course," Dylan said and turned to follow Conner to the pasture.

Lissa, Kira, Jade and many of the others swung onto their horses, excited to go on the journey with them. Marshall took the leads to the team and sat down beside the old man.

"This way," he pointed.

Rebel was so curious she couldn't contain herself. She couldn't imagine a space large enough to protect the large number of animals. How the hell would they feed them? She tried not to get her hopes up realizing that this was a long shot.

The small party made its way through the timber around the mountain. The terrain turned very rugged as they crossed a small creek and rambled into a small valley. It was more like a crevice surrounded by massive rock cliffs that reached high into the sky above them.

Lone eagle held up his hand for them to stop and pointed to a hole in the solid stone. "There."

Rebel looked at him curiously and couldn't help smiling back into his happy face. She dismounted and hiked to the crack in the rock.

Conner came up behind her with a lantern and stepped inside. The passageway was only about eight feet tall and three or four feet wide. It took them about twenty yards into the mountain then opened into a massive meadow.

Rebel stopped absolutely dumfounded. "Can this be real?" she asked looking at the huge space. It was two football fields wide and several more long. A creek happily bubbled along the edge and vegetation grew thick, hanging down the rock walls.

Lissa and Kira stood in awe unable to speak.

"I can't believe it," Dylan breathed. "This is amazing. Where is the light coming from?"

"It's just like the room in the big cave," Lissa said. "We have never found the light source."

Rebel once again felt as if she were dreaming. She couldn't believe that they had come here and found this Shambhala buried deep in the mountains of Montana.

Conner climbed up one of the rocks looking up. "It's the crystals. Look, the rock overhead is full of crystals."

"Amazing. I wouldn't have known," Lissa said. "I'm beginning to wonder about the implications here."

Rebel nodded and turned to Dylan. "How many will it support?"

"It will hold all of them but it won't feed them. We need to gather up some hay. I will make it our priority. We can use dad's wagon and big team to haul it. Come on, let's get to work," he said excitedly.

They walked back out to the wagon and couldn't help feeling some hope in the face of the impending doom around them.

They silently traveled back to the camp, each lost in thought.

Rebel glanced at the old man who sat perched on

the wagon with a big grin and thought about how strange this whole thing was.

As soon as they got back to camp, Dylan organized a group of men to help him harness the team and search for hay. They planned on finding the feed store and see if any of the grain was still good.

"Rebel, find a place to stash the tack we just might need it again," he said hopefully as they left on their quest.

Two days later, they were all gathered around the fire eating dinner and talking excitedly about successfully finding enough feed for the animals and getting them all moved to their new home. Rebel watched silently as her brothers interacted happily with the other men in the large group.

Lone Eagle stood up and the room instantly fell silent. He raised his hands and said, "The two brothers have returned. The time has come to move into the mountain. There is still one more journey we must face.

Larry looked at his grandfather expectantly and said, "What journey?"

Everyone looked at the old man curiously.

"This journey is for The One, the warrior woman," he said looking at Rebel.

The entire group of people followed his gaze to her.

Kira and Jade both held their breath.

Rebel looked into his eyes wondering what the hell he was talking about.

"The ancestors will test us. They need proof that we are worthy," he continued. "If she is successful, they will protect us from the war of the suns."

Conner stepped forward and said nervously, "What do you mean successful? What does she have to do?"

"I do not know. Only they know."

Conner looked at Rebel, his eyes full of worry. "I don't like this. You have been through enough. What more could they want?"

She glanced at him then to her brothers. She looked

at her mother and Jade then around the room at the hundred and fifty or so people looking back at her. She turned back to Conner and said, "Well, there is only one way to find out. Let's pack it up and move into the mountain." Then she thought about the old man's words and turned back to him and said, "Who are the two brothers?"

He pointed toward the door, "Two brothers."

Rebel walked outside and looked up into the sky and damn near choked when she saw the two large comets that had just appeared out of nowhere.

"Red kachina," Lone Eagle said pointing to the planet. "Two brothers."

Conner looked at Rebel in shock. "I don't believe this. It is just too much."

Rebel nodded in agreement and looked back into the evening sky.

"Come, the mountain calls us," the old man said.

Everyone started talking at once. The entire group erupted in movement as the people picked up their stuff and prepared for the journey into the cave.

Lissa walked up to her and said, "Rebel, I don't know what is in store for you down there but I know that everything will end well. I have seen the spirits that reside in this mountain and truly believe that they will protect us."

Rebel nodded and said, "Good, I'm feeling the need for some protection."

Conner and the brothers waited until the people had gone back inside then stepped silently beside her as she looked into the sky.

She turned to them and said, "I've studied the legend of the Kachinas and the two brothers. One of the brothers is the guardian of the North Pole and the other of the South Pole. They are here to help their uncle, the Red Kachina, the purifier, return the earth to its natural rotation. That just happens to be the opposite direction that it is spinning now. Everything makes sense. The pole shift, the earth's rotation slowing. This is it. The earth is going to stop and start rotating the other way."

They nodded their heads, nervously pondering what

she was saying.

"Rebel, I'm worried. I have a weird feeling about this," Dylan said.

"I have been doing a lot of soul searching since we got here and first talked to that old man. I don't understand all of this either but it feels right. Somehow, I feel like this is how it is supposed to be. Whatever it is that I have to do down there may be our destiny. I'm starting to believe that we were supposed to find our way here. Everything that has happened so far can't just be chance."

She could still feel their tension and couldn't help teasing them. "Don't worry guys, I mean after all, I am The One," she said sarcastically then laughed.

They all laughed with her taking some strength from her words.

"Come on, let's get moved in and go prove our worthiness."

Later that night, they had all found a little cubby up in the walls of the huge cavern. Jade and Lynn were on one side of her and Kira was on the other. The brothers had settled in up one level and Uncle Neil and Evie were down next to Lissa and her family on the lowest level.

"There are a lot of stairs," Jade complained. "I can't believe how many rooms there are in here."

"At least I won't be claustiphobic," Rebel laughed. "Do you have enough blankets? Are you going to be comfortable?"

She nodded and said, "We are going to be just fine, mom."

Rebel smiled and hugged her. "Come on, let's go sit by the fire."

They climbed down and gathered with everyone around the big fire. It sat burning in the center of the room in front of a very large alter that was shaped somewhat like a chair.

Rebel looked around the room suddenly overwhelmed by an ominous presence that she couldn't see. She edged closer to Jade, instinctively feeling the need to protect her from it. She watched Lone Eagle sit down in the chair shaped altar and one of the Native American boys set a leather bound box beside him.

The room grew silent as the old man stood and said, "It is time that the suns fight in the sky. The Red Kachina is here to restore the balance on earth and purify her. We seek refuge in our ancestors' mountain until the earth is pure again and on its right path. Our ancestors seek proof that we are worthy of being saved. The warrior woman has arrived to show them. Her Hopi ancestors have guided her here and will stand by her in her quest. If she is successful, the ancestors will protect us."

Rebel looked at Kira wondering which one of her parents had Hopi ancestors. Kira looked at Marshall who shrugged.

"She has brought the key," Lone Eagle said pointing to Jade. He turned to the box and said, "Open the box."

Jade looked at Rebel nervously. Her great grandmother had told her many stories about the Hopi and had given her a jade pendant that she had gotten as a girl from a small group of Native American people that lived near Portage, Utah. Her hand went to her neck and she pulled out the pendant that she always wore on a chain.

"Yes," the old man said with a smile.

Jade stood up and walked to the altar. She slid the piece of stone into the hole then jumped slightly as the lid popped open.

"This is the weapon the warrior woman will use to prove our worthiness," he said waving to Rebel. "It has special powers, made by our ancestors for this quest.

Rebel walked up beside Jade and peered into the box. It was a knife. She reached in and picked it up, admiring the razor sharp obsidian blade and beautifully carved bone handle. She looked curiously at Lone Eagle knowing now that she would have to fight.

"Ready?" he asked.

"Can you give me some idea of what to expect?"

"You will prove your strength fighting the ancestor warrior. Then you will prove your pure heart saving the jade key," he said.

Rebel tilted her head in confusion. She understood the fighting part but why save a key that opens an open box? She shrugged and stepped down onto the stone floor in front of the alter and said, "I'm ready."

Conner had silently watched Rebel pick up the knife and ready herself for the unknown. He wasn't comfortable with any of this. His anxiety level rose higher when she said that she was ready.

Suddenly the flames in the fire erupted into a dance from an eerie wind that swept past them. Drums started beating around them echoing faintly throughout the entire cavern. Lone Eagle stepped away from the altar and sat cross-legged in front of the fire. Jade followed him and sat down beside him.

Rebel felt the ominous presence again and the hair on the back of her neck stood up as the drums grew louder, pounding out a distinct beat. Tension filled the air as the flames of the fire danced and the lanterns went dark.

Suddenly, out of the darkness, warrior dancers appeared as if out of thin air. They surrounded the fire, dancing to the drumbeats that continued to grow louder and louder still.

Rebel looked at Conner, unsure of what exactly she was doing here. This seemed to her to be a ridiculous display of some kind of magic.

The flames in the fire erupted higher drawing her attention then out of the flames, a large man appeared. He jumped out of the flames landing right in front of her. The drumbeats stopped in a deafening silence and the warriors around the fire froze.

Rebel looked over the man in front of her. He was very large, standing almost a foot taller than her. He was dressed only in a leather loincloth and a beautiful turquoise neckpiece. He held a knife in one hand and a feather in the other.

She held her ground as he stepped toward her. He raised his blade to her throat and slid it under the five-inch mountain lion claws that hung in between those of the grizzly around her neck. He looked into her eyes and nodded his approval then lifted the feather in the air and let it drop. She didn't watch it fall, instead, stared deep into his eyes. He grinned at her and stepped back into a fighting stance. She mirrored him and prepared to spar. He waited until the feather hit the floor then moved.

They stepped around each other for a moment feeling each other out then he came in and swung with his knife. Rebel dodged the swipe and swung her own blade. He smiled as he jumped out of the way then came in again and this time he meant business. He followed the blade with a fist and she barely ducked them both.

Her adrenaline was starting to kick in as she focused on her adversary. She stepped in and raked her blade across his chest. He sneered as his blood stained her knife then swung his leg under her and nearly toppled her to the ground. She jumped over his legs and spun around landing her elbow in his face.

He swung his blade before she recovered and sliced her shoulder open. She jumped into the air and kicked him hard in his temple. He staggered back a step then launched up at her with a brutal swing. She dodged sideways and kicked him in the abdomen before he landed. He went to the ground. She stepped back allowing him to get to his feet. This fight had just begun and somehow it didn't feel right to kick him in the face.

He climbed to his feet, obviously surprised that she hadn't moved in and stepped back into his stance. Once again she followed his lead and prepared for attack.

Conner pushed his way through the crowd to get closer to the fight. He had been watching her closely and couldn't figure out why she was holding back. He knew she could be much more aggressive but she was dancing around this guy.

Rebel could sense that something wasn't right here. This guy she was fighting was much better than he was letting on. Why was he toying with her? She turned the knife in her hand so that the blade was pointing to the back and wrapped her knuckles around the bone handle hoping it would give her fist a more solid impact. She decided to box with him and see how he reacted.

She brought her fists up and danced in close then slammed him in the jaw with a right jab and followed with a left hook to his eye then quickly danced back out of his reach. He looked at her almost stunned and she didn't waste the hesitation. She stepped back in and pounded her fist into his nose.

He responded with a swipe of his knife then spun around with a kick that slammed her in the shoulder sending her sprawling. She climbed to her feet and stepped in again taking his breath with a rocket to his abdomen then spun around plowing her elbow into his bleeding nose.

She stepped back to recover and noticed that he was eyeing her in surprise. He crouched down and sprang at her, swinging his knife. Once again she dodged the blunt of the blow but ended up bleeding. She hit him again while he was in mid swing and felt his ribs break.

His face paled as he swung around to face her again. She didn't wait for him to square up. Her fist split his lip and knocked him backward. She could sense the anger growing inside him as he spit blood onto the stone floor and practically growled at her. She knew that he was going to unleash a split second before he did and managed to dodge most of the blows from his outburst. His knife caught her across the collarbone and she felt the warmth of her blood roll down her chest.

This was getting serious. Until now, she wasn't certain that he would actually kill her, but now she knew. She calmed herself and faced her opponent with a new determination. They clashed in battle each drawing blood, blow after blow, gouge after gouge until both were exhausted. They were almost perfectly matched and the winner wouldn't be the best fighter. It would be the one with the most heart.

Conner watched as the woman he loved was sliced with the blade over and over. He watched her take hit after hit and his gut wrenched in pain for her as her blood splattered the stone floor. He glanced at the brothers who were all gritting their teeth in anguish. Jade was covering her face with her hands, crying. He didn't even look at Kira who had probably passed out by now.

Rebel was getting tired but knew that the man in front of her was just as winded. She spun around and using her small size to her advantage, tucked herself between his huge arms with her back to his chest and slammed her knife behind her into his flesh then quickly stepped away.

He stood still staring at her in amazement as he bled then dropped to his knees.

The drums started pounding and the warriors around the fire started dancing and chanting loudly. Then out of the corner of her eye, she saw two of the warriors grab Jade and drag her to the altar, holding her firmly.

The man she was fighting snarled at her then leaped into the air, aiming to drive his blade into her daughters' chest.

Kira screamed and Lissa gasped.

Rebel reacted without thinking, without hesitation. She launched herself in front of the knife and heard Jade scream as she felt the blade penetrate deep into her heart. Everything around her went quiet. She could see Conner hurdle toward the warrior that had stabbed her but he flew through the man as if he were a ghost. A ghost? Rebel knew she was dying when the man disappeared right in front of her eyes. Then darkness overtook her.

Conner watched the blade move toward Rebel as if it were in slow motion. He jumped at the man holding the knife but passed through him as if he were vapor. He turned in confusion then crumbled down next to Rebel and took her into his arms. He held her close to him as her blood drained from her heart.

Suddenly, as he held her, all of the writings around the altar started glowing. The petragliphs on the walls glimmered. Then a beautiful light climbed slowly down from the ceiling of the cave.

It spiraled out as if it had fingers that weaved toward

them enticing them, hypnotizing them. The light slowly took the form of a beautiful woman dressed in white leather. She touched down on the bloody stone in front of him and smiled down at Rebel. The drums stopped again and the warriors stood at attention in the deafening silence.

"She is strong and true. Noble and unselfish. She has fought bravely and sacrificed herself for the key. She is the firekeeper of the spirit. The caretaker," the woman said softly.

"The key?" Conner asked with tears in his eyes.

The being looked up at Jade who was sitting in the chair behind him. She waved her arm toward the crying young woman and said, "Jade is the key."

"The key to what?" Jade breathed.

"Knowledge. You will unlock the knowledge that will save the worthy people here from the purification. The messages will be found written in the living stone. Only in the ancient teachings will the ability to understand the messages be found. You will read the writings of the ancient ones and survive to rebuild the earth."

She turned and waved her hand at the glowing images in the stone then looked back at Jade and said, "The spiritual watcher will help you. He is the guardian of the ancient writings. Together you will unlock their secrets."

Larry stood up in amazement. He had been named the spiritual watcher but didn't know exactly what that meant. He looked at the altar remembering the last time he had been here. There was an opening that required a key. Jade was the key. He looked at his grandfather who still sat cross-legged in front of the fire with a brilliant smile on his face.

Conner looked at the white being and said, "Who are you?"

Larry stepped forward and said, "This is white dove, the giver of eternal life."

The being smiled and nodded then looked down at Rebel. "You have passed the test. You have proven your strength and given your life unselfishly. You will protect the key. I give you new life, Firekeeper of the Spirit." She wrapped her fingers around the knife that was still buried deep in Rebel's chest and slowly pulled it out.

Conner held his breath as the blade was removed. Rebel moaned in his arms and he couldn't stop the tears that flowed down his cheeks.

"I will leave you now worthy ones and will return after the Red Kachina is departed. The time is near."

She floated upward and faded back into the white swirling light. The warriors faded into darkness and the fire dimmed back to its original state.

Conner looked around completely stunned then turned his attention to Rebel as her eyes fluttered open and she moaned again. He pulled her up to his chest hugging her tightly, completely overtaken by emotion.

Jade was so stricken that she couldn't move. She just sat in the big chair on the altar and tried to breath.

Rebel sat up and looked up at her fearfully. "Jade! Are you ok?"

Jade nodded slowly and tried to smile.

The people in the cavern were completely silent, no one untouched by the overwhelming experience they had all just witnessed. Rebel stood up and looked around the room. Her wounds were bleeding and she looked like she had just walked through a maze of razor blades.

Lone Eagle stood up and walked up to her. He wrapped his arms around her and said, "I knew you were The One. You have given us protection from the purification. We will live." He turned to the crowd of people and held one of her arms in the air. "She has given us new life!"

Everyone cheered and the cavern erupted in movement.

Kira, Marshall, and the brothers rushed to Rebel.

"My god, I had no idea that this was going to happen," Dylan said. "I thought I was going to lose my mind watching you fight. He was slicing you to pieces."

"Ya, but you were slicing him right back, Rebel," Warrick said with a grin. "You kicked his ass!"

Rebel smiled at her brothers.

"That dove lady might have given her new life but it won't last long if we don't stitch these knife wounds," Kira said angrily. "Here sit down."

Shane waved to Gabe who had already retrieved her medical bag. Ric followed her to Rebel still wiping tears from her eyes.

"Oh Rebel, I always hated it when you fought but this was truly agonizing. I never want to see you fight again," Ric said taking her hand.

Darien stepped up to Jade and held her shaking hand as she climbed down to her mother.

She sank to her side and said, "You saved me. You took the blade for me."

"And I always will," Rebel said with a smile then hugged her daughter tightly.

Lissa had been silent, unsure of what to say. She knelt down beside Rebel and looked at her wounds then said sadly, "I'm sorry Rebel. I didn't know that this is what they meant. I'm so sorry."

"Don't be, Lissa. If this is what needed to be done then that is how it is. I'm fine. Somehow this is all fine."

Lissa smiled at her new friend and squeezed her hand. "You do fight well, Rebel. I'll go warm some water so we can clean you up." She turned toward the fire and yelled, "Get her a place by the fire. Find a chair."

The people rushed to do her bidding and Conner lifted her up and sat her in the chair by the fire. Gabe started stitching the deep gashes that seemed to cover her entire torso. The brothers hovered nearby getting her coffee and watching the progress. Kira paced in front of the fire shaking her head.

Rebel could feel the anxiety filling the room. No one knew what to say to her. She knew that they wanted to celebrate but felt bad that she had been injured. Finally, she couldn't take it anymore. She waved to Gabe to hold on a second and stood up.

"Listen people. I volunteered for this. I knew that I

would be fighting. I knew that there would be blood. I don't want you to feel bad about it or feel obligated in any way. This is just how it played out. Nothing more. I don't understand everything that just happened but I'm sure that you will help me figure it out eventually. So let's just be happy that it turned out in a positive way, ok? We should be celebrating."

Everyone cheered, finally relaxing a little. They started talking excitedly so she sat back down and watched Gabe work on her wounds. One by one, the people came up to shake her hand and thank her.

Larry smiled at her and said, "Good fight Rebel. I am truly amazed. I can't wait to see what happens next."

Everyone cheered again.

Conner's face paled a little and he suddenly stood up, "Now everyone just hold on a minute."

The room fell silent.

"Before one more crazy god damned thing happens, before she damn near dies in my arms one more time, I am going to marry this woman!" he said then knelt down beside Rebel and took her hand.

"What do you say Rebel, will you marry me? Right now?"

Rebel looked at him completely shocked. She had assumed that when he had asked her on the mountain, it was because he wasn't planning on any of them surviving the night.

She smiled into his face and said, "Yes!"

Kira looked at the brothers who were all completely taken back. "Well," she said, "do we have anyone here who can perform the ceremony?"

"Manny is a Justice of the Peace," Lissa said smiling excitedly. Then she waved at everyone to help prepare a place for the ceremony.

The brothers all stood beside Conner and Kira, Jade, Ric, Lissa and Gabe stood beside Rebel.

They repeated simple vows then Conner surprised her again when he pulled a gold band out of his pocket and slid it onto her finger.

She looked at him curiously.

"I got it in the little town where we met Ric. I was in town getting supplies and saw a jewelry store. There wasn't a very big selection left and it's not a diamond…" he trailed off.

"It's perfect."

Conner smiled and kissed his bride. And she kissed him right back.

Everyone cheered and Kira and Jade wiped the tears from their eyes.

Lone Eagle turned to Larry and said, "Coffee would be good. And some of your mothers fry bread."

Rebel smiled at the old man and watched the crowd of people gather around the fire together to celebrate their newfound hope for the future.

She walked over to the altar and sat down on the step. Conner followed her and together they watched the celebration.

Rebel looked down at her ring and said, "You've had this the whole time?"

"I've wanted to make you mine since the first time I saw you."

She shook her head and said, "You really took me by surprise that first day. You lit a fire in my soul that I had never felt before. I fell for you before I walked out that door."

He grinned and said, "I'm so glad I followed you. I really thought you were going to shoot me when I caught up to you though."

"Well, I would have missed cause when I saw your handsome face, my blood fired through my veins so fast, I couldn't hold my weapon steady. Who knew that all that would lead up to this?"

"Ya, who knew that I would find The One? The woman who would save all of our lives," he laughed. "By the way, I feel much better about you kicking my ass now that I know you really are a warrior princess," he smiled at her.

Rebel laughed and said, "I didn't kick your ass. I was

just pissed off."

"I don't know Rebel." He looked down at the blood on the floor and shuttered. "I don't know if I could have beaten that guy. He was tough."

Rebel laughed again and said, "I feel much better knowing that I learned to fight for a reason. Now I don't feel like such a weirdo, maybe it was all supposed to happen."

He pulled her up onto his lap and said, "I never thought you were a weirdo. I admired you from the first day we met. You are my little spit fire."

She looked in his eyes and said, "You are my erotic sun god."

He laughed and picked her up. "And you are definitely the keeper of my fire," he said then he packed her to bed.

The next morning, Rebel took a thermos of coffee and hiked to the surface. She needed some fresh air and a look at the sun. She had dreamed all night about the events that had taken place and still couldn't make sense of them.

She didn't believe in ghosts and was struggling with the idea that they existed after all. It wasn't hard to justify the images appearing out of the darkness and the big man she fought could have just stepped back into the darkness as well. She was unconscious when the woman in white leather appeared so she didn't see how that worked. The drums could have been real. She shook her head as she thought through all the things that she had learned last night.

Somehow, she had Hopi ancestors and they believed that Jade was some kind of key. To what, she had no idea. The old man was happy and believed that now they would survive the purification, whatever he thought that was. The red star was supposedly the Red Kachina, here to purify the earth and the two comets were his nephews, the two brothers, here to help him restore the balance on earth. The comet that flew by last year was supposedly the Blue Kachina and now she was the fire keeper of the spirit, the caretaker that had been given new life.

She whistled for Jake and swung onto his back

without a saddle. She rode to the top of the ridge and looked toward the corner of Wyoming and tried to focus on the real things that she did know.

She knew that the volcano would erupt and that they would more than likely survive the initial blast but with the number of people now in the cave, she didn't know if they would survive very long afterward. Their supplies would only last so long and they weren't renewable at this point. She knew that they were about to crawl into the earth and live like ants with the possibility of never resurfacing. She knew that the red sun would either reverse the earth's rotation or tip her on her ass and it would be a miracle if the cave survived the movement of the earth's crust. If the mountain failed, they would all certainly perish.

She sighed with regret. All of this may have been for nothing. She hung her head and rode back down the mountain.

Conner and her brothers met her at the corral. The brothers were ready to take the remaining ten horses around to their new home. She sadly slid off Jake and removed his halter. She softly stroked his muzzle silently saying goodbye then turned away.

They watched her walk away and all of them knew that she really didn't expect to see her horse again.

Conner followed her and took her hand. "Rebel, you believed all along that we would live through this. Please don't lose faith now."

She tried to be strong and looked into his eyes. "I'm fine Conner. No matter what happens, at least we're together."

"Lone Eagle told me to tell you not to worry about your horse."

Rebel inhaled sharply in surprise.

Conner shrugged and said, "I don't know how he knows."

She smiled and said, "Well, he says we will live. Maybe he's right about that too."

They sat together talking into the afternoon.

The brothers returned and chatted with them for a while before going inside.

Then it happened. It started with a faint rumble and a slight tremor.

Rebel knew instinctively what it was and stood up facing Wyoming. Conner stood next to her and together they watched as a huge cloud of billowing ash and steam boiled up into the atmosphere.

"E.L.E," she mumbled as the earth shivered again under their feet.

Conner looked at her curiously.

"We are witnessing an Extinction Level Event," she said softly and strangely felt calm as she watched the end of time erupt in front of her. The ash plume grew larger and larger as the magma punched its way out around the massive cauldera. Then, the entire corner of the state blew into the sky.

Rebel took Conners' hand and slowly backed toward the cave opening. She knew that the pyroclastic flow from an eruption this big would reach a hundred miles but the shock wave from the blast would certainly reach them here. She couldn't take her eyes off of it. Fire rained down around them and she could feel the air warm against her face as she counted the seconds before they would have to dive underground.

They were witnessing the end of the world as they knew it. She looked into the sunset, knowing that this was the last time she would see it for a long time then tugged Conner into the cave entrance followed closely by the fast moving, boiling hot cloud of death.

The brown dwarf had arrived, the great purification had started and the Mayan calendar had ended all on December 21, 2012.

THE END

CPSIA information can be obtained at www.ICGtesting.com
Printed in the USA
LVOW060156300313

326726LV00022B/318/P